HALLOWEEN CANDY

Thomas M. Sipos

ISBN: 0-75963-748-2

This book is printed on acid free paper.

Cover art by Stuart Smith, stusmith@ntlworld.com
Author website: www.HalloweenCandy.net

1stBooks - rev. 06/25/01

By Thomas M. Sipos

Novels

Manhattan Sharks

Hollywood Witches

Vampire Nation

Anthologies

Halloween Candy

Contents

Tricks and Treats:

An Introduction to Horror

I entitle this book *Halloween Candy* for two reasons. One, because its single longest entry is my horror anthology screenplay of the same name. And two, because *Halloween Candy* is a Jack O'Lantern of a book. An anthology of horror fact and fiction, newly stuffed after a night of trick-or-treating with film critiques, short stories, haunted house reports, punditry, even a screenplay and celebrity interview. Writings dark and serious and whimsical, and all else that is horror.

Before I detail this book's contents, I will recount "the making of *Halloween Candy*." Or rather, how the film almost got made, again and again and again. If it seems odd publishing an unproduced screenplay, well, there is precedent. Darius James's *Negrophobia* was published in 1992, to wide critical acclaim. It remains acclaimed and unproduced.

* * *

I began outlining *Halloween Candy* in a computer science class, in December 1982. *Creepshow* had recently been released and I anticipated another horror anthology cycle. And since John Carpenter's *Halloween* was the most lucrative independent film to date, I thought to combine the two concepts in a Halloween-themed horror anthology. *Halloween* meets *Tales from the Crypt.*

I conceived a wraparound story to fit the title: A modern witch punishes some nasty trick-or-treaters with her nightmare-inducing Halloween candy. Each nightmare, a tale in my omnibus. Each tale written to stand on its own horrific best, even if at the cost of logical connectivity to the wraparound. Some people later complained of this loose connectivity, others not.

To root *Halloween Candy* in tradition, I opened with a revenant corpse story: "We Have an Opening in Biology 101." For my tentpole, I saved my strongest, edgiest tale: "The Lady Who Ate Dolls." Over the years, this darkly erotic gorefest was every reader's favorite. I ended on a satirical note with: "Because Beauty Is Only Skin Deep."

"Beauty," adapted from my short story of the same name, had been accepted for publication in *Nightguant,* a zine that folded after two issues. "Beauty" was to appear in their third issue.

Halloween Candy initially included a fourth tale: "They Came from Outer Space and Went Bump in the Night." Yet despite a generous body count, this alien gorefest had little story or characterization. In its defense, it featured *Halloween Candy*'s grisliest deaths. Nevertheless, I excised "Outer Space," partially because it compared poorly to my other three tales, storywise, and partially to lower the screenplay's budget.

I ended up with a 77-page screenplay. Short by Hollywood studio standards, but not unusual for indie horror. Many low-budget gorefests run 75 to 80 minutes.

Armed with my ignorance, I began marketing *Halloween Candy.* I phoned every studio, distributor, and production company mentioned in *Daily Variety* and *The Hollywood Reporter.* Unaware of industry directories, I phoned Los Angeles information from New York every time I needed a number. I spent lunch hours abusing my employer's long-distance bill. I submitted *Halloween Candy* to every P.O. Box "production company" with a classified ad seeking horror scripts. I submitted to "former studio script-readers" whose *American Film* classifieds promised they'd forward worthy scripts to their "studio and agency contacts." I placed my own classified ads, seeking producers and investors, in *Weekly Variety* and *Fangoria.*

My *Fangoria* ad drew a sizable response, mostly written on loose-leaf paper. A 15-year-old from Texas, planning an acting career in slasher films, stated: "Your script could be my big break." A 13-year-old from Maryland, who regaled neighborhood kids with his super-8 movies, wrote: "I can pay you $35, or more if you want." A special effects artist in California, seeking his first directorial project, wrote that while he enjoyed *Halloween Candy,* current technology did not allow "Beauty" to be filmed as written. (*The Hollow Man* demonstrates this is no longer true.)

And then I replied to an ad in *Fangoria* placed by a production company seeking horror scripts. This drew my first promising response.

The production company turned out to be David, a Mississippi native and USC film student, and his partner in Greenville, who, at age 26, was the youngest TV station manager in the US. Their plan was to shoot *Halloween Candy* on video, using station equipment. David would direct, his partner produce. The budget was $50,000.

David requested a rewrite to "We Have an Opening in Biology 101," to make its twist ending "less predictable." I happily complied. Made me feel like a real Hollywood writer.

David flew to New York to hand-deliver a contract that his local Mississippi lawyer had copied from a practice guide. We discussed film schools, David being from USC, I from NYU. We discussed script-readers, David opining that they were all frustrated writers. David had instructions to buy me dinner at whatever Manhattan eatery I chose, on his partner's credit card, no expense too great. I chose McDonald's. The one near NYU.

After David returned to Mississippi, I sought advice from a script-reader I'd previously submitted *Halloween Candy* to, a Los Angeles woman with an English accent. She referred me to New York agent Ron Bernstein.

Bernstein declared David's contract "horrible" because it only paid me net profits. I knew this, but replied that the budget was low, and these people seemed trustworthy. Bernstein said I could do as I please (I was not his client), but that in all his years in the industry, he had never seen a dime of net profit paid to anyone. Not once.

I thanked him, and now thoroughly depressed, phoned David for some upfront money. After a strained conversation, and time-out to confer with his partner, David agreed to send me a revised contract promising me $4,000 upfront. Several days later, David phoned to say that rehearsals had not gone well. *Halloween Candy*'s dialogue proved "too complex" for their local actors to memorize. So he and his partner would instead shoot a silent film, then dub the dialogue during post-production. A simpler film, from a script that David would write.

Although our deal collapsed and we never had a signed contract, I regard this episode as *Halloween Candy*'s first option. As for David's silent film, I've not heard or read of him anywhere since.

This "collapsed deal" soon seemed a good thing when in 1985, after I replied to a classified ad in *American Film,* the American Film Institute Alumni Association's Writers Workshop chose *Halloween Candy* for their monthly reading. I was surprised an AFI-affiliated group would sponsor a low-budget gorefest, but the Workshop's head and founder, Willard Rodgers, told me that he sought quality scripts regardless of genre. Good man.

I flew to Los Angeles for the event, held at the AFI campus on April 9, 1985. In the Louis B. Mayer Library, Mark Goodson Screening Room. The follow-up Q&A was moderated by Robert Wise (director of *The Sound of Music*—but also *The Haunting*). I was feted at a gala reception and shown L.A.'s nighttime vista from the AFI's hilltop mansion. I felt I had arrived. I felt like Kevin Bacon in *The Big Picture.* Fifteen minutes of glory, and then I was yesterday's news.

Major studios and legitimate production companies reviewed *Halloween Candy.* I was so impressed by the letterheads, I almost didn't mind the rejection letters. At least now I was attracting a better class of rejections.

I signed with my first agent, Diane Fallon, of the Diane Fallon Agency. She submitted *Halloween Candy* to Robert Wise's production company. No sale.

In 1986, I advertised my writing services in *National Review* and received a response from Norman, a North Carolina film critic, who introduced me to North Carolina filmmaker Bill Olsen (*Rockin' Road Trip*). After flying to New York to meet me, Bill optioned *Halloween Candy* for his upcoming slate of projects, which included remakes of *Mars Needs Women* and *Cabinet of Dr. Caligari.* This time, I was to get upfront money.

Wanting to meet Stevie Nicks, Norman suggested that Stevie, with her "white witch" image, was ideal for the role of Cheavan in *Halloween Candy.* I'd never heard of Stevie Nicks, but I had no objections. With nothing to lose, Bill suggested Stevie for the cast in his prospectus. That Stevie was likely unavailable proved unimportant, because Bill failed to raise financing and *Halloween Candy*'s option expired in 1987. Shortly thereafter, Diane closed her agency.

Having written several screenplays by now, I placed an ad in *The Economist* seeking producers and investors, and drew responses from Saudi Arabia, Singapore, West Germany, England, and Manhattan.

The Manhattanite was a mystery man who asked over the phone that I leave my scripts outside his apartment door, located in a seedy downtown building. I never saw him in the flesh. Over the phone, he asked what sort of deal I wanted. I said I'd want to consult an agent. He groaned, adding that he did not deal with agents.

The West Germans met me in New York, stopping along their way to Los Angeles to seek clients for their product placement firm. A short beefy blond, and a towering swarthy one named Udo. They were cordial, but less interested in *Halloween Candy* than in building industry contacts and picking the brain of anyone "connected" to Hollywood. I expect I disappointed them.

The Englishman was the most colorful. Always phoning at 5:00 a.m. EST, talking for hours while saying nothing, his dog barking in the background. Writing letters replete with typos and semi-coherent phrases. Declaring me a "genius" and *Halloween Candy* "amazing" and "magnificent." Announcing that his assistant was meeting with Spielberg and De Laurentiis to set up deals for me, and that he and his assistant would shortly be flying to New York with a "big cheque" for me. Figures were never discussed.

At first I listened because, you never know. But I phoned De Laurentiis's office, and was told they'd never heard of either the Englishman or his assistant. I assumed the same for Spielberg. From then on, I listened to the Englishman out of courtesy. He became a joke to my family and friends, a symbol of the "big deals" *Halloween Candy* was attracting. In time, the Englishman stopped talking deals, but his enthusiasm and optimism never diminished. He kept me informed of his own projects, of his scripts and novels. We never met, but exchanged Christmas cards for another decade, until his death. He was, I gathered from his widow, in his sixties.

In early 1987, I responded to another *American Film* classified seeking horror scripts. This ad was placed by a Manhattan-based music management firm hoping to expand into film production. Two managers (promoters?) wanting to become producers. They forwarded *Halloween Candy* to makeup artist Tom Savini, who expressed interest in it being his directorial debut. (It would be four years before I first spoke to Savini, on the phone, and I have yet to meet him.)

The two managers and I agreed to option terms (including upfront money), after which I secured an agent from the WGA signatory list to supervise the contract. Once again, a one-woman agency.

As she was new to agenting, she had no idea what an option contract looked like. Nor did the managers. Each side insisted the other draft the contract. To break this impasse, I gave the managers my Bill Olsen contract, as a sample, to be revised according to our new terms. Specifically, I'd reserved all print publication rights (novels, novelizations, short stories, comic books) to my screenplay.

Upon receiving the revised contract and option check, my agent was so thrilled (she later told me) that she ran through the office hallways brandishing the check to all her co-tenants. *Halloween Candy* was her first sale, you see. (Not really; I'd sold it before she was ever in the picture). She then deposited the check into her client trust account without my consent.

I was horrified upon seeing the contract. According to its terms, I reserved no print publication rights, but was merely to novelize the screenplay. All rights were granted (by implication) to the managers, who were hiring me to novelize what was now their property. This problem arose partially because neither manager understood the fine legal concepts inherent in a screenplay option, and partially because they mechanically copied the Olsen contract with little revision. Looking back, I doubt the managers even understood what they were agreeing to when I requested that I reserve the novelization rights.

We had a problem. By cashing the check, *my* agent had legally bound me to a contract that I refused to sign. Too late, I hired an entertainment attorney who drafted a contract favorable to me, but which worried the managers. So *my* agent suggested that they show the contract to their attorney.

The managers hired an attorney, who advised against *both* contracts. The first contract (which my agent agreed to by cashing the check) did not explicitly grant or convey any rights to the managers; it merely did so by implication. So this attorney drafted a third contract. Thus began an eight month exchange of papers, during which time the managers soured on their original attorney and hired a third attorney, who advised against all contracts up to that point and introduced his own set of contracts.

Meanwhile, I considered backup plans. I had appealed to William F. Buckley to help finance my yuppie satire, *Manhattan Sharks.* Perhaps thinking to dispel two birds at once, Buckley introduced me to Ben, a Long Island liquor distributor who'd tried to option Buckley's Blackford Oakes series. When *Manhattan Sharks*'s budget proved too rich for Ben, I suggested *Halloween Candy,* in the event its ongoing negotiations collapsed. But Ben was uninterested in horror. His dream project was a politically conservative version of *Porky's*, hopefully written by P.J. O'Rourke and starring Howard Stern.

In April 1988, a six-month option contract with the managers was finalized. My attorney had eaten most of my option fee. The managers' two attorneys doubtless charged more. The option was later extended for four months, expiring in February 1989. All rights to *Halloween Candy* reverted to me.

First lesson learned: An agent *may* have authority to bind you legally, even against your wishes, depending on facts and circumstances. When my agent cashed the option check, I had legally "agreed" to the contract, and this impaired my attorney's negotiating maneuverability. It was only because the managers' own attorneys (and thus, investors) also disliked that first contract that I was able to renegotiate and secure print publication rights.

Best defense: When retaining an agent, agree in writing that she can negotiate, but only you can agree to and sign a contract with buyers, and that buyers will be informed of this. Then make sure they are. This "solution" is problematic, because it indicates a distrust in your agent and places her in a potentially embarrassing position with buyers. And it's hard enough finding an agent without driving her off with your distrust and paranoia.

Next best defense: Choose a competent agent. Bad agents are worse than no agent. I should have known there were a few cards missing in her Rolodex when she said to me, "You're on your way, kid-o!" She liked calling me *kid-o.* I guess it made her feel like a real agent. Like the ones in old Hollywood movies.

Second lesson learned: The WGA signatory list is no guarantee of competence. It sets a minimum standard, no more. Diane Fallon was a WGA signatory and did fine. My second agent was a WGA signatory, and was worse than no agent.

Third lesson learned: If the buyer suggests you draft the contract, *do so.* Or have your attorney do so. Whoever drafts the contract has the advantage. (However, it's unlikely that any but the greenest producer would concede this advantage.)

Fourth lesson learned: Do not encourage the buyer to show your contract to his attorney; that's his responsibility as an adult. You (and your agent) should be looking out for you.

In the summer of 1988, I began novelizing *Halloween Candy* in anticipation of the film. I had completed a short story version of "The Lady Who Ate Dolls" and polished my *Nightguant* version of "Because Beauty Is Only Skin Deep" when my agent learned that publishers won't negotiate novelization deals for a film that has yet to secure a distributor. I suspended my novelization efforts until that eventuality, which never occurred.

By 1991, I was living in Los Angeles and working for a low-budget producer who, because of his litigious nature, I will call Andy (not his real name). I'd hoped to interest Andy in *Halloween Candy,* but he disdained horror. He imagined himself to be an A-lister, deserving of star-driven prestige projects rather than the how-to videos and nonunion projects brought to him by people he contemned as "amateurs."

Naturally, I hoped to entice some of those amateurs into producing *Halloween Candy,* but Andy's contacts were barely Z-list. Daily, a motley cross-section from the showbiz underbelly traversed his Hollywood offices. I met paranoid screenwriters with bound and illustrated tomes, flaky starlets, unlicensed agents, wealthy businessmen looking to cast their daughters or girlfriends in projects, and lookiloo "investors" with no money.

I learned that everyone in Hollywood (*everyone*—special effects artists, lighting technicians, writers, actors), claims they can raise half the budget for a film, if you can raise the other half. Once, we had four investors with four halves of a budget, and not a dime between them. I discovered that "half the budget" doesn't mean money, but free labor. Actors, writers, and crew working for *deferred pay* (which often means *no pay*). These "investors" each wanted to invest the "monetary value" of their friends' labor. Trouble is, you can't produce two films merely because you have four films' worth of cast and crew; someone has to buy the film stock.

One investor/video producer invited us to a business meeting at a pricey Malibu restaurant, only to announce upon our arrival that he wasn't very hungry after all. We took our meeting in the bar, where he and Andy each extolled his own extensive funding, while trying to squeeze money from the other. I nursed an overpriced diet coke while observing these two Hollywood power-brokers at play. First the investor opened, moving to impress by pointing out Dudley Moore eating in the dining area. Andy countered by getting thoroughly sloshed. Later that night, we performed due diligence by examining the investor's video library inventory, kept secure in his car trunk. Then I helped Andy stagger to a nearby Pizza Hut for some solids. During dinner, Andy began sobbing over his unrequited love for some realtor. I'd never met the woman, but I assured Andy that she loved him. Anything to make him stop crying.

Not that working for Andy was all glitz and glamour. His current employees were always fielding abusive and threatening phone calls from Andy's past employees, former investors, utility companies, his landlord, car dealer, grocer, and ex-wife, all claiming Andy owed them money. All of them, Andy assured us, were liars, frauds, or dangerously insane. In any event, everyone would be paid off, just as soon as Andy landed that one big investor to put him on the A-list.

This world of wannabes and low-budgeters is accurately profiled in Rod Lurie's *Once Upon a Time in Hollywood: Moviemaking, Con Games, and Murder in Glitter City,* a probing examination of the Emr murders. As it happens, I had argued with producer Jon Emr on the phone a week before his untimely death. After his murder hit the news, one producer called to ask if this meant that her own project would now be bumped up on Andy's production schedule.

My time spent in that Hollywood office was a learning experience. I learned that writers must have a script in hand, directors and actors must have a reel, but anyone can call himself a producer.

I decided to produce *Halloween Candy* on my own.

Rather than seek investors through classifieds, I now knew that to attract investors and studios I must first attach "bankable names" to my property. I ignored the A-list, assuming they were unattainable, and concentrated on B-list horror stars.

I tracked down Tom Savini's home phone, and spoke to him for the first time. He confirmed he was still interested in directing *Halloween Candy* should I raise financing. But he never sent the Letter Of Interest he'd promised, and which I'd hoped to include in my prospectus. Candy Clark and Jonathan Frid were kind enough to reply, but both declined any interest in even reading my script.

Horror was dead. It was so . . . Eighties. I concentrated on other projects, aside from an occasional query. I'd learned to ignore P.O. Box producers. I ignored Andy's calls requesting a loan. The man had nerve. He still owed me back pay.

In 1995, I submitted "The Lady Who Ate Dolls" and "Because Beauty Is Only Skin Deep" to Taurus Entertainment, as possible episodes for their upcoming *Creepshow* TV series. I re-contacted Taurus in 1997 and 1998. Anna, in development, asked that I be patient for a decision. In any event, the series never materialized.

In 1996, Stephen, a Canadian producer, expressed interest in *Halloween Candy*. I allowed him to "show it to investors" to help them decide. After four years, his investors remained undecided. Stephen never optioned *Halloween Candy*, but he did send me a Christmas card.

I continued submitting the short story versions of "Lady" and "Beauty" from my aborted novelization. In 1996, *Wicked Mystic* magazine published "The Lady Who Ate Dolls." Shortly thereafter, Dimension Films released *Scream*.

Horror was hot again.

Not that *Scream* was aesthetically innovative. An indistinguishable slasher film, *Scream* would have bombed in 1986. It succeeded a decade later because of marketing and timing.

Scream's marketing campaign distinguished the film for its "smart humor." But 1980s horror teems with smart humor (*Motel Hell, Creepshow, An American Werewolf in London, Re-Animator*). *Scream*'s marketing also credited the film with introducing strong women into horror, giving that as the reason for "horror's new female audience." But aside from validating the anti-horror prejudices of feminists and fundamentalists alike, it's untrue. The lone female survivor (often Jamie Lee Curtis) was so common in 1980s slasher horror, she had transcended from cliché into archetype. (For an overview, see *Men, Women, and Chain Saws: Gender in the Modern Horror Film,* by Carol J. Clover, Princeton University Press, 1992). It's unfortunate that horror's heritage was distorted to promote *Scream*. (*Scream* further misrepresents horror's history by having its characters repeatedly say "horror movie" and "scary movie" when they mean "slasher movie," thus reaffirming the popular lay myth that the 1978-86 slasher cycle is all of horror).

As for timing, audiences were so parched for horror by 1996 that anything was welcome relief. Even a film that, despite its slasher iconography, is in some ways nearer suspense than horror (see my essay, "But Is It *Horror*?: Defining and Demarcating the Genre").

But whatever its genre, *Scream* was *perceived* as horror, and so Hollywood's demand for horror rose. I prepared *Halloween Candy* for a new round of submissions. Intending a quick polish, I read it for the first time in a decade.

I was shocked.

Halloween Candy had only been my second feature screenplay (my first, a dreadful spy non-thriller: *The Executioner*). I had written much since then. I'd written script coverage for producers and for Willard Rodgers's National Writers Workshop (which by 1995, a decade after *Halloween Candy*'s reading, had dropped its AFI affiliation).

I was shocked by how poorly *Halloween Candy* compared to my recent work. Shocked that it had received so much acclaim. Shocked that people had paid thousands to option it. Instead of a polish, I did a thorough rewrite.

Horror wasn't the only hot genre in 1997. Independent films were exploding. Producers wanted "edgy." Dark and dangerous and erotic and envelop-pushing. A *Beavis and Butthead* writer told me the MTV show had given him a lucrative reputation as "that edgy writer." David Lynch too is edgy. *Eraserhead* and *Blue Velvet* and *Twin Peaks,* very edgy.

Halloween Candy had opened with the traditional "We Have an Opening in Biology 101," darkening with the edgy "Lady Who Ate Dolls," and ending on a laugh with "Because Beauty Is Only Skin Deep." I evened the tone. Every tale became dark and gory and edgy, and rife with black comedy and social satire.

"We Have an Opening in Biology 101" became "Weird Science in a Diverse University." The protagonists now ignoble, their love no longer mutual, the setting very PC 1990s.

"The Lady Who Ate Dolls" became "Witches Need Love Too." A slight tonal shift, humor now heightening its satirical counterpoints to *Fatal Attraction.* The elderly storekeeper replaced by Amir. Everyone's favorite, I changed this story the least. The short story version in *Wicked Mystic* is based on my original script, and will show the changes are minor.

I interwove a Michael Jackson satire into "Because Beauty Is Only Skin Deep." Originally, it was only Jackie's tale.

I resurrected "They Came from Outer Space and Went Bump in the Night," interweaving an *X-Files* parody into what had been a simple alien gorefest. With its addition, *Halloween Candy* grew from 77 to 107 pages. What had been low-budget/direct-to-video length was now major studio length.

In 1998, while attending an IFP/West screening, I ran into an actress from *Halloween Candy*'s AFI reading. Curious coincidence, for soon thereafter I began marketing the revised *Halloween Candy.*

Halloween Candy was a Finalist in the 1999 Blue Cat Screenplay contest, and Quarterfinalist in the Empire Screenplay contest. Blue Cat bought a full-page ad in *The Hollywood Reporter* announcing the Winner and Finalists (September 14-20, 1999, p. 99). Stephen in Canada (now with Tsunami Entertainment) agreed to read the new *Halloween Candy.* Literary agencies, production companies, and studio executives reconsidered *Halloween Candy.* ScriptShark.com rated it a Consider; better than Pass, less than Recommend. ScriptShark told me most submissions get a Pass. A Consider puts *Halloween Candy* onto ScriptShark's online coverage board, accessible only to legitimate agents, managers, producers, and development executives.

For all I know, *Halloween Candy* is still on those boards.

Why publish *Halloween Candy*? Because I can't afford to produce it. If you can't see it, at least now you can read it.

In publishing *Halloween Candy,* I considered three alternatives: (1) maintain its sparse screenplay format, (2) pad its narrative into something more "literary," (3) novelize it.

Screenplay styles change, but are mostly sparse. One must write nothing that cannot be seen or heard by an audience. No character thoughts. And no restrictive physical descriptions, such as hair and eye color, or exact age. Writers are not in charge of casting. Do not direct on paper. Actors don't like every glance and gesture scripted, as though they were puppets. Parentheticals describing a character's delivery should be kept to a minimum. It is the director and actors who interpret the script.

This makes for a less than literary reading experience.

One can pad a script with descriptions to enhance its literary appeal, but then the script loses its true form. A response to this may be that a script is a blueprint, not literature. Its true form is the finished film, and so if one publishes a script, it needs padding.

In which case, one should perhaps not merely pad, but novelize it. I did so with *Manhattan Sharks,* which I'd originally written as a screenplay. I had already halfway novelized *Halloween Candy* during its last option.

But I opted for the first alternative. The version in this book is the 1998 revised *Halloween Candy* screenplay, reformatted for easier reading. Unlike *Manhattan Sharks,* I don't think *Halloween Candy* works as a novel. It's intended as an audiovisual treat, a visceral shockfest, a loud and colorful funhouse roller coaster.

I can't provide that on paper. I can only suggest that the reader, in screening *Halloween Candy* within his or her theater of imagination, visualize it with campy acting and expressionist camera angles, colorful lighting and atmospheric smoke effects. Much like *Creepshow,* the impetus for *Halloween Candy.*

You are the director, and special effects artist, and casting agent.

* * *

What else? Aside from the screenplay, this book contains the following tricks and treats:

"They Came from Outer Space and Went Bump in the Night: Haunted Houses in California" appeared in *Horror* #8, 1997. It chronicles my experiences performing at Universal's Chamber Of Chills in 1996, and reviews other Halloween horror funhouses. (I'd been wanting to use that title ever since excising my alien story from the original *Halloween Candy.*)

"Spirit of '68" is based on my skit, "Love Beads and Shrapnel," which was performed on the UCLA campus in autumn 1991. I wrote the short story in 1995. It won Honorable Mention in the 1996 *Writer's Digest* contest.

"'*Sans* Fangs' with Jonathan Frid" is from my 1986 interview of Mr. Frid (Barnabas Collins in *Dark Shadows*). It was first published fifteen years later in *Filmfax* #83 (February/March 2001). The version herein contains additional material, mostly about Frid's childhood. I suspect *Filmfax* thought few readers would be interested in such trivia; I restore that information for those who are.

"Vampire Nation" was first published in *Horrors! 365 Scary Stories* (Barnes & Noble Books, 1998). It also serves as prologue to my 2000 novel, *Vampire Nation.*

"Communist Vampires" appeared on FrontpageMagazine.com, December 8, 2000.

"The Career Witch" is based on my 1986 spec teleplay for TV's *Tales from the Darkside.* Diane Fallon liked it, but not Laurel TV. This short story version originally appeared in *100 Wicked Little Witch Stories* (Barnes & Noble Books, 1995).

"But Is It *Horror*?: Defining and Demarcating the Genre" was to have appeared in *Midnight Marquee*, but the magazine changed direction (becoming *Midnight Marquee Monsters*) before my piece was published. Thus, this is its first print publication.

"Horror Goes Hollywood: A Call for Saturn Reform" originates from my July 1997 coverage of the 23rd Annual Saturn Awards for *Horror*, which folded before my report appeared. The version herein is essentially what I wrote then. I've deleted some stale news items, but my underlying critique remains valid four years later.

"Planets in Motion" was written in 1995. This is its first print publication.

"Stalking the Truth" appeared in *Sci-Fi Universe,* December 1997.

"Five Paranoiacs, All in a Row . . ." appeared in *Horrors! 365 Scary Stories* (Barnes & Noble Books, 1998).

"The Pragmatic Aesthetics of Low-Budget Horror Cinema" appeared in *Midnight Marquee* #60 (Summer/Fall 1999) under the title: "Art of the Low-Budget Horror Film."

"The Actor as Horror Villain" appeared in *Horror* #8, 1997.

"The Lady Who Ate Dolls" appeared in *Wicked Mystic* #25, Spring 1996. Among my influences for that story was Ray Bradbury's "Drink Entire: Against the Madness of Crowds."

Some of my book and film reviews may be found at Tangent Online (www.sfsite.com/tangent) and HorrorFind.com.

HALLOWEEN CANDY

EXT. PEABODY HOUSE - DAY

A suburban street in present-day New England. Trim lawns colored with autumn leaves. Halloween in the air.

Only one house is rundown, paint peeling. Freshly splattered with broken eggs. A rock sails through the air, shattering a window.

CHILDREN: Witch! Witch! Witch!

MRS. PEABODY, a shrewish fiftysomething, peers through the broken window. Four CHILDREN on her lawn, hiding behind bushes: ARTHUR, MEGAN, WOLF, JACKIE, all third-graders. No costumes.

MRS. PEABODY: You brats get off my lawn!

CHILDREN: Burn witch, burn! Burn witch, burn!

MRS. PEABODY exits the house, wielding a broom. The CHILDREN run away, squealing.

CHILDREN: Burn witch, burn! Burn witch, burn!

The CHILDREN race down the sidewalk, crashing into SARAH, a perky young woman with short blond hair, carrying a wicker basket.

SARAH: Whoa! What's the big hurry?

ARTHUR: We're gonna burn the witch!

MEGAN: Yeah, make her suffer!

SARAH: Oh dear. Where's your Halloween spirit? You should be dressing as young witches and warlocks. They're spooky, but not evil.

ARTHUR: No kidding. Witches are wimps. I wanna Charles Manson costume. Rack up a real body count.

SARAH: Oh dear.

WOLF: Witches are boring. I'd rather dress like Marilyn Manson.

SARAH: Rather than a warlock?

MEGAN: Witches are old. I hate old people. I hate generation X.

SARAH: Generation X is old?

JACKIE: Witches are ugly.

SARAH: I'm old?

JACKIE: Like ugly old Mrs. Peabody.

CHILDREN: Yeah, we hate Mrs. Peabody!

SARAH: Children, children. Age brings wisdom. Witch means wise woman. I can't wait to grow old.

MEGAN: Who says you have to wait?

SARAH: Furthermore, most witches are pretty. Even sexy. Only bad witches are ugly.

ARTHUR: Like ugly old Mrs. Peabody!

CHILDREN: Yeah, burn her! Burn her!

SARAH: No, no, children. You mustn't even burn leaves. Pollution makes our planet very sad.

SARAH removes a textbook from her basket, skimming . . .

SARAH: In fact, those of you planning a career in gender studies will be fascinated to learn that Wicca, the religion of witches, is actually an ancient form of nature worship, mischaracterized by Western industrial patriarchy—

WOLF: Witch!

The CHILDREN pummel SARAH with eggs.

CHILDREN: Burn witch, burn! Burn witch, burn! Burn witch, burn!

The CHILDREN run away, screams fading with the rustling leaves.

Smiling wryly, SARAH wipes herself with a handkerchief as she approaches MRS. PEABODY's house.

MRS. PEABODY sees SARAH's clothes, then indicates her house.

MRS. PEABODY: Trick or treat. Cute name for legalized extortion.

SARAH: Oh dear. That's certainly not the Halloween spirit.

MRS. PEABODY: Little monsters still remember last year. I never give treats.

SARAH: In olden days, only dead spirits were entitled to treats.

MRS. PEABODY: I'm all for traditional values. Do you suggest poisoned apples or razor blades?

SARAH: Now, Mrs. Peabody. We both know you could never do anything like that. They're only children.

MRS. PEABODY: So was Billy The Kid. I wish I was a witch. They'd be sorry.

SARAH: Well, I've got Halloween shopping.

MRS. PEABODY: For a pack of ungrateful brats, no doubt.

SARAH departs with a friendly smile.

INT. SUPERMARKET - DAY

Aisles of Halloween decorations and merchandise. SARAH pushes a shopping cart through crowds of shoppers. She reaches for a bag of candy corn and does not see TRUDY (age 6) sneak up and steal the wicker basket from Sarah's cart.

Turning, SARAH is surprised to find the basket gone. She searches and finds it poorly hidden on a shelf. TRUDY giggles from a hiding spot. SARAH pretends not to notice and returns the basket to her cart.

But when SARAH turns around, TRUDY steals it again.

As TRUDY is hiding it, SARAH creeps up and seizes the basket from TRUDY. TRUDY nervously eyes SARAH. Smiling, SARAH wags a finger at the naughty child.

INT. SARAH'S KITCHEN - DAY

A modern kitchen. Halloween paraphernalia covers the countertop. A stove heats a plain aluminum pot, boiling water.

SARAH takes a jar from a spice rack, pours herbs into her hand, adding to a blend of herbs, spices, and powders. She takes her concoction to the boiling pot.

A black cat, MORTIMER, watches her.

SARAH: All ready for tricks or treats, Mortimer?

SARAH casts the concoction into the pot .

An EXPLOSION of colored smoke. Eerie theme music swells as mist, sparks, and magic spiral from the cauldron, spelling the

OPENING CREDITS

And transmuting Sarah's modern clothes into the traditional black cape and pointed hat of Halloween witches everywhere. Her pert blond hair lengthens, thickens, blackens. The pot distends into a huge black cauldron, fire raging beneath.

Wind billows Sarah's black hair and cape. Her smile is maniacal but cheerful. An evil but happy witch.

SARAH takes a candy bar.

SARAH: Refined sugar. Saturated fat. Know what that means, Mortimer?

SARAH dunks the candy bar deep into the cauldron's bubbling brew, up to her elbow. She extracts her hand, unharmed. The candy bar is now a big gleaming skull candy.

SARAH: Lose weight now, or lose it later.

SARAH selects a piece of candy corn.

SARAH: Nobody likes poor candy corn. Know why?

SARAH dunks it into the brew. She extracts a bright orange Jack O' Lantern candy, grinning with one tooth.

SARAH: It rots your teeth!

SARAH selects a green mint candy, dunks it into the brew, extracts a gray alien candy. As in The X-Files.

SARAH: That's not the one I wanted.

SARAH dunks the gray alien into the brew. She extracts a vicious green alien candy, drooling saliva. Like H.R. Giger's Alien.

SARAH: Now that's the Halloween spirit!

SARAH reaches for an apple. MORTIMER growls.

SARAH: Good point. Too wholesome.

SARAH dunks a cupcake, extracting a Frankenstein monster candy. Then she reaches for a cookie. MORTIMER growls louder.

SARAH: All right already! You and your male ego.

SARAH bypasses the cupcake for a black licorice stick. She dunks it into the brew, extracting a black cat candy. She compares it to MORTIMER, then dunks the cat candy in again. She extracts it and the cat candy is fatter. MORTIMER growls.

SARAH: I sculpt it as I see it.

MORTIMER snarls.

SARAH: Diet! Don't blame the artist.

END OPENING CREDITS

EXT/INT. SARAH'S FRONT PORCH - NIGHT

ARTHUR, MEGAN, WOLF, JACKIE ring the doorbell. Their Halloween costumes are of modern celebrities. No traditional monsters.

SARAH opens the door, blond and perky, dressed in a hokey witch's costume rather than in her previous dark glory.

CHILDREN: Trick or treat, smell my feet, give me something good to eat!

Beside SARAH, hidden from the children, are two dishes of treats. One holds commercial candy. One holds her home-brewed candy. SARAH's hand hovers above the normal candy.

SARAH: Oh my! You all look so fearsome!

JACKIE: I'm a Spice Girl. How can I look fearsome?

SARAH: Not fearsome? How sad! Why, in olden times every costume evoked death, for only that represented the true meaning of Halloween, a time for harvesting fallen crops and contacting dead souls. Like my witch's costume, because wise women communed with the dead and—

ARTHUR: Trick or treat, you stupid witch!

SARAH's hand shifts to her special candy, hovering indecisively.

SARAH: Not stupid. Witch means wise.

MEGAN: Yeah, she just rhymes with witch.

SARAH: Children. Halloween is a scary day. Even a solemn day. Not a nasty day.

JACKIE: The only thing scary is your face.

WOLF: Are we getting something or not, you stupid "rhymes with witch."

SARAH: How about some scary candy? To put you in the Halloween spirit.

SARAH gives ARTHUR the black cat candy, to MEGAN the Frankenstein monster, WOLF the alien, JACKIE the skull. The CHILDREN leave without a word of thanks.

SARAH: Pleasant nightmares.

After SARAH closes the door, it is pummeled by eggs.

EXT. SARAH'S NEW ENGLAND TOWN - NIGHT

A peaceful autumnal suburb. Clouds swirl past a full moon, indicating a TIME LAPSE. Dogs (or wolves?) howl ominously.

INT. JACKIE'S BEDROOM - NIGHT

A princess telephone, makeup kit, Barbie dolls. Piles of candy wrappers. No wonder JACKIE twists and turns in her sleep. The half-eaten skull candy grins fiendishly.

INT. WOLF'S BEDROOM - NIGHT

Sci-fi movie posters. The half-eaten alien candy amidst empty candy wrappers. WOLF also has difficulty sleeping. Twisting, turning, moaning in bed.

INT. MEGAN'S BEDROOM - NIGHT

A room less girlish than Jackie's. More tomboyish. But the same pile of empty candy wrappers, the partly devoured Frankenstein head grotesquely deformed. MEGAN in bed, twisting and turning.

INT. ARTHUR'S BEDROOM - NIGHT

The sloppiest room of all. Empty wrappers everywhere, the black cat candy eaten to its paws. ARTHUR in bed, twisting, turning.

His PARENTS' voices emanate from downstairs.

MOTHER: *(downstairs)* I warned him. But, he says, all my friends eat all their candy on Halloween night. Sick holiday.

FATHER: *(downstairs)* Maybe he'll throw up. Teach the boy a lesson.

MOTHER: *(downstairs)* Did you check the unwrapped candy?

FATHER: *(downstairs)* Yes, yes. There were no pins.

MOTHER: *(downstairs)* I hope they weren't poisoned.

As ARTHUR twists and turns, we DISSOLVE to Arthur's nightmare.

EXT. CHEAVAN'S HOUSE - NIGHT

A dark street, glistening from recent rain. In an upstairs window of a two-story house, a violet neon sign burns: Good Witch—Let Me Help You!

Superimpose: WITCHES NEED LOVE TOO

INT. CHEAVAN'S PARLOR - NIGHT

Occult paraphernalia, low tables, plush furniture. The neon sign buzzes behind scarlet drapes. Many dolls, some manufactured, but most handcrafted. A big dollhouse.

ARTHUR, approaching forty but looking older, sits on a low plush cushion. A dirty raincoat covers his slouched frame.

CHEAVAN, a tall attractive woman past forty but looking younger, sprawls on a sofa, looking down on ARTHUR. Her blood-red robe accentuates her curves, its crimson contrasting the gold occult chains encircling her neck and waist, her cascading blonde hair, her gold high-heeled pumps.

ARTHUR: I'm just as good as Bixby. But he's so pushy. Coming in early. Volunteering to do my work. He steals my work. He stole my . . . He steals everything.

CHEAVAN: Did you complain to your boss?

ARTHUR: My boss hates me. He likes it when Bixby steals my work.

CHEAVAN: But I don't hate you, Arthur. You were right to seek my help.

ARTHUR: Yeah. It's funny. At first I wasn't sure about hiring a witch. But now it feels like the right decision.

CHEAVAN: It was the right decision, but it wasn't yours to make. Fate drew you to me. The stars in the sky.

CHEAVAN rises from the sofa, statuesque in her pumps. She approaches a horoscope chart, sensuous curves rippling beneath her robe. She indicates a point on the chart.

CHEAVAN: Your arrival was delayed.

ARTHUR: Damn rainstorm.

CHEAVAN: I expected you earlier. Much earlier.

ARTHUR: Seems nobody can predict the weather.

CHEAVAN: Cats can. Unlike men, cats are sensitive to the shifting moods of Mother Nature.

ARTHUR: Sounds just like a woman.

CHEAVAN: I want you to know, I don't help everyone. Most clients receive a basic reading. My power, I reserve for the worthy.

ARTHUR: If you think I'm worthy, you're one of the few. So what's the damage? An hourly fee?

CHEAVAN looks askance at him. She removes a male doll from the dollhouse and caresses it with her long fingernails.

CHEAVAN: I shall promote your career and enrich your life. I will fight your battles and destroy your enemies. How do you price that?

ARTHUR: I wanna be fair. You sound like you know your job.

CHEAVAN: I should. *(grips the doll, anger rising)* All my work and study and sacrifice. Years of experience. Ten dollar readings for smirking teenagers. Potions for fat customers who won't lose weight because they don't follow instructions. Obnoxious widows demanding a refund just because their husbands' ghosts are glad to be rid of them, never mind I just wasted my Saturday night summoning the creep. Do you think that's fair?!

ARTHUR: *(meekened)* No.

CHEAVAN: I'm sorry. Of course you don't. You and I are so alike. Career-oriented. Unappreciated.

Bending, CHEAVAN replaces the doll in the dollhouse. ARTHUR can't help admiring her curvaceous figure.

CHEAVAN: You don't have many friends. I can tell.

ARTHUR: Same as the next guy, I guess. Same as you.

CHEAVAN: I have no friends. None at all.

ARTHUR: Women can be jealous. It's hard to believe you'd have trouble with the guys.

CHEAVAN: How perceptive you are. Of course, I've had many opportunities. But my career frightens men. And I'm choosy. I'm no beggar.

ARTHUR glances toward the drapes. No sound of rainfall.

ARTHUR: Stopped raining.

CHEAVAN: Before you arrived.

ARTHUR: Oh. Well, good.

Rising from a cramped position, ARTHUR stumbles over a low table, struggles to quickly regain his balance.

ARTHUR: I better be going. Haven't even had dinner yet.

CHEAVAN: You don't enjoy eating alone. I can tell.

They exchange an understanding glance. Two lonely-hearts.

INT. EXPENSIVE RESTAURANT - NIGHT

ARTHUR and CHEAVAN in a corner booth. CHEAVAN wears a dress that might be described as New Age gypsy.

CHEAVAN: Arthur, it was such a good idea to come here. You must tell me all your favorite spots and secret places. You obviously know the best places to eat. How do you know so much about restaurants?

ARTHUR: I don't really. Usually, I just grab a burger.

CHEAVAN: Because you don't like eating alone? I know you so well.

ARTHUR: It's not that. I'm no boy scout. I just figured you deserved someplace nice.

CHEAVAN: Well thank you so much! You chose an excellent place, Arthur. Thank you again for your fine judgment.

BIXBY appears, a tall man with an easy grin.

BIXBY: Arthur? A fine judgment? Hardly ever hear that in the same breath.

ARTHUR: Oh, hello Roy. Ah, Cheavan, this is Roy Bixby.

BIXBY: Cheavan. It is a pleasure.

Leering, BIXBY kisses CHEAVAN's hand, then slaps ARTHUR's back.

BIXBY: Hey Arthur, where have you been hiding her? She's quite a dish. Mind if I butt myself in?

BIXBY slides into the booth beside CHEAVAN, pressing against her, closer than necessary.

BIXBY: I'm with a client, but he went to the little boy's. So Arthur, doing all right. You hooked a new lady fast enough.

ARTHUR fails to notice CHEAVAN's questioning glance.

BIXBY: Plenty of fish, eh Arthur? Love 'em and leave 'em. It's the way of the world. So, what are we talking about?

CHEAVAN removes some hairs from BIXBY's shoulder.

BIXBY: Whoa, not too friendly! I already have a lady. Right, Arthur?

CHEAVAN: Just tidying up.

BIXBY: Hey, this one really knows how to pamper her man. Better take care of her, Arthur, or someone will take care of her for you.

Neither men notice CHEAVAN wrap the hair into a napkin, then slide the napkin into a small drawstring pouch.

Across the room, Bixby's CLIENT glances about. BIXBY spots him.

BIXBY: Whoops, it's a work night. Means I have to go. *(to Cheavan)* Work is a foreign word to Arthur. But just for tonight, I can't blame him.

BIXBY squeezes her thigh, then returns to his CLIENT.

ARTHUR: Lord, I hate the man! He steals everything from me!

CHEAVAN: Don't fret, darling. I'm already committed to your side. And a witch's commitment is sacred.

ARTHUR: It's bad enough seeing his face at the office every day without running into him after work.

CHEAVAN: I'm glad he came. He saved us much time and effort.

ARTHUR: How do you figure?

CHEAVAN: Tonight was no coincidence. He came because we came. Our destiny, united, is a powerful karmic force. I know the signs.

ARTHUR: You're the expert.

CHEAVAN: I'm so glad you agree.

EXT. STREET - NIGHT

ARTHUR and CHEAVAN on a dark, wet street corner.

ARTHUR: Sorry I can't drive you home.

CHEAVAN: Not to fret. You'll afford a car before long. With my help, a Rolls Royce.

ARTHUR: In that case, you're the best investment . . . By the way, how much do I owe you?

CHEAVAN: Tonight, nothing. Pay me when I deliver. Fair enough?

ARTHUR: More than fair enough.

A brief moment of uncertainty. CHEAVAN leans a bit forward, just in case. But ARTHUR is awkward. No kiss. They shake hands and go separate ways.

EXT. BRIDAL SHOP - NIGHT

CHEAVAN walks lonely rain-slicked streets, giddy from her "date." She halts before a closed bridal shop, poses so her reflection in the display window is superimposed over a mannequin in a bridal gown. She smiles, gladdened by the image.

INT. 24-HOUR GROCERY - NIGHT

AMIR sits near the cash register, reading a skinmag. Tinted prescription lens. Polyester shirt opened low. Bushy black chest hair and a tonnage of gold chains.

CHEAVAN enters. A fat ugly CAT snarls.

AMIR: Shut up you stupid cat. What's the matter with you? Are you a homosexual?

CHEAVAN peruses the aisles quickly, discomforted by AMIR's loud conversation with the CAT.

AMIR: Look at her. She is a very pretty lady. You don't like that? I don't want a queer cat in my store.

CHEAVAN selects a few items and goes to the register. AMIR totals her purchases. Slowly.

AMIR: My cat is a queer. He doesn't like you. Only a queer would not like to look at you.

CHEAVAN nods, glancing around the store to avoid looking at him.

AMIR: Me, I like to look at you very much. You are a real fox. So, do you like my store?

CHEAVAN: It's very nice.

AMIR: I see you admiring it. I make good money. And I am my own boss. If I like, I can close right now and buy you a drink.

CHEAVAN: I don't think so.

AMIR: Why don't you look at me when I talk to you?

Reluctantly, CHEAVAN turns toward him.

AMIR: I am not an ugly man.

CHEAVAN: I really don't need this tonight. Just bag!

AMIR: Why are you such a bitch?

CHEAVAN turns away, drumming her long nails on the counter. AMIR shoves her items into a brown bag.

AMIR: Your breasts are big, but they are not that big. They are not so big that you can be a bitch.

CHEAVAN: Don't call me a bitch.

AMIR: I can see you have no boyfriend. You are very frustrated. You should take any offer you get.

CHEAVAN sighs, her fingernails increasing speed.

AMIR: Your breasts are big, but you are not so young anymore.

CHEAVAN's fingers stop.

AMIR: If you let a man pleasure you, you would not be such a bitch.

CHEAVAN: I said, don't call me a bitch!

CHEAVAN grabs AMIR's hair and SLAMS his head down on the counter, repeatedly JACKHAMMERING his head in an adrenaline rage, POUNDING AMIR into semiconscious stupor, EMBEDDING broken eyeglass shards into his bloody face.

CHEAVAN tugs and drags AMIR by his hair, setting her foot against the counter for leverage, pulling AMIR across the counter so they both CRASH to the floor on the other side.

CHEAVAN stands, AMIR groaning at her feet. Clumps of black hair entangled around her fingers. She gleefully extracts a RAG DOLL from her drawstring pouch, weaves the hairs around the doll in an occult pattern.

AMIR grabs CHEAVAN's legs and pulls her to the ground, his hairy arms grasping her legs, groping for her neck.

AMIR: You fucking bitch! I fucking kill you! Fucking dead bitch!

CHEAVAN kicks and crawls away, AMIR grabbing after her legs. She rises and staggers. He chases her, pounces on her, throwing her against the shelves. Soup cans tumble upon them.

AMIR gropes CHEAVAN's neck. CHEAVAN grabs a can, hammers AMIR's skull, splashing blood upon her hands and face.

CHEAVAN: I said don't call me a bitch! My name is not bitch!

When AMIR subsides, CHEAVAN throws the can away. She locates the doll and finishes weaving Amir's hair around it, binding the doll with bloody hair in an intricate occult pattern.

CHEAVAN stands beside AMIR and stares at her doll.

AMIR opens his eyes, glasses broken. His POV is bloody, blurry, groggy. AMIR flexes a hand, as though preparing to jump CHEAVAN.

CHEAVAN glares at the doll, eyes flaring a sinister energy of rage and hate. Pitiless and beyond appeal.

AMIR jumps up, screaming rage.

CHEAVAN smiles down at AMIR, now six inches tall.

AMIR: *(a squeak)* I kill you, you bitch! I fucking kill you!

AMIR halts, slowly gazes up at CHEAVAN, a giantess looming over him. CHEAVAN crouches before him, tears open her blouse, thrusts her naked breasts at him.

CHEAVAN: Big enough?

AMIR squeals fearfully and runs away.

CHEAVAN laughs, her towering legs taking small steps so as not to out pace AMIR. Finally, she knocks him down with her toe.

She places her foot over AMIR, then steps down. CRUNCH!

CHEAVAN removes her foot from the pulpy red mess. AMIR's body is injured, yet his head still moves. CHEAVAN sets the high heel of her gold pump over AMIR's head . . .

AMIR: No, please, please, you're not a bitch, you're not—!

CHEAVAN steps. The skull cracks like a walnut, bleeding gray.

CHEAVAN scrapes her pump's sole along the edge of a shelf, as though removing dog shit.

The CAT meows.

CHEAVAN: Here little kitty.

The CAT races forward and attacks AMIR's corpse with a voracious appetite. CHEAVAN pets the CAT.

CHEAVAN: You like him, do you? Maybe you are a queer little kitty, after all.

INT. ARTHUR & BIXBY'S OFFICE - DAY

ARTHUR slouches behind his desk, wearing a rumpled business suit. Awards and trophies cram Bixby's (unoccupied) side of the office. LINDSAY, their beautiful secretary, reads from her message pad.

LINDSAY: . . . and Frank wants to know when the chart will be ready. You promised you'd have it two days ago. George is still waiting for the Miami Market Analysis. And Lyona still isn't pleased with your San Diego survey. She wanted to see you first thing this morning. She can't understand why you're late again.

Groaning, ARTHUR glances at a clock radio. After ten. He reluctantly accepts his messages from LINDSAY.

ARTHUR: Okay.

LINDSAY begins to leave, then spins around on her heel.

LINDSAY: Oh. Roy saw you at Chez Shalimar's last night. He said you were with a girl. Did you have fun?

ARTHUR: It was okay.

LINDSAY: Good.

LINDSAY begins to leave again.

ARTHUR: Oh, Lindsay.

She halts and faces him.

ARTHUR: We're just friends.

LINDSAY: Oh. Well, I hope things work out for you eventually.

ARTHUR: I think they will. She's going to help me.

LINDSAY: Good. I want you to be happy.

LINDSAY exits.

INT. ANTEROOM - CONTINUOUS

LINDSAY enters and goes to her desk.

INT. CHEAVAN'S KITCHEN - DAY

A modern kitchen, but dark and cluttered. Window shrouded behind plants and curtains. Jars, potions, and herbs crowd the counter.

CHEAVAN, in loose-fitting red robe, removes Bixby's hair from the napkin and begins weaving it around a naked KEN doll, licking her lips hungrily, eyeing KEN with girlish glee.

INT. ANTEROOM - DAY

BIXBY enters from the hall, kisses LINDSAY's cheek. He wears his power suit like a fashion model.

BIXBY: Finished one meeting, off to another. Wish me luck.

LINDSAY: Luck. Not that you need it.

BIXBY: Can't hurt. Market's getting tight. Stiff competition.

LINDSAY: You'll pull through. It's poor Arthur I'm worried about.

BIXBY: Hey, I thought you two were history.

LINDSAY pecks BIXBY's cheek.

LINDSAY: You know we are. I can't help feeling sorry for him.

BIXBY: You're too sweet for your own good. But I guess that's what I love about you.

INT. CHEAVAN'S KITCHEN - DAY

The KEN doll sits on the counter, an intricate occult pattern of Bixby's hair binding his nude torso. Towering before him, CHEAVAN drops her robe and is naked.

CHEAVAN takes KEN, massages her stomach with him, presses him up along her body, between her breasts, up to her mouth, licks him, presses her long tongue between his little legs, into his groin, clamps him in her mouth, caressing him with lips and tongue.

INT. ANTEROOM - DAY

LINDSAY and BIXBY are kissing passionately, groping while trying to maintain some office decorum.

INT. ARTHUR & BIXBY'S OFFICE - DAY

ARTHUR at his desk, staring at the door, listening to Lindsay and Bixby's moaning and groaning. ARTHUR clenches a pencil, pressing his thumb against it, rubbing the pencil . . .

The phone RINGS, jolting ARTHUR, who SNAPS the pencil in two. He drops the pencil pieces, grabs the receiver.

ARTHUR: Hello! *(meekens)* I'm sorry. No, George. The market analysis is not quite ready . . . I know it's been a while.

The moaning and groaning from the anteroom intensifies.

INT. CHEAVAN'S KITCHEN - DAY

CHEAVAN sucks KEN into her mouth, deep throating him head first. She slowly extracts him, saliva glistening on his nude body. She grips her boy toy, swallows hard, licks her lips in anticipation.

INT. ANTEROOM - DAY

LINDSAY and BIXBY force themselves apart, not comprehending their sudden lust, nor its sudden break. Faintly embarrassed, yet also excited, BIXBY nods and departs. LINDSAY stares after him.

INT. ARTHUR & BIXBY'S OFFICE - DAY

No longer on the phone, ARTHUR sits motionless, listening for any sound. He hears Bixby leave. ARTHUR grabs his phone.

ARTHUR: Lindsay. Can I see you for a second? It's important.

LINDSAY enters, resetting her hair, blushing but cool.

ARTHUR: Please sit down.

LINDSAY sits. ARTHUR searches his desk for a task.

ARTHUR: Uhm, I need . . .

ARTHUR gives LINDSAY the broken pencil.

ARTHUR: Can you please sharpen this?

LINDSAY takes the pencil and slides it into the electric sharpener on Arthur's desk. ARTHUR watches it sharpen.

INT. OFFICE HALLWAY/ELEVATOR - DAY

BIXBY and PASSENGERS await an EXPRESS elevator. When it arrives, it's already crowded, but all squeeze in.

INT. CHEAVAN'S KITCHEN - DAY

CHEAVAN clenches her molars over KEN's arm, gyrating his arm between her teeth. She growls. Voracious sexual hunger.

INT. ELEVATOR - DAY

A FAT WOMAN bumps into BIXBY's arm. BIXBY winces.

FAT WOMAN: I'm sorry. My, what a lovely watch! I was thinking of buying one just like it for my nephew. May I see it?

BIXBY: Certainly.

The FAT WOMAN takes Bixby's wrist and examines the watch.

FAT WOMAN: Just lovely. Look at this.

The FAT WOMAN pulls Bixby's wrist over to show her FRIEND.

INT. CHEAVAN'S KITCHEN - DAY

CHEAVAN growls, bites, and rips KEN's arm from its socket.

INT. ELEVATOR - DAY

As the FAT WOMAN extends Bixby's arm to her FRIEND, Bixby's arm falls from its socket.

BIXBY and the FAT WOMAN stare at Bixby's severed arm, limp in her hand. His shock overpowering pain. Her whimpering intensifying. PASSENGERS gawking.

Then the blood geyser splashing from Bixby's torn socket hits home . . .

The FAT WOMAN drops the arm. EVERYONE screams at once.

INT. CHEAVAN'S KITCHEN - DAY

CHEAVAN swallows KEN deep into her mouth, crushing him under her teeth, squishing him, gnawing, grinding, chewing.

INT. ELEVATOR - DAY

BIXBY crumples to the floor, trembling like an epileptic fish out of water, flip-flopping and foaming.

Screaming PASSENGERS shove against each other, jostling away from BIXBY, even as his blood drenches everyone. They pound vainly on the doors, pressing random buttons. Somebody hits the ALARM. No use. No stops until the lobby.

BIXBY's clothes shred apart. Giant teeth marks indent his flesh, tearing red gashes along his chest and stomach.

INT. CHEAVAN'S KITCHEN - DAY

CHEAVAN pulls KEN from her mouth until only his soft plastic head remains hidden past her moist lips. She runs her tongue around his head a few times, then slides KEN deep into her mouth, slowly lowering her molars, squishing his head out of shape, moaning in sexual ecstasy as his head collapses under her teeth.

INT. ELEVATOR - DAY

BIXBY grips his head as it collapses, screams as his head cracks, splinters, falls into his brain. Brain matter spills through his broken skull, first as pustules beneath his scalp, then exploding as gray brain pus.

BIXBY's hands shake, his body quakes, trembling from neurological trauma. Still, he manages to grasp his head even as brain matter pours past his fingers.

The FAT WOMAN swoons, collapses, and disgorges a torrent of half-digested donuts and coffee upon BIXBY.

BIXBY's imploding head ejects an eye into the FAT WOMAN's mouth.

INT. CHEAVAN'S KITCHEN - DAY

CHEAVAN slides KEN from her moist mouth, saliva glistening along his wet nakedness. She dries KEN upon her own naked body as she approaches her blender. She removes its top.

INT. OFFICE BUILDING LOBBY - DAY

PEOPLE patiently await the elevator. Although the alarm is RINGING, the lights indicate a normal descent. A BUILDING ENGINEER waits calmly, expecting a false alarm.

INT. CHEAVAN'S KITCHEN - DAY

CHEAVAN drops KEN into the blender.

INT. OFFICE BUILDING LOBBY - DAY

The elevator arrives. PEOPLE shift toward its doors. The BUILDING ENGINEER makes a slight effort to hold them back until he can confirm all is well.

INT. CHEAVAN'S KITCHEN - DAY

CHEAVAN presses a button. The blender hits full blast.

INT. OFFICE BUILDING LOBBY - DAY

Elevator doors open, disgorging a geyser of blood and organs and hysterical PASSENGERS stampeding into the waiting PEOPLE.

A foot lands in a WOMAN's shopping bag. She gapes, then screams as the foot hops about, toes popping and flying off.

A DOG chases a juicy, bloody, bouncing thigh across the lobby.

Bixby's mangled head bounces from the elevator like a punctured basketball, rolling willy-nilly across the lobby, facial bits breaking off and zig-zagging along their own courses.

INT. ELEVATOR - CONTINUOUS

A blood whirlpool, Bixby's limbs and organs twirling and twisting within its crimson vortex. As in a blender.

INT/EXT. CHEAVAN'S PARLOR - NIGHT

CHEAVAN gazes from the window, her anxious face lit by the purple neon sign. Outside, the street is dark, wet, empty.

She finally smiles when she sees ARTHUR running toward her house, his unbuttoned raincoat flapping in the wind.

INT. CHEAVAN'S ENTRANCE - NIGHT

ARTHUR throws open the door, sweating, panting, red-eyed. CHEAVAN stands at the top of the stairs.

ARTHUR: Cheavan!

CHEAVAN: Up here, darling.

ARTHUR rushes upstairs.

INT. CHEAVAN'S PARLOR - CONTINUOUS

CHEAVAN leads ARTHUR to a low cushion. ARTHUR is too numb to resist. CHEAVAN sprawls on a sofa overlooking ARTHUR. A low table sits between them.

ARTHUR: Cheavan, it was so horrible!

CHEAVAN: My poor Arthur, you look dreadful.

ARTHUR: Head crushed like a cantaloupe. Blood splashing against walls. Flesh flying out the window.

CHEAVAN: *(claps hands, laughing)* Oh, Arthur! You are a poet. I wish I was there to see Bixby.

ARTHUR: I'm not talking about Bixby. I'm talking about Lindsay!

CHEAVAN: Lindsay? Who's Lindsay?

ARTHUR: Lindsay was our secretary. Mine and Bixby's.

CHEAVAN: But how is Bixby?

ARTHUR: Bixby? He was . . . like Lindsay.

CHEAVAN: Well then, there's no problem!

ARTHUR: Why did you kill her? I didn't ask you to harm Lindsay.

CHEAVAN: It's perfectly obvious. Some of the hairs on Bixby's jacket must have belonged to Lindsay. So now Bixby is dead and so is his little tramp.

ARTHUR: And I'm responsible. Oh God, I don't want to live!

CHEAVAN: Arthur, you mustn't say that! You had no way of knowing who Bixby was diddling. If it was this Lindsay bimbo, well, good riddance. She belonged to your enemy's karma. Our karma defeated theirs.

ARTHUR: You should have been more careful. You're no expert. I planned to marry Lindsay! *(covers his face, crying)*

CHEAVAN: But, Arthur. What about us?

CHEAVAN is barely audible over the buzzing neon sign. She reaches a trembling hand across the low table.

CHEAVAN: Arthur darling?

ARTHUR swipes aside her hand. CHEAVAN freezes, for a moment.

CHEAVAN: Bastard!

CHEAVAN overturns the table, scattering tarot cards, shattering a crystal ball. Leaping up, she grabs Arthur's hair.

CHEAVAN: I love you, you bastard!

ARTHUR stands, legs quivering, suddenly aware. CHEAVAN grips his hair, in his face, glaring as though he were a slug.

CHEAVAN: How dare you betray me after all I've done for you? You saw what I did!

ARTHUR: Oh God. I'm sorry. Cheavan, please let me go.

CHEAVAN: *(mimicking)* Cheavan, please let me go.

ARTHUR: Please, Cheavan.

CHEAVAN: Please, Cheavan. Listen to yourself. You're not even a man. Who are you to take my love and throw it back in my face?

ARTHUR: Please . . .

CHEAVAN: You're all alike. Full of lies and betrayal and ingratitude.

ARTHUR: I like you, Cheavan. I really do. We can be best friends—

CHEAVAN: I never wanted to be your best friend!

CHEAVAN yanks her hands from his hair, turns away, folds her arms across her chest. She is trembling. He is trembling.

ARTHUR creeps toward the door, desperate to leave quietly. The floorboards CREAK with every step. CHEAVAN seems not to notice. She seems to be praying. Or crying. ARTHUR can't be sure. He opens the door. CREAK!

CHEAVAN does not turn.

CHEAVAN: Please don't go.

ARTHUR closes the door behind him. His footsteps recede down the hall, down the stairs.

CHEAVAN opens her hand. Arthur's hair. She selects a rag doll.

INT. CHEAVAN'S ENTRANCE - NIGHT

ARTHUR hurries down the stairs, glancing nervously behind him.

INT. CHEAVAN'S PARLOR - NIGHT

CHEAVAN works quickly with the rag doll, using practiced skill to weave Arthur's hair into a quick & easy occult pattern.

EXT. CHEAVAN'S HOUSE - NIGHT

ARTHUR exits the house, closing the front door behind him. For a while he pauses and places his hand across his body. Has he felt some pain, or does he merely expect to?

He hurries down the path to the front gate.

INT. CHEAVAN'S PARLOR - NIGHT

Crude pattern finished. CHEAVAN sits the rag doll on the floor, wraps her finger around its belly. She yanks the doll backward.

EXT. CHEAVAN'S HOUSE - NIGHT

ARTHUR has gone a block when an invisible force grips his belly, drags him screaming back to the house. He tries to grab something, but only scrapes his hands raw upon the sidewalk, against the front gate, up the path to the front door.

The force does not open the door, but uses ARTHUR's body to SMASH open a hole, pulling and dragging ARTHUR through the hole, cutting and bruising him against the splinters.

INT. CHEAVAN'S PARLOR - NIGHT

CHEAVAN is breathing harder, salivating hungrily. She squeezes the doll, as though kneading dough for an upcoming meal.

INT. CHEAVAN'S ENTRANCE - NIGHT

ARTHUR lies immobilized on the floor, struggling under the force of Cheavan's fingers, turning blue, breathing difficult.

INT. CHEAVAN'S PARLOR - NIGHT

CHEAVAN rubs her thumbnail over the doll, presses its soft cloth. She hears Arthur's SHRIEK from downstairs. She buries her long nails into the doll.

INT. CHEAVAN'S ENTRANCE - NIGHT

ARTHUR's clothes shred apart. Gashes open along his torso.

INT. CHEAVAN'S PARLOR - NIGHT

CHEAVAN presses the doll's arms to its sides, digs long fingernails into its torso, tearing open its belly.

INT. CHEAVAN'S ENTRANCE - NIGHT

ARTHUR's arms are pinned against him. He stammers and screams as gashes rip open along his body.

INT. CHEAVAN'S PARLOR - NIGHT

CHEAVAN lays down the doll. She slides a gold pump off her foot, sets the shoe's heel over the doll's belly.

CHEAVAN: That should keep you in place, little man.

INT. CHEAVAN'S ENTRANCE - NIGHT

ARTHUR lies pinned to the floor. CHEAVAN descends the stairs. She approaches him, gazing down icily.

CHEAVAN: You still owe me. You agreed, remember? Payment when I deliver.

ARTHUR: Please God, help me.

CHEAVAN: God didn't help you. I did.

CHEAVAN kneels beside him. ARTHUR screams as she slides her fingers into a gash, digging ever deeper past his rib cage until her entire hand is inside him. Then CHEAVAN buries her other hand.

When both of her hands are inside ARTHUR, CHEAVAN feels about for his organs, smiling at his screaming blue face. Blood flows from his torso, across her wrists, onto the floor.

CHEAVAN pulls strands of flesh from him.

CHEAVAN: Look at this! You can't leave. You're coming apart at the seams.

CHEAVAN smells the blood on her hands.

CHEAVAN: And your blood alcohol content is way too high. Best friends don't let best friends drink and drive.

ARTHUR: Please don't kill me!

CHEAVAN: Arthur darling, I would never hurt you. You belong to me.

CHEAVAN glares at ARTHUR, cold, savage, blank.

ARTHUR: Please, Cheavan, please . . .

ARTHUR's pleas grow faint, as though he is shrinking. Yet we do not see what's become of him.

INT. CHEAVAN'S PARLOR - DAY

CHEAVAN stands by the window, smiling at a new day, sunlight warm on her face. Arthur nowhere in sight.

CHEAVAN: You hurt me, Arthur. But I understand. You were confused. Fate. Destiny. The stars. Men just don't get it.

CHEAVAN releases the scarlet drapery, sinking the room into darkness. She approaches the dollhouse, crouches and peers in.

CHEAVAN: I forgive you. We certainly understand each other now.

INT. DOLLHOUSE - CONTINUOUS

ARTHUR lies tied with string to a toy bed, his tiny arms and legs securely bound to its plastic bedposts. He is covered with dried blood. He opens his eyes, sees the giant sorceress peering in.

CHEAVAN: And Arthur, we are going to be together for a very long time. Isn't that wonderful, Arthur?

INT. CHEAVAN'S PARLOR - CONTINUOUS

ARTHUR does not answer. CHEAVAN frowns, reaches in, pinching him with her fingernails. ARTHUR emits a mouselike SQUEAL.

CHEAVAN: I asked you a question, Arthur!

ARTHUR replies faintly, barely audible.

CHEAVAN: I can't hear you.

CHEAVAN places her fingernails between his legs. Each time she repeats her question, she pinches, he squeals.

CHEAVAN: Isn't it wonderful, Arthur? I still can't hear you. Isn't it? Speak up. Isn't it . . . ?

THE END OF YOUNG ARTHUR'S NIGHTMARE.

INT. MEGAN'S BEDROOM - NIGHT

MEGAN is twisting and turning in bed. Sarah's half-eaten Frankenstein head candy glowers as we DISSOLVE to Megan's nightmare.

INT. COLLEGE CLASSROOM - DAY

A low rent community college. Dull, slovenly STUDENTS observe a cheap science demonstration: electricity sparking between two metal balls over a glass bowl of biochemical sludge.

Superimpose: WEIRD SCIENCE IN A DIVERSE UNIVERSITY

Professor HUGO VAN FERNEAU, middle-aged, wild-haired, intense (in a 19th century sort of way) shuts off the demonstration.

HUGO: And so, after billions and billions of years, lightning struck life into our primordial oceans. Oceans formed from trillions and trillions of atomic star stuff. Millions and millions of years later, we still ponder our origins. Mind-boggling quest, yes?

HUGO scans the class of bored, snoozing faces.

HUGO: Yes. But before we examine life, let us explore death. I know you've all read the text. Who wishes to summarize Reichstein's theory of death?

No volunteers. HUGO chooses SANJO, a heavyset dullard.

HUGO: Mr. Sanjo. Enlighten me.

SANJO: I didn't hear the question.

HUGO: Louder, Mr. Sanjo! Fill the room with your intelligence!

SANJO: I said, I didn't hear the question.

HUGO: Why does Reichstein believe cells are destined to die?

SANJO shuffles his notebook paper, hoping to find a clue. Some STUDENTS snicker. SANJO blushes. HUGO holds up a dime.

HUGO: Mr. Sanjo, here is a dime. I want you to call your mother, and inform her that there is serious doubt of you ever becoming a biochemist.

SANJO whips out a cell phone and speed dials.

SANJO: Hello ma? I ain't ever gonna be a biochemist . . . I know you're watching Oprah, but the teacher made me call . . . Well screw you, bitch!

SANJO shuts his cell phone. STUDENTS laugh.

HUGO: Mr. Sanjo. After class.

SANJO: Again?

HUGO: Can anyone answer my question?

HUGO nods to MEGAN LIPTON. She groans and raises her hand.

HUGO: Yes, Miss Lipton?

MEGAN: A clock?

HUGO: Yes, very good. Cellular lifespan is restricted by a genetic clock. The alarm rings, and the cell dies. Now, Miss Lipton, what if we could alter this clock with, say, an enzyme of sorts? What then?

MEGAN: You'd make a lot of money?

STUDENTS laugh.

HUGO: Yes, very good. That's very intuitive.

MEGAN: That's what you always say.

STUDENT laughter turns to hisses, whoops, and sexual grunts.

HUGO: Yes, she's quite right. I would indeed make a fortune. Because class, stop Father Time, and you stop aging. Eternal life!

FEMINIST STUDENT: Father Time is gender specific!

HUGO: Yes, I meant Mother Time.

FEMINIST STUDENT: The nonsexist form is Parent Time.

HUGO: Of course. Thank you for the correction. But getting back, as everyone is already asking, if we stop aging, what of wear and tear? Tissue damage? If I cut myself, and my cells no longer reproduce, will my cut never heal? Thoughts?

No volunteers. HUGO looks to MEGAN. She groans.

MEGAN: A rejuvenation hormone?

HUGO: Excellent! Yes, an enzyme to stop cellular aging. A hormone to maintain cellular health. Eternal life and eternal youth!

STUDENTS scowl at MEGAN.

HUGO: Anything you don't understand, ask Miss Lipton. That is why I have a TA.

SANJO: Tits and ass.

MEGAN: Fuck you.

Bell RINGS dismissal. STUDENTS begin to exit.

FEMINIST STUDENT: Professor, you cannot allow that remark to go unaddressed!

MEGAN: Fuck you too, dyke.

SANJO: Fuck you both, bitch.

MEGAN: Eat shit and die.

HUGO: Mr. Sanjo. My desk.

SANJO: What the fuck?

FEMINIST STUDENT: Professor, you are responsible for your TA as well as class decorum.

MEGAN: Lay off him, bitch.

FEMINIST STUDENT: Professor . . . !

HUGO hustles MEGAN and the FEMINIST STUDENT out of the room.

HUGO: I will handle it, Miss . . . ?

FEMINIST STUDENT: Ms.

HUGO shuts the door. With only HUGO and SANJO still present, HUGO sits behind his desk.

HUGO: Been studying for finals?

SANJO: Yeah. I guess.

HUGO: Good. Because unless you score a hundred, you will likely fail the course.

SANJO: Because of that dyke—?!

HUGO: *(slams desk)* You have no love of science, Mr. Sanjo! Science is a harsh and demanding mistress. And you failed over half her tests.

SANJO: Those questions were killer!

HUGO: They were true-false.

SANJO: They were trick true-false.

HUGO: I should assign essays. It'd be easier to grade a blank sheet. But my experiments are so time-consuming.

SANJO: Big man, with the big experiments!

HUGO: That will be all.

SANJO: You just wanna fuck your TA!

HUGO: That will be all!

SANJO: You ain't gonna fuck with me!

SANJO rushes out and SLAMS the door behind him.

INT. COLLEGE HALLWAY - CONTINUOUS

SANJO enters and is joined by SKIP and ROSCO. ROSCO is thuggish. SKIP is weak and scruffy.

ROSCO: Hey bro. What happened?

SANJO: Man, no way am I gonna pass bio.

ROSCO: Crazy Van Ferneau? I failed him too. Who gives a shit?

SKIP: Nobody in this school.

SANJO: Screw the test. Van Ferneau's been pissing on me all semester. I'm gonna make him into one sorry motherfucker.

INT. GODFREY'S OFFICE - DUSK

Dean GODFREY sits behind his desk, lighting a pipe. HUGO studies the sunset from the window. GODFREY's imperturbability contrasts with HUGO's megalomania.

HUGO: Billions and billions of times throughout Earth's history, our sun dies beyond the horizon, only to arise again. Reborn!

GODFREY: Had some more complaints about you, Hugo. Our goal is to teach these kids, not fail them.

HUGO: Hundreds and hundreds of cultures have made the sun their symbol of eternal life.

GODFREY: Let's talk turkey. We rely on tuition to balance the budget. If students drop out, we lose their state loans.

HUGO: The sun has served this role for thousands and thousands of years.

GODFREY: These kids may not be bright, but hey, this ain't MIT. Try and cut some slack, okay?

HUGO slams the window ledge.

HUGO: Nobody sees my true greatness!

GODFREY: Well, that may be. But what do you say? Go easy on the kids?

HUGO turns ponderously, ominously, toward GODFREY.

HUGO: You are right. This is not MIT.

GODFREY: Thanks. I know you'll do your best.

HUGO: You know more than you know.

GODFREY: Thanks again. Something else. Strange rumors. I feel silly asking but, Hugo, what do you do in your laboratory?

HUGO: You mean my little closet in the basement? I prepare classroom demonstrations. For the students.

GODFREY: No, I mean, late at night. After dark. After midnight. When it's dark.

HUGO: Why do you say I'm in my lab?

GODFREY: Night watchman spotted you. You and Ms. Lipton.

HUGO: Miss Lipton is my assistant. We often prepare for class the night before.

GODFREY: That's all? Night watchman reported strange noises and unusual lights coming from your lab.

HUGO: All right, yes! Miss Lipton and I conduct experiments. Bold and daring experiments beyond the imaginings of mere mortals. Experiments piercing the veil separating life and death. Experiments unlocking secrets that will make men into gods!

GODFREY: That's all? Nothing weird or kinky?

HUGO: No.

GODFREY: Well, that's okay then. This school does not need any more sexual harassment suits.

EXT. COLLEGE CAMPUS - NIGHT

Lightning flashes across the night sky, followed by thunder.

INT. HUGO'S BASEMENT LAB - NIGHT

A mad scientist's realm. Beakers, test tubes, flasks, funnels. Electrical gizmos with needles and knobs and dials, all silent. Dusty slab with leather straps, shoved into a corner. Coiled copper cable spiraling from machines to a lightning rod jutting out a basement window. Many caged ANIMALS.

MEGAN is feeding a RABBIT. HUGO enters.

MEGAN: Oh professor, this rabbit is having a hard time.

HUGO: Impossible.

HUGO approaches the RABBIT. MEGAN grabs HUGO, kisses him, presses her knee between his legs.

MEGAN: Oh! Now you're the one having a hard time.

They kiss until HUGO breaks it off.

HUGO: Did the night watchman see you?

MEGAN: Who gives a fuck?

HUGO: I give a fuck. I cannot allow Dean Godfrey to terminate my employment contract. I need this miserable broom closet.

MEGAN: Up to you. But enjoy it while you can. You only got a week.

HUGO: Oh no, we have eternity.

MEGAN: Don't kid yourself. We have until finals. Then I'm out of this crummy school. Out of this crummy town.

HUGO: But wouldn't you rather leave town on the arm of a Nobel-winning scientist? A rich and famous scientist?

MEGAN: Sure. Where can I get one?

HUGO unlocks and opens a secret metal drawer under the table. He removes a thick notebook.

HUGO: My notes. Eternal life and eternal youth.

MEGAN: Yeah, yeah. The enzyme and the hormone. Real great.

HUGO: When we are married, I will wine and dine you in New York, Paris, London.

MEGAN: I wanna go to Lollapalooza.

HUGO: I will buy you the best table at Lollapalooza.

MEGAN: Okay, well, like I said last year. When you can afford all that, I'll marry you. But I'm graduating this semester, so you got a week to cash in your research.

HUGO: The enzyme is nearly perfect. The hormone is almost there.

MEGAN: Yeah, yeah. The enzyme and the hormone. Get one to work and I'm yours forever.

HUGO: Just one? Mine forever?

MEGAN: Sure. In the meantime, all I want is my A-plus.

HUGO: You will get your A. And rubies. And diamonds—

MEGAN: An A-plus!

HUGO: An A-plus. You've earned it.

MEGAN: You bet I did. So don't fuck with me. *(laughs)* At least, not after next week. I wouldn't wanna have to go fuck a lawyer.

They embrace and kiss.

EXT. COLLEGE CAMPUS - NIGHT

Lightning, thunder, and rain, signifying a TIME LAPSE.

INT. HUGO'S BASEMENT LAB - NIGHT

The gizmos buzz and hum and spark electricity. The beakers, test tubes, flasks, and funnels smoke and bubble with colored liquids. Bunsen burners flicker blue fire. The coiled copper cable tapers into a beaker containing the formula.

HUGO is alone and fervid, checking gizmos and bunsen burners.

HUGO: An ideal thunderstorm! The atmospheric ions are perfect. Soon the labors of a lifetime shall reward me with infinite lifetimes to come.

HUGO carries a caged RABBIT to his formula. He pours his formula into a dish for the RABBIT. He pets the RABBIT as it drinks.

HUGO: Drink up, old friend. The enzyme in this formula will stop your genetic clock. You shall live forever. And its hormone will rejuvenate your cells. You shall not decay as centuries fade into eternity.

INT. COLLEGE STAIRWAY - NIGHT

SANJO, ROSCO, and SKIP creep down a darkened staircase.

ROSCO: Man, this is crazy. We ain't gonna find no secret lab.

SANJO: Well he's gotta have someplace to fuck his TA. Just look for a room with a mattress.

SKIP: I heard Van Ferneau's got a Frankenstein monster in his lab.

ROSCO: Aw man, those are just rumors. Hey, how do we even know he shacks up in the basement?

SANJO: Some chick told me.

ROSCO: What chick?

SANJO: The one who hates Megan Lipton.

ROSCO: That's every chick in school.

They reach a landing and face a heavy steel door. They CREAK open the door.

SANJO: Easy with the door.

INT. COLLEGE BASEMENT HALLWAY - CONTINUOUS

SANJO and ROSCO enter, then SKIP, who lets the door SLAM shut. The BOOM echoes throughout the dark cluttered hallways.

SANJO: *(shouts)* I said be quiet!

SANJO's echo drowns out the door's echo.

INT. HUGO'S BASEMENT LAB - NIGHT

HUGO hears the BOOM. Then Sanjo's garbled SHOUT. HUGO transfers his notebook into his secret metal drawer, locks it, then enters the basement hallway.

INT. COLLEGE BASEMENT HALLWAY - CONTINUOUS

HUGO looks in both directions, but sees only darkness. He hesitates, looks back on his experiment, then sets off in the wrong direction.

Soon thereafter, from another direction, SANJO, ROSCO, and SKIP approach the lab. Light emanates from its open door, providing the only source of illumination in the basement.

ROSCO: Hey man, somebody's down here. We better split.

SANJO: Stay cool, stay cool. Let me just check it out.

SANJO edges past the open doorway and peeks inside.

SANJO: It's all right. Nobody's here.

INT. HUGO'S BASEMENT LAB - CONTINUOUS

SANJO, ROSCO, and SKIP enter and gawk.

SANJO: Oh man, this is fucking insane.

ROSCO: Those crazy rumors were true.

SKIP: Where? I don't see any Frankenstein monster.

Then SKIP spots the slab in the corner.

SKIP: Hey, but there's his bed.

ROSCO: *(mocking)* Seems the monster got loose.

SANJO: Well this beats ripping up some old mattress. Party!

SANJO and ROSCO go wild, toppling tables, shattering flasks and beakers, smashing machines. Chemical clouds and electrical explosions fill the lab. The caged ANIMALS panic. ROSCO and SANJO toss and catch some cages, drop others. Some ANIMALS escape.

SKIP lifts the caged RABBIT, tilting it about.

SKIP: Check this rabbit. It's scared of me.

Giggling, SKIP spins the cage like a ferris wheel, enjoying the RABBIT's torment. He opens the cage.

SKIP: I'm gonna squish me a wabbit, hu-hu-hu-hu.

HUGO appears in the doorway.

HUGO: Damn you to hell!

HUGO rushes SKIP and grabs the cage.

HUGO: Give me that!

SKIP bolts. HUGO grabs him, throws him against the table, shattering flasks, beakers, drenching both of them with chemicals. SKIP grabs the beaker with the formula, flings it into HUGO's face. Into his mouth. HUGO gags, but does not loosen his grip.

SKIP: Let me go! Help! Help me!

ROSCO and SANJO rush to the door, stop, look back at SKIP.

SKIP: Somebody help me!

SANJO runs back in and attacks HUGO. HUGO loses his grip. SKIP bolts out the door past ROSCO.

SANJO and HUGO struggle, knocking over a bunsen burner, setting aflame the spilled chemicals. Flames spread onto HUGO's soaking smock. SANJO backs off as flames turn HUGO into a human torch.

SANJO stares, mesmerized. ROSCO rushes in and grabs SANJO.

ROSCO: What do you wanna do? Toast marshmallows? Let's go!

INT. COLLEGE BASEMENT HALLWAY - CONTINUOUS

SANJO and ROSCO are two dark silhouettes, running. Behind them, flames erupt from the lab. Smoke alarms RING. Sprinklers come alive and drench them. Outside, lightning and thunder.

SANJO: Where's Skip?

ROSCO: Back home with mommy.

SANJO: Scumbag!

INT. HUGO'S BASEMENT LAB - NIGHT

Everything aflame. The RABBIT is free of the cage but surrounded by fire. It runs about, erupts into a flaming furball, continues running, then succumbs near HUGO, whose corpse is burning bright.

EXT. COLLEGE BUILDING - NIGHT

Lightning, thunder, and rain. SANJO and ROSCO jump from a broken window onto the lawn. SKIP is running in the distance. Flames glower from a basement window, the lightning rod jutting into the night sky.

INT. GODFREY'S OFFICE - DAY

Dean GODFREY at his desk, lighting a pipe. MEGAN in a chair.

GODFREY: I'm not here to judge. You and Hugo. Nobody's business. But that fire spread way too fast.

MEGAN: He didn't identify the chemicals.

GODFREY: No use playing dumb. I've seen your grades. Perfect score on every test. Yes or no?

MEGAN: *(hesitant)* Yes.

GODFREY: Obviously, a very bright girl. A biochemical genius, even.

GODFREY shifts a pad and pen across his desk.

GODFREY: I want a complete list of every chemical compound you two used.

MEGAN: They were . . . ordinary chemicals.

GODFREY: Fire Marshall disagrees. He can't identify those compounds. Highly flammable stuff. Makes him suspicious.

MEGAN: Of what? Arson?

GODFREY: Or an accident. Perhaps while manufacturing explosives. Or drugs?

MEGAN: Hugo . . . the Professor, never did anything dangerous or weird.

GODFREY: Hope not. Weird science means higher insurance rates. Which increases tuition. Which is bad for diversity.

MEGAN: So now I'm the excuse?

GODFREY: No excuses. I'm proud of our diversity record. If I were you, I'd worry about manslaughter charges.

MEGAN: Manslaughter?

GODFREY: The night watchman. He died this morning.

MEGAN: Fuck.

GODFREY: In a fire for which you share criminal liability.

MEGAN: No way! I wasn't making any weird or dangerous chemicals.

GODFREY: Hope not. But they came from somebody's lab. Did Hugo have any students capable of arson? Students who hated him?

INT. HALLWAY OUTSIDE GODFREY'S OFFICE - CONTINUOUS

ROSCO passes by, halting at the mention of "arson." He stops to eavesdrop.

MEGAN: *(office)* Well, a lot of students thought Hugo was boring, but they liked his tests. All true-false. You had to be a real moron to fail.

ROSCO scowls, but maintains vigil.

GODFREY: *(office)* So no one was failing?

MEGAN: *(office)* Sure, some. Let's face it, this ain't MIT.

GODFREY: *(office)* Quite.

MEGAN: *(office)* I mean, Hugo's tests were dummied down. Open book, open notes. But some of these students can't even read their own notes.

ROSCO curses silently.

GODFREY: *(office)* Among the more . . . academically challenged students, any potential arsonists?

MEGAN: *(office)* Hugo didn't say who was failing. Wasn't a big deal. I can check his class records.

ROSCO has heard enough and dashes off.

INT. GODFREY'S OFFICE - CONTINUOUS

GODFREY: No records found in his office. And his lab, nothing but ashes. We'll likely give the entire class a B.

MEGAN: I was gonna get an A-plus!

GODFREY: You may have to settle for a B-plus. B, plus ten-to-fifteen in state pen.

MEGAN pales, gulps.

EXT. CEMETERY WALL - NIGHT

Dark and foggy. Two grave robbers, SCAREDY and BOSSY, toss their shovels over the wall. Then SCAREDY hoists BOSSY over and in.

SCAREDY: Ow. Why do I always have to boost?

BOSSY: Shut up before you wake the dead!

BOSSY lands inside the cemetery, tosses a rope over the wall, and pulls SCAREDY in. They grab their shovels and pull flashlights from their pockets.

EXT. CEMETERY - CONTINUOUS

The grave robbers are two silhouettes running past tombstones.

BOSSY: This one's worth it. You'll see.

SCAREDY: Sometimes I wonder why I'm not a normal crook.

BOSSY: Because scum like you don't have the guts to rob the living. At least these stiffs don't scream for help.

SCAREDY: I wouldn't want to be around if they did.

They finally reach their target grave. We don't see the name on the tombstone. Is it Hugo?

BOSSY: Here. Dig. And hurry.

They begin digging. After a TIME LAPSE they hit a coffin. BOSSY begins to open it. SCAREDY climbs out of the grave to give BOSSY room, then leans over the tombstone to watch BOSSY.

BOSSY: Ow!

SCAREDY: What?!

BOSSY: Dropped the lid on my hand. Wait a minute . . . I got it.

SCAREDY nervously backs off, walking over the grave behind the one they're unearthing.

BOSSY: Oh my God!

SCAREDY: What now? Ah!

HUGO's earth-blackened hand reaches from the grave under SCAREDY, grabbing his ankle. SCAREDY trips forward, his head SLAMMING the tombstone to the grave BOSSY is unearthing.

Inside the grave, BOSSY gazes at a wealthy spinster's corpse.

BOSSY: What did I say? Look at the size of those rocks!

BOSSY pulls rings off the corpse's fingers.

BOSSY: Sorry, lady. Can't take it with you. Against the rules. *(to Scaredy)* Get down here and gimme a hand.

Blood drips onto the corpse's face.

BOSSY: What the . . . ?

BOSSY aims his flashlight up, revealing SCAREDY's head resting on the tombstone, which reads: Just Resting.

BOSSY: Hey, is this a joke?

BOSSY stands on the corpse's head, breaking it with a dry CRUNCH. He grips the tombstone, pulls himself from the grave, then nudges SCAREDY.

BOSSY: Come on, no sleeping on the job.

He feels something. He aims the flashlight at his sticky hand. Blood. He aims lower and sees SCAREDY's bashed head. Startled, BOSSY screams, slips, falls back into the grave. CRACK!

BOSSY lies at the bottom of the grave, head askew, neck broken.

In the distance, HUGO's silhouette staggers among the tombstones.

EXT. COUNTRYSIDE - NIGHT

A storm approaches, wind gathering strength. HUGO's silhouette staggers along the road. He appears well-dressed, but we do not see whether he is burnt, rotted, or rejuvenated.

The VOICEOVER of his thoughts sounds articulate and normal.

HUGO: *(voiceover)* I am alive. Alive! My formula mocks the gods! My mistress—science!—generously rewards my years of faithful devotion.

INT. HUGO'S BASEMENT LAB - NIGHT

Burnt and blackened walls and tables. Scattered cages. Animal corpses. Shards of glass. Smashed machinery.

MEGAN hits a switch: ceiling lights work. She ducks under police tape and approaches the table with the secret metal drawer. She unlocks and opens it. Its contents untouched by fire.

MEGAN finds and opens the grade book: a row of A's after her name, some without pluses. She produces a pen and adds pluses.

MEGAN: You said I earned it. Now . . . let's see who's academically challenged.

She searches for F's.

MEGAN: Ted is failing? Loser. Too bad you're such a wimp, Ted. Nobody'd buy you as an arsonist. Lisa? Another mouse.

MEGAN sees Sanjo's name with a row of F's.

MEGAN: Yes! We have our patsy. Hugo dissed him every day, and the entire class is a witness. If the frame fits . . .

She shuts the grade book and is about to close the secret drawer, when she sees the notebook containing the formula. She removes the notebook and begins reading:

HUGO: *(voiceover)* Today I begin my experiments in my quest for eternal life.

EXT. SKID ROW STREET - NIGHT

Distant thunder. Dumpsters and police sirens. HUGO's silhouette staggers past lethargic WINOS who see nothing amiss in HUGO's appearance.

WINO: Hey buddy, spare some change?

HUGO: *(voiceover)* The world scorned me, but soon the multitudes shall grovel for my formula. But first, I must return to my lab, before some miscreant steals my notes.

WINO: Fuck you too.

INT. HUGO'S BASEMENT LAB - NIGHT

The POV of a ground-level creature crawling toward MEGAN's feet. We do not see the creature. MEGAN reads Hugo's notes, immersed.

HUGO: *(voiceover)* By God's Law the rabbit should be dead, but I give it life! Life! My enzyme works! But what of my hormone?

The POV creeps toward MEGAN, nearing her foot . . . then touches! MEGAN jolts and YELPS. She looks down, shocked by what she sees. We never see the creature in this scene.

MEGAN: It's Hugo's rabbit!

EXT. COLLEGE CAMPUS - NIGHT

Wind and thunder are stronger, heralding the first drops of rain. HUGO's silhouette CLUMPS toward the college. The door is locked. He searches for and finds an open window. He climbs in.

INT. HUGO'S BASEMENT LAB - NIGHT

With notebook and grade book, MEGAN prepares to leave. We still do not see the rabbit.

MEGAN: Un-fucking-believable. Bugs Bunny survived the fire. Lollapalooza, here I come!

A noise from the hall. MEGAN looks toward the doorway. Soft CLUMPING sounds. She creeps toward the doorway . . .

INT. COLLEGE BASEMENT HALLWAY - CONTINUOUS

MEGAN peers in one direction. Nothing. She turns and collides with SANJO. ROSCO and SKIP behind him.

ROSCO: Hey bro, look what you found.

The three GUYS back MEGAN into the lab . . .

INT. HUGO'S BASEMENT LAB - CONTINUOUS

Backing away, MEGAN tries to be inconspicuous with the grade book and notebook.

SANJO: What you got there?

MEGAN: Nothing.

SANJO: Let's see "nothing."

SANJO grabs the grade book and skims through it. MEGAN drops the notebook and reaches for it. ROSCO kicks it from her grasp.

SANJO: Crazy Van Ferneau's grade book. Where'd you get it?

MEGAN: Dean Godfrey's office.

ROSCO: That's bull.

SKIP: Hey Sanjo, we got the book. Let's get out of here.

SANJO: *(to Megan)* You know what's in here?

MEGAN shakes her head.

ROSCO: Yeah. She knows.

INT. COLLEGE BASEMENT HALLWAY - CONTINUOUS

SKIP peers into the HALLWAY. He sees shadows. Perhaps movement. Hard to tell if anyone is really there.

INT. HUGO'S BASEMENT LAB - CONTINUOUS

SKIP turns from the hallway.

SKIP: Sanjo! Something's moving out there.

ROSCO: Yeah. I think it's the Frankenstein monster.

SKIP: Hey Sanjo, let's check it out.

SANJO: You check it out.

ROSCO: Yeah, go out there. If it's Eddie Munster, say hi for me.

SKIP remains still.

ROSCO: Move your ass!

SANJO: Hey, cool it. We gotta figure out what to do with her.

ROSCO: No! He ran like a dick last night! *(to Skip)* Time to stick your neck out. Move!

Reluctantly, SKIP exits.

INT. COLLEGE HALLWAYS/STAIRCASES - NIGHT

Darkness. The only illumination is from Hugo's lab and occasional lightning flashes outside. SKIP creeps like a frightened rabbit, turning corners, creeping down corridors.

Past one corner he sees something that makes his eyes bulge.

SKIP: O-O-Oh God! Help me!

HUGO's silhouette CLUMPS toward SKIP. SKIP stumbles back.

SKIP: Help me! Somebody help me!

HUGO: *(voiceover)* How appropriate that we meet.

SKIP grabs a fire ax, but can't unclamp it from its moorings. He grabs a fire extinguisher, breaks it loose, tries to spray HUGO, but accidentally sprays himself. Blinding himself. He drops the extinguisher.

SKIP: Help! I can't see! Somebody please help me!

HUGO grabs the fire ax, breaks it free, approaches SKIP.

HUGO: *(voiceover)* Are you calling the night watchman? I wonder where he is?

SKIP clears his eyes of foam, just in time to see HUGO swing the ax, burying its blade in SKIP's face. Blood and brain surge from SKIP's cleaved face. His body collapses with a THUD.

INT. HUGO'S BASEMENT LAB - NIGHT

SANJO and ROSCO back MEGAN against a wall. SANJO flicks open a switchblade.

SANJO: Now be a good bitch and drop your pants.

MEGAN: You are in so much trouble. This is sexual harassment.

SANJO: No, bitch. This is rape.

INT. CHEMICAL SUPPLY ROOM - NIGHT

HUGO's silhouette moves among the tables. His hands reach for a large container from a supply shelf. Sulfuric acid.

INT. HUGO'S BASEMENT LAB - NIGHT

MEGAN on the ground, shoulders pinned by ROSCO. She's screaming. SANJO kneels between her legs, fumbling with his zipper.

ROSCO: Hey man, save me a piece.

ROSCO looks up and sees the horror approaching from behind SANJO. ROSCO goes numb and weakens. MEGAN begins to rise.

SANJO: Fuck man, hold the bitch down.

SANJO sees ROSCO gawking at something.

SANJO turns around. Looking up, blinded by the ceiling lights, he only sees a dark silhouette. He raises a hand to shield his eyes. He sees HUGO. SANJO screams.

HUGO pours acid into SANJO's wide open mouth, splashing it across his face, into his eyes. SANJO grabs his face, acid pouring upon his hands, smoke hissing through his fingers.

SANJO kicks and screams as the acid dissolves his flesh, dribbles across his arms, down his chest, into his eyes and brain.

MEGAN is stunned into silence. ROSCO rises and backs away.

ROSCO: Hey man, it's cool. I was just leaving. Hey, the bitch wanted it, know what I mean? Stay away from me! I mean it! Back off!

As HUGO approaches, ROSCO grabs a stool, swinging it as a weapon. HUGO yanks it from him. ROSCO throws a cage at HUGO, then ROSCO stumbles to the ground.

MEGAN looks toward the exit, but HUGO and ROSCO block her path.

HUGO shoves ROSCO into a cage, and locks it shut.

HUGO: *(voiceover)* Billions and billions of years ago, lightning created life on Earth!

HUGO grabs the end of the coiled copper cable, touches it to the cage.

HUGO: *(voiceover)* Lightning you are! To lightning you shall return!

Lightning strikes the rod extending from the basement window, its current traveling along the cable and through the cage. ROSCO screams as his flesh is smoked, blackened, burned.

HUGO drops the cable and faces MEGAN. She clutches his notebook. For the first time since his return from the grave, we hear HUGO speak. Unlike his VOICEOVER, his voice is hoarse and raspy.

HUGO: I see you found my notes.

MEGAN: Hugo?

HUGO: My cells are alive. I shall live forever.

MEGAN: Forever?

HUGO: My enzyme works!

MEGAN: But not your hormone!

HUGO glances at a window. In its reflection we finally see HUGO since his return from the grave. Burned, rotted, decaying flesh hangs from his bones. Maggots crawl across his face.

We finally see the rabbit, huddled in a corner. It too is a living barbecue.

HUGO: The enzyme, but not the hormone. A disappointment that is offset by our impending nuptials.

HUGO clumps toward MEGAN.

HUGO: You said if I got one to work, you were mine forever.

A TIME LAPSE and we CUT TO:

HUGO strapping MEGAN to the slab, as in a 1930s Frankenstein movie.

HUGO: Mine for eternity!

Lightning and thunder. MEGAN screams.

THE END OF YOUNG MEGAN'S NIGHTMARE.

INT. WOLF'S BEDROOM - NIGHT

WOLF twists and turns in bed. Sarah's alien candy has been eaten to its teeth, its alien drool glistening with Wolf's saliva as we DISSOLVE to Wolf's nightmare.

EXT. CAMPFIRE - NIGHT

A blazing UFO plummets from the dark sky, its white fire skimming treetops, then landing somewhere within the forest.

Superimpose: THEY CAME FROM OUTER SPACE AND WENT BUMP IN THE NIGHT

At the forest's edge, oblivious to events in the sky, five campers encircle a smoldering campfire. Four preteens: DAVIE, BOBBY, BETTY, and STEVIE (the youngest). And WOLF, mild-mannered, soft-spoken, thirtysomething.

WOLF aims a flashlight under his face, casting ominous shadows.

WOLF: A hundred thousand years ago, a hundred million light years away, an ancient race was dying. Their planet's food supply was dwindling. Their livestock, nearly extinct. And so they sent explorers into the galaxy, seeking a world that had the nutrients they needed, before it was too late. Their odds were one in a million.

EXT. FOREST CLEARING - CONTINUOUS

A classic 1950s FLYING SAUCER lies in the clearing. A pulsating hum emanates from its smooth golden hull. Smoke and steam hiss from underneath it.

A ramp descends. An ALIEN emerges. Dark, hairy, tarantula-like. Many legs or appendages. It enters the forest.

WOLF: *(voiceover)* Once, they had been a wise and noble race, but bitterness over their fate made them cruel. They killed without mercy, and in their rage destroyed many weaker civilizations. They were an ugly people.

EXT. CAMPFIRE - CONTINUOUS

The children have huddled closer to WOLF. He hugs BETTY with one arm, his other hand holding the flashlight. He scans his listeners. Nobody notices that STEVIE has left.

WOLF: The centuries rolled by, and their civilization crumbled. All that remained were a few starships scattered across the universe. They had lost contact with their home planet generations ago. Eventually, these ships too passed away, until only one remained, its crew insane with hunger.

EXT. FOREST - CONTINUOUS

The POV of the ALIEN creeping through the brush, ANIMALS hurrying fearfully from the path of its hairy tentacles.

WOLF: *(voiceover)* Finally, one dark night, they discovered a distant planet at the edge of their galaxy that had exactly the food they needed. A planet on which they could slaughter entire herds of food, and feast to their evil stomachs' content.

EXT. CAMPFIRE - CONTINUOUS

WOLF pauses, surveying his attentive audience.

WOLF: The name of the planet was Earth. And the name of the food was human being!

The children scream. WOLF grabs BETTY, BOBBY, and DAVIE, groping and growling like a scary monster.

SAMANTHA: Stevie! Bedtime!

For the first time, we see that the campfire is in the backyard of a rural house. SAMANTHA, thirtysomething, is leaning out of an upstairs window.

WOLF rises languidly, dusting his black FBI suit.

WOLF: Seems he went inside already.

SAMANTHA: Did you scare him away?

WOLF: I just told him a story.

SAMANTHA: What story?

WOLF: Oh, some story from work.

SAMANTHA: Honestly, Wolf!

INT. UPSTAIRS HALLWAY - CONTINUOUS

The second floor of a nice middle-class home. SAMANTHA leaves the window, approaches Stevie's bedroom door, knocks lightly.

SAMANTHA: Stevie?

A SCREAM from downstairs. SAMANTHA runs to the staircase landing.

SAMANTHA: Is everything all right?

JILL: *(downstairs)* No, everything is not all right.

SAMANTHA hurries downstairs.

EXT. FOREST - NIGHT

STEVIE meanders through the woods, kicking pebbles and rocks. He hears rustling. He slows and peers ahead.

Movement in the brush. A dark and hairy shape bobbing, partly concealed by foliage. STEVIE stops. From the brush pops a large ALIEN, thrice bigger than Stevie. Big moist eyes, goofy grin. A cuddly, kooky tarantula.

STEVIE: Wow!

The ALIEN moves forward. STEVIE edges back. They both halt. Now STEVIE edges forward and the ALIEN backs off. STEVIE stops. So does the ALIEN.

STEVIE: Are you from outer space?

STEVIE edges forward. The ALIEN trembles at his sudden approach, but makes no move. STEVIE attains touching distance.

STEVIE: *(softly)* I'm gonna take you home with me.

STEVIE slowly touches the ALIEN's hair, then gently pets it. The ALIEN titters. STEVIE smiles.

The ALIEN bites STEVIE's hand!

STEVIE screams, collapses, writhes in pain. Blood and foam drool from the ALIEN's chomping jaws, mangling and sucking the arm into its wet orifice, suctioning flesh from bone, skin tearing as it's sucked into the ALIEN's mouth faster than the bones themselves.

STEVIE shrieks as he's skinned and devoured by the "cute" E.T.

INT. BASEMENT REC ROOM - NIGHT

Halloween decorations abound. The thirtysomething JILL carves a Jack O'Lantern with difficulty, her black FBI suit spattered with pumpkin pulp. SAMANTHA, dressed as a homemaker, is helping JILL.

While they carve Jack at one end of the basement, at the other end, WOLF, DAVIE, BOBBY, and BETTY crouch around a plastic tub, bobbing for apples.

WOLF: Who's next for apples?

CHILDREN: Me, me, I do, I do!

WOLF: Okay, ladies first.

BETTY squeals, delighted, and begins bobbing.

DAVIE: Uncle Wolf, can we play a spooky game?

SAMANTHA: *(perks up)* No! No spooky games!

WOLF: *(to the children)* You heard what your mother said. No spooky games. *(murmuring)* Not until she leaves.

CHILDREN: Yea!

Watching WOLF, SAMANTHA and JILL exchanges smiles.

SAMANTHA: My brother has such rapport with the kids. He loves children.

JILL: I've noticed.

SAMANTHA: Do you ever think that someday, you and Wolf . . . ?

JILL: One thinks of many things. But for now, Wolf and I are married to the Bureau.

SAMANTHA: You'd make a lovely couple.

JILL: I think this Jack's just about done, don't you?

SAMANTHA: Fine. I can take a hint. I'll go get a candle.

JILL: I'll go with you. I want to wash up.

SAMANTHA and JILL carry the Jack O'Lantern, tray, knives, and all paraphernalia upstairs.

WOLF: They're gone.

CHILDREN: Yea!

WOLF: Okay. Here's a spooky game. It's called Alien Abduction. I'm a monster from outer space, come to capture Earthlings.

CHILDREN: Ooooooo!

WOLF: If I catch you, I take you aboard my secret spaceship upstairs, that mommy doesn't know about, where I perform medical exams with my rectal probe.

CHILDREN: Oooooooooooooo!

WOLF: The rest of you are FBI agents. You have to zap me with your ray guns before I jump on you. If you capture me, you get to examine me with rectal probes.

BETTY: I don't like this game.

WOLF: Sure you do. It's a fun game. It's just like playing doctor.

BOBBY: Uncle Wolf, if we capture you, can we cut you into pieces, and pass around your body parts?

WOLF: No, that's the October Game. This is Alien Abduction.

DAVIE: Real government agents don't use ray guns.

WOLF: Yeah we do. We got them at Roswell. One more thing. This game is a lot more fun with the lights turned off.

WOLF switches off the lights.

CHILDREN: Ooooooooooo!

EXT. FOREST/SAMANTHA'S HOUSE - NIGHT

The ALIEN bobs through the forest brush, dragging a SAC. When it sees Samantha's house, the ALIEN stops. An organic light in its underbelly, covered with a filmy membrane, pulsates blue-white.

EXT. FOREST CLEARING - NIGHT

The flying saucer, surrounded by mist. At the base of an antenna, projecting from the saucer's domed roof, a light pulsates blue-white, communicating with the ALIEN outside.

EXT. SAMANTHA'S HOUSE - NIGHT

The ALIEN's belly-light pulsates, then darkens. It creeps toward the house, enters the backyard, probes the house for an entrance. A basement window is ajar. The ALIEN presses it open.

INT. KITCHEN/DINING AREA - NIGHT

An open kitchen with a broad view of the dining and living rooms. A door leads to the basement.

SAMANTHA is lighting the candle within the Jack O'Lantern. JILL is drying her hands after washing up.

WOLF emerges from the basement, carrying something shiny.

SAMANTHA: Wolf, look what Jill made.

WOLF smiles amiably and approaches the Jack O'Lantern, its poorly carved face having been somewhat repaired by Samantha.

WOLF: Looks like ol' Jack had some reconstructive surgery. Who botched the first attempt?

SAMANTHA: Don't blame Jill. Just not her field of medical specialty.

WOLF: I guess not.

JILL: Muller, what do you have in your hand?

WOLF: It's nothing.

JILL and WOLF refer to each other by last names. JILL approaches WOLF and sees that he's carrying a long silver probe, simple but with tiny dials and led lights.

JILL: Muller, you weren't supposed to take that with you.

WOLF: C'mon, Scuppy. Remember all the fun we had? It's just a souvenir.

SAMANTHA: Fun? You two?

WOLF: Ask Scuppy about Hanger 18 sometime.

JILL: Muller, this is serious. If the government finds that missing . . .

WOLF: How can it be missing? It never existed in the first place.

SAMANTHA lifts the Jack O'Lantern.

SAMANTHA: Hey, one of you lovebirds wanna help me get this outside?

WOLF pockets the probe, takes the Jack O' Lantern from SAMANTHA.

WOLF: I'll get that. Oh, by the way. We're playing hide and seek, so don't tell the kids where I am.

SAMANTHA: Oh, we won't!

SAMANTHA and JILL exchange mischievous smiles.

INT. BASEMENT REC ROOM - NIGHT

Dark, aside for flashlights held by DAVIE, BOBBY, and BETTY. All children have eyes shut.

DAVIE: Ninety-five. Ninety-six. Ninety-seven.

The ALIEN crawls along the ceiling. Its upside-down POV sees the children across the room. It creeps behind a door into another room.

DAVIE: Ninety-nine. One hundred!

All eyes open. BOBBY blasts a pretend ray gun.

BOBBY: Zap, zap, zap!

DAVIE: There are no aliens down here.

BOBBY: They could be hiding.

BETTY: Where's Uncle Wolf?

DAVIE: The alien monster! That's what we have to find out. Do we all have our ray guns?

BETTY and BOBBY raise their right hands, held like a gun.

DAVIE: Rectal probes?

BETTY and BOBBY raise their left hands, index finger pointed up.

DAVIE: Great. We'll split up. Me and the lieutenant will climb this mountain. You explore this area.

BOBBY: Roger.

DAVIE and BETTY climb the stairs and exit.

BOBBY flashes his light about the rec room. Cluttered with toys, furniture, party paraphernalia. Various doors lead to washroom, boiler room, storage room, etc.

BOBBY creeps toward the washroom, yanks open its door . . .

INT. WASHROOM - CONTINUOUS

BOBBY "shoots" his finger.

BOBBY: Zap, zap, zap.

Washing machine, dryer, ironing board, etc. No monsters. BOBBY shines his flashlight throughout the room. Up the walls. Along the ceiling. Nothing. Then a NOISE.

INT. BASEMENT REC ROOM - CONTINUOUS

BOBBY spins around. Soft CHITTERING sounds emanate from the boiler room. BOBBY creeps toward it and opens the door . . .

INT. BOILER ROOM - CONTINUOUS

BOBBY gyrates his flashlight, but spots nothing. Hard to see anything with the boiler hogging so much space. BOBBY enters. Soft CHITTERING.

BOBBY: I know you're in here, you monster! You can't escape!

BOBBY creeps around the boiler. He trips. His hand caught in something. He drops the flashlight. It rolls away. Darkness.

BOBBY: Hey, time out!

BOBBY struggles, becoming entangled. He whimpers, reaches for a light switch, flicks it on . . .

Giant spider web! BOBBY is caught.

BOBBY thrashes about, crying. He looks up and sees STEVIE, now a mangle of bones and shredded flesh, partly encased in a silken SAC. Leftover lunchmeat in a doggie bag. BOBBY screams.

The ALIEN drops down, snatches BOBBY, glides swiftly and silently up its silken thread, carrying the screaming boy.

INT. KITCHEN/DINING AREA - NIGHT

An idyllic coffee commercial atmosphere. Languid conversation as JILL and SAMANTHA serenely sip coffee.

JILL: Must be difficult, raising four children without a husband.

SAMANTHA: I won't say it's easy. But I wouldn't trade my life for the world. More coffee?

JILL: Please.

SAMANTHA tears open an instant coffee pack, pours its contents into a china cup, adds hot water.

JILL: No more French Vanilla?

SAMANTHA: Try Swiss Mocha.

JILL: Mmmmmm. I can smell it.

SAMANTHA: Wolf loved chocolate as a boy. After the . . . incident, mom let him drink all the hot chocolate he wanted. At first, I was so jealous. I thought he'd made the whole thing up.

JILL: I can sympathize. Muller's stories can be . . . incredible.

SAMANTHA: I refused to believe he'd been . . . I'm sorry.

JILL: You can say "abducted." Muller and I are very open about it.

SAMANTHA: You two seem close. So why the last names?

JILL: Just professional courtesy, I guess.

DAVIE and BETTY rush down from the second floor.

DAVIE: Anyone see a space monster?

JILL: Space monster?

BETTY: His spaceship's upstairs—

DAVIE: That's a secret!

BETTY: Oops.

SAMANTHA can barely contain her smile.

SAMANTHA: I think space monsters usually hide outdoors.

DAVIE: Thanks, mom!

BETTY: Yea!

DAVIE and BETTY rush outdoors. The women sip coffee.

SAMANTHA: Does Wolf ever discuss his abduction?

JILL: A little. The details are still a bit personal.

SAMANTHA: Classified, you mean. I can take a hint. It takes time to heal.

JILL: Yes. Yes, it does.

SAMANTHA: I am proud. He hasn't let it affect him. Or his work.

JILL: No. No, that's very true.

SAMANTHA: Care for some Hazelnut?

JILL: Please.

JILL proffers her empty cup. SAMANTHA selects an instant coffee packet from a large tin, then tears it open.

JILL: This is delicious coffee.

SAMANTHA: Agent Cooper thought so.

JILL: Agent Cooper?

SAMANTHA: When Wolf had that identity crisis, and he'd dress in women's—

JILL: Yes. Yes, I remember.

SAMANTHA pours the Hazelnut coffee powder into JILL's cup, then adds the empty packet to a growing pile.

SAMANTHA: I have some Mint-Java when you're finished.

JILL: Mmmmmmm. Please.

SAMANTHA: So what's all this about Hanger 18? A new nightclub?

EXT. SAMANTHA'S HOUSE - NIGHT

DAVIE and BETTY skulk alongside the house. Rustling, up ahead in the brush. BETTY squeals. DAVIE hushes her. They creep forward.

WOLF jumps from behind them, groping and pawing.

WOLF: Booga-booga! Arrrgh!

BETTY screams, drops her flashlight, runs. DAVIE runs in another direction. WOLF chases DAVIE, groping and pawing his ass, but not grabbing him up. Extending their moment of "play."

WOLF: Booga-booga! Booga-booga!

EXT. FOREST - CONTINUOUS

WOLF chases a laughing, screaming DAVIE into the woods behind the house.

WOLF: Booga-booga! I'm gonna abduct this Earthing! Booga-booga!

DAVIE: No, no!

WOLF: Booga-booga! Yes, yes! I'm giving him a medical exam!

DAVIE: Nooooo!

WOLF: Booga-booga!

A blue-white light pulsates up ahead, matched by a pulsating hum. WOLF halts immediately, turning pro. He draws a gun. DAVIE continues running.

WOLF: Davie! Get back here!

WOLF tensely creeps toward the light. Ahead of him, DAVIE halts near the flying saucer.

DAVIE: Hey, look Uncle Wolf!

WOLF: Davie, don't go near that!

A dazzling Christmas display of Spielbergian lights suddenly goes ablaze across the body of the craft. The light atop twirls blue-white, complementing a loud SIREN.

The ramp descends. ALIENS emerge single file, their underbellies pulsating wildly. DAVIE retreats, screaming. He runs past WOLF.

WOLF: Run, Davie, run!

Atop the ramp, from behind the line of marching tarantula ALIENS, emerges a GRAY ALIEN (a humanoid in silvery skintight body suit). WOLF stares transfixed at it. The GRAY ALIEN is LIMPING. WOLF's eyes bulge.

WOLF: You come back for a piece of me? Is that it? Eat this!

WOLF shoots at the GRAY ALIEN, bullets ricocheting from the hull of the craft. But the tarantula ALIENS close in, so WOLF runs.

CUT TO:

DAVIE is running through foliage, gunshots behind him. He looks back. Black hairy forms bobbing in the distance, rustling.

CUT TO:

WOLF running through the woods, ALIENS rushing about him. Ahead? Behind? Can't be sure. He hears a SCREAM.

WOLF runs past some brush and sees DAVIE caught in a huge spider web, cast between several trees.

WOLF: Davie!

DAVIE: Help me, Uncle Wolf!

WOLF starts toward him. But ALIENS emerge from the surrounding shadows and block WOLF from DAVIE.

WOLF flicks open a cell phone, speed dials.

INT. KITCHEN/DINING AREA - NIGHT

A huge pile of empty coffee packets near SAMANTHA and JILL, still sipping coffee. Across the room, BETTY watches "Tarantula" on TV in the living room. SAMANTHA opens another packet.

SAMANTHA: Orange Kahula Kava?

JILL: Please.

JILL's cell phone rings. She answers.

EXT. FOREST - NIGHT

WOLF watches the ALIENS converge on DAVIE. From the ground, from the trees, from above. WOLF shouts into his cell phone.

WOLF: Scuppy! I need backup!

INT. KITCHEN/DINING AREA - NIGHT

SAMANTHA pours hot water into JILL's cup.

JILL: Muller, where are you?

EXT. FOREST - NIGHT

WOLF on the cell phone, watching DAVIE in the web.

WOLF: Out back. About five hundred yards from the house.

JILL: *(cell phone)* I'll be right there.

WOLF: No. Wait a minute.

From every corner of the web, dark tarantula silhouettes converge on DAVIE's struggling silhouette, until all silhouettes merge into one. WOLF's face glistens with sweat and tears.

WOLF: We're too late.

INT. KITCHEN/DINING AREA - NIGHT

SAMANTHA is contemplating her unopened packets of flavored coffee.

JILL: Too late for what, Muller?

WOLF: *(cell phone)* Is Samantha with you?

JILL: Yes. Yes, she is.

SAMANTHA: Is that Wolf? Ask him if he'd like some Amaretto when he gets back with Davie.

EXT. SAMANTHA'S HOUSE - NIGHT

WOLF runs from the woods. Tarantula ALIENS follow but keep their distance. WOLF runs toward the front door.

INT. ENTRANCE - NIGHT

SAMANTHA runs downstairs toward JILL, who's comforting BETTY near the front door.

SAMANTHA: Stevie's not in his room!

JILL: Listen to me, Samantha. It is very important that you do not panic.

SAMANTHA: Where's my baby boy?!

BETTY: Mommy, I'm scared.

JILL: There's nothing to be afraid of, dear.

WOLF swings open the front door and rushes in.

WOLF: Scuppy, I've never seen aliens so horrible! So monstrous!

BETTY cries. SAMANTHA attacks WOLF with her fists.

SAMANTHA: And you left him out there! You killed Davie!

JILL: Samantha, please calm down.

SAMANTHA: Where's Stevie? Where's Bobby?

BETTY: Bobby's in the basement.

SAMANTHA rushes toward the kitchen, toward the basement door.

BETTY: Is Bobby in trouble?

JILL: No sweetie, Bobby's not in any trouble.

INT. BASEMENT REC ROOM - CONTINUOUS

SAMANTHA flicks on the light and rushes downstairs. At the landing, SAMANTHA gapes. A basement draped in silk webbing.

SAMANTHA: Wolf! Jill! What the hell's going on?!

She hears CRUNCHING. She scans the room, scans the ceiling, then screams upon seeing the ALIEN, upside down on the ceiling, MUNCHING on BOBBY's remains.

The ALIEN pops BOBBY's sucked-out skull into its mouth, the boy's head collapsing under its jaws with a final DRY CRUNCH.

SAMANTHA screams, flails, and entangles her arms in webbing. She struggles to escape and STEVIE's corpse drops before her, a dried and shriveled pendulum swinging before her on a silken thread.

The ALIEN hurries toward SAMANTHA.

WOLF grabs SAMANTHA, pulls her from the ALIEN's reach, and drags her upstairs.

The ALIEN hurries after them.

WOLF pulls SAMANTHA through the doorway into the KITCHEN, slams and locks the door on the onrushing ALIEN.

INT. KITCHEN/DINING AREA - CONTINUOUS

WOLF hugs a hysterical SAMANTHA. An imperturbable JILL holds a whimpering BETTY.

BETTY: What's wrong, mommy?

JILL: Nothing, honey. Muller?

WOLF: Whatever's down there ate Stevie and Bobby.

JILL: Oh no.

BETTY cries.

JILL: Don't cry, dear. Everything's fine. Muller, are you sure that door's strong enough?

WOLF: I'm more worried about the ones outside!

SAMANTHA: They're dead, they're all dead!

BETTY runs crying to SAMANTHA. They hug.

Liquid silk squirts from under the basement door, onto SAMANTHA's feet and ankles, yanking her down, dragging her toward the door.

BETTY: Mommy!

JILL pulls BETTY to safety.

WOLF grabs SAMANTHA. Even as SAMANTHA is pulled toward the door, fresh silk squirts out, gripping other parts of her body.

WOLF: Samantha!

SAMANTHA: Save me, Wolf!

SAMANTHA is dragged toward the door, where the webbing continues pulling, tearing her skin, sucking it through the crack under the door. Fresh silk squirts in, carpeting the floor.

JILL lifts BETTY. JILL and WOLF hop about, their feet dodging the silk spray, compromising WOLF's attempt to save SAMANTHA.

The silk grasps SAMANTHA's exposed organs, pulling them under the door, mangling them into bloody pulp as heart and lungs and liver are squeezed under the door. Blood inundates the floor, soaking its silk carpeting.

WOLF grabs SAMANTHA's arm, its flesh sliding off her bones like a glove. She is a skinned-and-gutted skeleton.

WOLF: Samantha!

JILL: Muller, you're frightening Betty.

BETTY is crying hysterically, staring at her mother's remains.

WOLF: They killed my sister, Scuppy.

JILL: I'm sorry, Muller. But our first priority is to report this to the authorities.

The house lights go out. Moonlight streams through the windows.

INT. ENTRANCE - CONTINUOUS

WOLF and JILL, guns drawn, rush with BETTY from the kitchen.

Strange blue-white lights pulsate outside, bright enough to shine through the curtains. The lights shift direction for no apparent reason, other than that it looks cool. The Venetian blinds cast shifting shadows across the walls. Very cool.

WOLF: Damn the Bureau, Scuppy. Those monsters killed my sister. And now they're paying.

BETTY is bawling hysterically.

JILL: Muller, calm down. You're scaring Betty.

WOLF crouches and hugs BETTY.

WOLF: I'm sorry, dear. Please don't cry.

JILL: Muller, you're in no state to go out there. Stay with Betty. I'll go out and talk to them.

JILL opens the front door, revealing rows of pulsating blue-white lights, silhouetting dark tarantula shapes.

EXT. SAMANTHA'S HOUSE - CONTINUOUS

JILL exits, flashing her badge, gun raised.

JILL: Federal officer! Stand right where you are!

The tarantula ALIENS part, making way for the GRAY ALIEN.

JILL: Sir, do not move. Do not come any closer.

The GRAY ALIEN approaches, LIMPING, hand on its hip.

JILL: Sir . . . oh my God. Muller!

JILL rushes back into the house, slams shut the door.

INT. ENTRANCE - CONTINUOUS

JILL enters in time to see WOLF hugging BETTY, his hand moving under her skirt . . .

JILL: Muller, what are you doing?!

WOLF pushes BETTY away.

WOLF: I'm comforting my niece.

JILL: Come here, dear.

BETTY runs to JILL.

JILL: Did your uncle hurt you?

WOLF: You're imagining it, Scuppy.

JILL: No, Muller, no more! I covered for you at Area 51. At Hanger 18. But now you're doing it to humans. To children.

WOLF: Don't be crazy, Scuppy.

JILL: Do you know who's out there?

WOLF: Our friend from Hanger 18.

JILL: You knew?

WOLF: I saw him! Just before they killed Davie.

JILL: Do you know why he's here?

WOLF: Because he's a fucking pervert. They all are.

JILL: I don't think so, Muller.

JILL aims her gun on WOLF.

WOLF: Scuppy, what are you doing? They killed Samantha!

JILL: But they came for you, Muller. Because of your . . . problem.

WOLF: They did it to me first, Scuppy! Don't forget that. They . . . *(breaks into tears)* They touched me first!

JILL: I know, Muller. And I'm sorry. But this cycle of abuse must end.

JILL opens the door. The GRAY ALIEN's silhouette approaches from the light.

WOLF: Don't do this to me, Scuppy!

JILL: I'm sorry, Muller! I'm sorry!

WOLF: Scuppy!

The GRAY ALIEN enters. Blazing white light fills the room, until there is nothing but whiteness.

INT. ALIEN SPACECRAFT - NIGHT

WOLF lies prone on a metal examining table, air blowing into his face. He opens his eyes. A GRAY ALIEN holds what resembles a high-tech tire pump, pumping air into WOLF's face to awaken him.

Several GRAY ALIENS observe WOLF, some brandishing rectal probes.

WOLF: No! Not again!

The GRAY ALIENS lower the probes. WOLF sighs, relieved. But he remains immobilized on the table, naked. The GRAY ALIEN with the pump LIMPS to a tarantula ALIEN crouched in a corner.

WOLF: Didn't feel so good on the receiving end, did it?

The GRAY ALIEN opens the pump's chamber, positions it beneath the tip of the tarantula ALIEN's torso.

WOLF: What are you doing over there?

A slimy EGG SAC dribbles from the torso, into the pump.

WOLF: Make mine a Spanish omelette. Those creepy-crawlers don't taste too good after they hatch.

The GRAY ALIEN seals the pump's chamber, now full of eggs soon to hatch into giant tarantulas. He LIMPS toward WOLF.

WOLF: Oh no, you gotta be kidding. Oh please God, no!

The GRAY ALIEN raises the pump, and aims for WOLF's ass . . .

WOLF screams.

THE END OF YOUNG WOLF'S NIGHTMARE.

INT. JACKIE'S BEDROOM - NIGHT

JACKIE twists and turns in her sleep. The lower jaw of Sarah's half-eaten skull candy glistens white as we DISSOLVE to Jackie's nightmare.

INT. DRUMMER BOY'S THRONE ROOM - DAY

A giant toy train track traverses the room, joining two huge mouse holes. A white horse (with a prosthetic unicorn horn) eats candy bars from a silver tray. Painted on a vaulted ceiling, Michelangelo-style, cherubs cavort with gray aliens.

Superimpose: BECAUSE BEAUTY IS ONLY SKIN DEEP

DRUMMER BOY, a young black man in a sequined drum major uniform, sits on a golden throne, flanked by BODYGUARDS and LAWYERS. DR. VINE (older male) and DR. IVY (younger female) sit before him.

DRUMMER BOY: You understand, I only wish to even out my skin tones. I'm proud of my African heritage.

DR. VINE: Of course. Le Renard is a powerful skin tone evener.

DRUMMER BOY: I understand there's a side effect . . . ?

DR. VINE: Correct. Le Renard's patented dermal enzyme softens and evens skin tones, erasing moles, acne scars, age spots. Unfortunately, it also decreases melanin levels.

DRUMMER BOY: You understand, it's not what I want. It's for my fans. So my uneven skin shading will not distract them from my music.

But DRUMMER BOY's skin tones are even. No blemishes.

DR. VINE: Understandable.

DR. VINE opens his briefcase. A BODYGUARD stiffens. DR. VINE extracts a small jade jar, its label bearing a grinning red fox. He hands the jar to the BODYGUARD, who hands it to DRUMMER BOY.

DRUMMER BOY: Oooooooo, what a pretty fox!

DR. VINE: Naturally, we employ no animal testing of any kind.

DRUMMER BOY: That is so important. Foxes are one of my most favorite animals.

DR. IVY: *(flirtatious)* Really? What kind of foxes do you like?

DRUMMER BOY ignores her come-on. DR. VINE intervenes.

DR. VINE: Knowing that your music promotes positive, wholesome values, we're confident you'll be delighted with our message . . .

DRUMMER BOY: *(reading the jar's label)* "Revealing your inner beauty. Because beauty is only skin deep." That is so inspired. So educational.

DR. VINE: We feel strongly about it.

DR. IVY: Although we can lose it to make room for your lyrics. Look great on that label, don't you think?

DR. VINE: But before we discuss your lyrics, we must discuss . . .

DR. VINE pulls a contract from his briefcase, hands it to the ATTORNEY heading the ROW OF ATTORNEYS.

DR. VINE: As per our conversation. You use our cream. If it pleases you, you agree to endorse it.

DRUMMER BOY: I hope that will be the case. I don't believe any physician has ever appreciated my creative need for even skin tones.

DRUMMER BOY turns to the ATTORNEYS huddled over the contract.

DRUMMER BOY: That is why I am forever seeking new physicians. New employees.

Jolted by his remark, the ATTORNEYS look up in unison.

DRUMMER BOY: Gentlemen, is the contract in order?

The ATTORNEYS hesitate, glance at one another, then nod.

INT. JACKIE'S BEDROOM/MARY LOU'S BEDROOM - NIGHT

Two teenage girls on the phone, JACKIE and MARY LOU. During their phone conversation, we CROSSCUT between their bedrooms.

In JACKIE's bedroom: clothes and magazines are strewn across the floor. A spoiled girl, lacking gratitude. Walls plastered with posters of actors, fashion models, rock stars, and Drummer Boy.

JACKIE has blond hair/dark roots. She is PRETTY.

JACKIE: Aaaaaand, I bought a new pair of jeans, a jacket, and some shoes.

MARY LOU: Oh Jackie, I wish I could dress like you. I'm so fat and ugly.

JACKIE: Don't say that. You're not so fat. You're just fat.

MARY LOU: I'm a whale! You're so lucky. You're skinny. And it's easy for you, too.

JACKIE: What about the pills I gave you?

MARY LOU: They made my chest hurt.

JACKIE: Oh, blame the pills. Blame me. Blame everyone but yourself.

MARY LOU: I'm sorry.

JACKIE: If you're not willing to make a little sacrifice for your looks, I can't help.

MARY LOU: You're right. I'm sorry. I'll take some more later.

JACKIE: Oh, and I broke my nail today.

MARY LOU: Oh no!

JACKIE: Yeah, and it's my favorite one. It's always been my favorite.

MARY LOU: But you're still sooooo beautiful.

JACKIE grabs a mirror, flares her nostrils into it.

JACKIE: Brown bag it! I got a big nose, short neck, close set eyes, no cheekbones. I'm a monster!

All NOT true.

MARY LOU: I'm the monster!

JACKIE: Well lose some weight. Oh! Guess what else I got?

MARY LOU: What?

JACKIE: Le Renard. A new skin cream. And guess what? I got it for free!

JACKIE grabs the jade jar, its label featuring a sleek red fox.

MARY LOU: Free? How come?

JACKIE: Some test market thing I saw in a magazine. It's got a fox on it and everything. That's 'cause it'll make you look like a fox.

MARY LOU: Get me some!

JACKIE: The label says: "Lofty thoughts and noble dreams, yield heaps of inner bliss to reap. Ancient gods gave man this cream, to show true beauty lies skin deep."

MARY LOU: That's deep. What does it mean?

JACKIE: Gahd! You're so ignorant!

MARY LOU: I'm sorry.

JACKIE: It's from Drummer Boy's new CD.

MARY LOU: Oh, I love Drummer Boy! Let me borrow some.

JACKIE: No, it's mine. Get your own.

MARY LOU: How can I get some?

JACKIE: You can't. It's a limited program.

MARY LOU: Oh. Okay.

JACKIE: Besides, I'm ugly. I need this.

MARY LOU: I'm ugly too.

JACKIE: Yeah, but you're hopeless.

MARY LOU: I know. I'm sorry.

JACKIE: Lose some weight. I need this cream for Joey. It's not like you have a boyfriend. Who cares if you look like a monster?

MARY LOU: Nobody. I'm sorry. You're right.

EXT. JACKIE'S HOUSE - NIGHT

Clouds swirl past a full moon, indicating a TIME LAPSE.

INT. JACKIE'S BEDROOM - NIGHT

JACKIE in pajamas. She opens Le Renard. Bright peppermint green cream. She sniffs.

JACKIE: Wow. Strong!

JACKIE scoops some out, rubs her fingers against it.

JACKIE: Gosh. Tingles!

JACKIE smears the cream on her face.

JACKIE: Mmmmm. Nice!

JACKIE puts Le Renard onto her dresser, among the crowd of beauty aids. She turns off the light, and goes to bed.

Moonbeams and shadows flicker on the jar. Some cream is smeared onto the jar. It glows green.

EXT. HIGH SCHOOL PROMENADE - DAY

A cheerful, sunny day. STUDENTS stroll the tree-lined promenade, JACKIE and MARY LOU among them.

MARY LOU: Oh Jackie, let me keep looking! I'm so jealous! You're more beautiful than ever!

JACKIE: I know. My skin is amazingly to die for. You don't even notice the close set eyes. I look so much better than Judy Big Nose.

MARY LOU: Better than me.

JACKIE: Duh. Better than—Omigahd!

CUT TO:

JOEY and VINNIE in the distance, in 1950s black leather jackets.

CUT TO:

JACKIE: Hide me! Quick! Hide me!

JACKIE ducks behind MARY LOU, begins fussing furiously with her hair, scrutinizing herself in a compact mirror.

CUT TO:

VINNIE: Hey Joey, ain't that your chick?

JOEY: Yeah? Where?

VINNIE: Over there. *(shouts)* Hey Jackie! Why don't you get inside the tent. Oh! 'Scuse me. I see Mary Lou's already in it.

VINNIE is still chuckling as the BOYS reach the GIRLS. JACKIE shoves MARY LOU aside.

JACKIE: Joey. What a surprise.

JOEY: Aaaaaa Jackie! How's it going?

JACKIE: *(thrusting forth her face)* Everything's going fine.

JOEY: Lookin' fine. Fine and sweet.

MARY LOU: Does she now?

JACKIE elbows the giggling MARY LOU.

JOEY: *(to Jackie)* But you look a little different.

JACKIE: What are you talking about? I always look this way.

JOEY: Nah. You're more beautiful every time I see you. You do something to your hair?

MARY LOU: Not her hair!

JACKIE stomps MARY LOU's foot. MARY LOU takes a hint and limps toward VINNIE.

JACKIE: *(to Joey)* No way. I've always been blond.

JOEY: Well I'll see you tonight, blondie.

JACKIE: Know where you're gonna take me?

JOEY: Someplace nice and quiet.

MARY LOU reaches VINNIE, who's staring nonchalantly into space, cigarette dangling between his lips, like James Dean.

MARY LOU: Hi, Vinnie.

VINNIE: How's it going?

MARY LOU: I really like your hair. It smells nice.

VINNIE nods distantly, eyes crinkling coolly against his tobacco fumes. JOEY embraces and kisses JACKIE, long and hard.

INT. JACKIE'S CLASS - DAY

An aging, bearded HIPPIE TEACHER, wearing a green Army jacket, drones before disinterested STUDENTS. In the back of the class, JACKIE doodles supermodels and fashion designs.

HIPPIE TEACHER: So we know that DNA's got a pretty heavy word in determining the physical stuff. Color of my skin, size and shape of my nose . . .

CUT TO:

Two GIRLS whispering, occasionally glancing back at JACKIE.

FIRST GIRL: Joey's taking Jackie out again tonight.

SECOND GIRL: That dropout! Where'd you hear?

FIRST GIRL: Esther told me.

SECOND GIRL: Tell me everything!

After a TIME LAPSE, the HIPPIE TEACHER wipes the blackboard.

HIPPIE TEACHER: . . . so you ladies just remember. If you don't dig my pretty face, don't blame me. Blame my folks.

Some STUDENTS laugh at his joke.

HIPPIE TEACHER: You can always blame the older generation.

More STUDENTS laugh.

JACKIE has looked up, interest piqued, yet we don't see her face.

FIRST GIRL glances back, then does a double-take. Shocked and horrified. She nudges SECOND GIRL, who also looks at JACKIE.

SECOND GIRL: Oh my God! Oh gross!

SECOND GIRL turns away, repulsed. STUDENTS turn to look, some standing to get a better view of JACKIE. All become nauseated, horrified. No smiles, no laughs.

STUDENTS: Oh Gahd! Gross! Grody!

JACKIE: What, what's the matter?

FIRST GIRL: Jackie! Your face!

JACKIE grabs her compact mirror.

The HIPPIE TEACHER moves toward the focus of attention, gently pushing through the crowd of students.

HIPPIE TEACHER: All right, everyone settle down. Nobody's gross. Nobody's grody. We got a problem, let's not slam anyone. Let's rap. Everyone's beautiful. Everyone's *(cringes upon seeing Jackie)* Sweet Jesus, that's disgusting!

JACKIE's mirror slips and SHATTERS on the floor as she SCREAMS. Its shards reflect her legs escaping from class.

INT. HIGH SCHOOL HALLWAY - CONTINUOUS

As JACKIE runs, the bell RINGS. STUDENTS pour from classrooms, impeding JACKIE. She pushes through the growing throng, faces staring after her in horror.

STUDENTS: Did you check her face? What was it? Must be from the special class.

JACKIE runs past some VALLEY GIRLS cringing in disgust.

VALLEY GIRL: A double-bagger for sher.

JACKIE nears two conversing SCHOOL COUNSELORS.

COUNSELOR ONE: I don't care if you're black or white or yellow, or even green with pink polka-dots.

COUNSELOR TWO: Absolutely. Or purple stripes.

COUNSELOR ONE: Or rainbow checkerboard. Race, looks, makes no difference—

JACKIE shoves past them. They gawk, then one turns aside and VOMITS.

JACKIE reaches her locker, fumbles with its lock, swings it open, grabs her LUNCH BAG, dumps its contents.

EXT. STREET - DAY

JACKIE running home, head covered by a brown paper LUNCH BAG.

INT. JACKIE'S ROOM/HALLWAY - LATE AFTERNOON

CROSSCUT between: JACKIE staring into a dresser mirror, her door locked and barricaded with furniture; her MOTHER in the hallway, POUNDING on the door, shaking the doorknob.

MOTHER: Jackie! Open up! I'm your mother, and I'm ordering you to open this door at once. Do you hear me, young lady?

JACKIE's pallid face is almost translucent. Red and blue capillaries spread miniature road maps across her face. JACKIE raises a hand to her face, moaning when she sees the tiny veins in her nearly translucent hand.

Her phone RINGS. JACKIE answers it.

MARY LOU: *(phone)* Hello, Jackie? Jackie, are you there?

JACKIE: Mary Lou?

MARY LOU: *(phone)* Oh Jackie, I was so worried! What happened to you? I heard it was something awful!

MOTHER: Jackie darling, if you have a problem, please tell me. I only want to help.

MARY LOU: *(phone)* Helene heard that someone threw acid in your face in chemistry lab.

MOTHER: Jackie, I'm your mother! You have no right to treat me this way!

MARY LOU: *(phone)* But Judy heard someone say to her friend that something exploded in your face in physics, and that you have warts and radiation poisoning and everything! And, oh Jackie, you had a date with Joey tonight—

JACKIE: I gotta go, Mary Lou.

MARY LOU: *(phone)* But Jackie—

JACKIE hangs up. She scans her cosmetic counter while silently mimicking her MOTHER.

MOTHER: Jackie, when your father comes home he's going to knock this door down, and go in there, and he's going to be so mad at the way you treat your mother!

JACKIE: Leave me alone! I'm just tired! Don't I have a right to be tired?

MOTHER: You're tired? Think how tired your father and I are! Jackie, I'm warning you, we're fed up with your nonsense!

JACKIE snatches Le Renard, almost opens it, then sees her face in the mirror. She hesitates. She almost sets down the jar. Then she sees a Drummer Boy poster reflected in her mirror.

JACKIE: I am so ignorant. If you can't trust Drummer Boy . . .

JACKIE unscrews the jar, scoops out much cream, applies it to her face. Much green cream remains in her hands. She shrugs, smears the peppermint pudding onto her arms, neck, shoulders.

MOTHER: After all the sacrifices your father and I made—

JACKIE: Shut the fuck up!

MOTHER: What did you say?!

JACKIE: It's because of you and dad I was born a monster!

MOTHER: You're not my Jackie—

JACKIE: DNA! Look it up!

EXT. JACKIE'S HOUSE - NIGHT

JOEY pulls up in a dented old car. He HONKS, jumps out, lopes to the front door. He RINGS the bell repeatedly.

JACKIE and her PARENTS are yelling inside. The front door opens, JACKIE exits. She looks radiant. She SLAMS the door behind her.

JOEY: Aaaaaa Jackie! Lookin' fine and sweet.

They kiss.

JACKIE: Thanks. Let's go.

JACKIE hurries JOEY to his car. Her FATHER opens the front door, her MOTHER crying behind him.

FATHER: You were grounded, young lady!

MOTHER: She never says where she's going . . .

FATHER: Get back here now!

MOTHER: . . . or when she's returning.

JOEY's car ROARS away from the curb.

EXT. DRIVE-IN MOVIE - NIGHT

Inside Joey's car. Parked at the rear of the drive-in, where it's DARK. JOEY and JACKIE are making out, then . . .

JACKIE: Mmmm. Joey. Joey wait.

JOEY: What?

JACKIE: I gotta go to the lady's room.

JOEY: Now?!

JACKIE: I'll be right back.

JOEY sullenly stares ahead. JACKIE buttons her blouse.

JACKIE: I won't be long.

JOEY: Just hurry up!

JACKIE exits the car.

INT. SNACK BAR - NIGHT

A one-story building. Brightly lit, glass walls, one small door. Dozens of teenaged PATRONS sit around small tables.

JACKIE enters. No one looks in her direction. We do not see her face as she approaches the COUNTER GIRL, looking down, wiping the counter.

JACKIE: Where's the lady's room?

COUNTER GIRL: Over by the—

The COUNTER GIRL looks up. Horror-struck. She edges away, pale, trembling.

JACKIE: Why are you looking at me like that?

JACKIE leans forward. The COUNTER GIRL screams, trips over backward. A male COWORKER rushes to her aid, sees JACKIE, freezes.

JACKIE: Wha, what's wrong . . . ?

JACKIE edges forward. The COWORKER grabs the faint COUNTER GIRL, drags her into a back room, SLAMS shut the door, BOLTS it.

JACKIE stands frozen with dread, feeling all eyes on the back of her head. Slowly, she turns . . .

As in a 1950s monster film, EVERYONE screams, knocks over tables and chairs, storming the exit as though JACKIE were that monster.

Bottlenecked by the one small doorway, the mob surges against the glass walls, SHATTERING them, spilling people underfoot. Brawny jocks shove scrawny nerds upon the broken glass, trampling them. Boys trample screaming girls. Teens trample crying children.

JACKIE spots a cigarette machine: it has a mirror. JACKIE staggers toward it, looks. We finally see her face.

A riot of crisscrossing blood vessels. Bright red arteries, dark purple veins, extending from her hairline, across her face, down her neck and arms, reaching her fingertips. More extensive than before. More visible.

JACKIE screams, covers her face, hands and arms also translucent.

The mob gone, JACKIE staggers toward the doorway, stumbling over the fallen, crying, bleeding bodies.

EXT. DRIVE-IN MOVIE - CONTINUOUS

Chaos outside. JACKIE exits the snack bar, searching frantically for the drive-in exit. Teens run to escape her, shoving past one another, locking themselves in cars, rolling up windows.

JACKIE trips against a car: inside, two TEENAGERS necking. Seeing JACKIE, the GIRL screams. The BOY turns angrily, sees JACKIE. Anger drains from his face. He hurriedly rolls up the window. JACKIE sees her nightmarish face reflected in its glass.

JACKIE staggers through the drive-in, leaving riots in her wake. Crowds race madly in opposing directions. A car CRASHES into a YOUNG GIRL and sends her body FLYING into another car. Other girls fall and are trampled, their screams lost in the BLARE of car horns, the CRASH of fender benders, the glare of headlights.

CUT TO:

JOEY waits impatiently in his car. He hears increasing pandemonium, turns, sees the rioting. A screaming mob runs past his car.

JOEY: Suddenly, everyone has to go. Assholes.

EXT. DRIVE-IN ENTRANCE - NIGHT

An elderly SECURITY GUARD struggles to guide traffic into an orderly exit. JACKIE runs into him. He grabs her, holds her, sees her face.

SECURITY GUARD: Oh my God . . .

The shock of JACKIE's face causes him to loosen his grip. JACKIE breaks free and escapes.

EXT. ROAD - NIGHT

Torrential rain. JACKIE staggers along a muddied highway shoulder. Cars hiss by, silhouetting her within the glare of oncoming headlights.

INT. CAR - NIGHT

A boorish HUSBAND. A shrewish WIFE. The HUSBAND drives.

WIFE: Can't you drive any faster? We'll miss the entire party.

HUSBAND: We wouldn't be so late if your makeup didn't take so long.

WIFE: You didn't complain before we were married.

HUSBAND: I didn't know you'd pile it on so thick every night. It's like sleeping with a paintbrush.

WIFE: All right, I'll take it off!

The WIFE yanks off her HUSBAND's toupee, wipes her face with it.

HUSBAND: Hey!

The HUSBAND grabs for his toupee, driving one-handed. They tussle until something up ahead catches the WIFE's attention.

WIFE: Hey! What's that thing coming down the road!

JACKIE stumbles into the glare of the car's headlights.

HUSBAND: Oh my God!

WIFE: Watch out, you're gonna hit it!

EXT. ROAD - CONTINUOUS

The car careens, barely missing JACKIE. She falls into the highway shoulder. Now completely drenched in mud, her face and arms obscured by its wet blackness, she staggers home.

INT. DR. IVY'S EXAMINATION ROOM - DAY

DR. IVY with JACKIE and MOTHER. JACKIE's translucence has spread since last night. Face, neck, shoulders, arms: all tinged red by her underlying muscles, traversed with red and blue blood vessels and spidery white nerves.

DR. IVY: It appears as though your daughter is experiencing an epidermal pigmentative discoloration.

MOTHER bites a clenched fist, moaning fearfully. DR. IVY quickly intervenes, quick to reassure, quick to deter a malpractice suit.

DR. IVY: Aside from which, Jackie is an astonishingly healthy young lady!

MOTHER: Thank goodness.

DR. IVY: And even the discoloration isn't an illness, or a medical problem.

MOTHER: I was so worried when I saw her looking like this.

DR. IVY: Hey mother, let me decide when we start worrying, okay? Right now, I say we wait for those test results. I'm sure it's nothing.

MOTHER: I felt so guilty about signing that consent form. Only Jackie said the cream was for a school science project.

DR. IVY: They can be a handful at this age.

MOTHER: I don't even know if that's legal.

DR. IVY: Please don't worry about it. All that matters is Jackie's health. My advice is, you take her home.

MOTHER: Yes.

DR. IVY: Give her a hot nutritious dinner.

MOTHER: Always.

DR. IVY: Chock full of vitamins, and minerals, and all that good stuff you moms do so well.

MOTHER: Yes.

DR. IVY: But nothing she may have eaten these past few days. It may be food poisoning.

MOTHER: *(to Jackie)* You hear that? No junk food!

DR. IVY: And get her to bed early. No more cramming for school.

MOTHER: *(to Jackie)* Go to bed early!

DR. IVY: And when the results come in, I'll let you know.

MOTHER: Oh thank you, doctor. Thank you so much.

INT. DR. IVY'S RECEPTION ROOM - CONTINUOUS

A BEAUTIFUL NURSE puts an arm around JACKIE as she escorts JACKIE and MOTHER out. The NURSE's beauty, melodic voice, and charming manners provide a painful contrast for the hideous JACKIE.

BEAUTIFUL NURSE: Well Jackie, it was nice to see you again. I'm sure everything will be fine.

MOTHER: Yes, you see, she is a little worried that her boyfriend won't like her anymore, because she isn't beau-ti-ful!

JACKIE: I don't care about that!

BEAUTIFUL NURSE: Oh, fiddlesticks! I'm sure he's waiting at home right now, worried to death over you.

JACKIE: I don't want to see him!

MOTHER: *(ignoring Jackie)* Yes, but you know how they are at this age. Jackie wants to be a beauty queen!

JACKIE: I do not! I just don't want to look like a monster!

BEAUTIFUL NURSE: Why, she looks lovely even now. You know, Jackie, beauty is only skin deep. I'm sure you have no reason to worry. I'll bet your lucky boyfriend will see the real you, deep down inside.

EXT. CONCERT - NIGHT

An outdoor night concert. DRUMMER BOY leaps from a ring of fire, dressed in a drum major's uniform, hands and face plastered with peppermint green skin cream. The AUDIENCE roars its adulation.

DRUMMER BOY moon walks toward a wind machine.

DRUMMER BOY: *(singing)* Lofty thoughts and noble dreams, yield heaps of inner bliss to reap. Ancient gods gave man this cream, to show true beauty lies skin deep! Wooooooooo!

DRUMMER BOY halts. Water cascades upon him, washing away all cream, baring his skin. While we don't see him after his stage shower, the AUDIENCE does. They rise to their feet, shrieking. Thrilled . . . or terrified?

EXT. JACKIE'S HOUSE - DAY

JOEY drives up, parking just as PARAMEDICS load a stretcher into an ambulance, bearing a covered patient. Jackie's parents watch, MOTHER crying hysterically, FATHER comforting her.

JOEY dashes to the PARENTS, just as the ambulance drives off, lights flashing.

JOEY: What's happening? Where's Jackie?

MOTHER: Oh, my baby! My poor baby!

FATHER: Please, young man. Leave us be.

JOEY: Was that Jackie?

MOTHER: Oh, my baby!

FATHER: Young man, you're not welcome here. Leave us alone.

JOEY: Where'd they take Jackie?!

FATHER: I said, leave us alone!

MOTHER and FATHER enter the house, SLAMMING the door in JOEY's face. JOEY runs to his car, SCREECHING away from the curb.

EXT. STREET - DAY

JOEY spots the ambulance afar. He speeds toward it, dodging cars and pedestrians, racing past red lights, until a car ahead of him stops at a red light. JOEY can't get by, but he sees the name on the ambulance: Hope Medical Center.

EXT. HOPE MEDICAL CENTER - DAY

The ambulance speeds past the parking area, halting outside ER. As PARAMEDICS remove their patient, a MEDICAL TEAM rushes from ER, led by DR. BERNARD. He lifts the sheet to check the patient. What does he see?

DR. BERNARD: Quarantine her! Now!

EVERYONE strides into ER, wheeling the covered patient.

EXT. HOPE MEDICAL CENTER - DAY

JOEY's car speeds through the parking area, stopping before the main entrance. JOEY rushes into the hospital.

INT. HOPE MEDICAL CENTER LOBBY - CONTINUOUS

JOEY runs to the reception desk, serviced by a FAT NURSE eating a plateful of donuts.

JOEY: I'm looking for my girlfriend. Name's Jackie. They just brought her in.

FAT NURSE: *(disinterested)* Jackie what?

JOEY: Jones. Jackie Jones.

The FAT NURSE checks a computer, then labors from her chair to flip through a Rolodex, shuffle some forms. JOEY's impatience increasing. The FAT NURSE sighs and trudges back to her chair.

FAT NURSE: No Jackie Jones.

JOEY: *(slams desk)* They just brought her in here!

FAT NURSE: You'll have to wait until I receive further infor . . .

The FAT NURSE realizes JOEY has run off. Sighing, she reaches for the phone, then changes direction and reaches for a donut.

INT. HOPE MEDICAL CENTER HALLWAYS/ROOMS - DAY

JOEY races down hallways, rushing from room to room, interrupting bed-wetters, vomiters, burn victims, quadriplegics, shoving his way through corridors crowded with the sick, the dying, the dead.

INT. QUARANTINE CORRIDOR - DAY

Bright fluorescent lighting. White tiled walls. Spacious and antiseptic and barren, in contrast to the filthy, crowded hallways traversed by Joey.

A stoic DR. BERNARD and exuberant DR. GROSS stroll the corridor.

DR. GROSS: So what you're saying then, doctor, is that this is an entirely new phenomenon in the field of medicine?

DR. BERNARD: Presumably so. As of yet, no known documentation of any such incident can be found. Not by us, nor by our computers.

DR. GROSS: Fascinating! What would you suggest is the prognosis for a cure in a case such as this?

DR. BERNARD: While we do not know, as of yet, what we are confronted with, at this point it appears likely that the damage itself is permanent.

DR. GROSS: Mind-boggling! And no one has any theories as to the cause of this illness?

DR. BERNARD: None whatsoever.

DR. GROSS: Extraordinary! At least the pigmentative deterioration has ceased progression. The patient is fortunate in that respect.

As DR. BERNARD and DR. GROSS round one corner, JOEY rounds another, racing in the direction from which the two doctors have just come. A video camera monitors JOEY as he SLAMS open a door.

INT. QUARANTINE ROOM #1 - CONTINUOUS

A dying OLD MAN is the sole occupant, lying under an oxygen tent. JOEY scans the room and leaves.

INT. SECURITY ROOM - DAY

A GUARD watches a bank of video monitors. JOEY appears on one. The GUARD snatches a phone.

GUARD: Dispatch security to Quarantine Corridor Five.

INT. QUARANTINE CORRIDOR/ROOM #2 - DAY

JOEY slams open the door: an empty room. He leaves, rushing for the next room . . .

INT. JACKIE'S QUARANTINE ROOM - CONTINUOUS

JOEY throws open the door, looks in, and shudders.

A bed containing a skeleton and organs, connected by a network of blood vessels and nerves. JOEY almost exits, then yields to morbid curiosity and approaches the pulsing organs . . .

As if just now seeing him, the organs sit up and JACKIE screams!

JOEY screams back.

JACKIE has ZERO pigmentation. Her transparent skin provides a clear view of her insides, like those plastic models in school. JOEY sees her heart pump, her lungs rise and fall under her ribs, her muscles contract and loosen as she moves her bones.

JACKIE covers her eyes, muscled eyeballs staring expressionlessly from behind muscled finger bones. Eyelids transparent, save for the capillaries and nerves traversing them. Transparent eyelids gliding futilely over ever-seeing eyeballs.

JOEY cowers against a wall, still screaming when GUARDS burst in and drag him away.

DR. BERNARD and AIDES shove the madly screaming JACKIE onto her bed, strapping her down, muscled bones struggling as DR. BERNARD fills a syringe with medication . . .

INT. DRUMMER BOY'S THRONE ROOM - DAY

DRUMMER BOY sits on his throne, yet we don't see him. ATTORNEYS, ACCOUNTANTS, ASSISTANTS, and BODYGUARDS are standing nearby. DR. VINE and DR. IVY sit before him, mouths agape.

DRUMMER BOY: I was wondering if you had anything stronger?

DR. VINE: You want something stronger?

DRUMMER BOY: Just to even out my skin tones, you understand.

DR. VINE: Ahem, I don't mean to contradict your assessment, but since I last saw you, your skin tones have evened out . . . considerably.

We finally see DRUMMER BOY. His transparent lips smile indulgently. He is as much a plastic model as Jackie.

DRUMMER BOY: Of course, I expect you to say that. I understand your obligation to defend your product. But I hope you'll agree that I am the best judge of my own skin?

DR. VINE: Of course.

DRUMMER BOY: I'm glad you don't dispute my judgment.

DR. VINE: No. Not at all.

DR. VINE scans the entourage hovering beside DRUMMER BOY. Not a one says a word.

DR. VINE: You know your skin best.

DR. IVY: Can we assume, then, that you are no longer concerned about, uhm, any depigmentation that may result in lighter skin tones?

Ignoring her, DRUMMER BOY addresses DR. VINE.

DRUMMER BOY: As I stated previously, I'm proud of my African heritage, and would regret lightening my skin. However, your cream has so far failed to lighten my skin, as you can plainly see.

DR. VINE gawks at the silent entourage, glances at DR. IVY, then turns to DRUMMER BOY.

DR. VINE: Of course. Your skin is no lighter than before, yet your tones are a shade uneven. A stronger cream is appropriate.

INT. JACKIE'S LIVING ROOM - DAY

FATHER holds MOTHER, dried tears staining her face. DR. BERNARD lays out some paperwork. DR. GROSS enjoys a tray of confections.

DR. BERNARD: The state of a person's mind is largely conditioned by its environment. Therefore, the loss of your daughter's sanity should come as no great surprise.

FATHER is already signing the paperwork, eagerly.

FATHER: And this is in her best interest?

DR. BERNARD: I can assure you, there can be little hope for your daughter to enjoy a normal life in the outside world. This way, you can rest assured in that she will always enjoy the constant attention of the finest minds in medicine. And you need never worry about expenses.

DR. BERNARD accepts the signed forms. FATHER squeezes MOTHER.

FATHER: It will be comforting to know that Jackie will receive such fine attention. What about the . . . ?

DR. BERNARD: The sum we discussed has been agreed to. You may expect a check shortly.

MOTHER: Thank you for all your help, doctor.

FATHER: We're deeply in debt to you.

EXT. JACKIE'S HOUSE - DAY

DR. BERNARD and DR. GROSS exit the house, and approach a black car parked by the curb. A power window hums down. DR. BERNARD leans into the car and hands DR. VINE one of the forms. DR. IVY seated beside DR. VINE.

DR. BERNARD: They've waived all claims.

DR. VINE: Excellent. You may expect a check shortly.

DR. IVY passes a folder to DR. BERNARD.

DR. IVY: Her medical records. As agreed.

The window hums up, the car drives away, leaving DR. BERNARD and DR. GROSS at the curb.

DR. GROSS: What a marvelous arrangement, doctor! Think what a boon to medical science!

INT. HARVARD MEDICAL CLASS - DAY

About 150 students, taking notes. Strapped to a table before the class is the living, naked body of JACKIE. A PROFESSOR indicates her organs with a pointer.

PROFESSOR: As you can see, the blood enters the aorta through the vascular canal—

STUDENT: Excuse me, professor. We're having trouble seeing it back here.

A murmur of agreement from his section.

PROFESSOR: Oh, excuse me.

The PROFESSOR rotates the table on a pivot, tilting it toward the STUDENT. JACKIE remains catatonic, mute.

PROFESSOR: Is that better?

STUDENT: Yes, thank you.

PROFESSOR: Can you all see?

THE END OF YOUNG JACKIE'S NIGHTMARE.

EXT. SARAH'S NEW ENGLAND TOWN - MORNING

The morning after Halloween. Beautiful and serene. Clear blue sky. Crisp air rustling autumn leaves.

INT. JACKIE'S BEDROOM - MORNING

Young JACKIE lies stiffly in bed, as if strapped onto an examination table. Open eyes blank. Hair on end. Face frozen in fear. An irreversible catatonic coma, forever trapped in her nightmare.

Her panicked MOTHER and FATHER in the room.

MOTHER: *(shouting)* Why is she staring like that? John, do something! What's wrong with my daughter?!

INT. WOLF'S BEDROOM - MORNING

WOLF lies immobilized on his stomach, as if strapped onto a table. His open eyes catatonic, hair on end, face frozen in fear, trapped in a nightmare. His PARENTS shouting.

MOTHER: Did you call the doctor?

FATHER: Yes, for the fiftieth time! I called the doctor!

MOTHER: When will he be here?

FATHER: I don't know!

INT. MEGAN'S BEDROOM - MORNING

Immobilized on her bed, MEGAN's blank, catatonic eyes see nothing except her nightmare. Face tight with fear. Hair on end. Her MOTHER is crying. Her FATHER slaps MEGAN, to no avail.

FATHER: *(slapping Megan)* Wake up! Wake up!

MOTHER: Oh God, what's happened to her? Look at her! Oh God!

FATHER: *(slapping Megan)* Wake up! Wake up! Wake up!

INT. ARTHUR'S BEDROOM - MORNING

ARTHUR lies spread-eagled, as though tied to a toy bed. His hair on end. Face contorted with fear. Open eyes seeing nothing. His MOTHER and FATHER present, arguing.

MOTHER: I told you to check the candy, damn you!

FATHER: I did check the candy!

MOTHER: Not well enough, you bastard!

FATHER: I'm sorry! I'm not God!

MOTHER: I hate Halloweeeeeeen!

EXT. SARAH'S HOUSE - MORNING

Pleasant, birds chirping. SARAH exits her house for the morning paper, wearing a hokey black-and-orange Halloween bathrobe. She spots MRS. PEABODY several houses down.

SARAH: Good morning, Mrs. Peabody!

MRS. PEABODY: You think so? Look what those brats did now!

SARAH strolls to MRS. PEABODY's house. It's covered with shaving cream. And her bushes.

SARAH: Oh dear.

MRS. PEABODY: I stayed up all night to see this wouldn't happen. And now look!

SARAH: Well that's no fair. Playing tricks the day after Halloween.

MRS. PEABODY: Little monsters. Wait till next year. I'll give them a treat. Pins and razors!

SARAH: Now, now. Nothing traditional about pins and razors.

SARAH returns to her house, and is about to enter when she hears giggling. She looks about and spots TRUDY hiding behind a tree. TRUDY drops a can of shaving cream, and grabs it up again.

SARAH: Little girl? Oh little girl?

TRUDY stops giggling and peeks out. SARAH produces the Jack O' Lantern candy from her bathrobe sleeve. As if by magic.

SARAH: You don't believe those silly stories about witches, do you?

TRUDY shrugs.

SARAH: You know the nicest thing about Halloween? It's the one day of the year when it's okay to take candy from strangers. Even from witches.

Hiding the shaving cream behind her, TRUDY edges toward SARAH.

SARAH: Don't be afraid. Only ugly witches are bad. I'm not ugly, am I?

TRUDY shrugs, so SARAH mocks a frown. Then TRUDY shakes her head, so SARAH grins. But when TRUDY nears, SARAH pulls back the candy.

SARAH: But even good witches get very mad at naughty children who don't have any Halloween spirit. You do have Halloween spirit, don't you?

TRUDY nods coyly, then snatches the candy from SARAH.

TRUDY retreats a few quick steps, keeping the shaving cream hidden. Without taking her eyes from SARAH, TRUDY bites the candy. She smiles gleefully, as if she's fooled SARAH.

TRUDY darts away.

SARAH reaches her front door, then glances back at TRUDY running down the street.

SARAH: Accepting treats the day after Halloween. That is definitely not the Halloween spirit.

SARAH smiles, then laughs, then CACKLES in a manner both pleasant and maniacally evil. As her cackling intensifies, in both pitch and menace, she enters her house and closes the door.

THE END . . . UNTIL NEXT HALLOWEEN!

They Came from Outer Space and Went Bump in the Night: Haunted Houses in California

"Help me. Please help me. You've got to get me out of here before he comes back." The young woman's head is clamped within a guillotine, her pleas directed at the people shuffling into the Torture Room. Torn bodies stretch across two racks, one with a whirling buzzsaw. The woman continues pleading until everyone is in the room. "He's crazy. He wants to kill me. *Why are you all just staring at me! Get me out of here!"*

The knife-wielding Torturer pops out of a doorway, rushes at and startles the crowd before backtracking toward his guillotine. His leather apron is splattered with blood. "This is Robin, my ex-girlfriend. It didn't work out. She's a vegetarian. I'm not."

"Please help me!"

"Listen to her. Every day it's the same thing. Whine, whine, whine. Should I kill her?"

"Noooooo!" screams Robin.

"Yeah," mumble a few voices in the crowd.

"Should I kill her?" shouts the Torturer.

The crowd grows louder. "Yeah."

"I can't hear you! SHOULD I KILL HER?"

"YEAH!"

"YOU'RE SICK!" screams the Torturer, then counts, "One, two, three!" releasing the guillotine, dropping Robin's head into the basket. The countdown is important. It cues the actress to lower her head, away from audience view.

Show over, the Rover hustles the crowd into the next room.

The Torture Room lay at the heart of the **Chamber Of Chills,** a joint venture of Universal Studios and Imagine Entertainment operating in eleven locations nationwide this past Halloween. The Universal Citywalk Chamber was a plywood haunted house containing some twenty rooms and hallways jerrybuilt on the ground level of a mall garage, its concrete floor stenciled with COMPACT parking spots. Audiences were shepherded through by Rovers, tour guides in black robes and skull masks. Not all haunted houses have Rovers.

A "haunted house" may be defined as a carnival funhouse featuring performers in macabre roles. The Chamber's heavy dramatic emphasis, particularly the events in its Torture Room, evokes the French Grand Guignol. But not all haunted houses are theatrical. Many of the haunted houses in southern California eschewed actors improvising darkly comedic dialogue in favor of mute performers and humorless shocks. Chamber theatrics also emphasized movie monsters, many (not all) inspired by Universal's 1930s pantheon. Weekend nights, I played the Devil in the Exorcist Room.

A pink room. The audience enters to see the Exorcist Girl already squirming in bed, pleading to them, "Mommy, please help me. He wants to take my soul. Mommy what's happening?!" I hear the cue from my cubicle next door, darken the room, activate the strobe light. The Exorcist Girl arises from a hole in the bed, a plaster body cast strapped perpendicular to her chest under a bedsheet. She appears to levitate. "What's happening mommy!" She gags, her voice deepens. "I'm happening, mommy! Her soul is mine and YOU'RE NEXT!"

I shift the floor thrice with a mechanical lever, bang open the Devil Door (a low door disguised as a mirror), rush to attack the crowd behind the railing, grope without touching, my red face and black beard flickering in the cold strobe, laugh demonically, scream throatily, "Your soul is mine! Muh-ha-ha-ha-ha!"

Surprise is key, the shock of a sudden attack from the dark. I've turned crowds into domino chips, people falling against each other, screaming or laughing as a whole row tumbles. I play the music of horror. I begin on a high note, strive to maintain the shock, hold the note. If they catch their senses, no longer fear you, you drop the note. Rarely do you regain a note after losing it. Slamming open my Devil Door, I hurl my attack at the weakest link in the crowd, the screamers. I corner young screaming girls afraid to run past my groping hands for the Exit. I try to maintain the note, keep them screaming, stomp the ground, flail arms, shout demonic threats to prevent their senses from returning and reminding them it's only a show.

Each show I strive for a domino tumble, or at least one fall down. Each show about a minute long, give or take. A hundred or two shows a night, give or take. Rovers herd the crowds through like cattle, in and out. If I can scare some off their feet, the Exorcist Girl gives me thumbs up.

Haunted houses are primordial events. Women clutch their menfolk, who (small wonder) enjoy seeing the women melt into pulp, enjoy shielding them from my groping hands. Yet some women laugh at my act. One grabs my horns. Patrons vary. Some stride past looking bored. Others smile politely, then move on. Some profess Jesus. Others offer their souls. Worst are those who assault the actors (mainly rowdy, drunken male teens). Oddest are the parents who laugh when their toddlers burst into tears. Between shows, some Exorcist Girls express disgust at the parents who come through.

I've performed with ten Exorcist Girls and one Exorcist Boy. Actors are rotated but I'm always the weekend Devil, aside from a night as Dracula, two as the Headless Frankenstein, and a night in the Hand Room. We're told roles are cast according to merit. Some actors grumble nepotism and favoritism are involved. Others suspect punishment, as some roles are considered especially demeaning. The Exorcist Boy wears the same big-boobed plaster body cast for the levitation trick as the Exorcist Girls.

The Chamber Of Chills features many monsters. Other haunted houses are single-themed. Santa Monica's **Alien Terror** is what it sounds like: a haunted house devoted solely to alien terror.

Sponsored by The Puzzle Zoo, a toy, game, and novelty store, Alien Terror operates out of a former video & music store. Upon entering, I am met by an American "astronaut" who informs me that our government discovered the debris of an alien spacecraft and some live aliens at Roswell, all of which were rushed to this secret location in Santa Monica. He shows me pickled alien fetuses and crash debris to prove he's not crazy. The Truth Is Out There.

I know I'm close to it because I hear the theme music to *The X-Files* piped into every room. The Chamber's sound system pipes a mix of recorded effects into its rooms (screams, chains, spooky music, news bulletins of escaped lunatics). Alien Terror only plays *The X-Files*'s opening theme, but it works.

Next door a harried technician is shocked to see me entering this Top Secret facility—amidst a red alert. He mutters something about a "carnage" and "chaos in there," asks if I have authorization, is so panicked he takes my word for it and waves me in with a: "God bless you, you're on your own!"

I am indeed. Unlike the Chamber, no Rovers accompany me. I am alone. Even if due to a lower budget, it's spookier this way. Unlike the Chamber, Alien Terror has smoke machines, apparently set at full blast. Billowy clouds hide its plywood walls, creating an illusion of infinity, a sense of outdoors. I am beside an alien crash site, outdoors, at night. A tense Marine shouts into the fog, "One civilian coming through!"

I run past groping aliens, and something in this murky smoke doesn't make sense. I was told I'm still in Santa Monica, yet signs read Area 51, Roswell, Hanger 18. During an alien autopsy, I witness an *Alien* spawn erupt from the alien on the table; a gray alien hosting the kind that drools. Incongruities blur. I rush through too fast to ponder the huge slug devouring the screaming guard or the gray humanoid disemboweling the shapely, shrieking scientist, the iconography from a half century of alien mythology compressed into a surreal fever dream of contradictory nightmare images, constructing a dialectical, if irrational, conspiracist's vision of reality. If Fox Mulder ever dropped acid, this is what he'd see on a bad trip.

Special effects are by Michael Burnett, who also did effects for *Evil Dead II* and TV's *Monsters.* Burnett tells me he often keeps his work. The slug devouring the guard previously appeared in *Monsters*'s "Shave and a Haircut, Two Bites." Nice to see he hasn't been typecast as a Lovecraftian vampire. He gave a strong performance as an alien, although failed to perform on my second visit (and no understudy).

Alien Terror's manager, David Saffron, says he's experienced no problems from audiences. Unruly groups are split into smaller groups before being admitted. Saffron pats a walkie-talkie under his sweater, ready to call security should trouble erupt. Before every show, he assures audiences that actors will not touch them, and admonishes them not to touch the actors.

Haunted houses vary in many respects but those two rules are ubiquitous. I later go through with a crowd, pausing to gawk at the humanoid disemboweling the sexy scientist in the observation booth, the shrieking victim smearing the glass partition with her blood. The humanoid pops open the door, rushes at us, groping. A laughing boy shoves him in the chest. The humanoid nabs the kid, lifts aside his rubber alien mouthpiece. "Don't touch the people!"

Mom grabs her kid. "You heard what he just said? I swear, if you can't behave yourself I'm not taking you anywhere . . . "

Assaults happen in haunted houses. One night I pop open my Devil Door, rush the crowd, screaming for souls in the dark, feel water hit my face, continue screaming, feel more water in my face. Now certain something's not right, I stop the performance. I drop the note, break the spell of horror. The Rover is already on the walkie-talkie, calling security. He points to the man who tossed several swigs at me. "Sir, will you come with me?"

"That better not be urine!" shouts the Exorcist Boy, also wet. Audience members ask one another what happened. An embarrassed silence, filled by ghostly screams and rattling chains. Security and management rush into the Exorcist Room. The culprit is removed. The Exorcist Boy and I are asked if we're all right.

The Chamber draws its roughest crowds on weekends, when the nearby amphitheater hosts rock and rap concerts. Drunken, stoned gang members visit us afterwards. Actors are told to stay three feet behind the railing, for our own protection. That detracts from the show. Many of us ignore the rule. We're told that if we're assaulted, no charges can be pressed unless we can identify our attacker and are willing to press charges. Since no one asks me if I want to press charges, I assume none are.

Haunted houses are dangerous workplaces. A teen girl punches me in the nose. A teen boy kicks an actress. "I couldn't see his face in that Headless Frankenstein thing," she complains the next night, her leg still aching. "Otherwise, I'd of kicked him back." A father escorts his toddler through the Exorcist Room. As she stares up at me, all googly-eyed, dad instructs her with, "Go ahead honey. Kick him. Kick him in the balls."

Security is extensive at the Chamber. L.A. gangs are a constant concern. Patrons pass through a metal detector. An Exorcist Girl tells me a sawed-off shotgun was found on one youth.

"If he had a gun, why'd he go through the detector?" I ask. "Didn't he know he'd get caught?"

"Oh, he wanted to get caught," she replies. "He was showing off to his friends."

Another youth races through the Chamber, ignoring every performance, only staying long enough to "shoot" each actor with his fingers. Actors are told that if there's "trouble" we are to run to the safety areas and lock ourselves in. No heroics. I don't know where those areas are, but I'm reckless enough to believe I won't need to. Security guards here are professional and plentiful. They do a good job keeping the horrors of reality outside.

Bringing those horrors *into* a haunted house was the idea behind the **House Of Terror.** Operated by Newport Entertainment, the House Of Terror was situated on the first three floors of a four-story Anaheim office building a few blocks from Disneyland. Its president and owner, Jeffrey Immediato, thinks the horrors of the real world surpass monsters and aliens. With House Of Terror he wanted to "open the edge of reality, just a bit," and bring that reality into a haunted house.

House Of Terror has Pinhead and Freddy Kruger (but the Chamber's Freddy has dialogue). It even has an *outdoor* Roswell crash site in its atrium (but Alien Terror's foggy indoor crash site is more expressionistic, more Caligarian). What House Of Terror has that other haunted houses don't are rooms devoted to real-life murderers Charles Manson, Jeffrey Dahmer, John Wayne Gacy, and OJ Simpson. The Manson Room's walls drip bloodily: "Helter Skelter" and "Die Pigs." The Dahmer Room's refrigerator is stocked with human limbs. The OJ Room resembles the patio on which Ron Goldman and Nicole Brown Simpson were found dead. Initially, a blond actress lay on the floor, blood streaming from her throat.

Then came the protesters. Soon after came the media. Radio stations called, broadcasting Immediato's voice deep into Canada. Brown family attorney Gloria Alred grilled Immediato on her radio show. The wire services picked up the story. By the time I met Immediato [two days before Halloween] 782 newspapers worldwide had run a story on the OJ Room. Leeza Gibbons wanted an interview. Oprah wanted him on her show. "But I have no time just now," Immediato explained to me in his hectic office. "Maybe after Halloween."

Which side did the protesters claim to represent, Nicole or OJ? Immediato doesn't know. He's gotten calls from across the country, both praising and condemning his "statement" on OJ. Yet Immediato claims he intended no statement and expected no controversy. As he points out, the OJ Room is only one of four that dramatize real-life murders and nothing distinguishes the OJ Room from the other three. Immediato refused to close the OJ Room, as some protesters demanded, though after a phone call with Denise Brown he did remove the actress portraying Nicole, "in deference to her sister's wishes."

As for the audience, Immediato says, "We've had 50 to 60,000 customers since we opened [about two weeks ago]. Maybe one tenth of one percent complained of the OJ Room, and 90% of those complained that we had removed the actress."

Patrons are frisked before entering the House Of Terror. No metal detector, but more security than at Alien Terror. Aside from some soldiers' dialogue capped by a rainstorm in the Roswell atrium, shows are unstructured. Patrons wander through the rooms nonstop. Actors speak no lines. Sometimes they growl. Often they suppress grins. Mainly they just menace crowds with staring eyes and outstretched arms. As at Alien Terror, no railings hold them back. Crowds must negotiate their way through a delightfully disgusting madhouse area, filthy bare mattresses strewn about, straightjacketed psychos sauntering ahead and behind them.

Immediato says he and his staff are always arguing about the exact number of rooms, and whether hallways count. Current tally is 161 exhibits within 50 to 70 rooms but that's always changing, depending upon audience response. Some rooms are traversed, some are off to the side, for display only. Such as the murder rooms. I almost missed the OJ Room, which is small and dim, its light bulb having burned out. An actor wears a #32 USC football jersey and wields a bloody knife.

The rooms exit into a lobby containing rental booths hawking Halloween and horror kitsch. Serial Killer Inc. sells t-shirts, sweatshirts, caps, and beanies featuring the faces of . . . well, of people you'd expect from a company called Serial Killer.

An actor informs me that House Of Terror's cast is comprised of high school volunteers. He's worked in several haunted houses over the years. It's his hobby. He "enjoys scaring people." He's surprised to hear that Alien Terror and the Chamber use paid professional actors. Alien Terror hired a casting agency, Prime Casting. Chamber recruited its initial cast through trade paper ads and auditions (first they asked me for a werewolf howl, then to mime driving over someone with a motorcycle). Later, due to a high turnover rate, non-actors were hired without auditions. One Exorcist Girl only came to get ideas for her church's annual haunted house. The Chamber offered her a part instead.

Haunted houses allow for such cavalier casting. The Chamber is one of the more theatrically-structured, yet even its better delineated characters don't require subtle internalizations; just broad, bloody showmanship. Haunted houses are less a stage for the Method Actor than for the Ham. Less Stanislavski, more P.T. Barnum. Haunted houses are the splatter houses of theater, and its acting style of showmanship supports a horror aesthetic of shocks over quiet terror. And as in splatter cinema, some shows offer straight shocks, others infuse black comedy.

The Torture Room inspires a new schtick every night. One irritating Victim, clamped in the guillotine, shrieks incessantly for help. The Torturer arrives and shouts, "SHAD-UP! SHAD-UP! SHAD-UP!"

"Yeah, shud-up!" a patron screams from another room.

"Shad-up!" scream actors from every room. "Shad-up!"

The Chamber's makeshift plywood rooms are roofless. Everyone can simultaneously hear every actor's performance, and the chainsaw and guillotine, and the sound system's screams and chains and wind and music, and patrons screaming and tumbling against walls, and horns from the Car Room and the garage surrounding us. The Chamber resounds like a madhouse in Hell, its Ninth Circle centered in the Torture Room. Some rooms drown out others, but the Torturer's schtick is always heard everywhere. A less inventive Torturer releases his guillotine with, "If you want to get ahead, you gotta get a head!"

Comedy relieves boredom and enlivens small parts. The actor in the Car Room merely has to push a car's hood past a curtain at the crowd, headlights on, horn blaring. But actors want lines, so he gives himself some, quipping after every near fatality, "Can anyone direct me to the 405?"

Rooms that don't shock or inspire black comedy can still be saved with standup. The Trophy Room is mounted with stuffed monster heads. An actor-as-Dracula sticks his head through the wall, popping out at passing crowds. People usually guess the gag in advance. Smart alecky kids point to the actor, explaining it to anyone who's still in the dark. It's all pretty lame. So if my surprise rush to the railing is met by silent stares, I say in a Lugosi accent, "Don't all scream at once."

Patrons break into smiles, tension eased. Tension, because the Trophy Room is the Chamber's second show, following a Crazed Clown who just pops out of a giant Toy Box. If the Crazed Clown fails to scare them, and I fail, patrons begin to worry about an $8 admission flushed down the toilet. I acknowledge their anxiety by turning it into a joke. When my vampire snarls are met by blank stares, I make an unexpected 180° turn, break into laughter and say, "So, are we scared yet?"

A brat says, "No."

"Well, don't worry. It gets even scarier!" It does. Only by now my Lugosi sounds like Count Floyd. "Wait till you see the Frankenstein Room next door! Ooooo-boy! It even scares me!"

A woman eyes my vampire makeup and natural beard. "What *are* you? Are you a vampire? A werewolf? I don't even know what you're supposed to be."

"My mother was Elvira and my father was Wolfman Jack, so you tell me! Even they don't know!" In time, my Count Floyd becomes Shecky Floyd of the Catskills.

"This show sucks," a young thug complains.

"Hey look, I didn't write the script. I just pop out of the box. We're not talking *Hamlet*. There's only so much you can do with a box. You get in. You pop out."

Worse is when one drunken teen guesses the gag, leans over the railing before I pop out, and screams into my face.

It helps if the Crazed Clown warms up the audience. I hear one Clown pop from his box beside the Player Piano, shouting to the audience, "Every night the same song! It's driving me crazy! Somebody please make him play something new! Anything! Mozart! Menudo!"

The Exorcist Boy's stubbly face over a big-boobed levitation body cast inspires surreal comedy. Unlike the actresses who go silent when my Devil appears, he continues spewing Spanish invectives. Makes no sense storywise (if the Devil has left his body, why is he still possessed?) but the Exorcist Room never held to scrutiny ("I don't remember you from the film," a man says to me). I ask the Exorcist Boy how to say *your soul is mine* in Spanish. *Tengo tu alma.* I am now a bilingual Devil.

Showmanship doesn't require sense, only an audience. People point down at us from the second floor of the garage, which forms a balcony overlooking our rooms. If security doesn't shoo them off, I wave. If they wave back, the Devil takes a bow.

Showmanship does require storytelling. Not all haunted houses tell stories. **Shipwreck '96** is less show than nightclub. Operated by Long Beach's *Queen Mary* ocean liner, Shipwreck '96 promises two haunted houses for the price of one ($10). Patrons begin at the Londontowne Of Terror, two floors of two houses (not plywood mazes). Afterwards, you enter the *Queen Mary* herself for the Haunted Hull Of Horror.

Shipwreck '96 is the Spinal Tap of haunted houses. It earns the distinction of being southern California's loudest house. As in House Of Terror, patrons traverse Londontowne without benefit of Rovers or railings, running past actors in horrific makeup who slam plastic knives, machetes, and axes against walls. Makes a nice loud bang. They don't talk. They're there to bang walls. Eardrum-shattering noise is Londontowne's motif.

Londontowne is a heavy metal madhouse, assaulting patrons in every room with deafening grindhouse rock. Many rooms are barren aside from horrific day-glo masks tacked to walls. Laser lights slice through heavy smoke. Spotlights change colors, disco-style. Londontowne is smoke, light, and music. No acting, no storytelling, no humor. A few rooms have displays. Visually, the first room has a classical horror atmosphere—cobwebs, smoke, violet lighting, silent Goth actors amidst Victorian furnishings. Silent not to support the atmosphere, but because no one can hear actors in the heavy metal din. Another room contains a medical examiner's table, unattended. Mainly, Londontowne is about banging walls in a noisy nightclub.

An unrelenting mind-numbing sameness pervades Shipwreck '96. After Londontowne's two same houses, we enter the Haunted Hull Of Horror inside the *Queen Mary*, where we are confronted with . . . more of the same. Smoke, laser lights, and heavy metal madness beset our designated path of stairwells and catwalks. Actors pound the *Queen Mary*'s metal hull and pipes with plastic knives, machetes, axes. Makes a nice loud echo. Inside one sealed room, an actor pulls innards from a supine body. Aside from such incidentals, Haunted Hull Of Horror is Londontowne on a boat. Not having been inside an ocean liner before, I find the hull more interesting than its horrors.

The horrors culminate when the Hull exits onto a smoky discotheque. For real. Food, drinks, and Halloween kitsch are sold in a gallery overlooking a dance floor.

Maybe I'm too old to appreciate Shipwreck '96's disco/metal fusion horrors. Most patrons enjoyed it immensely. Most patrons were in their teens, by a far greater proportion than at other haunted houses. While waiting to enter the *Queen Mary,* on line conversations centered on MTV, pot, and homework. I spent my time studying the *Queen Mary*'s history, and easily found room before the photo display.

The *Queen Mary* has a supernatural past: 49 deaths in its 60-year history and numerous ghost sightings. *A Guide to the Haunted Queen Mary* is available in its gift shop. Those legends (plus mermaids, Davy Jones's Locker, Moby Dick, sea monsters) might have been incorporated into Shipwreck '96. They weren't.

Queen Mary Seaport PR manager, Elizabeth A. Borsting, tells me that 5,000 people visited on Halloween night. I'd seen many the night before, and a concert-sized crowd on Halloween. One line snaked around a block toward the gate, dribbling people to a second line for tickets. A third line to enter Londontowne. A fourth to enter the *Queen Mary.* Inside which (no, you're not there yet) a fifth line continued toward the Haunted Hull. Security, medics, and PAs everywhere. Shipwreck '96 is *huge.*

Spooky House is small but growing. Seven years ago, friends Bob Koritzke and Dave Rector opened a haunted house in a garage. Not for profit, but for the sheer love of scaring people. Spooky House grew each year, spreading from garage into backyard. As it grew in acreage, so did the number of people who drove to see it, bringing with them kids, noise, and traffic. In 1995, neighbors complained to the city. Spooky House was cited for permit violations.

This year Bob and Dave went by the book. Several months to research, file for, and obtain about a dozen permits from various city agencies, and from the swap meet upon whose lot they erected this year's Spooky House.

A cute little house from the outside, Norman Bates's home in miniature. Not ghastly. Not horrific. Spooky sums it up nicely. Once inside, hallways, rooms, and furniture slant crookedly. Spooky House is more Caligarian than Alien Terror's Roswell crash site. A skewed Exorcist Room has an Exorcist Girl, but no Devil. Between its two railings, the walkway moves (as does the Chamber Exorcist Room's floor). A young man fries in an electric chair, convulsing, frothing at the mouth, emitting much smoke during his prolonged death throes. An atmospheric cemetery with violet lighting, similar to the one at Disneyland, lies in Spooky House's courtyard.

Spooky House is dark, easy to get lost in, maze-like. Unusual for a haunted house. Shipwreck '96 boasts two mazes (Londontowne and the Haunted Hull), a misnomer since patrons can only advance one way. Chamber also claims a maze, but it's just a dark passage with many turns. In normal usage, a maze is a confusing pattern of multiple paths within which one is easily lost. In haunted house terminology, a maze is not confusing, contains only one path, and is impossible to get lost in. Otherwise the meanings are identical.

About thirty volunteers perform at Spooky House, all friends or family of Bob and Dave. Horrifically made up, actors pop out and shock patrons, or stalk them through the rooms. They have no lines. Performances are simple. These volunteers lack direction and the improvisational training to get by without it. (However, one PA told me that Shipwreck '96 hired paid professional actors through trade paper notices, and to no greater effect than at Spooky House or House Of Terror).

Bob Koritzke tells me he broke even on Halloween night (1,432 patrons) and may show a profit this year to share with volunteers. Horror has always been revitalized at its grass roots, done more for art than profit. Spooky House exhibits lush colorful art direction. As with Roger Corman, I suspect Bob and Dave know how to stretch a buck (low-budget filmmakers may want the art director's number in their Rolodex).

If Spooky House isn't yet the AIP of American Grand Guignol, it's a notch above Ed Wood. If Shipwreck '96 is a mega-concert, Spooky House is a decent garage band. Bob Koritzke has modest goals for expansion. Maybe next Halloween, two locations.

Until then, Bob will return to his day job at an ad agency.

Where once there stood a Spooky House, there'll sit an empty lot. Perhaps real ghosts will again haunt the *Queen Mary*'s hull, their current presence obscured in smoke and lights and music. Jeff Immediato plans to convert his Anaheim office building into "an intimate concert/dinner theater" with a stage for musicians in the atrium, upon the former Roswell crash site. Investors already sit outside his office when I return from the OJ Room. David Saffron's not certain what they'll do with Alien Terror's retail space. "Something entertainment-related." Perhaps a nightclub or dinner theater.

Haunted houses, like other forms of theater, are strenuous. At the Chamber we apply our own makeup. Glue from my Devil horn drips into and congeals my eyebrow. The glue-remover doesn't remove. I snip off my eyebrow. It'll grow back. An Evil Scarecrow grows woozy from the chainsaw's gas fumes. They replace it with an electric model. A more healthful chainsaw, although not as scary-sounding when sawing off the Farmer's Daughter's arm. We trip over our capes and Frankenstein boots, sometimes scrambling up in time to save the note, sometimes amusing crowds with our pained struggles on the floor. Actresses have it harder than actors, wearing the same one-size-fits-all capes and boots. An Exorcist Girl tells me her entire body is black-and-blue from the plaster body cast strapped to her chest and back and shoulders, and from chafing within the Evil Scarecrow's straw suit. Another actress cricks her neck in the guillotine. We are beat after every night, yet have reason to be proud of our art.

Final night at the Chamber quiet. A cold Sunday in November with few guests. Closing nights are sad, no matter how arduous a show. We close early, about 10:30 p.m. Large trucks already wait outside to demolish the Chamber Of Chills. Where tonight Crazed Clowns and Devils and Torturers performed the music of horror, tomorrow there'll be COMPACT parking spots.

* * *

[Addendum: Spooky House has grown. On my last visit, on opening night, September 29, 2000, I saw Spooky House now has a companion attraction: the Haunted Forest. Tickets to both are $12.50. Up from $5.50 in 1996. Spooky House 2000 also boasts promotional tie-ins with a radio station and Tower Records. And a website: www.spookyhouse.com.]

Spirit of '68

"If I may interrupt, sir . . . " John focused his concentration on the silver tray within his delicate grip, heavily laden with a glass of cognac. "Mr. Peterson sends this small token to express his congratulations on sir's admission into the club."

"Ah! Most kind, most kind." Lowering his newspaper, Oliver reached for the glass. "Send Peterson my heartiest—*John Evans!*"

Years earlier, the waiter might have blushed. Now his pale complexion was incapable of displaying shame.

"Remember me? Oliver Haywood?"

"Yes sir, indeed I do."

"Hey everyone!" Chortling heartily, Oliver jabbed his cigar toward the waiter. "I know this asshole!"

A few staid club members glanced in their direction. One gentleman raised an eyebrow. His conversational partner scowled. Everyone disregarded the waiter's presence, apparently not seeing him, apparently looking right through him.

John Evans was used to it. He knew that his face was not agreeable. Most people averted their eyes. In some ways that was preferable to . . .

"When did I last see you, Evans?" grinned Oliver, shifting within the armchair to better observe John.

"I believe, sir, it stands close to fifteen years." John Evans scanned the darkly paneled lounge, hushed and dimly lit. His pale thin lips strained a tight smile. The murky illumination was perfect for his plans. He'd await midnight, when most members will have retired. Knowing Oliver, he'd still be here. Drinking past the point of inebriation. Drunk and helpless and alone in the dark.

Revenge was a dish best served cold, in darkness and seclusion.

John Evans cleared his throat. "Should sir require further services, I shall be in the kitchen."

"Nonsense! Stick around!" Oliver gulped the cognac. He shook the empty shot glass toward Peterson, the club's chairman now murmuring with some financiers at the far end of the lounge. "Hey Peterson! Kind of chintzy on the free booze! Next time try opening your wallet for a full glass."

Peterson grimaced at Oliver before returning his attention to his colleagues, his face now a shade redder.

Oliver elbowed John, his meaty arm meeting no resistance against the frail waiter. "So Evans, what's with this waiter gig? Remind me. What were you gonna be? Actor? Dancer?"

"Sir may recall, it was my hope to achieve some success as a poet."

"Poet, poet, that's right. Oh, and some more of this cognac stuff when you leave?" Oliver glanced askew at Peterson, shouting, "I want the good stuff! Not watered down next time!"

Oliver chuckled as Peterson pointedly ignored him.

Turning to John, Oliver added, "Poet, right. Yeah, you were quite the hippie back then, weren't you? Long hair!"

"The callowness of youth, sir, engenders easy indiscretions. I do not say I regret everything—"

"*Looooooong* hair!" laughed Oliver. "I did too! I did too! Let you in on a secret, Evans. Never washed it. Not for three years. It was a statement. Remember?"

"I recall a lice epidemic at the commune—"

"A statement. But you! You shaved your head!"

"Only after discovering blood on my pillow."

Oliver chuckled. "After which *everyone* shaved. We looked like cue balls, except you. You were the three ball. The red one. Red and scabby. Man, your scalp was one giant raspberry!" Laughing, he lit another cigar. "Remember the riots? Chicago, 1968? You and me?"

Tobacco smoke veiled and permeated John. "I recall being kicked in the head, rather severely, by the police." Swooning, feverish, enraged, floating. . . . "Regrettably, I fail to recall sir's participation. Perhaps my head injuries at the time—"

"I was coordinating. Back at the hotel. Tense situation. We ran out of weed. None of my so-called comrades would share. Selfish bastards." Oliver leaned over conspiratorially. "Good thing I hid my stash."

"Regrettably, the police later discovered sir's stash on my motorbike."

Chuckling, Oliver mused aloud, "Good, good times."

John concentrated on the tray, determined not to let it slip through his fingers.

"Remember love beads, Evans?"

"Sir may recall, I owned a turquoise string until the Columbia riot."

"That's right! The pigs dragged you down the stairs with that damn necklace."

John fingered the white scars beneath his white collar. "I recall, sir, the beads were particularly sharp."

"Sharp? You were bleeding at the neck! *Bleeding!* And then the fuzz discovered I'd locked them inside the building! So they dragged you back up the stairs, then down again, then all through the dorm, searching for an exit!" Oliver trembled with laughter. "Good times! Good times!"

"Sir may recall, they were the only love beads in history to be recalled by the manufacturer."

Oliver sighed. "I made a fortune on those love beads."

John gripped the tray, almost felt its sharp edges.

"Good, good times." Oliver puffed his cigar, wistful, not seeing John's bone-white fingers tense along the silver tray. "You went to Vietnam, didn't you, Evans?"

"I was drafted."

Oliver scowled in mock anger. "Traitor!"

"I went as a conscientious objector."

"Traitor!"

"I served in the ambulance corps."

"Traitor to the Revolution!"

"I was finally discharged when a burst of hot shrapnel exploded in my—" Dropping the tray, John covered the web of white scars on his pale face.

Oliver chuckled.

John was choking, yet his throat was dry, empty. "I suffered two years of skin grafts. Then an infection set in and worsened . . . "

Grinning, Oliver puffed his cigar. "Should have taken a college deferment."

"Sir may recall, my modest means did not allow for a graduate education."

"I took three deferments. BA, JD, MBA. Look at me today. Money in the bank and a clean conscience to spend it with."

John fumbled for the fallen tray, numb fingers gliding over its surface, feeling nothing, difficulty making contact.

Oliver puffed smoke rings. "Whatever happened to Janet, Evans? Sunshine, as we used to call her?"

"Regrettably, sir, she chose not to await my return."

"Sunshine sent you a Dear John, eh John? Ah, what a shame!" Scowling, Oliver shook his head. "Shame. Shame."

Although John felt no tears on his scarred white cheeks, his vision blurred. He arose, abandoning the tray. "Sir will excuse me. Janet, she . . . she was the only woman I ever loved."

"She was a good woman, Evans."

"Yes sir, she was that." John recalled haunting memories of a gentle nineteen-year-old, of tender gray-green eyes behind soft strawberry blond hair. "A kind and generous woman."

"A lot of men will agree with you, Evans. Believe me, after you went to Nam, *a lot of men* at the commune came to feel the same way about our little Sunshine. A generous woman, shining her light freely upon *all* men."

"Sir?!"

"Upon men of every race, creed, color, age, class, national origin, marital status . . . free love is a wonderful ideal, Evans."

John Evans could endure no more.

Enraged beyond the point of madness, unable to wait until the club had cleared of witnesses—atmosphere be damned!—John raised his pale fingers toward Oliver's neck, watching and guiding those fingers that could not feel, then raised them still higher, raised his arms until they could reach no higher, then raised them still higher, raised them until his feet rose off the ground . . .

Floating.

"Boo!" shrieked John. "Boo! Boo! Booooooooo!"

"That's right, Evans. Cry. Cry for lost causes. Cry for lost ideals." As always, Oliver looked right through John, not noticing that this time, he really was looking *through* John.

Jabbing his cigar at John, its smoke suffusing John's pale effervescence, Oliver shouted, "Hey Peterson! You got a real revolutionary working for you right here! He's ten times better than you, and he knows it!"

Peterson turned, scowling. Seeking the troublemaker.

But by then Evans had faded away, his spirit finally broken.

"*Sans* Fangs" with Jonathan Frid

"Look at this!" Jonathan Frid points to *The Dark Shadows Files,* its cover featuring himself in bared fangs. He begins flipping through the book. "One . . . two . . . three . . . four. Four! They know I hate this. They know I hate these fangs, and yet the first four pictures all show me in fangs. I know it's all part of the game. But four!"

Best known as Barnabas Collins on TV's *Dark Shadows,* Frid has other complaints about the book. He points to a fanzine on his coffee table. "They claimed I wrote an introduction to the book, and I didn't. They were misinformed by the publisher."

I had met Frid the week before, on a rainy March afternoon in 1986. We were to conduct an interview in a Manhattan eatery, but he'd forgotten and arrived late. All bundled up in spring, he came despite a cold, apologizing profusely. "I really thought it was for next week. Then I looked at the calendar and saw it was for today. Well, I rushed down as soon as I could."

I say it's okay, but he insists on paying for my lunch. As Frid is in no condition for a long interview, we postpone it for the following week.

Then Frid interviews *me,* inquiring about my background. He listens intently. "I think I can trust you," he concludes. We go to his East 18th Street apartment. (Frid has since returned to his native Canada). Once there, Frid lends me a video cassette of *Seizure* (a Canadian horror film starring himself, then unavailable in the US), and his scrapbook of press clippings. "This will help you in your research for our interview."

I sense this gesture is part of his apology for being late. Frid's reputation among fans for his courtesy and consideration is well-earned.

And so the following week, I am in Frid's apartment watching him lose his temper. But he isn't angry for long, and soon regrets castigating *The Dark Shadows Files*'s author. "He was here earlier today, before you arrived. The poor guy. He brought this copy. He was so proud. He thought I would be pleased and I just let him have it!"

This is because Frid does not share his fans' interest in vampires. "I'm not interested in horror movies. I'm interested in villainy. I'm interested in what makes ordinary people, like yourself, *tick* the way you do. And the way I tick. And the way somebody else ticks. I see horror every day, when people reveal themselves. It's like, 'Oh, that's what he's like! That's why he does something.' I'm constantly watching people. Watching their strengths and weaknesses. I find myself going into theaters less and less, let alone horror. I gave that up when I was seven or eight years old."

That was also about when Frid had his first acting role: as part of a choo-choo train in a Sunday school play. "Probably a middle car. I wasn't even an engineer or the caboose." Despite the minor role, Sunday school nurtured Frid's dormant acting bug in other ways. "As a young boy I used to think I wanted to be a minister, because my grandmother thought I wanted to be a minister. I used to dress up and put gowns on and make like I was a priest. I used to hold forth on the stairwell and pretend it was a chancel. So I guess I got my gothic roots pretending that the stairs was a gothic church."

But over time, Frid realized he lacked the calling to be a priest. "I was just using church ritual as a way of expressing my love of ritual. I must say I didn't get much inspiration from the Presbyterian Church, which my family were connected with, because their services are pretty sparse. I should of been an Anglican or Episcopalian. The Episcopalian Church does a very elegant service. Even the Catholics, Romans as we called them. Anyway, be that as it may, that's how I got my start."

In prep school, Frid discovered the joy of acting. "I was about twelve or thirteen or fourteen, and I was in a class play and I just loved it. It was the greatest excitement of the year. I wasn't aware of this being my life's work, I just enjoyed doing it." The turning point came at age sixteen. "The *great* decision in my life, probably more important than making a decision to go into the professional theater, was to ask to go into the *school* play. Not the class play, but *the school* play. It took me a week to get up enough *nerve* to *ask* to be in it."

Frid's request was deemed unusual because few boys at his all-male prep school wanted to do plays. "Especially when they had to dress up and play girls. [The school] just *commandeered* people to be in the senior play. The brightest students in the Latin of two senior years, you simply were drafted. I of course *dreaded* being called a sissy just because I *wanted* to be in the play. That's what took such nerve. And secondly, I wasn't one of the brighter students. I got two prizes in prep school. One was for Industry and Progress. I came from the bottom of the class to the middle, and that's as high as I ever got. And I got the Reading Prize in my final year."

Not being a top student, Frid required approval from both the Headmaster, and English Master in charge of plays. The day Frid approached the latter is forever seared into his memory. "Oh I was nervous, that was a nerve-wracking day. Everything is so important when you're young. To ask to be in that play was the biggest decision I ever made in my life. I've always remembered that. I don't remember when I decided I wanted to be a professional actor. Sort of vague ideas about it. But I not only got in the senior play, I got to play a very important role!"

The play was *The Rivals,* by Sheridan Brinsley Sheridan. Frid's role was that of Sir Anthony Absolute. "He was the father of the young male hero. So I started playing heavies from the very beginning."

That beginning also nearly ended Frid's acting career. "I can remember waiting in the wings. I thought I was never gonna get my breath, I was so nervous. Then I came on. I was on Hell on Earth. Fortunately, I didn't have to say anything for the first two minutes." Frid played opposite the character of Mrs. Malaprop, origin for the term *malapropism.* "She gibble gabbles for two minutes. Gave me a chance to catch my breath. So when my first line came out, I said, 'Where's Jack?' or something meaning my son. I had a big pompous line, and I was so big because I had all this gas in me from nerves. I was so pumped up with air, I couldn't breathe. And just on cue, I was able to release all this, and I surprised myself and everybody in the place. I was this great voice suddenly. Now, if I had had to speak earlier, I probably wouldn't have had a theatrical career. At all. Because I wouldn't have been able to speak. It was just a miracle that I was on cue with my breath."

Frid doesn't credit any particular play with his decision to act *professionally.* "Actually, I think what made me go into the theater was a chap. We were both in the Canadian Navy back in 1944, '45. And *he* had made up his mind that he was gonna be an actor. I used to listen to him, and we talked naturally a lot about the theater, because we were the only two in our platoon, or whatever, that cared about such things. He came from a little town way up in northern Saskatchewan. And I thought, anybody who has the nerve to come from northern Saskatchewan in Canada, and come down and wanna be an actor in New York, had a lot of guts, and I thought I can do that too."

Stan made good on his talk. He auditioned at the American Academy and was enrolled when Frid visited New York in 1946. "He was a baker's son from northern Saskatchewan, and now he knew New York, and he was hobnobbing with all these people at the American Academy, and I was terribly impressed by it. My closest friend in the Navy was gonna be an actor, why can't I be an actor? A professional actor. I made up my mind I was gonna be an actor too."

Frid visited the American Academy and thinks he met its head, Gellinger. Ironically, Frid doesn't remember whether he auditioned, and if so, if he was accepted. He thinks not on both counts. "In any case, I didn't follow through. I went to London instead, and went to the Royal Academy."

Whatever became of Frid's old navy buddy, whose theatrical career looked so promising in 1946? Forty years later, Stan was still living in New York. An executive with Grey Advertising.

Coming from the Royal Academy, Frid attained a reputation as a Shakespearian actor, albeit secondary to his renown as Barnabas. But Frid disputes that label. "I've been in a lot of Shakespearian plays, but I don't call myself a Shakespearian actor. I'm not a scholar of Shakespeare. There are loads of plays of Shakespeare's that I don't know. I don't think I'd ever sit down and *read* a play of Shakespeare's unless I were in it. And when I do get in them, I have to study them. Reading Shakespeare is still to me like reading a foreign language. I won't say it's that difficult, but almost. When I get a role, I pick at the pieces, the *pieces*. And worry my way through it. *Richard III*, I spent a month before rehearsals, every day for hours on end, picking at, trying to figure out what it was all about. I was still working on it the final night when we closed. I was still finding new things." Whatever he found, Richard III remains Frid's favorite Shakespearian role. "I did that at Penn State and got very good notices. I was very pleased with that except, as I say, I was still left *unfinished*."

Frid even questions the notion that he has a Shakespearian reputation. "Everybody in the press says it, so I guess that's the reputation. It comes from the press. I'm flattered, but I don't think it's real. I haven't played Shakespeare in twenty years. And even then, I wouldn't play it that regularly. I had two years where I played in a Shakespearian company in Toronto. Six plays in a row. I had fairly substantial parts. And then I had two years at the American Shakespeare Festival. I didn't have that many good roles there, but at least I was working with good people. That was it." That was enough for the press, but not enough for Frid. "Most Shakespearian actors that are called Shakespearian actors have played *all* of his plays over a period of years. But I've only been in, maybe a dozen. Not that many."

Frid differentiates a Shakespearean *reputation* from typecasting. "When you play Shakespeare, you are anything but typed. The very fact that you can do Shakespeare opens you up to everything. I think being 'typed' is playing these dumb things on television all the time, or in the movies. Just an everyday thing where you're playing a gangster, and all you do is come home with a fedora or whatever. Or you're playing any of these cutie-pies in Hollywood, these glamour boys. They're all just playing themselves, playing their own sex appeal. Which is fine, but that's all they're doing. That's being typed. But when you're playing Shakespeare, you're not being typed. It's the very *last* word you should use for anybody in Shakespeare, because the *demands* that Shakespeare makes on you opens you up. You get these *types* from Hollywood. You mention me one actor in America that isn't typed. But you try to put him in Shakespeare, he'll just go on playing Humphrey Bogart. He won't hide himself or disguise himself in a role."

I note that many Hollywood stars try to prove themselves by performing Shakespeare. Frid acknowledges the point, with reservations. "They don't do it too well. Sometimes they do, but on the whole they don't. They're usually exploited in their own gimmick. They made a movie of *Midsummer Night's Dream* in the Thirties. They had Mickey Rooney doing his Mickey Rooney number. In his puck, I guess. Everybody played themselves."

Frid then distinguishes English actors from Hollywood stars. "What makes [Laurence Olivier] so great is that he was constantly disguising his own real personality. Obviously, he imbued these parts with his own personality, in a sense. But in another sense, he hid his own personality. It was his character that filled these roles. The guts within the man. Let's use the word *charm* instead of personality. A Hollywood actor will never give up his charm to play these roles. They want to be attractive. Katherine Hepburn is caught in that same trap. She will never play a role that doesn't allow her to play her *charm* into it, *a lot.* She doesn't *break* from her own personality, her own charm. Olivier would do that. Olivier did it constantly. He would just release himself *totally* from his charm. He couldn't wait to obliterate that. He wanted to get rid of that charm and sex appeal or whatever. But very few actors want to do that."

I suggest Peter Sellers as an actor who hid himself. Frid almost agrees. "His humor was always there. Did he ever play anything where he didn't have a sly sense of humor in it? He was brilliant. Yes, he got away from [his charm]. He loved disguise. But he always had that twinkle in his eye. But I liked him for that. He was an interesting actor. He was unpredictable."

A seasoned stage actor by 1967, it was sheer luck that Frid landed the role of Barnabas Collins. After he'd finished a tour in Florida, Frid notified his agent that he would stay there for a month or so. "I just happened to be back in New York, coming into my apartment. The phone was ringing. It was my agent. I said, 'I told you I wasn't gonna be back for a long time. How did you happen to ring just now? I'm just coming in the door.' He said, 'I just called you on a chance that you might be there because there's a soap opera called *Dark Shadows*, and they're looking for somebody to play a vampire.' And I said, 'Oh knock it off. Besides, I told you I'm gonna go to the west coast, to move there. I want to pursue teaching.'"

Frid had by now earned an MFA in directing from Yale. He hoped to land a job in a university drama department. But his agent persisted, arguing that since

Frid would spend another month in New York getting organized, he may as well earn a little extra money. Exasperated and not wanting to argue, Frid agreed to see the *Dark Shadows* producers. "I didn't audition. I was just interviewed for it. I went up and I kind of landed the role."

Frid credits one of the writers for getting him the part. "It's *my* belief that Ron Sproat was instrumental in getting me that role. I've never *asked* him. No one ever *told* me that. It's just my guess because he had gone to Yale with me. He'd been in the class behind me. He was a playwright, but he had seen my work. We were in a lot of shows together up at Yale. I had a reputation for playing villains, and playing against the villainy. I would always justify it. I would motivate him with his own motives, and make the rest of the world villains. To give myself two poles to play between. Instead of just playing villainy, I would look for the strength in the character, put it up, and then play in between. You can come up with all kinds of nuances.

"I think Dan Curtis really wanted a monster. He wanted a vampire who was going around gnashing his teeth and biting necks all the time. And I think the writers—this is my supposition, I don't know for sure—but the writers wanted to give [Barnabas] more colors. And that's why Ron said, 'Well, I think we have the person. I think Jonathan Frid would be ideal because he has a look about him that's villain. But he plays against it, he can play nuances.' Anyway, they wanted to talk to me about this. And they did. And we even went into rehearsal talking about this."

Frid supposes those discussions were the basis for subsequent press reports that he helped develop the role of Barnabas. But he disputes collateral reports that the producers had no clear idea of what they wanted.

Dark Shadows is known for its copious bloopers, indicating a low budget and short rehearsal time. But Frid believes the show had "a very high budget." Then why so many bloopers? "Well, the production values were so stressed. They had ambitious things to do. All these effects and everything."

I ask Frid his take on the characters Barnabas encountered. Angelique tormented Barnabas yet, at times, she softened toward him. Did she have any goodness in her? "She was softened, but by design. She was a designing woman. All designing women play it soft. That's a classic term. A designing woman. And when she softened, she softened for effect. She was written as a complete villain. They wrote Barnabas in such a way that he hated her all the time. There was never a moment that he really liked her. He may have softened a little. He was a designer himself, in a sense. He was manipulating. There were times when he tried to manipulate her out of his life. And to do that, he had to be civilized with her. At *best*, they were civilized. Never did they like each other."

But Angelique said she loved Barnabas. Did he think she was ever sincere? Frid reconsiders. "Yes, that's true, she did. She loved him, and he didn't love her. It was unrequited love."

So was Angelique's love for Barnabas perverse? At times, she rescued him; at times, she tried to destroy him. "Ah well, she was a perverted woman to start with. She was a witch. I never really tried to analyze her character that much. She was a love/hate thing. To bring it into the world of reality, people that are rejected will come back at people, hating. *Hating.* They're jealous. Frustrated. Unrequited love can do terrible things to people if they're not too strong. They can come back *biting,* so to speak."

At the time of my interview, *Dark Shadows* was airing on PBS's New Jersey Network, running the episodes in which Angelique plots to marry Quentin. Having seen Frid volunteer for NJN's pledge drive, and assuming he followed the show, I ask if he thinks Angelique ever truly loved Quentin.

"Well I'll tell you Tom, you're barking at the wrong tree, because I don't know anything about the plot of *Dark Shadows.* I've lost interest in it. I don't remember the plot. I never knew the plot very much at the time. Only in so much in what I had to do from day to day. What her relationship to, whatever his name is, Quentin? I didn't know and I never saw that. It's playing but I don't watch it." Frid says his TV barely receives channel 50, and he likes it that way. "That gives me an excuse not to watch it. I hate to watch it."

I'd also wanted Frid's perspective on Reverend Trask. In 1897, Trask was a hypocrite. But in the 1795 episodes, he seemed a sincere witch-hunter. And he was right, there was a witch and she was evil. His error was in identifying her. Thus, the 1795 Trask was not a complete villain.

"That's interesting your saying that. I've always thought of Trask as being just a plain black villain. Unlike Barnabas. Barnabas had other assets to it. But this crusty old guy was always just the same. I suppose it could have been exploited that way. If I had had that role, I probably would have thought that through." Frid enjoys multi-dimensional villains; he found Trask a bore. "They're so predictable. I'm half asleep after they've opened their mouths for ten minutes. That's why they're usually small parts. Trask could not carry a whole series. You get bored after two days of him in every scene."

But although he recalls Trask, Frid can't distinguish between the two timelines other than by what I tell him. "See, I don't know that story. I don't remember it. There have been two or three occasions recently where somebody's shown me, it was at somebody's house and they put it on and I watched it. I had no idea what I was doing or where I was in the story. It was as if I had never done it. I was told it was the 1795 story, the Quentin Collins story. I couldn't have told you what I was gonna say next or where I was going. It was a total blank."

Preferring to discuss his present work, Frid compares his approach to Barnabas to his reading in a play last night at the Chelsea Theater. The play dramatizes the true-life woes of Norwegian painter Edvard Munch ("The Scream"), portraying him as a stereotypical genius; an alcoholic and womanizer torn by personal demons. Frid read the role of Dr. Jacobson, the man who cures Munch. Once sober, Munch worries that he's lost his artistic edge, his new work inferior to that of his wilder days.

Absent and lackadaisical when discussing *Dark Shadows,* Frid sparks renewed passion when relating his current project. "The director, who I went to Yale with, another one of my Yale mates, he's run this theater for years and years and years. I hadn't seen him until this recently. And I said, 'Now Bob, you drive me nuts. I never understand the plays I'm in with you.' I kid him to death. It's got twenty-five people in it, and they're all playing about six roles, and there's stream of consciousness. You never know what's real. It's really this mad painter's mind. But at times there's reality in the play, and sometimes it's what he's seeing. So it's very difficult to follow this damn play. Finally, I had to stop him in his tracks the other day. I said, 'Bob, you've got me behaving like all these patients, and people that are in his mind. I'm the stable one in this play, I think. I don't really understand it, but I think you're going too far with me being a silly ass. He's the one that cures this guy in life, and in the play it's recognized.' [Munch] goes to this clinic, and he finds salvation. He's a womanizer, whores to virgins to all these girlies. And he comes out of all of that. He's taken off all of his alcohol. And he comes out on top. So I said, 'Bob, you cannot have me just going around like a crazy man.' I'm always doing this with roles. I'm always saying to the director, 'You're going too far here. You want to make a broad statement with me, and I won't have it that way. These are real people. They're not just effects.'"

Frid likewise tried to ground Barnabas in reality. "I don't even know what a vampire is. I read a little about it. I did a little research on vampirism. I found [the producers] making so many mistakes according to the rules, which I thought were, you know. I think people that are interested in the occult are kind of all crazy. However, if you're gonna play their game, play it properly. If a vampire doesn't have a shadow, he shouldn't have a shadow. My God, not only did you see my shadow all over the place, but they actually exploited it one time. The very first time that I meet Maggie Evans is in a restaurant, when she's closing up. My shadow overwhelms the corner where she's getting her coat. And she turns around, 'Oh, Oh!' And I say, 'Oh, did I scare you?' I'm always saying 'did I startle you?' That's the cliché where I'm at. I was just going over to help her with her coat. But they used my *shadow* to exploit a scene. And you're not supposed to see a shadow."

Frid was more interested in Barnabas's "playing a lie" than his being a vampire. The latter aspect simply meant having to "gnash my teeth and bite somebody every once in a while just to get attention. I was always a threat. But that was all taken care of in the writing. So I was always able to play other things. That's the one thing I liked about doing *Dark Shadows.* I liked playing that character. I'd never play another vampire in my life. I would never. But I would play Barnabas again, if it were written carefully enough. Because there's nothing an actor wants more than to have a role where the character is a threat in some way or other. It just gives a whole dimension, a *dynamism* to a person, when they can be a threat. And the more you *hide* it, the more you play it *subtly,* the more effective it is." Which is why Frid hated the fangs. "I always felt like a damn fool, going 'AARRRGH!'" Raising his head, Frid points to an imaginary camera, then to his teeth. "There's the camera, and I'm going 'AAARRRRGH' SEE?! SEE MY FANGS?! AAARRRGH!" He drops character. "Just stupid! Just stupid! It was so awful! And to my mind, took all of the threat out of the man by doing it that way."

Frid was required to raise his head before every bite, but failed the first time. "The first time I did it, I had to disobey their orders, because it was the first time I did it, and I put the teeth in upside down, wrong way around. Everything. I couldn't put them in. So I *couldn't* do that. So I came in sideways." Frid demonstrates, head low, mouth only partly open. "By far, it was the most effective bite I ever did. Do we see something there, or do we *not* see something there? I think they saw a piece of a fang hanging down. It was just so subtle."

As the show progressed, the producers took increasing liberties with the supernatural, inventing things with no basis in the literature. Only in *Dark Shadows* have I ever seen the *I Ching* used for time travel.

Frid grows impatient. "I don't know anything about that. They did everything, sure. That's par for the course. That was legitimate, to do all that. That's what the show was about. They had to do *all* the stories. You see, *Dark Shadows* ran out of gas after four years because it was so special. They limited themselves. I mean, there were love interests, it was always a soap opera. But most soap operas are about nothing, and so they can go on forever. But *Dark Shadows* had specific materials to work with. It was working in a very restricted area."

Stephen King made the same critique of Dan Curtis's *Kolchak: The Night Stalker.* The show required a new monster each week. By season's end, they'd run out.

Frid sighs. "I never saw that stuff so I don't know. Maybe you're right." He's said all he wants to about *Dark Shadows,* so we move on to his one-man show, *Villains.*

For years, Frid had contemplated doing a one-man show on the nature of villainy and evil. Either that, or a lecture tour on soaps. "I'm a frustrated teacher. I guess I like being up on stage by myself rather than with other actors. I never thought about it until late in life, because I've always wanted to be an actor and that meant being with other people on stage, sharing the stage, which is all right too. I like doing that. But I also like to be up there by myself. As a teacher would. Or a lecturer." The impetus was something Frid had long avoided: attending a convention. "I was asked to these things and I wouldn't come out of hiding. I wanted to stay out of *Dark Shadows* completely."

That changed around 1981, when Frid attended Shadowcon in Los Angeles. "They treat you like a king. They fly you there, and they put you up, and look after you, and all the rest of it. They don't give you, at least I never asked for, an honorarium or whatever you call it. It was just the fun of going out there and doing it. A free trip. I always looked at it that way."

But the trip had its price. Aside from much autographing, Frid was required to attend a Q&A session. Answering questions he'd already answered *ad infinitum.* Two years after his return to fandom, he was bored. "Not for me, but for them. They'd heard everything already, a thousand times. I thought, I'm not going back the *third* year and do that all over again. I've answered all those questions. Any number of times. I'm gonna take them something that's different. And if they want me to do the question and answer thing, I'll do it. But I want to bring something *fresh* of myself to it. Some new material."

And so Frid developed a one-man show, *Genesis of Evil.* Part One comprised excerpts from early roles that influenced his interpretation of Barnabas. "What *led* to Barnabas. I was honest to a certain point. In some respects, I cheated a little. Not really. Because everything you do, before you do something, affects it." Part Two was composed solely of material the fans wrote about Barnabas or *Dark Shadows*.

And there was much to select from. "Way back in the old days, it was a tremendous amount. Tons of it I never read. Some of it was very good. Most of it was pretty awful. A good percentage of it, let's say, was mash. Proposals. Not that many proposed marriage, but there were a few hundred. Out of tens of thousands of letters. I used to have letters from people that would write once a day, for months on end." One married woman wrote prolifically. "I mean *thick* letters. The equivalent of a couple of books." Bela Lugosi claimed 90% of his mail came from women. The same held true for Frid. "There'd be a handful of men who ever wrote."

Frid's correspondence is now more manageable. "I get mail still to this day. Not that much, of course. There's no way to get a hold of me. No one knows quite how to send mail to me. In any case, I'm just on reruns. But I get it. A few. An odd mail today." And less flaky. "Normal mail, because they know me. I'm more familiar with the fans now, because I don't have that much other to do. In the old days, I never had time to even think about them."

Fans also send poetry to Frid, which he incorporated into *Genesis of Evil.* "I read a lot of their poetry. Tons of it. And I picked what I thought was the best." He performed *Genesis of Evil* at two or three cons. "Then the following year, I decided not to do anything about *Dark Shadows.* Keep it out completely. Do original materials."

Soon thereafter, Frid considered developing *Genesis of Evil* into a commercial show for off-Broadway or the college circuit. Now called *Villains* and still in development, Frid performs it for his fans at his apartment. He invites me to attend. "This one on Wednesday will be a lot of odds and ends. The people that are gonna be here Wednesday were all at the festival two weeks ago."

Villains has less poetry. "Maybe about five or ten minutes. Or comment on it. Obviously, I can't forget the gothic themes." Included are readings of Poe's "Tell-Tale Heart" and "Cask of Amontillado." Frid had performed the former on WNJU, during a pledge drive. "I do other things, like ghosts and so forth. I'm beginning to introduce short pieces, like from James Thurber. Comedy things. But they're usually about foibles of human beings. Which of course, monster things are built basically around. People's vulnerability."

As examples, Frid cites "The Ghost" and "Bed Call." The former tale concerns a man who thinks he sees his wife's ghost. In reality, he's the ghost and she's alive. The latter concerns a man (Frank) who receives a phone call from a dead friend, who convinces Frank that suicide would be preferable to his troublesome life. The friend eggs Frank to retrieve his gun. "And as we fade, 'Gun, gun, gun, gun . . . ' Blackout. Then I come up. I say to the audience, 'Things aren't going too well for you, are they? You've been having problems, right? I think it's important that we talk. Isn't that your phone ringing? I think we better have a talk.'" Thus, Frid brings the message full circle to the audience. "So I'm doing that kind of story. Which are of the occult up to a point, but they're not really monster stories. They're not vampires, and they're not werewolves, and all that stuff. They're dead callers and the ghost, but they're really human stories. The humanity in them is much more strong."

Villains also includes relationship tales. One concerns a couple who have long been married. Their tale begins happily enough, during a Sunday stroll. Then the wife notices her husband admiring other women. At first she feigns amusement, but as he continues girl-watching, she grows angry. They argue and agree to divorce. After a brooding moment, they continue as before, all talk of divorce forgotten. The audience realizes this is a constant ritual between them, and will likely continue well into old age.

"To me, that's horror. To see two people who are ostensibly in love, and they are. He keeps saying, 'I *love* you, but I can't help looking at the girls.' The last thing in the story, she gets up in this restaurant, she goes over to the phone, and he's looking at *her* legs. 'God, she's got nice legs.' His own wife, you see. But to me, that's horror. That's the horror of life. To make a marriage work. To make friendships work. Make *relationships* in life work, and see where they go awry, is horror. I don't need *monsters*, for God's sake. I don't need vampires and werewolves to enthrall me with the *mystery* of life. The mystery of life is all around us, all day long. Our [interview] right now has got all kind of mysteries going.

"To me, horror is when I see somebody lying. I mean a person I know. A friend. And he's telling me something that I accept. And then suddenly, as he or she is telling it, there's something that gives them away. They're not telling me the truth. And I discover it myself, just in the way they're not telling it like it should be told. They're slipping. You see somebody *slip.* And they know that they're lying to you. That sends chills, shivers, right up and down my spine. It's *horror.* It's *horror.* In the cold light of day."

Frid's interest in people, trying to guess what makes them tick, motivated another selection for *Villains.* "I'm not always right, you know. I make lots of goofs about other people. But I'm willing to admit that. I think too many people have too many strong opinions. 'He's got that look that I don't like. He's got that look of a real crook.' And then he turns out to be a lamb." The story concerns a yuppie who spots a burglary in progress: two ugly, scar-faced men loading up a van with goods from an electronics store. He phones the police. When he realizes they won't arrive in time, he plays hero and attacks one of the men. "At this point, the cops get there. It turns out the guy he's beating up, he owns the store and they're moving. So the cop arrests this poor guy, this sanctimonious character, and says, 'Don't you know that crime doesn't pay?' The thing that I find amusing about the story is that you never know why a person looks [like they do]. Everybody thinks they can know the look of a crook. He thought he knew what the look of a crook was, and it wasn't. He was totally wrong. They were just two guys coming out of the store."

The promotional material for *Villains* states that "the indifference of the universe to man's fate and his predilection to do evil are inexorably connected." Would Frid describe his show as reflecting a nihilist or existentialist philosophy?

"I don't know. I studied those things in school and I always forget those terms and what they mean, but if that's what it sounds like, that's what it is. I don't have any particular philosophy. I guess I'm a pessimist. I think mankind doesn't succeed in conquering nature. We're constantly done in. And there's a certain resilience, a certain fighting back. But it never really succeeds.

"Every civilization thinks they got the ultimate answer. Believe it or not, when I was brought up by well-meaning people, the British Empire was the greatest blessing the world had ever had. And I really believed it. I was told to believe it. In fact, in our own lifetime it's gone to nothing. Really, the writing was long on the wall, long before I was born. But it was still in its form. I grew up having [been] paraded out to these parades. They were never like these American parades. They were always military parades, and the arms, and the color guards, and the pipe bands, and the King's face. I mean he was like a *god* to us! He was King of England! He was everything. The British Empire was the greatest empire the world had ever known. Borders never end, and the sun never sets." Frid laughs at this point. "No one had ever told us that it hadn't lasted very long, and it was a constantly evolving empire. I'll give them one bit of credit. They can still say that they got the Community of Nations. The Queen still goes every year to that. She's head of the Great Commonwealth. The Empire still does exist in some form or another, which you'd never know reading the American papers.

"But anyway, that's beside the point. The point I'm trying to explain [in *Villains*] is that nature is omnipresent. It's there. It always will be. And it slashes down like we stamp on an anthill. You don't even realize that you wiped out a whole civilization of little workers. That's what happens to us. In the scale of things, we're just like ants in the ground."

Villains's pessimism evokes the work of "Brother Theodore" Gottlieb, a monologist who frequently appeared on *Letterman.* However, although Gottlieb's monologues began on a dark note, he'd stretch them to the point of hilarious absurdist comedy. Frid's humor in *Villains* falls short of absurd. "Theater of the ridiculous, I can understand. It's the theater of the absurd I don't quite understand. I saw [Gottlieb] once. It must have been fifteen years ago. It was an after-hours kind of theater, down in the village. After the regular show finished, he'd come on at twelve o'clock. I couldn't quite get him. He just makes arbitrary switches. I found him a bit surly. I didn't follow him. I didn't get his gig. Probably had too much to drink anyway."

In 1970, Frid appeared in *House of Dark Shadows.* His film portrayal of Barnabas was darker, less sympathetic, more of a monster. "That was Curtis. He had his way with that. That's what Barnabas would have been like in the series if it hadn't been for the writers."

Frid's belief is corroborated by Curtis's later remarks. In 1991, Curtis stated that his NBC prime time *Dark Shadows* was what the soap would have been had ABC provided a larger budget. Although he was specifically referring to the lusher production values, one may infer that the NBC series more closely reflects Curtis's vision in other areas too. Certainly, he enjoyed greater creative autonomy, having just picked up an Emmy for *War and Remembrance.* Whatever the reason, the 1991 Barnabas was sadistic and feral, even more so than in *House of Dark Shadows.*

This darker Barnabas was why Frid abstained from *Night of Dark Shadows.* "I wouldn't have anything to do with the show after that." After the series ended in 1971, Frid was deluged with horror roles, most of which he declined. He accepted a small non-monster role in the 1973 TV-movie, *The Devil's Daughter,* one of the few times he'd been out to Hollywood.

Following that, Frid appeared in Oliver Stone's directorial debut, *Seizure* (1974, aka *Queen of Evil*), as Edmund Blackstone, a horror novelist plagued by nightmares. He and his wife (played by Christina Pickles of TV's *St. Elsewhere*) host a dinner party for an odd bunch, including an obnoxious millionaire, his mistress, her gigolo, a Russian Count, and others. The party is crashed by three bizarre types in S&M garb: Henry Baker, Hervé Villechaize ("Da plane, da plane!"), and Martine Beswick. Are they demons, escaped lunatics, or creations of Blackstone's mind?

Despite Frid's distaste for horror, he thinks Blackstone had potential. "I could play that kind of role. Because he wasn't a monster. There were monsters *around* him. But it was relating monsters, ideas, to a human being." Stone's screenplay was a work-in-progress when Frid agreed to it, and remained so into production. "I tried to make that role. [Blackstone] should have been more central. It's his nightmare. All those other people! All had too much to do."

Frid likens Oliver Stone to Dan Curtis. "All they really want to do is get into the *horror*. AAAARRRGH! Both of them are exactly the same way. They have to control their instincts, and unless they have writers, other people to control them, they go crazy. Stone had a good idea, but he wasn't interested in that. He's interested in the absurd. This absurd, arbitrary, cut to this and that and this. Instead of following some human predicament. And follow it carefully and quietly. *Seizure* could have been a marvelous story. But it was just too buggered up with all of his silly monsters. All third-rate looking monsters, anyway.

"I think the idea of it, the personification or the actualizing of [Blackstone's] horror in his head was effective. But it's a confusing idea. It's a very difficult concept. All Oliver Stone did was made it more complicated, instead of clarifying it." Such as by having so many peripheral characters. "They were all dragged into it too much. It should have concentrated on Blackstone and these horror things in his head. How he couldn't shake them. And were symbolic of the demons within him."

In 1986, *Seizure* was available in Canada, but not in the US. Frid suspected that Stone had pulled strings to prevent its video release in the States. Circumstantial evidence supports Frid's theory. When *Platoon* (1986) was released, I read press reports describing *The Hand* (1981) as Stone's directorial debut. Apparently, publicists were trying to erase embarrassments from Stone's early filmography. *The Mad Man of Martinique* (1979), which the Internet Movie Database (www.imdb.com) credits to Stone, was also forgotten by 1986. In 1988, *Seizure* was released in the US by Prism, but is once again out of print. Stone would not have liked Prism's video box, which screams: *Created, Written, and Directed by ACADEMY AWARD WINNER OLIVER STONE ("WALL STREET," "PLATOON").*

Although both Frid and Stone would rather forget *Seizure,* the film has merit. Yes, it is dramatically confusing. For instance, although the story indicates the characters have long known each other, their dialogue contradicts it. But as it *is* Blackstone's nightmare, its surrealism is appropriate.

Frid is less forgiving, dismissing the notion that any contradiction can be justified by it being a dream. "That's a cop-out. Nuts to that. That's why dreams are very dangerous things to do. And so are drunks. A drunk can do anything. The greatest challenge to a writer is for him to deal with sharp, intelligent people, and to have them fuck themselves up. That's the problem. That's a real challenge to a writer. But if he has a lot of nitwits, you can do anything you like with nitwits. Or dreams. Or drunks. You can get away with any kind of nonsense."

Reviewers have labeled Blackstone a villain, but if so, his villainy is one of cowardice rather than evil. His wife accuses him of willingness to sacrifice their son to save himself. But would he? Or does he only suspect his wife of thinking him a coward?

Frid thinks it enough that it's on Blackstone's mind. "If you *feel* that you could sacrifice your son, you're potentially there. And somewhere or other in the back of his mind, he thinks that's in the back of her mind, and probably is. That's the horror of the dream. He realizes that she thinks that he's a coward. The story could have been about his relationship with his son and his wife, and his writing. His dealings with his wife, his son, and his writing. The weekend house party was a good idea. Although I'm not so sure it was even necessary. I used to wonder, would Blackstone have those kinds of friends? I didn't think they belonged in his life. They were certainly God-awful hosts, to have that mixture." Frid chuckles. "Blackstone deserved what he got, just by having that kind of collection together on a weekend. He ought to have had more sense than that. Awful. Just a rag-a-tag group."

Not only was Frid disappointed with the film, he found the shoot itself unpleasant. "It was an awful experience. We went up to Canada, and it was an underground picture, and we're all supposed to be up there on a holiday, and all the rest of it. It was a screwed-up kind of affair." The production company had rented the house from some English Canadians in Quebec. Blackstone's bedroom doubled as Frid's bedroom. "A lot of people in the company were on pot and drugs. The house got smashed up the last day. I hope the company got sued. It was just dreadful. It was like living with a bunch of pigs. For a month. Awful people." Frid excludes Martine Beswick from his reproach; they remain good friends.

Seizure was one of Frid's rare brushes with the Hollywood drug scene. "I usually had friends outside the theater. I don't have very many actor friends, so I don't know what they're into." Frid is also unimpressed with the notion of drugs as a status symbol. "I suppose anybody can create a status symbol. Suppose I call that tray of liquor over there a status symbol? I don't know. Some people would think it's disgusting."

Dark Shadows remains the only gothic horror soap opera to date. Attempts to copy its format have so far failed. Aaron Spelling tried it with *Dark Mansions,* a prime time soap he developed for ABC. Spelling's people never contacted Frid. "Somebody from New York wanted to submit me. I sent them a tape, but I never heard back. Well, just because it has the same title doesn't mean to say it has a role in it for me. I know about three or four leading ladies that were supposed to be up for it." *Dark Mansions* was released in 1986 as a TV-movie. It ends on a cliffhanger because the "movie" was really a two hour pilot. Naturally, the cliffhanger was never resolved.

That same year, Edwin Vane, former vp of daytime programming at ABC during *Dark Shadows*'s run, and now head of Group W Productions, made another stab at a daytime horror soap: *Salem's Children.* Intended for syndication, the plot concerns two powerful families, one good, one evil. The latter draw their power from "The Book of Shadows." Although *Daily Variety* (12/18/86, pp. 20, 28) reports that Martin Tahse produced a pilot reel, I have found no evidence of this pilot ever being released. Certainly, the series was never produced. Much as Frid hates his fangs, *Dark Shadows* remains unique.

Over the fourteen years since I interviewed him, Frid has continued working in theater and developing one-man shows. He currently has three shows: *Fools and Fiends*, featuring "murder, mischief and heartbreak" with selections from Saki, Poe, Stephen King, and others; *Shakespearean Odyssey*, with readings from the Bard; and *Fridiculous*, emphasizing "mayhem, wit and whimsy in story and rhyme," drawing from James Thurber, Groucho Marx, Jack Finney, and others.

Frid performs his shows *gratis* through Charity Associates (his own creation) for registered charities in Southern Ontario, Canada (where he now lives). He's performed at churches, synagogues, clubs, community centers, private homes, and intends to expand into hospitals and retirement homes. He tailors his material to every audience. Interested charities can contact: CharityAssoc@jonathanfrid.com. Requests from outside Ontario (including the US) are welcome, but travel expenses may need to be reimbursed.

Not that Frid no longer finds paid acting work. In June and July 2000, he appeared in *Mass Appeal* at the Stirling Theatre Festival of Ontario, playing an elderly priest whose orderly life is challenged by an idealistic young seminarian. *Mass Appeal* is described as "a touching yet funny examination of the nature of friendship, courage and the infinite variety of love." In other words, it explores human relationships, long one of Frid's primary interests as an actor.

Frid promises to keep his website updated with news from his career: www.jonathanfrid.com. At seventysomething, Jonathan Frid is still going strong.

Vampire Nation

"You accept that your . . . *ancestral castle,* is now property of the people of Rumania?"

"With your doctors' kindness, I understand . . . " What was this century's proper honorific? "*Comrade* Colonel."

Colonel Popiescu snorted, skimmed the report. "Farkas. You are Hungarian?"

"My ancestors . . . " Count Farkas waved the subject aside with the delicate hand of an aristocrat, pulled his hand away from the pale sunlight spilling through the grimy window, illuminating air heavy with dust. He stared at the dour, sluggish soldier. Peasant. Despite the bright red stars piercing his drab brown uniform, Colonel Popiescu was still just a slothful, anemic peasant. Weak blood nourished on potatoes and vodka.

"You also understand, Transylvania has been liberated by the Rumanian People's Army from Hungarian fascist occupation?"

Count Farkas smiled with thin red lips. "I am happy to hear it." The dusty calendar on the wall read 1977. Until he awoke a month ago, it had been a hundred and twenty years since he walked the earth. Luckily, he knew Rumanian, now apparently the dominant language in this portion of the old Hapsburg Empire.

Colonel Popiescu set the report aside, pressed a button. “Of course, the Constitution of the Socialist Republic of Rumania guarantees equal treatment to every citizen, regardless of ethnicity. Did you not find this to be true at our state psychiatric hospital?”

Count Farkas eyed the Colonel’s medical certificates hanging beside portraits of pasty-faced bureaucrats. An office without vitality, aside from that blood-red flag. A nation of cattle, patiently awaiting slaughter. As soon as Farkas established himself . . . “The doctors are very . . . agreeable.”

Popiescu nodded, pressed the button. “The people considered prosecuting you for criminal assault, but the people’s psychiatrists diagnosed you mentally ill.” Popiescu pressed the button, slammed it, bellowed toward his door, “Nurse! Water!” He turned to Farkas. “The report states, *Count,* you no longer believe your delusion of aristocracy.”

The Count winced on cue. “Please, Comrade Colonel, refer to me only as Comrade Farkas.”

Popiescu grunted, satisfied.

A fat woman with thick ankles shuffled into the office carrying an aluminum tray, glasses, bottles of mineral water. She set the tray atop Popiescu’s papers, wiped her sweaty brow with her stained apron. She found a bottle opener, wiped a glass with the apron, opened a bottle, poured its water into the spotted glass.

Count Farkas narrowed his red eyes, snatched a bottle, saw a dead fly and bits of insect debris floating atop the water.

The woman took the bottle from him, glanced at it, saw the fly. Expressionless, she opened the bottle, poured the fly and debris onto Popiescu’s floor, poured the remaining water into another spotted glass, handed it to Farkas.

Popiescu watched this incident with glazed eyes, limply held his own glass in a dirty hand.

The woman shuffled out of the room, gray hair spilling from her babushka. Farkas espied one of her hairs stuck to his glass.

Popiescu drank before continuing, dribbling onto his soiled tunic. “It is good, Comrade Farkas, you no longer suffer from these delusions. The people require clear-headed workers, uncontaminated by ancient superstitions.”

Farkas leered. This was the best news upon awakening. “The doctors cured me of all such superstitions. I no more believe in aristocracy than in Christ, heaven, or . . . vampires.”

Popiescu nodded sleepily. “Comrade General Secretary Ceausescu is correct in stating that once atheism is firmly anchored in the class consciousness of the proletariat, then revolutionary Marxism-Leninism shall enter a new stage of dialectic materialism in which scientific socialism . . . ”

Count Farkas let the Colonel drone on. This was better than *Monsieur* Voltaire’s influence in France. If the vampire’s strength is that no one believes in him, what more could he ask than to awaken in a nation of atheists?

* * *

Farkas exited his apartment, shuffled along Brasov's broken sidewalks, seeking quarry. He squinted against an overcast sky. Still enough sun to burn him. Shrugging, he scratched a lesion, wiped the pus against his trousers.

Peasants and laborers, faces blackened by nearby refineries, slumped against empty store windows, clutching liquor bottles. A soft breeze stank of benzene. A slovenly group of soldiers, red patches upon shabby uniforms, bantered beneath a large bleacher, one of them urinating in public.

Farkas squinted at the bleacher, empty and dilapidated. Its sole vitality derived from massive blood-red banners, hung beside colossal portraits of bureaucrats. Everywhere, scarlet banners draped buildings, lampposts, monuments, bleeding the nation.

Comrade Farkas browsed for prey. Everyone was too distant, or too unruly, or too much trouble. Shrugging, he shambled back to his state-owned apartment.

Communist Vampires

A woman approached me at a book-signing. Twentysomething, Asian-American, with cherry-red hair, she said she "belonged to the MTV generation" and developed a reading habit while in the Navy. She wasn't into history or politics. She'd only bought *Vampire Nation* the previous week because she was a vampire fan. Yet she enthused over it, enjoying it enough to seek my autograph. Seeing her, I knew I'd reached an audience who'd never read *The Black Book of Communism.*

Until now. For *Vampire Nation*'s suggested readings include the *Black Book* and *Victory*. Just as *Maus* teaches adolescents about Nazism through its comic book tale of some cats' genocide of mice, so *Vampire Nation* is my attempt to introduce mainstream readers to Communist horrors.

Despite an 85-100 million death toll, Communism still finds apologists. Castro has fans. Artists and academics romanticize Communist "idealists." Generation Y is blissfully ignorant of the Cold War, prey to their professors' revisionism. The *Black Book* is heavy reading; *Vampire Nation* is written as a popcorn movie with a message.

Insight describes *Vampire Nation* as "a satiric horror fable about life in Communist Rumania." One reader compared it to *Animal Farm*, in that both novels feature fantastical Communist creatures. And *Prometheus* (newsletter of the Libertarian Futurist Society) said *Vampire Nation* "combines political dystopia, horror, espionage thriller, and black comedy . . . even a Boy Meets Girl story. But surprisingly enough, all these elements hold together. The binding force is a single central idea: vampirism as the ultimate form of communism, in which blood is redistributed from producers to parasites."

The problem with popular entertainment is not its sex and violence, but its lack of diverse viewpoints. In every tale of land developers vs. environmentalists, you already know who's sleazy, who's honest. Republicans are always bigots, and bigots are always white. Gun collectors are always crazy. *The Apostle* is an outstanding film partially because it dares to be different: a film about a Bible Belt minister who isn't unremittingly evil.

Conservatives and feminists decry the horror genre for its sex and violence, yet horror is the most inherently diverse of genres. It can be graphic, but also subtle. *National Review* writer Russell Kirk wrote ghost novels. Low-budget horror films include the feminist (*The Devonsville Terror*) and fundamentalist (*Day of Judgment*). Horror is the only genre replete with sympathetic clergy, and not a few good witches. Evil ones too, from both camps. Horror literature includes such profound works as *Frankenstein* and *The Exorcist* (forget the pea soup—read the book).

Rather than fretting over TV sex and violence, what America really needs is more diversity from its myth-making media. Popular entertainment spins our hopes and dreams and nightmares, our heroes and villains. It is the prism through which the populace interprets all it sees. Couch potatoes see Bush on TV and their "gut feelings" recoil. Lurking in their subconscious are thousands of fictional portrayals of drunken fratboy, Southern-accented, Bible-thumping, ex-military, country-club Republican bigots. Stereotypes as false as any other, yet positive facts are a poor defense against negative "gut feelings."

Whatever the problem, censorship is not a solution. Some conservatives flirt with censorship in the form of voluntary (but government-pressured) ratings, advisories, and Internet filters. They are not alone. Everyone from Christian fundamentalists to the Anti-Defamation League proffer Internet filters. But I'd leave such "solutions" to campus PC tyrants. Good people with good ideas should never fear opposing views.

The proper solution for anyone misportrayed or ignored by the media is to join the dialogue, to fight culture by creating more culture. People want to be entertained. They will always view or read or listen to something, and you can't fight something with nothing. You can't create positive portrayals by censoring sex and violence. In the 1980s, Spike Lee and Robert Townsend independently produced *She's Gotta Have It* and *Hollywood Shuffle*, respectively. Conservatives too are a minority group, and can learn from Lee and Townsend.

The excuses are running out. *The Blair Witch Project* was shot with a camcorder. CD burners are empowering garage bands. Print-on-demand is revolutionizing self-publishing. Amazon.com distributes all of the above. And the Internet is publicizing everyone. Conservatives should stop flirting with censorship, and start contributing to the dialogue. My contribution is *Vampire Nation*.

Stephen King says authors don't choose their subjects, the subject chooses them. I was born in New York, yet spent summers visiting relatives in Communist Transylvania. It always felt different behind the Iron Curtain. As when you enter a roomful of strangers and sense a shared mood, yet see no reason for it. Behind the Curtain was a mood of fear, despair, paranoia. You saw no clear reason for it. The sun shone. Birds sang. Yet the despair was omnipresent, oppressive, weighing you down.

After I wrote *Vampire Nation*, it was rejected by all major publishers, unread. So I self-published it through Xlibris, one of many print-on-demand presses mushrooming across the Internet. A few bookstores carry *Vampire Nation*: Dark Delicacies and Laissez-Faire Books. So do all major online booksellers.

Promotion is difficult, but not impossible. I did a Halloween interview on Tennessee's WJCW 910 AM. Germany's Utoprop Agency is representing translation rights to *Vampire Nation* in Europe. I commissioned music for my website, www.CommunistVampires.com: a RealAudio-streaming, vampiric version of the Communist anthem, *L'Internationale.*

Conservatives will never influence "the MTV generation" via TV advisories against sex and violence. But new technologies are empowering everyone, leveling the playing field for all minorities and subcultures.

The Christmas Box and *Celestine Prophecy* demonstrate that self-publishing can work. Anyone who dislikes the current culture can now create his own.

The Career Witch

Alex was alone in the darkened room, seated before the Ouija board.

"Oh spirits! Can anyone hear my voice? Give me a sign so that I may speak to Cassandra. Give me a sign!"

There came three loud raps!

He tensed. "Cassandra, is that you? Have you returned to me as promised?"

More raps, then shouting. "Alex! Can you hear me?"

Alex opened his eyes, sadly realizing that both the raps and shouts came from outside. Adjusting his power tie, he opened the front door to his empty house.

Outside in the dark stood a thirtysomething flower child in a granny dress. "Alex, I was so worried something had happened." Kissing his cheek, Meg entered. "You sounded so anxious over the phone. Is everything all right?"

"My wife is dead."

"I'm sorry. I know how much you loved my sister. But Alex, it's been nearly a year. Isn't it time you started . . . seeing other people?"

"I'll never find anyone like Cassie. Besides, her death is only temporary. She promised she'd return."

"But you've tried tarot cards, crystal balls, séances. You still haven't reached her."

"But I haven't tried the Ouija yet!"

Meg saw the Ouija board, its wooden surface shimmering from the glow of the red candles burning in the candelabra.

"Meg, darling," he said, "you have to understand, my skills are nowhere near as powerful as Cassie's. She was the witch in the family. Whenever I needed supernatural help in business, she handled it."

"If she was so powerful, *she* would have contacted you by now." Meg held him. "Alex, I think it's very noble of you to keep a torch lit for Cassandra. But look what it's doing to you. You're wasting away. You've got to get out. If only for one night."

"But I feel so close. As if at any moment, she'll break on through from the other side."

"Maybe she doesn't *want* to break on through. Death can be a powerful trip. Maybe she's changed."

Alex scowled.

"Not that she no longer loves you," Meg added. "But maybe she's happy in her new scene."

"I could never be happy without *her*."

"And I'm sure she'd *prefer* to have you with her. But as you said, she loved you, so she wouldn't want you to destroy yourself over her. Let me take you out tonight. Dinner's on me."

"I don't know. Cassie was very wise about metaphysics. If she preferred death, she would have known that before she died. She knew more about death than you or I."

"But not as much as she knows now."

Alex shook his head.

"Oh, Alex! I wish I could help you."

"You can! That's why I called you here."

Meg brightened. "Name it! Anything you want."

"You're Cassie's closest living relative. She told me you two were quite close growing up together."

"About six feet. We shared the same bedroom."

"I was thinking, if we merge our efforts to reach Cassie, we'd double our chances of succeeding."

Meg played with her mood ring. "It's not that I don't want to help. But there's a time for everything. A time to live. A time to love. A time to die. A cosmic harmony. Cassandra is dead. You have to accept it or you'll keep getting bummed out."

"I'll get a nervous breakdown if we don't reach her. At the very least we should *ask* Cassie if she's happy where she is. I owe her that much."

Meg sighed. "All right, Alex. For your sake, I'll try it this once. But you have to promise. If we don't reach Cassandra within the next half hour, you're going out with me tonight. And this way, you pay for dinner!"

Alex gave her a quick kiss. "I knew I could depend on you."

"You'll always be able to."

The two of them sat down at the Ouija, placing their fingers on the planchette.

"Like this?" Meg asked.

"That's right. Lightly, so it's free to move."

"I'll try my best."

"I'm surprised you asked. I thought you and Cassie were part of the same coven."

"Long ago."

Alex stared at the Ouija. "Beloved wife. Wherever you are. Your husband and sister eagerly await your return."

Meg looked askance before adding, "I sense she's in heaven right now. Happy and wanting you to live your own life."

"Then I want to hear her say it."

"Maybe she can't. Maybe it's against the rules."

"Wait a minute! It's moving!"

Astonished, they watched the planchette spell: HELP ME.

"Cassie's in trouble!" Alex exclaimed.

"Maybe it isn't Cassandra."

The planchette continued to spell: USE THE BOOK OF REMAKING.

"It doesn't make any sense!" cried Meg. "We'd better stop."

"Cassie! Is that you?" asked Alex. "Where are you?"

The planchette spelled its answer: HELL.

Meg sighed. "It's her."

* * *

Alex flipped through the book. "One of Cassie's most prized possessions."

Meg paced the living room, arms folded nervously. "The *Book Of ReMaking*? That's a book of alchemy. Transmuting reality by summoning demons. You can't get Cassandra out of hell with that. You don't know *what* you'll pull from hell with those spells."

"Cassie wouldn't have asked for the book if she didn't know its powers."

"If she knows what she's talking about, how did she get *downstairs* in the first place?"

"Obviously, a cosmic error." Book cradled in his arm, Alex pushed aside furniture, clearing a space in the middle of the room. "You knew Cassie. A good witch. A kind and loving wife. I always felt her death was a mistake."

"Even if it was, you're going about this the wrong way."

Chalk in hand, Alex drew a pentagram on the parquet floor, then a circle around it, careful so it matched the diagram in the book.

"Has it occurred to you," Meg asked, "that it might be her occult stuff that got Cassandra into the mess she's in? Maybe if we prayed for her? Catholics say enough prayers can free a soul from purgatory and send them to heaven."

"Cassie isn't *in* purgatory. And I don't want her in heaven. I want her with me!"

"You're playing with fire. Whatever your goals are, the *Book Of ReMaking* is not the right path. If you insist on fooling around with magic, there is some positive magic I can use."

"Positive magic? That sounds like something discussed on talk radio. Along with fad diets and pop psychology." Alex put away his chalk. "Meg, you're a sweet girl, but you always were a flake. Cassie was different. A professional. A career witch."

"Cassandra was greedy. I know we belonged to the same coven long ago, but we went two separate ways."

"Now she needs your help."

"I'm trying to tell you, I gave up that dark stuff. I *can't* help her. I don't know how."

"It's in the book. We just follow instructions."

"Dammit, I wouldn't help Cassandra even if I could! It's no mistake her being down there. She sold her soul to the devil!"

Alex paused, then continued searching for candles. "That's absurd. Her powers were pure. They came from within herself."

"They came from hell! Long ago my sister wanted something that belonged to me. And when she couldn't get it honestly, she had Satan stack the deck." Meg collapsed into an armchair. "Not that it was the end of it. Black magic is a heavy trip. You get addicted. You can't stop once you're hooked."

"My wife was ambitious. And why not? She was smart, talented, beautiful. She *deserved* the best."

"And she got it. Then her credit statement came due."

"No one has the right to imprison my wife in hell!"

"Her Master does. And you're wrong. They don't make errors like that down there. Hell can't stomach good people. It's like indigestion. They'd be . . . vomited out."

"She's my wife!" He placed candles at each pentagram tip. "If need be, I'll break open the gates of hell and yank her from Satan myself."

Meg sighed. "Alex, you're an amateur. You don't know what the *Book Of ReMaking* is capable of."

"I have faith in my wife and her guidance. Whatever she may have done to others, I know she loved me, and I intend to aid her in her hour of need." He lit each candle. "Ready."

As Alex read from the book, a gentle breeze blew through the enclosed room, building into a gust, then a gale. "Hear me, king of the dead! Obey my commands, ruler of the underworld! By the strength of my will, throw open the gates of inferno! Let free the sorceress Cassandra, whom you have unjustly enslaved!"

Pulling her wind-whipped hair away from her eyes, Meg stared at the circle. The wood within it melted away. But instead of a hole, there was a cauldron of reddish-yellow light. A portal to another dimension. Two female hands pressed against an invisible barrier separating her world from the living room. The rest of her was shrouded in a glowing reddish-yellow mist.

Alex saw the hands. "She's alive! My Cassie has returned!"

Meg trembled from cold and fear. "How do you know it's her? It could be anybody! It could be any*thing!*"

Alex watched the fingers frantically scratching against the invisible barrier. "Something's wrong! She can't get through!"

Meg grabbed him, shouting to be heard over the howling wind. "Alex, I'm scared. I don't know who or what is down there and I don't want to find out. Let's run as far as possible and forget tonight ever happened."

"How can I run now? I've waited a year to get my wife back. To hold her in my arms. To gaze into her eyes." His face glowed red from the portal fire. "And there she is. So near . . . " He reached down, as if to place his hands against the woman's.

"No!" Meg grabbed him, they struggled, she scratched his wrists. Tiny blood droplets struck the barrier, dissolving it.

A finger slipped through.

"Blood! That's the key!" Alex clawed at his wrists. New droplets created new holes. Tiny but expanding.

Meg realized what was happening.

Long fingernails pressed through the new holes.

Alex glanced about the room. "Too slow. I need a knife."

Meg swept her arm across the candles, knocking them down. Thunder shook the room, a tornado wrecked brief havoc, the magic force was sucked down whirlwindlike into the portal.

Within seconds the wind was gone. So was the portal.

* * *

"The problem lies in drawing sufficient blood to let Cassie in, while ensuring I don't bleed to death." Alex chuckled as he studied the diagram of human blood vessels in the medical book. "If I'm not careful, I'll end up trading places with Cassie, and then she'll have to rescue me."

"If you really think she would," Meg mumbled, then said, "If you're going to cut yourself, you should minimize the risks."

"Why do you think I'm wasting time with this book, when just by slashing my wrists I could have my arms around my beloved wife at this very moment?"

"So have a nurse at the blood bank do it."

"Blood banks don't let you take blood home. Even if they did, it would mean an extra day. I've waited long enough."

"You could buy blood. People go there to sell. All you'd have to do is outbid the blood bank. Or bribe somebody who works there. It would be smart trading. Cassie would like that."

He shook his head. "Not as romantic as slashing open my own flesh. There's something special about spilling your own blood to rescue your wife. Besides, I want Cassie rescued by clean blood. So many blood donors are disease-ridden addicts or back-street winos."

"Cassandra talked the same way about blood. Always speaking of blood mysticism and blood oaths and pacts written in blood."

"Blood is the stuff of life. A vital element in all magic."

"Only in black magic. Good witches don't use blood."

"Can *you* rescue Cassie without it?"

"No, if she *deserves* to be where she is, white magic won't save her."

"Why do you say *if* when you have no doubt?" Alex snapped. "Are you trying to spare my feelings?"

"Yes, I'm trying to spare your feelings! I'm trying harder than you ever tried with me when . . . when I loved you, long before you even met Cassandra."

Alex nearly popped his button-down. "You loved me?"

"And you loved me! We were both very much in love, until I introduced you to Cassandra. Until she sold her soul to the devil for the power to steal you from me. She couldn't have done that with white magic. A good witch can only make people aware of something they already feel. Only black magic can create an illusion of false love, which is what you feel for Cassandra." Meg was near tears. "My sister *deserves* to burn in hell!"

Alex turned away uneasily. "I've heard younger sisters are often jealous of their older siblings."

Meg slumped into the armchair. "If only you could remember. When you asked me here tonight, I thought her power over you had finally been severed. Ever since Cassandra died, I was waiting for you to feel again what you once felt so strongly. But I should have known my sister would do her best to pull you down into hell with her."

Alex ran the dagger's blade over a candle flame. "The lower forearm should do." He collected his blood in a chalice.

"Look what Cassandra's making you do! At all of this." Meg indicated the dim room. "Does it seem natural to you? Or healthy or normal? Ten years ago you wouldn't have fooled around with demonology and bizarre blood rituals."

Alex bound his arm with a strip of cloth.

"We used to believe in good magic," Meg continued. "You and I together. In a path of peaceful nirvana."

"You're sweet. But you're not Cassie. She was strong and exciting. The only woman I could *ever* love." Alex cradled the *Book Of ReMaking* in one arm, approached the magic circle with the chalice. The candles were already lit. "If you won't help, then please don't interfere. I'll just cut myself once again. And you won't be welcome here anymore."

"Tell me one thing, Alex. Since Cassandra died, have you ever felt anything at all for me?"

"Always. You're my sister-in-law. I care a great deal for you. But I love Cassie."

"Good." Then Meg said to herself, "Before she died, you stopped caring completely. Her power into this world *is* weaker. I just have to cut her off for good."

Again, Alex read from the *Book Of ReMaking.* The wind began. The portal appeared. Meg glanced nervously into the mist and light, saw the hands against the barrier.

Alex raised the chalice over the portal, began tilting, but before a single drop spilled, Meg knocked the chalice out of his hand, sent it flying past the circle, striking and splashing its blood against the wall.

"Just what do you think that accomplishes?" Alex demanded. "I just have to draw more blood from myself." He set the book down, went to his dagger, undid the cloth around his forearm.

Meg grabbed the *Book Of ReMaking,* tore out some pages, held them over a candle. "Don't waste your blood, Alex. You'll never open the gates to hell without these pages."

Disembodied screams hollered from the portal as paper caught fire.

Alex started toward Meg, but halted when she raised her arm and shouted, "I dump these candles now, the door to hell slams shut forever!"

"Meg! If you ever cared for me . . . "

"I loved you. I still do. That's why I have no choice."

Fingers were still scratching the barrier when Meg swept the candles. As before, a whirlwind blew through the room, sucking itself through the portal. The hands spun within the circle, as if the woman were caught in a whirlpool.

Still clutching the dagger, Alex rushed Meg, they struggled, she stumbled onto the blade. Her blood spilled and spiraled into the portal, melting through the barrier as lava through a frozen lake. Enraged at losing his wife, Alex stabbed Meg repeatedly, her blood reacting as gasoline to fire, until the light from the gaping hole was too bright for Alex. He stepped back. Meg's body crumpled and disappeared down the hole.

Cassandra spun up the whirlpool, her swirling body halting at floor level. The wind ceased. The portal vanished. Complete silence.

Cassandra stood on the pentagram, wearing a ceremonial robe, her hair golden against its crimson cloth, her arms outstretched to Alex. "Faithful husband. I *knew* I could depend on you."

Alex rushed into her arms. "My beloved wife!"

"Now we'll be together forever. Just as I promised."

"I knew you would defeat death."

She became hesitant. "Now, darling. I only promised death would not separate us. I never claimed I could *defeat* it."

"Nevertheless, whatever you've done, someone else needs your help. It's your sister. I've—" he broke into tears. "I've killed her."

"Of course you did. And I'm glad you did. Her blood opened the door for us. Now we are together again."

"*My* blood could have done that. She didn't have to die."

"Yes she did. Your blood was by choice. That was enough to open the door. But not enough to allow me to take you back. But with her blood on your hands, we'll always be together. You see, my Master won't let me stay up here. And so I came to get you!"

She grabbed him just as the floor crashed open beneath them, sending them into the fires below.

Soon, Alex's screams were heard no more.

The hole coughed. Meg's bloody body flew through the hole. The hole sealed itself before she crashed down on the pentagram.

She awoke dazed and confused. She saw blood on herself, but found no wounds. She glanced about the room.

"Alex? Alex, where are you?"

But Is It *Horror*?:

Defining and Demarcating the Genre

Horror is a squishy genre to define, and no wonder. Horror shows such as *The X-Files* are mistaken for science fiction, while suspense and fantasy films are marketed as horror. Non-horror fans, especially, define horror by its latest cycle, most recently slashers and chainsaw massacres. Those hating slasher films thus condemn all of horror, forgetting the bug-eyed monsters and old Universal classics. But remind them of *Dracula* and *Frankenstein*, and they remember that they like horror too.

Horror authors are no help. When horror book sales decline, horror authors try to recategorize their works as dark fantasy or suspense, making horror a genre that dare not speak its name.

* Genre is not Style

Horror is a difficult genre to define and delineate because its parameters are established by different criteria than for most other genres. Cinematic genres are usually delineated by a set of *story conventions*: by elements of plot, character, period, and setting.

Genre should not be confused with *style*: the techniques and manner whereby the story is told. *Film noir* is not a genre but a filmmaking style characterized by wet streets, gritty sets, night-for-night photography, high contrast expressionistic lighting, claustrophobic framing and art direction, a jazzy soundtrack, and heightened dialogue. Although noir is most often identified with mystery's hard-boiled subgenre, the noir style has been applied to science fiction (*Blade Runner*, 1982) and horror (*Werewolf*, Fox TV, 1987-88). The only noir element concerning *story* is its pessimistic/nihilistic thematic atmosphere. Yet a pessimistic atmosphere can inform many genres and does not alone qualify noir as a true stand-alone genre.

*** Horror as an Emotive Genre**

Although horror has its own story conventions, horror is an emotive genre, defined by its intent to scare.

Horror presupposes a *threat*, building tension with its promise that something hideous will occur, there is no escape. *Sleepaway Camp* (1983) opens on an idyllic lakeside setting. It looks to be a family film, but its audience knows better. By their own *genre awareness* the audience collaborates with the filmmaker to create tension as a speeding motorboat nears some exposed swimmers. Horror audiences stick their hands into a black box, knowing something will bite, only uncertain as to how and when.

Other genres strive to emotionally move an audience, but only horror and comedy solicit audiences primarily by promising a specific and consistent emotional impact: fear and mirth, respectively. And while other genres depict frightening scenes, only horror spotlights the fearsome, making it its *raison d'être.*

If horror is a squishy genre to peg, it comes from its being an emotive genre. Horror is a fearsome blob, absorbing new story conventions from every historical/societal shift. Horror always finds a new scary mask to resonate current concerns, finding the dark side to every wish, whether in outer space or in suburbia.

*** Horror requires an Unnatural Threat**

Because fear is a fundamental emotion evoked by many stories, both genre and mainstream, one cannot classify as horror any and every tale that frightens an audience or depicts horrific imagery. Such a definition is overly broad. If every film depicting the fearsome or the horrific is of the horror *genre,* then everything from *The Godfather* to *Titanic* is horror. In which case the term loses all meaning and horror ceases to be a distinct genre.

So as to differentiate itself, the *horror genre* must dramatize horrific events other than the commonplace, realistic, or historic. It must posit an *unnatural threat* that is outside the realm of normalcy, reality, or history. Defining the "weirdly horrible tale," H.P. Lovecraft wrote:

> A certain atmosphere of breathless and unexplainable dread of outer, unknown forces must be present; there must be a hint . . . of that most terrible concept of the human brain—a malign and particular *suspension or defeat of the fixed laws of Nature* which are our only safeguard against the assaults of chaos and the daemons of unplumbed space.[1]

Philosopher Noël Carroll distinguishes the horror genre from horrific reality. The genre "is different from the sort that one expresses in saying 'I am horrified by the prospect of ecological disaster,' or 'Brinksmanship in the age of nuclear arms is horrifying,' or 'What the Nazis did was horrible.'"[2] Carroll terms the latter *natural horror,* and the genre as *art-horror.*

War films evoke fear and horror. Yet war films that naturalistically depict horrifying war images (*All Quiet on the Western Front*) are no more horror films than are films about the horrors of poverty, domestic violence, urban crime, or genocide. But films about fearsome unnatural soldiers qualify as horror films (e.g., the revenant Confederate corpses in *The Supernaturals,* 1986; the Vietnam grunt/vampire in *Deathdream,* 1972; and the entire Nazi zombie subgenre: *Shock Waves*, 1970, *Oasis of the Zombies*, 1981, *Night of the Zombies*, 1983, *Zombie Lake*, 1985).

However, an unnatural threat can only exist in the context of a natural universe. As Alamo Joe observes in *Werewolf,* a talking flower is terrifying in a world in which flowers do not talk. His remark well defines horror: *When the world isn't the same as our minds believe, then we are in a nightmare.*[3] A story in which talking flowers are the accepted norm may make for fantasy—even dark fantasy—but not horror, because such flowers do not suspend the fixed laws of nature as understood by any character within that universe. This is why Alamo Joe scoffs at *Alice in Wonderland,* disbelieving that Alice would regard a talking flower with surprise rather than terror.

A horror story requires an unnatural threat, which is to say that in addition to being unnatural, the threat must be a *threat.*

---

[1] My italics. *Writer's Encyclopedia,* edited by Kirk Polking, Writer's Digest Books, Cincinnati, 1983, p. 153.

[2] *The Philosophy of Horror or Paradoxes of the Heart,* by Noël Carroll, Routledge, New York, 1990, p. 12.

[3] Frank Lupo's pithy teleplay for *Werewolf*'s TV pilot is replete with sharp observations and concise dialogue.

But what of *sympathetic monsters*? What if a fantastical "threat" is sympathetic or desirable? Is it horror if the monster is hero rather than villain?

Carroll writes, "[T]he monsters we find in horror stories are uniformly dangerous or at least appear to be so; when they cease to be threatening, they cease to be horrifying."[4] But increasingly, formerly threatening horror icons are depicted sympathetically. Horror historian David J. Skal writes, "By the mid-1980s, more people were reading about vampires than at any time in history, and for the first time, they were identifying with them positively."[5]

Is it still horror if the vampire is a hero? Sometimes.

There is no horror story if the unnatural "threat" is *wholly* sympathetic, positive, and desirable, and only mortals and mortal forces are villains. But note that an unnatural threat can threaten either mortals *or* the creature embodying it. A vampire who despises his condition may make for a horror story, even if he is sympathetic. In *Dark Shadows* vampirism is horrific, even though Barnabas is not.

Conversely, there is no unnatural threat in *NightBreed* (1990). Although the fantastical creatures were initially forbidding, they were later revealed to be moral and decent, once you got past their "differences." Nor was their condition unnatural or undesirable to themselves; they did not seek a cure. The only threat came from mortals using mortal weapons. Thus *NightBreed* is dark fantasy rather than horror.

The Craft (1996) also features sympathetic "monsters." Four outcast girls form a coven to take vengeance on the popular crowd at their high school. So long as every villain is mortal, and every witch a heroine who enjoys the occult, *The Craft* is not horror. Only when the Craft turns against the heroines, and they turn on each other, does *The Craft* thread (barely) into horror.

The Initiation of Sarah (TVM, 1978) likewise depicts a nerdy girl who unleashes unnatural powers on her tormenters. Although college frosh Kay Lenz is more sympathetic than *The Craft*'s high school witches, *Sarah* is more assuredly horror because (1) Lenz faces a moral struggle, fearing and rejecting her own unnatural powers early on (and is thus herself threatened by them), (2) a villain (sorority den mother Shelley Winters) enlists unnatural forces for evil ends, and (3) other sympathetic and vulnerable characters are threatened by Lenz's unnatural powers.

A horror story requires *sympathetic* and *vulnerable* potential victims. For a threat to *threaten,* the audience must sense that sympathetic characters (preferably the principals) are at genuine risk of serious harm. Had the audience

---

[4] *The Philosophy of Horror*, ibid, p. 28.

[5] *The Monster Show: A Cultural History of Horror,* by David J. Skal, W.W. Norton, New York, 1993, p. 344.

for *Sleepaway Camp* not sensed that the swimmers were vulnerable to the speeding motorboat, they would have felt no tension as the boat drew nearer.

A major weakness of many expensive big studio horror films (rarely a fault in low-budget indie horror fare) is that audiences correctly sense that the stars are safe from harm (a presumption Hitchcock betrayed to great effect in *Psycho*). *The Frighteners* (1996) is well structured with surprises, yet the audience just *knows* that Alvadar and Fox will enjoy a happy ending, even if they don't exactly know how. (I had thought that Fox would end up a happy ghost, as in *Ghost*.) An audience's perception of hero *invulnerability* (he cannot be seriously injured) and *invincibility* (he cannot lose) weakens the horror.

The Craft fails as horror partially because its heroine witches are ever strong, confident, and sassy. Even when the Craft turns against them, the audience just *knows* the heroines will triumph. Conversely, throughout *Carrie* (1976) and *Sarah,* Sissy Spacek and Kay Lenz remain insecure, threatened, and vulnerable. Both seem unable to handle either the school bullies or their own unnatural powers. This heightens the horror.

*** Moral Avengers as Threats in Horror Anthologies**

Horror anthology films, rooted in EC Comic's *Tales from the Crypt,* have a long tradition of the unnatural threat acting as moral avenger. Their most common storylines gleefully depict a revenant corpse killing an evil mortal. Yet most such films may be regarded as horror because (1) the corpse is often as unsympathetic as his mortal victim, (2) unlike some feminist Wiccans or romantic vampires, these corpses lead an undesirable existence (thus suffering from their own unnaturalness), and (3) audiences identify with the victim; even if they enjoy his comeupance, they cringe at his gory demise. Audiences empathize, even if not sympathize, with the victim.

In *Creepshow*'s "Father's Day" the revenant corpse, moral avenger though he may be, was a domineering tyrant in life, as unsympathetic as his worthless heirs. Plus, he's putrefying. And though the audience may enjoy Adrienne Barbeau's comeupance in "The Crate," the avenging monster is not purely moral—he kills good folk too.

However, because horror anthologies have long functioned as morality plays, they are ever in danger of sympathizing too much with the unnatural, thus weakening its threat to the point that it is no longer horror. One of the *Grim Prairie Tales* (1990) features an irascible old white man who desecrates an Indian burial ground by riding through it, mocking a dying old Indian in passing. As his comeupance, he is buried alive. The tale ends with Indian children playing on his grave. But because these Indians are not portrayed as evil or repugnant (unlike the monsters in *Creepshow*), this tale is suspense rather than horror, similar in attitude to "revenge films" such as *Death Wish* and *Billy Jack* (revenge fantasies of the political Right and Left, respectively). Indeed, the sublime spirituality of the Indians' retribution evokes Yahweh's vengeance on the Egyptians in *The Ten Commandments.*

*** Horror's Three Subgenres**

While a genre may be subdivided by various criteria, I find it practicable to partition horror by the genus of its threat. This is appropriate because an unnatural threat is fundamental to horror. All of horror's unnatural threats can be placed into one of three categories: The supernatural, the monsters of nature and science, and the dark side of the human psyche.

Are these natural demarcations? Skal writes, "With *Dracula, Frankenstein,* and *Dr. Jekyll and Mr. Hyde,* the psychic landscapes of castle, crypt, and laboratory were definitively mapped."[6] He doesn't label his threats, yet they are supernatural, horror/sci-fi, and the horror psycho. Yes, Jekyll uses science to transmute into Hyde, so he is monster rather than psycho. But Hyde remains human, albeit pure evil. He can pass for a psycho in a pinch.

*** Supernatural Horror and Dark Fantasy**

In *supernatural horror* the threat is mystical, lacking a rational, materialist explanation. Traditionally this has meant such sundry as vampires, ghosts, werewolves, witches, and demons. But this subgenre is increasingly muddled.

Supernatural horror is often confused with *fantasy.* To distinguish, remember that in horror the fantastical element must be (1) unnatural to its universe, and (2) threatening. Is it a good ghost, or a bloodcurdling ghost? *Ghost Story* (1981) is supernatural horror. From its opening frame it promises to frighten. It has romance, but a romance secondary to horror. Conversely, *Ghost* (1990), while it occasionally jolts its audience, is a romantic fantasy. *The Frighteners* is more problematic. Its storyline and playful supernatural milieu resemble that of *Ghost,* yet its more threatening supernatural villain pushes *Frighteners* toward horror.

Causing further confusion is the term *dark fantasy.* Dark fantasy is not a genre, but a subgenre of fantasy, being fantasy that's . . . dark. Some horror writers inaccurately use the term to distinguish their works from slasher stories. Yet what they're usually writing is not dark fantasy, but supernatural horror. This is because regardless of how unnatural the threat, if the setting is an identifiable naturalistic universe, the story is horror. (Although the creatures in

---

[6] Ibid, p. 145. Stephen King too singles out these three novels for special attention in *Dance Macabre,* Everest House, New York, 1981, pp. 60-88.

NightBreed first appeared to be monsters threatening our natural world, they were soon revealed to be inhabiting an alternative world that was both natural to them and non-threatening, even hospitable, to mortal visitors. Hence, not horror.)

*** Horror/Sci-Fi**

Horror stories featuring the monsters of nature and science, I term *horror/sci-fi* (by which I mean a subgenre of horror and not of science fiction). I use the term "monster" broadly, encompassing Frankenstein's monster, space aliens, mad computers, Cronenberg's plagues, swamp creatures, any unnatural threat beget by nature or science. Here it is important to note that a creature may be born of nature, yet still be contrary to Nature (i.e., the natural order), hence unnatural. Mutants and monsters are often referred to as "crimes against Nature."

Horror/sci-fi monsters are of material origin and have a scientific rationale. Yet these monsters represent an unnatural threat because, despite the scientific rationale underpinning their material origin, they are either newly discovered or newly created. Thus they are unnatural to our previous understanding of the universe. As with the talking flower, they reveal that things aren't as our minds believed.

*** Horror/Sci-Fi vs. Science Fiction**

Science fiction is an intellectual genre, speculating on the societal impact of future technologies. Horror is an emotive genre, merely using sf icons for its own ends. Rather than speculate about the societal impact of space travel, horror drools over exploding astronaut heads.

Horror/sci-fi films include *Alien* (1979), *Galaxy of Terror* (1981, aka *Planet of Horrors, Mindwarp: An Infinity of Horrors*), *Horror Planet* (British 1981, aka *Inseminoid*), *Forbidden World* (1982), and *Creature* (1984, aka *The Titan Find*). All these films depict futurist space travel, as in *2001: A Space Odyssey* (1968), and space weaponry, as in *Star Wars* (1977). But their aesthetic goals and emphases differ.

2001's HAL 9000 computer is fearsome, but *2001*'s emphasis is on examining technology's influence on human history and human nature, and on our place in the cosmos. HAL's story function is to stimulate such speculation, thus *2001* is science fiction. Conversely, while the drooling aliens in the above horror/sci-fi films may stimulate speculation on human greed, hubris, or whatever else motivates astronauts into space (where no one can hear you scream), their emphases is on creating an atmosphere of terror, building tension, then granting an emotional release by brutally butchering hapless astronauts in darkened corridors or caverns.

Darth Vader's genocidal destruction of an entire planet may qualify *Star Wars* as one of the most violent movies ever filmed. Yet despite its violence, *Star Wars* is a science fantasy/space opera (science fantasy being a subgenre of science fiction that borrows the latter's iconography without a serious attempt at scientific plausibility, as in Ray Bradbury's poetic *Martian Chronicles*). *Star Wars* is not horror for several reasons. The Death Star's threat is a natural progression in that universe's escalating arms race. The violence is fantasy violence; death is distant and quick. And the audience empathizes with the pretty princess rather than with her extinct people. Horror must threaten, but the audience knows Princess Leia is safe, just as surely as it knew the swimmers in *Sleepaway Camp* were not.

While most *Frankenstein* films are recognizably horror/sci-fi, Mary Shelley's novel is more problematic. Its serious speculations on the ethics of science are endemic to science fiction. Yet Shelley's answer—some things Man was not meant to know—is anathema to classic sf. Her answer is horror's answer. Furthermore, her cursory description of Frankenstein's technology, the references to Paracelsus's alchemy, the monster's spiritual turmoil, and the heavy emphasis on the physical, psychological, and spiritual sufferings of the protagonists, all suggest *Frankenstein* is horror rather than sf.[7]

* Science Fiction's False Claim to Horror Monsters

Some scholars still claim horror monsters for science fiction. Per Schelde justifies this by first divorcing sf literature from sf film; abandoning speculation to literature, and redefining the sf film as what sounds suspiciously like horror:

> [D]espite appearances, sf movies and sf literature have little in common and appeal to very different audiences. Science fiction literature is, at its best, not afraid of experiments, of intellectual speculation. . . . Sf movies are a very different kettle of fish: the closest relatives of the genre are the horror movie and the action/suspense movie. . . . Sf movies assiduously (with a few exceptions) avoid being intellectual and speculative. The focus is not the "what if's" of science, technology, and the future. The sf film focus is on the *effects* of science, on the junction where what science has created (usually a monster) meets people going about living their lives. Sf science

[7] See *Terror of Frankenstein,* aka *Victor Frankenstein,* Swedish-Irish, for a faithful film adaptation of Shelley's novel. Reference books variously state its year of release as 1975, 1976, and 1977.

> does not have to be logical. All that is required is a scary monster. How the monster came to be or where it came from is, if not irrelevant, peripheral.[8]

But if you redefine a film genre's sole requirement as having a scary monster, then you're describing horror. Especially if the science doesn't need to be logical so long as the monster is scary. So why not just call it horror?

Patrick Lucanio argues that 1950s "alien invasion" films are science fiction rather than horror. He states that one of sf's goals is to instill in audiences a *sense of wonder*. "This connection between the notion of wonder and mystery and the science fiction film is most pronounced in films that take their audiences to other worlds."[9] He cites *2001* and *Star Wars* as examples, but then continues, "Although such matters as aspiration and wonder may be obscure when exploring the alien invasion film, this type of film nevertheless is rich with similar insights into the human condition. . . . The alien invasion film depicts humanity at the mercy of either malevolent or benign rational (albeit alien) forces."[10]

Lucanio is correct in that a sense of wonder is an aesthetic goal of sf, but he is wrong to use it as a litmus test for sf and thereby claim it exclusively for sf. Horror too has its sense of wonder stories. So long as God and death and afterlife remain mysteries, we mortals will wonder, hope, and fear. In *Contact* (1997) Jodie Foster asked the aliens: "How did you survive your nuclear age?" A trivial, but typically sf question. Horror's mad scientists think bigger. They ask: "Is there a God, and what happens when we die?" Asked that in an old *Outer Limits* episode, a dying alien replied: "Unknown." (Yes, *The Outer Limits* is a horror show.)

Furthermore, if aliens are sufficiently malevolent, they are horror aliens. Lucanio errs in focusing on the monster's origin instead of intent (i.e., does it come in peace, or to steal our women?). Any monster with a rational explanation for its existence, Lucanio claims for science fiction. Indeed, Lucanio's broad criterion (of having a "rational explanation") sweeps many monsters into his "alien invasion" sf subgenre. Lucanio writes that "James Whale's *Frankenstein,* Rouben Mamoulian's *Dr. Jekyll and Mr. Hyde,* and Ernest B. Schoedsack's *Dr.*

---

[8] *Androids, Humanoids, and Other Science Fiction Monsters: Science and Soul in Science Fiction Films,* by Per Schelde, New York University Press, New York, 1993, p. 2.

[9] *Them or Us: Archetypal Interpretations of Fifties Alien Invasion Films,* by Patrick Lucanio, Indiana University Press, Bloomington, 1987, pp. 15-16.

[10] Ibid, p. 16.

Cyclops—all . . . are best seen as alien invasion films."[11] So too giant insects, such as *Tarantula* (1955).[12]

Lucanio contravenes his own methodology. He offers "proof" that *Invasion of the Body Snatchers, Attack of the Fifty Foot Woman, Killers from Space,* and *Tarantula* are science fiction by citing trailers ("Science Fiction Reaches A New High In Terror!" and "Science Fiction's Most Terrifying Thrill!").[13] But these trailers' promise of "Terror" as easily proves the films are horror. Furthermore, a poster for three of Lucanio's "science fiction" films, *The Spider, Beast with a Million Eyes,* and *Night of the Blood Beast,* explicitly screams: "3 HORROR HITS!"[14]

After such broad claims for science fiction, Lucanio necessarily defines horror narrowly, limiting it to the exotic. "The most important characteristic of the horror film is its emphasis on an alternate state of the actual world. . . . its exotic settings and characters . . . the use of one without the other does not produce the horror film. Transylvania is perhaps the quintessential setting of the horror film."[15]

That excludes much, and Lucanio knows it. He robs horror of all non-supernatural films. "By the term *horror film* I mean *Gothic film.* This term distinguishes those films that have historically been molded out of supernatural stories . . . from films dealing with slaughter and gore, the so-called 'mad-slasher' films. To my thinking such films as Hitchcock's *Psycho* and John Carpenter's *Halloween* are 'thrillers' and not horror movies in the traditional sense."[16]

But the proper question is not *Is it horror in the traditional sense?* but *Is it horror?* To Lucanio's way of thinking, horror is a very narrow and static genre.

But there's still less. Lucanio then excludes all supernatural films set in contemporary time and space. "A vampire prowling the streets of contemporary Los Angeles, as in Bob Kelljan's *Count Yorga—Vampire* (1970), or Dracula himself stalking London's 'miniskirt girls' in Alan Gibson's Hammer production, *Dracula A.D. 1972,* strains to the point of farce or satire the willing suspension of disbelief so crucial to the traditional horror tale."[17] By such stringent criteria, *Rosemary's Baby* is not horror (although inexplicably, Lucanio concedes *The Exorcist* to horror[18]).

---

[11] Ibid, p. 2.
[12] Ibid, p. 17.
[13] Ibid, p. 4.
[14] Ibid, p. 19.
[15] Ibid, p. 7.
[16] Ibid, p. 133, n. 20.
[17] Ibid, pp. 10-11.
[18] Ibid, p. 9.

For the most part, what Lucanio labels as "alien invasion" films, I term horror/sci-fi. But do these monsters belong to science fiction or horror?

Lucanio disputes critics who categorize films on the basis of a common foundation of fear. "[T]he tradition of horror and science fiction criticism, a tradition that ignores the difference between them, is based on a Freudian dogma concerning the depiction of our repressed fears and desires. When the alien invasion film is discussed . . . it is discussed in terms of the horror genre."[19]

Well, that's because malevolent aliens, being both unnatural and threatening, are indeed horrifying. Lucanio mistakenly ignores both genres' intended audience reaction: science fiction being an intellectual genre aiming to provoke speculation, horror being an emotive genre aiming to evoke fear. Both genres occasionally evoke a sense of wonder, so that's not determinative.

*** Cinematic Horror vs. Literary Science Fiction**

Notably, Schelde, Lucanio, and the critics Lucanio disputes, all of them, implicitly or explicitly, judge sf literature and sf films by different criteria. Sf literature is settled, but as a film genre, sf must be torturously redefined, otherwise many "sf films" reveal themselves to be horror.

This highlights a key point: *Horror is primarily a cinematic genre, whereas science fiction is primarily literary.*

As a genre of ideas, sf is best expressed in print, a medium in which it's possible to analyze complex scientific or sociological concepts. But scripts do not permit lectures. TV writer Carleton Eastlake observes, "[I]n the majority of feature films, science fiction is largely used to provide a little flavor for the icing on what is basically your same old action-adventure, guy-with-a-very-big-gun cake."[20]

True, but then Eastlake continues, "Television oddly enough, often does better: *Babylon 5* has miraculously risen to the level of good science fiction, and depending on your taste, the many faces of *Star Trek* are often creditable, as is *The X-Files.*"[21]

Here I disagree. My point isn't that authentic science fiction rarely makes it to the screen, but that when it does, it isn't very good. Horror *works* onscreen (big or small), whereas science fiction does not. The best "science fiction" shows are all horror, whereas true science fiction shows are usually dreary. Disregard horror shows like *The X-Files,* and science fiction is left with *Star Trek*'s somnolent pontificating.

---

[19] Ibid, p. 6.
[20] *The Bulletin of the Science Fiction and Fantasy Writers of America,* Fall 1996, p. 25.
[21] Ibid, p. 25.

This is not to say that horror is incapable of meaningful intellectual speculation in print form (e.g., Shelley and Blatty's spiritual ruminations). But being an emotive genre, horror doesn't require long speeches. As in *The X-Files,* dark suggestions suffice.

Indeed, horror not only suffices on sparse suggestions, it thrives! Lovecraft believed horror worked best when suggested rather than stated,[22] and cinema's sound-bite dialogue is enough talk for horror. Lighting, special effects, acting, and music can create an eerie atmosphere in a way that words alone cannot. And if a horror artist elects shocks over suggestion, as some splatter stylists prefer, cinema delivers a bigger punch than text.

*** Supernatural Horror vs. Horror/Sci-Fi**

Perhaps because they are both horror subgenres, the line can blur between supernatural horror and horror/sci-fi.

The characters in *The Haunting* (1963) rationalize Hill House's behavior and influence, prattling off both architectural and psychological explanations. But they are whistling in the dark. The story posits a supernatural explanation, hence the film is supernatural horror. *Bram Stoker's Dracula* (1992) depicts a traditional vampire, made so by affirming Satan, so he is supernatural. But the vampires in Richard Matheson's novel, *I Am Legend,* were created by germs, thus they are horror/sci-fi monsters. All three films based on, or inspired by, his novel (*The Last Man on Earth,* 1964, *The Omega Man,* 1971, and *Night of the Living Dead,* 1968) retain a scientific rationale, although the rationale itself varies. Other vampires straddle these two subgenres. A Satanic witch cursed *Dark Shadows*'s Barnabas Collins so that he became a vampire, but his condition was treatable through the scientific efforts of Drs. Julia Hoffman and Eric Lang.

The X-Files often grafts scientific explanations onto supernatural threats, but not so plausibly as to always convince us a threat was material rather than mystical. Never before have horror's seams between science and the supernatural been so hard to see. *Dark Shadows*'s Timothy Stokes raised Angelique from the dead through a blend of science and sorcery, yet we saw the test tubes apart from the pentagrams. Not so in *The X-Files,* which is the show's appeal. But while an occasional episode's subgenre may be difficult to peg, *The X-Files* is always horror, never science fiction. This is because an *X-Files* without science is conceivable; an *X-Files* without scares is not.

The vampire in "3" had no scientific rationale, and the psycho in "Irresistible" required none. But although "Irresistible" had neither supernatural nor sf elements, *X-Files* creator Chris Carter says of it, "I think it's one of our

---

[22] *Supernatural Horror in Literature,* by H.P. Lovecraft, Dover, New York, 1973, p. 42.

scarier shows."[23] And while Carter cites many influences, such as horror's *Kolchak: The Night Stalker* and spydom's *The Avengers,* he adds, "I was never what you would call a science fiction devotee . . . I've never read the classic science fiction novels, except maybe one of each by Ursula Le Guin and Robert Heinlein a long time ago, and I've never watched an episode of *Star Trek!*"[24]

Finally, whenever a story combines science with the supernatural, the result may be horror or fantasy, but never science fiction. Horror can feed on science; science fiction cannot stomach the supernatural. Science fiction either invalidates the supernatural with a plausible and rational explanation, or is subverted by it.

* The Problem of Zombies

Zombies too blur the line between science and supernatural. The earliest film zombies were products of science seen through native superstition. Narcotics and hypnosis created Lugosi's zombie slaves in *White Zombie* (1932), yet this horror/sci-fi film's photography created an eerie ghostly atmosphere, a tradition continued in *I Walked with a Zombie* (1943).

Later zombies shed all ethereal pretense for aggressive cannibal appetites in films that rooted them firmly in science. Zombies were created by a meteor in *Night of the Living Dead* and by chemical warfare gas in *Night of the Zombies* (Italian 1983, aka *Zombie Creeping Flesh, Zombie Inferno, Cannibal Virus, Hell of the Living Death*).[25] Even supernatural zombies embraced this new ravenous lifestyle, such as the Satanic zombies in *Burial Ground* (Italian 1979, aka *Zombie Horror, Zombie 3*) and *Children Shouldn't Play with Dead Things* (1972).

Children highlights another zombie classification problem: How to delineate between zombies and revenant corpses? Are the corpses in *Children* zombies simply because of their cannibalism? The earliest film zombies had scientific origins, while revenant corpses are traditionally supernatural, going back centuries and finding modern expression in EC Comics and horror anthology films. Unlike most zombies, revenant corpses have clear minds, intent on vengeance or Satanic evil (e.g., the "blind dead" in Amando de Ossorio's Spanish film series). Revenant corpses eat no flesh; the supernatural reserves that role for ghouls. Yet the corpses in *Children* want it all: flesh, vengeance, and evil. A conundrum.

---

[23] *X-Files Confidential: The Unauthorized X-Philes Compendium,* by Ted Edwards, Little, Brown & Co., Boston, 1996, 1997, p. 6.

[24] *The X-Files Declassified,* by Frank Lovece, Citadel, Secaucus, 1996, p. 4.

[25] This film's Third World cannibal zombies should not be confused with the Nazi zombies in another *Night of the Zombies,* also released in 1983.

* The Horror Psycho as Uberpsycho

In horror's third subgenre the threat is a human, usually with a warped psyche, but one whose abilities are unenhanced by science or the supernatural (otherwise this "human" would be a monster of some sort). I term this threat the *horror psycho.* But because other genres too have psychos (as does reality), horror must contribute "something extra" to distinguish its psychos from those of mystery, suspense, or the real world. And despite being unenhanced by science or the supernatural, the *horror* psycho must present an *unnatural* threat.

The classic horror psycho may be termed the *uberpsycho.* What makes him unnatural is a superhuman durability and tenaciousness setting him beyond the control of mortals. Indisputably insane (not always true of serial killers in mystery and suspense), the uberpsycho's insanity often originates from a physical or emotional trauma resulting in a severe psychic detachment. He feels neither empathy nor pain. He is oblivious to wounds inflicted upon him. What does not kill him makes him strong. He efficiently executes his victims with a skill beyond that of naturalistic psychos.

The uberpsycho is an impersonal force of nature, sometimes evil, sometimes dark avenging angel. In both *The Burning* (1982) and *Slaughter High* (1987) an innocent suffers extensive burns due to a bad prank, yet despite painful and crippling disfigurement, he leaves the hospital to wreak vengeance upon his former tormentors.

Conversely, the *suspense psycho* of mysteries and suspense thrillers is dangerous, but no superman. Prick him and he bleeds. Spook him and he runs. And though arguably the mundane man-next-door is all the more terrifying because he is next door, his is a different kind of terror. A naturalistic terror that lacks Lovecraft's "suspension or defeat of the fixed laws of Nature." The suspense psychos in *Frenzy* (1972) and *Silence of the Lambs* (1991) are all-too-human. Their neighbors probably described them as friendly, polite, but quiet.

A second unnatural trait shared by many horror psychos is an enigmatic quality. We rarely know the reason for an uberpsycho's indestructibility. In *Halloween* (1978) Donald Pleasence first explained Michael Myers as "pure evil," ultimately allowing that Myers was the bogeyman. And that was explanation enough.

As with many of horror's threats, horror psychos are often scarier unexplained. *Friday the Thirteenth*'s Jason Voorhees was initially as enigmatic as Myers, but as the film series progressed Jason's indestructibility was "explained" as resulting from an electrical storm. This late mix of science (bordering on the supernatural) created a logical mess, pushing Jason close to self-parody.

* Horror vs. Mystery vs. Suspense

Because psychos stalk all three genres, the line can blur between horror, mystery, and suspense. However, because the psychos in the latter two are similar, I refer to them collectively as *suspense psychos* as opposed to the horror psycho.

Apart from analyzing their psychos, another way to distinguish between these three genres is my *timeline test,* an inexact but useful method. Suspense films concentrate on events *preceding* a murder (*Strangers on a Train,* 1951). Horror on the *commission* of the murder. Mystery on events *following* a murder. Suspense films tease their audience with the question: Will X kill Y? Horror audiences already know; they came to watch it happen. Mystery stories begin with the body, asking: Whodunit?

Suspense probes the minds of cat and mouse. Mystery probes for clues. Horror probes the corpse.

Suspense films reveal the identity of their psychos early on, the better to examine their warped minds (*Silence of the Lambs*). Mysterics conceal their psychos for the sleuth to unmask. Horror too conceals its psychos, but for another reason: to empower them. Hidden, horror psychos remain a dark and enigmatic force of nature.

Horror's attempts at genuine mystery are usually half-hearted and lame. Either the "unseen" killer is obvious to audiences early on (so they wonder why everyone in the film is so stupid), or the killer is revealed to be someone so unexpected the choice appears arbitrary. Mystery audiences would feel cheated by such "surprise twist ending" killers. Not so horror fans, who seek a different thrill from horror. They wonder less about the killer's identity than about *Who will survive and what will be left of them?*

Film distributors often misrepresent films according to the current "hot" genre. In the early 1980s horror psychos were hot, so "bait and switch" marketers sold shoddy suspense and thriller films as horror. The skull poster for *Visiting Hours* (Canadian 1982) promised horror, but the film is a feminist revenge thriller in the vein of *Death Wish* and *Dirty Harry.*

Compare *Visiting Hours*'s psycho with Michael Myers. Myers is fearless, potent, enigmatic. *Visiting Hours*'s psycho is early on revealed to the audience, his life and lifestyle stripped to all its pathetic boredom, himself exposed as cowardly and weak, fearful of confronting his female victims. Myers is a dark force inspiring awe and terror. *Visiting Hours*'s psycho is a craven pervert, inspiring disgust and contempt.

As in *The Frighteners* and *The Craft, Visiting Hours*'s potential horror is diluted by its heroine's invulnerability and invincibility (especially up against a vulnerable naturalistic psycho). When the film opens with TV journalist Lee Grant broadcasting a personal crusade against the psycho, audiences correctly sense that the psycho has more to fear than does Grant. No tension derives from worrying over Grant's fate, no more than we would fret over Dirty Harry. Rather than evoking fear or suspense, *Visiting Hours* offers thrills derived from its heroine's vigilante vengeance.

Regarding my timeline test, *Visiting Hours* again fails as horror because it concentrates on Grant's sleuthing rather than on the killings. Yet the film is also not a mystery because we know the murderer's identity, even if Grant does not.

Eyes of a Stranger (1981) is yet another feminist revenge thriller falsely marketed as horror. *Love Boat*'s Lauren Tewes plays a TV journalist who broadcasts a personal crusade against a psycho, a weak and craven pervert . . .

Nevertheless, some feminist revenge films are horror rather than suspense or thriller,[26] although expectedly, horror handles the conceit differently. In *Demented* (1980) the rape victim *becomes* the horror psycho, fearlessly torturing, castrating, and killing her tormenters with easy efficiency, even licking their blood from her knife. As in many nihilistic horror films, *Demented* offers no clear hero/heroine, but rather a horror psycho as dark avenging angel. What sets *Demented* closer to horror than suspense is the female vigilante's psychosis and brutal overkill.

This horror-oriented feminist revenge formula also appears in *Last House on the Left* (1972, aka *Sex Crime of the Century, Night of the Vengeance, Krug and Company*) and *I Spit on Your Grave* (1978, aka *Day of the Woman*). Both have been marketed as horror, although neither have psychos, much less horror psychos. *I Spit on Your Grave*'s Camille Keaton seems near the edge of psychosis, but only *Demented*'s Sallee Elyse crosses the line.

* The Horror Psycho as Apparent Uberpsycho

Some horror psychos are as vulnerable as suspense psychos, but because their identity remains hidden, their murders surprising and unpredictable, they create the illusion of being an indestructible dark force. They appear to be uberpsychos because, unseen, neither victims nor viewers are certain of their strengths or weaknesses.

I term these horror psychos *sociable psychos* because they are lucid and articulate. Unlike Myers and Jason, they function in society. Sociable horror psychos appear in *Night School* (1980), *Curtains* (1982), *Pieces* (1983), and *Psycho* (1960).

---

[26] I differentiate suspense stories from thrillers in that the hero's victory is assured in the latter, as in the James Bond spy thrillers. However, screenwriter Ross LaManna informs his UCLA class that he regards films featuring a "skilled professional," such as Bond or Rambo, to be action films, whereas thrillers involve an "everyman" caught up in events (*Enemy of the State, The Fugitive*).

Whereas suspense films reveal their psychos early on, the above horror films depict the killings without revealing the killer. Yet despite the secrecy over the psycho's identity and motives, these films are not mysteries because little screen time is spent seeking the killer. Emphasis is on slaughter, not sleuthing. Victims are either unaware of any nearby serial slayings, or they trust the authorities to handle it. If authorities are investigating, they do most of it offscreen, only dropping by occasionally to interrogate or warn the heroine. To the extent the authorities are involved, they do a poor job. Usually, the psycho's identify is revealed rather than solved.

Horror psychos are empowered by masks. Their faces hidden, every horror psycho is potentially a disfigured uberpsycho.

In *Night School* Rachel Ward is a bright graduate student of anthropology, inspired by her study of primitive tribes to decapitate competing lovers while wearing a black leather motorcycle outfit, complete with helmet and tinted visor. Thus hidden from the audience, Ward becomes an unknown dark force, just as easily male or female, attractive or disfigured.

Ward's murders qualify her as a serial killer. Her motivation qualifies her as psycho. But it is her dark masked persona that qualifies her as a horror psycho. When she finally removes her helmet and reveals herself to us, she loses her uberpsycho persona. Even after all her butchery, she appears vulnerable, even sympathetic.

Curtains too depicts a series of brutal murders committed by an unseen killer, occasionally wearing a mask. But unlike *Night School,* in which an irrelevant police investigation finally corners the wrong suspect, the characters in *Curtains* aren't even aware that a killer is picking them off. There is no investigation, only a final revelation.

Ignorant victims (unaware of a killer in their midst) are common in horror psycho films. Although anathema to mysteries (because you can't solve a murder unless you're aware of it), this story convention is aesthetically appropriate to horror. Horror's goal is to evoke fear by threatening the inevitable doom of at least some characters, and psychos are more threatening if they stalk victims who are too ignorant to even attempt self-protection.

Another story convention in many horror psycho films is the police apprehending the wrong suspect *at the film's end,* with no time left for remedy (*Night School*; *Stage Fright*, Australian 1983, aka *Nightmares*; *Intruder*, 1989). Or they mistakenly determine the psycho is dead (*Friday the Thirteenth VIII: Jason Takes Manhattan*, 1989), or cured (*Psycho II*, 1983), or gone elsewhere (*Halloween*). More so than in mystery or suspense films, authority figures in horror can't be too competent because it would dilute the horror.

Pieces's horror psycho is even loonier than those in *Night School* and *Curtains.* He's stitching together his own handcrafted girlfriend using other women's body . . . pieces.[27] Even so, he has charm and status. And although he wears no mask, he is similarly empowered by secrecy; his identity is concealed from the audience, his deeds seen only through POV shots.

Psycho straddles genres. It starts as a suspense film, with significant screen time spent on cat-and-mouse events preceding the murders. But the suspense story is a red herring, as the suspense does not build toward the murders. The first murder is an unexpected shock, whereupon *Psycho* shifts gears from suspense into horror. Murders are neither planned nor solved, so much as they are used to shock. The psycho's identity remains hidden until the end. Is *Psycho* a mystery? No, because the psycho's identity is discovered rather than solved. And although a film's style is not determinative of its genre, it's indicative that the art direction and cinematography cast Norman's home as a haunted house.

*** Horror vs. Splatter**

Especially in the minds of many non-fans, horror is often confused with *splatter.*

John McCarty defines splatter movies as those striving "to astonish us with the perfection of their violent illusions, and, at their most extreme, mortify us with the gleefully presented realism of these often disgusting film tricks. Mutilation, or other forms of graphic mayhem designed to evoke in us a feeling of revulsion, is usually the theme; in the lesser of these films, often the only one. . . . Their plots are often openly derivative of other films, and usually dispense with logic or plausibility of any kind. Why? Because plot serves mainly as a springboard from one violent/splattery/FX-laden set piece to the next."[28]

McCarty mistakenly defines splatter and noir as genres,[29] but both are styles rather than genres, because they have no story conventions to call their own. When a genre filters its story through some stylistic prism, its thematic attitude and atmosphere may be altered, but the story remains rooted in its genre and subgenre, be it hard-boiled mystery, horror psycho, or horror/sci-fi. McCarty acknowledges this even as he denies it, writing that splatter is "a genre unto itself which has survived over the years by feeding voraciously off virtually every other filmic form, especially the horror film, a genre which it has all but consumed."[30]

---

[27] A project similarly attempted in *The House That Screamed,* aka *The Boarding School, La Residencia*, Spanish 1969.
[28] *Official Splatter Movie Guide Vol. 2,* by John McCarty, St. Martin's Press, New York, 1992, p. viii.
[29] Ibid, viii-ix.
[30] Ibid, p. ix.

What McCarty fails to recognize is that the reason splatter feeds voraciously off other film forms is because it has no story conventions of its own. Only a true stand-alone genre can make that claim. But he is correct in that horror has made especial use of splatter. This is unsurprising because (1) splatter can heighten both the unnatural and the threatening (e.g., the gory plasticity of the shape-shifting alien in *The Thing,* 1982), and (2) splatter and horror share synchronous goals. McCarty says splatter intends "to evoke in us a feeling of revulsion."[31] So too does horror; Carroll considers impurity necessary for horror, adding that "nausea, shuddering, *revulsion,* disgust . . . are characteristically the product of perceiving something to be noxious or impure."[32] The unnatural is often revolting.

But horror is more diverse and resilient than splatter. Gut-busting gore energizes 1982's *The Thing* with a delightfully revolting slam-bang punch. But 1951's *The Thing* relates the same horror/sci-fi story equally effectively with quietly atmospheric sets and lighting. No bloodied bodies or elastic aliens required. Horror does fine with or without splatter.

And the feeling is mutual. Splatter does not require horror. McCarty cites *Indiana Jones and the Last Crusade* (1989) and *Wild at Heart* (1990) as examples of non-horror splatter.[33]

Horror and splatter are synchronous, not synonymous.

* Horror vs. Snuff

In the minds of many ignorant non-fans, horror evokes images of *snuff.* But horror is not snuff. Horror is fiction. Snuff is real. Horror entices its audience with imaginary threats. Snuff promises reality, its fans encouraged to believe (however falsely) that the onscreen splatter is actual, which is snuff's chief "appeal."

When horror films depict splatter, it's usually achieved via special effects. I say usually, because real gore can also be gotten from stock footage companies licensing film clips of crime scenes, wartime combat, executions, slaughterhouses, surgeries, and autopsies. But when a horror film does contain stock news footage, it's only to support the fiction, not to subvert it. Stock footage is often cheaper than actually filming an event, so low-budget horror filmmakers sometimes try to blend stock footage into the fiction unnoticed. In *Night of the Zombies* (the Italian cannibal zombie film, not the Nazi zombie film) a nude actor was painted to resemble nude tribesmen in some anthropological stock footage. Then this footage was edited into the film to create the illusion of

---

[31] Ibid, p. viii.
[32] My italics. *The Philosophy of Horror,* ibid, p. 28.
[33] *Official Splatter Movie Guide Vol. 2,* ibid, pp. vii-viii, 165.

the actor interacting with the tribesmen. Thus real tribesmen were used fictively, as characters in a story.

Horror does not entice its audience with news footage. *Night of the Zombie*'s aesthetic goal was to hide (not highlight) its news footage's reality. But gory news footage is enough for snuff fans. The *Faces of Death* snuff video series is little more than a compilation of shockumentary footage.[34]

Aside from legally obtained footage, snuff may also be had by injuring or killing real-life "actors." Such films are periodically rumored to emanate from the Third World. This is snuff, not horror.

Snuff falls under what Carroll terms "natural horror," lacking Lovecraft's "suspension or defeat of the fixed laws of Nature," and is functionally closer to reality shows like *Cops* and TV newscasts (if it bleeds, it leads) than to horror. Horror is a scary roller coaster promising a safe return. Snuff appeals to lookiloos and rubber-neckers ogling a freeway pileup.

*** Humorous Horror vs. Comedy**

Is *comedy* a genre or style? A set of story conventions or a manner of presenting them? Both, really. Comedy is *sui generis.* Some comedic formats, such as TV sitcoms, have their own conventions. But other comedic forms, such as parodies, borrow conventions and icons from other genres. Yet because comedies *can* function alone (unlike splatter or noir) comedy is more genre than style.

Horror shares a special bond with comedy. These two emotive genres play off one another. Tension builds into fear. Fear is released through screams or laughs, often both in quick succession.

Yet through this interplay, horror and comedy fight a tug-of-war. This is because whenever comedy borrows another genre's icons, it subverts that genre in the process. Horror can apply splatter or noir stylistics and remain horror, but nothing horrifying remains of Dracula in *Love at First Bite* (1979). Too much humor is subversive to horror, although horror can survive, even benefit from, some humor. So when we ask *Is it horror?* we must distinguish between humorous horror and comedies borrowing horror icons. The first is horror, the latter comedy. This is their tug-of-war.

Here is a test: Does the fear survive the laughter? If so, it's a horror film. If not, a comedy.

The following films all ooze black comedy and dark social satire, but because fear prevails over laughs, they are horror: *Andy Warhol's Frankenstein* (1974, aka *Flesh for Frankenstein, Andy Warhol's Young Frankenstein, The Frankenstein Experiment*), *Mother's Day* (1980), *Motel Hell* (1980), *An*

[34] Although McCarty reports that various scenes in it have been proven fake. Ibid, p. 55.

American Werewolf in London (1981), *Re-Animator* (1985), and TV's *Tales from the Crypt.* But laughter overwhelms fear in the following comedies: *Abbott and Costello Meet Frankenstein* (1948), *Young Frankenstein* (1974), *Love at First Bite,* and *Teen Wolf* (1985).

Another way to distinguish between humorous horror and comedy is *emotional synchronicity.* Unlike comedy, horror synchronizes our emotions with the threatened character. Carroll defines horror as "one of those genres in which the emotive responses of the audience, ideally, run parallel to the emotions of characters."[35] In horror, we fear *with* them or *for* them. In comedy, we laugh *at* them. We fear for Jenny Agutter in *An American Werewolf,* but laugh at any hapless newcomer who espies Herman Munster.

Character vulnerability, so important to horror, is another distinction. In *Andy Warhol's Frankenstein* we dread what will befall the servant at the mercy of the two evil children. In comedies, we know the heroes are safe. Costello can fall from a skyscraper, yet remain indestructible. A far cry from the gory chainsaw realism of *Motel Hell.*

Yet comedy works *with* horror as it does with no other genre. As the above examples show, humorous horror (wherein the horror is not subverted by the laughs) is abundant. The same cannot be said for other genres. *The Hitchhiker's Guide to the Galaxy* is hilarious social satire, but contains no serious speculation on science, whereas there's much horror in *Tales from the Crypt.*

Horror is bound to comedy by a human impulse to relieve fear with laughs. Fear is a fertile womb for laughter. Other genres use humor, but only horror carries an innate potential for humor. For better and worse. No genre other than horror so risks unintentional laughs. Nothing inherently funny about detectives or astronauts, but a zombie or swamp monster is always at risk of shattering its delicate tension at the wrong moment.

William Paul sees another common thread tying horror to comedy, one similar to splatter. And like McCarty, Paul hopes to coin a new genre, calling it the *gross-out movie*, of which he writes:

> A gleeful uninhibitiveness is certainly the most striking feature of these films—of both the comedies *and* the horror films—and it also represents their greatest appeal. At their best, these films offer a real sense of exhilaration, not without its disturbing quality, in testing how far they can go, how much they can show without making us turn away, how far they can push the boundaries to provoke a cry of "Oh, gross!" as a sign of approval, an expression of disgust that is pleasurable to call out.[36]

---

[35] *The Philosophy of Horror,* ibid, p. 17.

[36] *Laughing Screaming: Modern Hollywood Horror & Comedy,* by William Paul, Columbia University Press, New York, 1994, p. 20.

Yet while the "gross-out" scenes in *Animal House* (1978) and *Carrie* (two of Paul's examples) may constitute a style, they do not a genre make. This is because although a story's thematic attitude and atmosphere is altered when filtered through a gross-out prism, the story remains rooted in its original genre. *Animal House* is funny. *Carrie* is scary. Thus the gross-out film is not a true stand-alone genre.

In summary, the bonds between horror and comedy are strong and unique, yet the two remain distinct genres, a film perhaps one or the other, but never both. The determining test is whether the laughs have stifled the fear; whether the horror is subverted by its own inherent humor.

*** Erotic Horror vs. Splatterporn**

Horror also shares bed with *erotica* and *pornography*. This is not surprising because although horror is an emotive genre, it is also a visceral genre. Paul's gross-out, McCarty's splatter, and Carroll's notion of horror as "terror plus impurity" all ascribe a visceral quality to horror.

Consider the bonds between horror and erotica/porn. Both seek to physically stimulate the nerves: erotica/porn to excite the flesh, horror to shudder it. Yet they posit opposing messages: erotica/porn encourages viewers to take it off, horror warns teen campers to keep it on.[37] David Cronenberg has been described as "the king of venereal horror,"[38] an appellation unlikely to apply to filmmakers of most other genres. His early themes may be summarized as the revolt of the flesh.[39] Clive Barker's *Hellraiser* film series threatens with S&M imagery, depicting flesh as simultaneously seductive and repulsive. Porn stars regard horror as their nearest rung up toward legitimacy. Porn actress Marilyn Chambers made her "legit" debut in *Rabid* (1977, aka *Rage*), and Traci Lords's first non-XXX film was *Not of This Earth* (1988).

Fear of sex and fear of death are also linked. "The bulk of academic research on the horror film has looked to Freud and his heirs for direction,"[40] writes

---

[37] E. Michael Jones interprets the entire horror genre, from Mary Shelley's novel onward, as the moral order's reassertion of natural law against its transgressors. *Monsters from the Id: The Rise of Horror in Fiction and Film,* by Jones, Spence Publishing, Dallas, 2000.

[38] *Cronenberg on Cronenberg,* edited by Chris Rodley, Faber and Faber, London, 1992, p. xvii.

[39] "The Visceral Mind: The Major Films of David Cronenberg," by William Beard, appearing in *The Shape of Rage: The Films of David Cronenberg,* edited by Piers Handling, New York Zoetrope, 1983, p. 4.

[40] *Terror and Everyday Life: Singular Moments in the History of the Horror Film,* by Jonathan Lake Crane, Sage Publications, Thousand Oaks, 1994, p. vi.

Jonathan Lake Crane, explaining, "The uncanny may . . . arise when infantile complexes, once banished from consciousness, are revitalized. When fears of castration, 'womb phantasies,' or 'animistic beliefs' are rekindled we are frightened."[41]

We should distinguish porn from erotica. Pornography may be defined as a straightforward depiction of graphic sex with little concern for story or character. This resembles McCarty's concept of splatter as a straightforward depiction of graphic violence with little concern for story or character. Sex and violence are gratuitous, respectively. Not surprisingly, porn and splatter function easily together, creating what I term *splatterporn.* Erotica pays greater heed to both story and character, combining with horror to create *erotic horror.*

As to the question *Is it horror?*, erotic horror is always horror. Splatterporn sometimes is, sometimes isn't.

Erotic horror cinema originated in Europe. "During the 1960's and 70's, the European horror film went totally crazy. It began to go kinky—creating a new type of cinema that blended eroticism and terror. This heady fusion was highly successful, causing a tidal wave of celluloid weirdness that was destined to look even more shocking and irrational when it hit countries like England and the U.S.A."[42]

Vampyres (1975, aka *Vampyres—Daughters of Darkness, Satan's Daughters, Blood Hunger*) is representative of this erotic horror cycle. The film depicts a lesbian vampire couple enticing motorists and hitchhikers into their gothic mansion just off a highway. When the older vampress falls for a man, she determines to keep him alive, and so bleeds him just a bit every night. Weakened and trapped, the man witnesses the vampire couple's nightly sexual blood revelries.

Beautiful and brutal, *Vampyres* succeeds as both erotica and horror, keeping sex, atmosphere, and splatter in perfect balance. Lyrical shots of the vampires traversing a misty cemetery in dark robes accentuate their supernatural ethereality. They are alluring and not without sympathy; yet they remain unnatural threats. "In the blink of an eye Miriam's bloodlust changes her from provocative plaything to raging psychopath."[43]

This careful balance between the sensuous, the surreal, and the savage, expressed with distinct characters, raises *Vampyres*'s sex and violence above gratuitous splatterporn.

---

[41] Ibid, p. 40, n. 9.

[42] *Immoral Tales: Sex & Horror Cinema in Europe 1956-1984,* by Cathal Tohill & Pete Tombs, Primitive Press, London, 1994, p. 5.

[43] *Vampyres: A Tribute to the Ultimate in Erotic Horror Cinema,* compiled by Tim Greaves, Draculina Publishing, Glen Carbon, 1996, p. 33.

Don't Go in the House (1980) is an example of *horror splatterporn.* Its story features a young man whose religious zealot mother (shades of *Carrie*?) burned his arms as a child to drive out the demons. After Mom dies he continues hearing her voice, so he keeps her corpse in her bedroom (shades of *Psycho*?). But because he partially realizes Mom is dead, he's free to take vengeance on other women. He lures victims home and ties them naked inside a fireproof steel room.

Here is where the splatterporn kicks in. The film "treats" the audience to lingering closeups of bound naked women, the camera moving slowly from head to toe, front to back. When the camera finishes examining a victim, the psycho enters wearing a welder's outfit (depersonalized behind his mask). He wordlessly pours kerosene over his victim while she begs for mercy, then torches her. Then the camera lingers over her burning, naked, screaming body.

Don't Go in the House contains some effective horror scenes, as when the psycho imagines his victims' charred corpses approaching him for vengeance. But the repetitive burnings are ugly, mean-spirited, and misogynistic. The clinically photographed and gratuitous use of nudity and gore qualify this film as splatterporn rather than erotic horror.

Ilsa: She-Wolf of the SS (1974) is an example of *non-horror splatterporn.* Its story structure is standard for porn. Ilsa is an SS officer who tortures naked men and women in S&M fashion, in order to prove her "scientific theories" about female supremacy. She castrates men who fail to perform, until she finds a POW with a unique talent: He can stay hard for as long as he likes. Pleased by his ability to avoid premature ejaculation, the well-endowed Ilsa forces him to perform nightly. His sexual prowess buys him time to escape.

As *Ilsa* demonstrates, not all splatterporn is horror. But because many ignorant non-fans equate horror with splatter, they now also equate horror with splatterporn. The *Threat Theatre* video catalog (claiming to specialize in "horror & sleaze," as though they were similar) is evidence of this genre confusion. *Threat Theatre* lumps *Vampyres* and films by Fulci and Argento into offerings that it variously terms "erotic horror, sex, gore, shocks, sadism, sleaze, S&M, sex-n-gore, gore-nography, animie, and Hong Kong action/fantasy/sci-fi." Sex and violence, not horror, appear to be the common theme. Here is one representative example from the catalog:

> *Daughter of Rape* (Hong Kong, 1992) Hysterical rape-comedy-gorefest may be incoherent as hell, never making up its mind whether it is a comedy, a sex film, or a horror film, but damn does it deliver on all three! The movie opens with multiple gory murders which lead to a police "investigation" . . . Pervert cop shows up, grabs corpse's tits, insults grieving family members ("Does everyone in your family have big tits?"), and sniffs dead girl's crotches to "tell if they've been raped"! It turns out that the daughter was

> being incestuously raped and blackmailed by her dad (who takes her up the ass in one scene happily singing, "Row, Row, Row Your Boat!"), and no one in her family would help her, so she killed them all in a fit of rage. Quality sleaze that's a laff riot![44]

Well, I suppose it's some people's idea of a "laff riot." But whatever it is—sleaze, porn, splatter—it is *not* horror.

The many genres and styles with which horror is confused indicate the need for objective criteria in categorizing film genres. I hope I've established such criteria for horror. If I've succeeded, then whenever my above criteria are applied to any particular film, by however many people, the answer to the question *But is it horror?* will always be accurate, objective, and consistent.

[44] *Sex, Shocks and Sadism! An A-Z Guide to Erotic and Unusual Horror Films Available on Video!*, by Todd Tjersland, Threat Theatre International, Olympia, 1996, p. 23.

Horror Goes Hollywood:

A Call for Saturn Reform

The 23rd Annual Saturn Awards show was held July 22, 1997, at the Century Park Hyatt Hotel in Century City. But this report is not about the awards show itself, although it concludes with a list of nominees and winners. But rather, this article explains what the Saturn is, why it's worthwhile, the extent to which it's failed on its promise, and how this failure has hurt horror.

The Academy of Motion Picture Arts & Sciences never extends Oscar consideration to every outstanding film in a given year, although it may claim otherwise, but primarily to films deemed serious and respectable. Despite a rare win (typically in "lesser" categories), odds disfavor comedy, action, science fiction, and horror. Were it otherwise, 1985's Oscar nominees would have been dominated by *The Company of Wolves, The Doctor and the Devils,* and *Re-Animator. The Brood* would have swept 1979. But if they won't let you join their club, you can either cry into your milk or start your own.

Horror's club is the Academy of Science Fiction, Fantasy & Horror Films, established in 1972 by its longtime President, Dr. Donald A. Reed. This Academy presents the Saturn Awards. A Saturn is like an Oscar, only nicer. A golden statuette of Saturn, rings and all. An Oscar is a nude eunuch. Which would *you* rather see on your mantle?

It's difficult to judge films of disparate genres against one another, because different genres pursue different aesthetic goals. The Oscar solution is exclusion. Horror's embarrassment of riches in 1985 were never seriously considered against *Out of Africa.* The Saturn folk are more inclusive, with first two, then three, and now *four* Best Film Saturns. One each for Best Science Fiction, Best Fantasy, Best Horror (which in 1985 went to *Fright Night*), and Best Action/Adventure/Thriller Film.

I have a problem with that. That's one Saturn *too* inclusive. By what rationale does an Academy devoted to Science Fiction, Fantasy, and Horror honor Action/etc.? The first three are all genres of the fantastique, not a patchwork hodgepodge. They share a centuries long history, their overlapping icons busying academics intent upon demarcating genre seams. Action/etc. is an interloper, its Saturn created in 1994 and first awarded to *Pulp Fiction.* Now, I agree that personality goes a long way, but if an Academy identifies itself as one devoted to SF/F/H, its awards should reflect it. What next, a Best Nighttime Soap Saturn?

Another problem is the Academy's wanton standards by which a film may qualify as SF/F or H. Consider the epidemic of action-comedies masquerading as science fiction: *Independence Day, Mars Attacks, Men in Black.* However worthy these films are in their own right (as something other than science fiction), genre purity should be one of the standards the Academy applies when adjudicating genre excellence. Best Science Fiction should mean Best *Science Fiction.*

Some background on the Academy: Anyone can join. Current membership fees are $120 per year, less for students. Members are admitted to (often pre-release) screenings of current films, sometimes a dozen a month, sometimes half as many. All screenings are held in Los Angeles, so if you're commuting from New York or Seattle, you may wish to reconsider joining. However, membership fees are deemed charitable donations (hence, tax deductible), so technically you shouldn't mind missing out on the screenings. It's all for a good cause. Members also get to participate in the Saturn Awards.

Sadly, the screenings reflect two negative trends within the Academy: (1) a shift toward the mainstream, and (2) a concurrent shift toward big studio product, at the expense of low-budget horror.

Even toward the late 1980s, one still saw much grassroots horror at Academy screenings. Low-budget horror such as *Dead Pit* (1989), *Brain Dead* (1990), and *Pumpkinhead* (1988, and whose late co-author, Mark Patrick Carducci, is eulogized in the current Saturn Awards program book). Non-genre films were screened, but SF/F/H dominated.

Today that is no longer true. Almost all screenings feature big studio fare, and over half are non-genre. Grassroots horror, always the genre's most vital lifeblood, is in anemic supply. Only one screening in over six months qualifies:

Texas Chainsaw Massacre: The Next Generation, a darkly humorous and spirited gem, lively and rich with quirky surprises, starring Renée Zellweger (*Jerry McGuire*) and Matthew McConaughey (*Contact*). A few bigger budgeted horror films were also screened during those six months (such as the gut-wrenchingly satisfying *Mimic*), and some big studio nonsense (*The Lost World, Men in Black, Batman and Robin, Contact*).

At least *Contact* is true science fiction. But over half the screenings were of mainstream studio fare. No consistency, no genre or thematic unity, just whatever came down from corporate marketing that week. During that six month period, screenings by the Academy included *Leave It to Beaver, Speed 2: Cruise Control, G.I. Jane, Seven Years in Tibet, U Turn, Face/Off, Operation: Condor, Copland, Air Force One, Hoodlum, My Best Friend's Wedding, Con Air, Out to Sea, For Roseanna, Addicted to Love, Buddy, Dream with the Fishes,* and *Bean.*

Now, I like Britcoms. But I worry if *Bean* doesn't dilute the Academy's *raison d'être.* There's a season for *Bean,* and a season for Royale with cheese, and a season for chainsaws. And the Academy is not the proper time or place for the former two.

One may postulate that Academy screenings only reflect the state of the genre. Certainly, while indie genre filmmaking thrived in the early 1980s with the rise of VCRs, it suffered with the bankruptcies of Cannon, Empire, Film Ventures, and De Laurentiis. Yet grassroots horror is out there, even if much of it goes direct to video. Full Moon, Concorde, and PM Entertainment continue to produce low-budget genre product (even if often cookie-cutter, lifeless, and lacking in vision). So too guerrilla filmmakers shooting 16mm and digital video, many lacking distribution. The Academy should seek them out, or at least welcome poverty row filmmakers who approach them with rough cuts. Does the Academy do so?

In the 23rd Saturn Awards program book, Dr. Reed writes that the Academy "honors filmmakers and encourages them to make quality genre films which are not only popular, but contribute to the arts and sciences." But what is a quality genre film? Is it something expensive, slick, loud, and rife with big stars and big explosions? Perhaps another clue emerges when Reed adds:

> As the Academy is geared to honor, recognize, and promote the genre film, I usually work closely with each studio in promoting their new genre releases. Whether it's providing an enthusiastic audience for an advance screening, or viewing a film to provide a nifty quote for publication, I've found myself working with a staff of studio representatives which are probably the most under-rated group working at the studios, namely the publicists.
>
> This tireless group of dedicated individuals have the job of building public awareness for their upcoming new films. Very often these people brainstorm into the night working on the latest strategy to help sell their

> newest film. It's not an easy task and it is one filled with plenty of stress. They know that their ad campaign could ultimately make or break a film and, with so much money riding on the films these days it's a daunting challenge. My hat is off to these great individuals. This year, we are honoring one of the best in publicity, promotion, and marketing: Edward Russell. Ed has done a successful job at Sony Pictures for many years. He is the recipient of the Service Award this year. Let this award be a symbol for all the work these people do at the studio. This Academy is cognizant of their efforts and we are happy to acknowledge them, especially Ed, for all their hard work.

It almost sounds as if the Academy is an arm of studio marketing. I'm sure it's all very exciting. However, with all due respect for the Academy's positive work, I humbly suggest that an Academy that hopes to honor and encourage genre excellence should perhaps be less concerned with "providing an enthusiastic audience" for studios than with providing discerning genre cinéastes with worthy films. Likewise, an Academy committed to excellence should be less concerned with providing "a nifty quote for publication" than with providing impartial critiques. An Academy devoted to quality should be less concerned with working "closely with each studio in promoting their new genre releases" than with seeking quality films from whatever source. What if a studio's latest film is garbage? Is it the Academy's job to supply an audience, a nifty quote, or help with promotion, regardless of merit?

Studios (and indie filmmakers) should be welcome to participate and support, but not dominate or dictate. Publicists are useful sources of information, but they are not unbiased. Conflicts of interest arise between corporate publicists and an organization with an independent aesthetic objective. What if a publicist has four films to promote that month: one genre, one borderline, two mainstream. A conscientious and discerning genre academy may request just one, perhaps two, films for screening. The publicist may insist on a package deal. Screen all four or nothing.

Academy screenings are rife with non-genre fare. What about the Saturns? Are rigorous standards enforced?

The Saturns *usually* go to genre fare, but even that's beginning to crack in the mania to celebrate studio product over genre excellence. The 1994 Best Fantasy Saturn went to *Forrest Gump.* Whatever one thinks of *Gump* on its own merits, one must greatly torture the definition of fantasy for it to encompass *Gump.* Incidentally, *Gump* also won the Oscar for Best Picture, so the two Academies are beginning to think alike. Nor is this a first. *The Silence of the Lambs* won a Best Picture Oscar and a Best Horror Film Saturn (despite being more of a suspense thriller than a horror film).

All this begs the questions: Why have the Saturns? Why were they established? To seek out and celebrate genre films disparaged by the establishment, or to rubber-stamp studio product? Have the Oscars come around to honoring genre films, or is it the Saturns that have sold out to the mainstream? It weren't always so. The first Best Horror Film Saturn went to *Blacula* in 1972. But today, the two Academies appear to be separate divisions of the same studio, like Disney and Miramax.

The Saturn's genre categorizations seem haphazard. Why was *The Island of Dr. Moreau* nominated for Best Science Fiction Film instead of Horror? Why was *Phenomenon* nominated for Best Fantasy instead of Science Fiction? (Really, it's more of a mainstream romantic drama.) Why was *Curdled* nominated for Horror, but *Bound* for Action/Adventure/Thriller? If *The Frighteners* qualifies for Horror this year, why did *Ghostbusters* win for Fantasy in 1984? Because there were few fantasy films that year and they wanted to award *somebody*? What if *no* worthy fantasy films emerged in 1994? Must the Academy award a Saturn anyway? Even to a *Gump*?

When one year the NAACP determined there weren't enough worthy candidates for its Image Award in a specific category, it nominated no one for that category. Studios preferred the NAACP nominate someone, *anyone,* but the NAACP's decision (1) signaled Hollywood about the paucity of black roles, and (2) maintained the value of the Image Award by only honoring *quality* black talent. Likewise, SFWA members have the option of voting "No Award" if they deem that no book or story merits a Nebula in a given category. Publishers may not like it, but it expresses the SFWA membership's displeasure over the paucity of quality science fiction being published, and it enhances the value of the Nebula.

Saturn reform should adopt that practice. If no Best Horror Film Saturn is awarded in a given year, it will inform the studios (*and* the independents) that their output is wanting. Even if the studios ignore the message, it strengthens the integrity of the Saturn.

How are Saturns awarded? I vaguely recall participating in both nominations and voting while an Academy member in the 1980s. I allowed my membership to lapse in response to what I perceived as a shift away from grassroots horror. When I rejoined in the mid-1990s, I found that members now have no say in nominations, and may only vote in the four Best Film categories; not for any of the people (directors, actors, etc.), and not in any of the television categories).

This year the Best Horror Film Saturn went to Wes Craven's *Scream,* a smartly-alecky (rather than smart) standard slasher effort. Although inferior to Craven's best work, *Deadly Blessing,* is *Scream*'s victory a sign that the Academy is at least reaching out to low-budget horror? Well, no. Craven is now well-established. The studios respect him. I wonder, what if today's equivalent of *Last House on the Left* knocked on the Academy's door? The Academy seems to prefer schmoozing with studio publicists over digging for grindhouse treasures. Which is not to say that studio product is always inferior to that of low-budget indies. *The X-Files* merits every award it gets. I only wish the Academy did more to level the field so we could better see all the players.

I wrote Dr. Reed in June 1997, inquiring about the screenings' selection process, and the history and rules for the Saturns. I also expressed my concerns over the aesthetic direction of the Academy, and my desire to discuss these issues with him. In a brief discussion after a screening, Dr. Reed explained he was too busy to give interviews until after the Saturn Awards ceremony. His assistant, Robert L. Holguin (a Saturn producer), arranged press passes for me and a photographer, for which I am thankful. But a week after the awards, Dr. Reed said he was unable to see anyone in the near future. I queried Mr. Holguin, but he did not respond to my request for an interview.

The Saturns need reforming. They should honor quality genre films, irrespective of distributor or budget. Instead, they seem to concentrate on promoting studio films. I'm not sure if greater participation by the membership would help, not while free screenings are dominated by mainstream studio product. I suspect such screenings attract members who perceive Academy membership as a season ticket to summer popcorn movies. What the Academy needs are members passionate and knowledgeable about SF/F/H. I wonder if that's true of even a majority of its current membership?

Here are my guiding principles for Saturn reform: (1) Only films clearly qualifying as science fiction, fantasy, or horror shall be considered for nominations within those genres. Practically, this means that genres shall be defined in writing, and nominations must justify, in writing, why a specific nominee qualifies. (2) Effort shall be expended to seek out worthy films with small budgets, or films lacking distribution, so that every genre film receives fair consideration. (3) Any genre film shall receive priority over any non-genre film for screening slots, irrespective of production value. (4) If it be adjudged, either through the nomination process or by final vote, that no worthy candidate exists in a particular category, then no Saturn shall be awarded in that category for that year. (5) No Saturn shall be awarded for any work unrelated to science fiction, fantasy, or horror. The Action/Adventure/Thriller Saturn shall be abolished.

If some of these rules are already in place, it is not evident from the nominees. My requests to see the Saturn rules were ignored, so I don't know what they are. I suspect the nominating committees (if there be such), and voting members (in categories other than for Best Films), are dominated by studio employees and those currying their favor. If so, the Academy is a front for corporate horror. Its decline in aesthetic integrity mirrors that of MTV, which has fallen from discovering and nurturing innovative music videos, to promoting politically correct corporate rock. Grassroots low-budget horror films are as scarce at Academy screenings as music videos on MTV.

Perhaps we need yet another Academy, one committed solely to horror. One that works with horror filmmakers, while maintaining a healthy independence from the marketers. We once had that, or close to it. In 1983 four Utah fans founded the National Horror Motion Picture Association. For two years they awarded the Edgar Allan Poe Awards. The Poes for short, perhaps to avoid confusion with the MWA's Edgars. For two years the NHMPA published a quarterly journal, featuring supportive letters from Stephen King and Debra Hill. But it folded, having never grown beyond fanzine status.

Horror needs an Academy to serve as its Sundance Festival. An Academy to discover and screen and publicize the next *Blair Witch Project,* rather than wait for Artisan to do the spadework. Can the Academy of Science Fiction, Fantasy & Horror Films become the Sundance of SF/F/H? Or is it too far off-track? Or maybe the Saturns do accurately reflect the state of the genre, in which case, horror's grassroots need watering. Certainly, there are deserving contenders among this year's nominees, along with much sludge. Much as I liked *Curdled,* someone should have stepped in and said: *Curdled* is not horror.

If you didn't see the 23rd Annual Saturn Awards, it's because you weren't there. At one time the Saturns were syndicated, now no more. During our brief conversation, Dr. Reed said that no network wanted to buy the broadcast rights this year, not even the Sci-Fi Channel. Without license fees to fund the Awards, the Academy instead charged $500 tickets and only those paying could attend. Otherwise, it might have been open to all members, *gratis*.

Do the Saturns represent the best of SF/F/H? Consider this list of nominees and winners. Categories and nominees listed in no particular order. Winners boldfaced. Yes, two Life Career Awards. Are these the best of 1996? Decide for yourself.

* * *

[Addendum: In March 2001, for the first time, I received a form from the Academy entitled: "Academy Processing Form for Serving on Voting Committees for the Saturn Awards." The form stated: *We are currently revising the committees which vote for the Saturn Awards. We request that you fill this form out and return it to us so you may vote on the committee of your choice. Members may serve on one or two committees depending on whether there is space available. If you serve on a committee, you will be sent a ballot allowing you to vote in the specific category of your choice.* Eight committees were listed: Direction, Writing, Music, Costume, Make-Up, Special Effects, Television, Video. The form also requested my age group (under 30, 30-50, over 50), and my genre preferences: Sci-Fi, Fantasy, Horror, or Other. This new committee form is a positive sign; although why should the Academy care if some members like "Other" genres?]

* * *

BEST SCIENCE FICTION FILM:
Independence Day
Mystery Science Theater 3000
Star Trek: First Contact
The Island of Dr. Moreau
Escape from L.A.
Mars Attacks!

BEST FANTASY FILM:
Dragonheart
The Nutty Professor
The Adventures of Pinocchio
James and the Giant Peach
The Hunchback of Notre Dame
Phenomenon

BEST HORROR FILM:
Scream
The Relic
The Frighteners
Curdled
Cemetery Man
The Craft

BEST ACTION/ADVENTURE/THRILLER FILM:
Fargo
Bound
Ransom
The Rock
Twister
Mission: Impossible

BEST DIRECTOR:
Roland Emmerich (Independence Day)
Tim Burton (Mars Attacks!)
Wes Craven (Scream)
Jonathan Frakes (Star Trek: First Contact)
Joel Coen (Fargo)
Peter Jackson (The Frighteners)

BEST WRITER:

Kevin Williamson (Scream)
Brannon Braga & Ronald D. Moore (Star Trek: First Contact)
Jonathan Gems (Mars Attacks!)
Dean Devlin & Roland Emmerich (Independence Day)
Fran Walsh & Peter Jackson (The Frighteners)
The Wachowski Brothers (Bound)

BEST ACTOR:

Eddie Murphy (The Nutty Professor)
Jeff Goldblum (Independence Day)
Bill Paxton (Twister)
Michael J. Fox (The Frighteners)
Will Smith (Independence Day)
Patrick Stewart (Star Trek: First Contact)

BEST ACTRESS:

Neve Campbell (Scream)
Geena Davis (The Long Kiss Goodnight)
Helen Hunt (Twister)
Penelope Ann Miller (Relic)
Gina Gershon (Bound)
Frances McDormand (Fargo)

BEST SUPPORTING ACTOR:

Brent Spiner (Star Trek: First Contact)
Brent Spiner (Independence Day)
Jeffrey Combs (The Frighteners)
Edward Norton (Primal Fear)
Joe Pantoliano (Bound)
Skeet Ulrich (Scream)

BEST SUPPORTING ACTRESS:

Alice Krige (Star Trek: First Contact)
Drew Barrymore (Scream)
Fairuza Balk (The Craft)
Glenn Close (101 Dalmatians)
Vivica Fox (Independence Day)
Jennifer Tilly (Bound)

BEST YOUNG ACTOR:

Lucas Black (Sling Blade)
James Duval (Independence Day)
Kevin Bishop (Muppet Treasure Island)
Jonathan Taylor Thomas (The Adventures of Pinocchio)
Lukas Haas (Mars Attacks!)
Mara Wilson (Matilda)

BEST MUSIC:
Danny Elfman (Mars Attacks!)
Danny Elfman (The Frighteners)
David Arnold (Independence Day)
Randy Edelman (Dragonheart)
Jerry Goldsmith (Star Trek: First Contact)
Nick Glennie-Smith, Hans Zimmer & Harry Gregson-Williams (The Rock)

BEST COSTUME:
Deborah Everton (Star Trek: First Contact)
Colleen Atwood (Mars Attacks!)
Kym Barrett (Romeo & Juliet)
Robin Michel Bush (Escape from L.A.)
Thomas Casterline & Anna Sheppard (Dragonheart)
Joseph Porro (Independence Day)

BEST MAKE-UP:
Rick Baker & David Leroy Anderson (The Nutty Professor)
Rick Baker & Richard Taylor (The Frighteners)
Greg Cannom (Thinner)
Jenny Shircore & Peter Owen (Mary Reilly)
Michael Westmore, Scott Wheeler & Jake Garber (Star Trek: First Contact)
Stan Winston & Shane Patrick Mahan (The Island of Dr. Moreau)

BEST SPECIAL EFFECTS:
Volker Engel, Douglas Smith, Clay Pinney & Joe Viskocil
(Independence Day)
Scott Squires, Phil Tippett, James Straus & Kit West (Dragonheart)
Wes Ford Takahashi, Charlie McClellan & Richard Taylor (The Frighteners)
James Mitchell, Michael Fink, David Andrews, Michael Lantieri,
ILM & Warner Digital Studios (Mars Attacks!)
ILM & John Knoll (Star Trek: First Contact)

Stefan Fangmeier, John Frazier, Habib Zargarpour & Henry LaBounta (Twister)

BEST GENRE NETWORK TV SERIES:

The X-Files (Fox)
Dark Skies (NBC)
Early Edition (CBS)
Millennium (Fox)
The Simpsons (Fox)
Sliders (Fox)

BEST GENRE SYNDICATED/CABLE TV SERIES:

The Outer Limits (Showtime)
The Adventures of Robin Hood (TNT)
Babylon 5 (Syndicated)
Highlander: The Series (Syndicated)
Poltergeist: The Legacy (Showtime)
Star Trek: Deep Space Nine (Syndicated)

BEST GENRE TELEVISION PRESENTATION:

Doctor Who (Fox)
Alien Nation: The Enemy Within (Fox)
The Beast (NBC)
The Canterville Ghost (ABC)
Gulliver's Travels (NBC)
The Lottery (NBC)

BEST GENRE TELEVISION ACTOR:

Kyle Chandler (Early Edition)
Avery Brooks (Star Trek: Deep Space Nine)
Eric Close (Dark Skies)
David Duchovny (The X-Files)
Lance Henriksen (Millennium)
Paul McGann (Doctor Who)

BEST GENRE TELEVISION ACTRESS:

Gillian Anderson (The X-Files)
Claudia Christian (Babylon 5)
Melissa Joan Hart (Sabrina, The Teenage Witch)
Lucy Lawless (Xena, Warrior Princess)
Helen Shaver (Poltergeist: The Legacy)
Megan Ward (Dark Skies)

LIFETIME ACHIEVEMENT AWARD: **Sylvester Stallone**

PRESIDENT'S AWARD: **Billy Bob Thornton**

LIFE CAREER AWARD: **Dino De Laurentiis**

LIFE CAREER AWARD: **John Frankenheimer**

GEORGE PAL MEMORIAL AWARD: **Kathleen Kennedy**

SERVICE AWARD: **Edward Russell**

Planets in Motion

Averting her eyes from the man seated across from her, Lara studied the horoscope on her coffee table. "I can see from your chart, you're a very unusual person."

Marvin paused before answering. "Okay."

"Now, I don't mean that as unusual *bad.* Unusual can also be very good."

"Okay."

"In your case, it's unusual *great.*"

A smug grin. Marvin nodded his approval. "Okay."

Lara saw no reason for his self-satisfaction. He was a porcine creep, reeking of sweat. His corduroy jacket shabby and unwashed. Receding hairline revealing a scabby red scalp.

If only he'd stop ogling her.

Lara knew she was beautiful. Just a fact. Tawny hair, emerald eyes, tanned and toned. She'd almost made a living as a fulltime model, then almost as an actress, then almost as an aerobics dance instructor. Speaking stoically, lest her client infer something from an inadvertent smile or glance, Lara added, "Your Jupiter aspect indicates you're highly creative."

"You think so?"

"The planets say so."

"Sounds accurate."

"I'm not surprised. You're obviously very intuitive, very sensitive to your talents." Lara also knew that everyone in Los Angeles imagined themselves as creative, and enjoyed hearing it confirmed. Along with an explanation as to why no one else thought so.

Lara obliged. "But your talents are unusual. I see immense talent and creativity in your chart. You could doubtless succeed in any number of areas. Writing, acting, the business side. But it's not a talent that the bottom-line people in Hollywood always appreciate, or even understand. You're not always gonna get the recognition you deserve."

"Yes. I always felt I deserved more."

"Yeah, I'm not surprised." Everyone felt that way.

"Show me my Jupiter aspect." Marvin heaved his sweaty bulk forward, straining the springs in Lara's old couch. "Explain to me how it works." Hunching over the horoscope, he leaned into Lara. Invading her space.

Leaning back, away from Marvin, Lara tapped Jupiter with her fingernail. "Your Jovian abilities are obscured by Pluto, a dark planet blinding people to your talents, what you can do for them. So they foolishly pick their no-talent friends, rather than pick the best and brightest."

"Yes! Oh this is so true! So true! What else do you see in the planets?"

"You're unappreciated at work."

"Yes!"

"Unappreciated by women."

"Yes!"

"You have wonderful abilities, but it's almost like, they're suited to another world."

"Yes! That is so true! I am from another planet!"

Lara hesitated. He seemed earnest. "Yeah, I saw that in your chart right away."

Falling back into the couch, Marvin pounded the armrest. "I *told* the Kangarazandan Star Senate you were the right oracle for the job." He groped within his jacket, found and gave Lara an azure business card, writ in silver calligraphy:

LARA LYSETTE:
Wiccan High Priestess! New Age Healer!
Soul Mate Matchmaker! Psychic Visionary!
Tarot Mistress! Professional Astrologer!
By Appointment Only!

Lara glanced at her card, then flicked it aside.

Marvin was adjusting his white sock. "Before invading a foreign planet, we first like to consult its holy people."

"I see."

"We don't want to offend your local gods."

"No, you don't want to do that."

"Mother taught me that."

"Taurans listen to their moms."

Marvin cocked his head, squinting. "Am I still a Tauran even if I wasn't born on Earth?"

"Ah, the planet of your birth isn't important. Since you're on Earth now, Earth astrology affects you as well."

"Okay. I thought so."

Lara groaned. Of all her weirdo clients, Marvin definitely ranked in the top 50%. Lara renewed her vow to move to Seattle. She'd turned thirty last fall. Why kid herself about a Hollywood career? Escape the loonies. Escape the riots, freeway snipers, brush fires, mud slides, power shortages, earthquakes . . .

Escape, before the Big One sundered California.

Only one reason to stay: her rent-controlled apartment, its balcony overlooking Venice Beach. Indeed, time to wrap this session and hit those sands, before the inevitable . . .

"Ahem . . ." Marvin cleared his throat, rumbling piglike. "I was wondering, since you admire my talents, I thought maybe, if you're not busy tonight—?"

"I'm very flattered," Lara snapped. "But I don't date clients."

"Weeeell, but you haven't seen the size of my rocket."

Lara blinked. "Excuse me?"

"It's powered by these two big nuclear balls. You should see how far they shoot my fuel!"

Lara gawked, disbelieving.

Marvin grinned. "Ride my big fat rocket, and you'll feel the Earth move!"

Snatching his horoscope, Lara began reciting her standard disclaimer. "In summation, I see an upswing in your career, but not right away. But within two years—"

"Two years! But the invasion is scheduled for next month."

"Well I am so sorry! But your transits won't support a career change for another twenty-two months."

Marvin cocked his head. "Transits? What's that?"

"They're aspects across time. You calibrate the planetary positions in your natal chart against their current positions, then interpret their angular degrees."

"Well, what's wrong with my transits?"

"NOTHING! They're just not ready for an invasion!"

"Well but," he whined, "*why* aren't my transits ready?"

Lara sighed through clenched teeth. Invent something and be rid of him. And then she was definitely ditching L.A. for Seattle. "See this chart? That's Mars in your seventh house. Mars is a blood-red warrior planet, a great ally for an invasion. But you gotta wait twenty-two months for it to move into Aries, which is ruled by Mars. That's when its influence is strongest. Even better if you wait another month, when Mars conjuncts Pluto, reinforcing their co-rulership of Scorpio. Now, with the moon square to Saturn, trine to the sun . . ."

* * *

Some weeks passed. The clients were weird, but only in the usual way. Weather was nice, as always. Lara forgot about abandoning California and her Venice Beach apartment.

One night, Lara was thrown from bed.

Into water.

She staggered upright, her world thundering, her nightgown drenched. Around her was darkness, the rumble of tearing walls, the clatter of breaking pipes.

Earthquake!

She groped in darkness, wading toward her moonlit balcony, her quickest route to the beach and safety.

The Big One!

She stood on her balcony, wading in six inches of sea water. Venice Beach gone. Where once was sand, was now ocean. The apartment beneath hers, submerged. Its tenants . . .

Damn, she should have moved to Seattle!

A shifting light caught her eye.

Lara watched the moon racing across the night sky, fast as a falling star, pulling the tide, water rising past her knees. The moon stopped, square to Saturn near the southern horizon.

Which was not where Saturn should be.

Lara scanned the sky. Mercury, Venus, Mars, Jupiter, all newly positioned. She even discerned the Martian canals. Mars was not only repositioned along its orbit, it was *closer.* And a new planet near Mars . . . Pluto?

Heart pounding, Lara waded into her apartment, grabbed her files. Pluto should be invisible to the naked eye, as should Uranus and Neptune. But back outside, she spotted two new twinkles in the sky, one blue, one aquamarine. Had she joked about planets exerting greater influence with proximity?

Under a moon twice its normal size, she searched her files for Marvin's horoscope, desperately trying to remember the transits she'd recommended, on a whim. She found his chart, tossed the rest into the current. The only heavenly body still in its proper place was the sun . . .

Dawn's gravity drained the ocean from Lara's apartment, and a noontime sun shone over the beaches of Las Vegas.

Stalking the Truth

About the time Fox Mulder's sister was abducted by aliens, a seasoned reporter was pounding Chicago's extraterrestrial beat. Had young Mulder contacted Carl Kolchak, together they might have recovered Samantha, thus nipping Mulder's UFO obsession early on. That this never occurred may be ascribed to Kolchak's obscurity: His otherworldly findings were seldom published.

Carl Kolchak was the creation of former reporter Jeff Rice, whose novel became the 1972 TV-movie *The Night Stalker.* Produced by Dan Curtis (*Dark Shadows*), scripted by Richard Matheson (*I Am Legend*), it was the highest-rated TV-movie till then, spawning a 1973 sequel, *The Night Strangler,* and an ABC series, *Kolchak: The Night Stalker,* running from 1974-75.

Kolchak pursued a Las Vegas vampire in the first film, an immortal Seattle ripper in the second, and was twice expelled by local authorities. The series found him in Chicago reporting for the INS wire service.

Like Scully, Kolchak never seeks supernatural explanations, yet each week another routine assignment becomes an X-file. He balks at covering the fashion show in "The Trevi Collection," but by some reporter's luck, discovers a model who's a witch. Now he's got his story! Mulder would pay a million credits for such luck. Not that Kolchak's luck ever holds. Either due to political pressure or a disbelieving editor, his best stories are spiked. The truth remains out there.

Chris Carter cites *Kolchak* as an influence, although adding, "sometimes the *Night Stalker* influence is overstated." In pitching *X-Files* to Fox's Peter Roth, Carter suggested that there was "nothing scary" on television, saw this as a window of opportunity, and proposed a modern version of *Kolchak* to fill it.

The X-Files is also indebted to *Twin Peaks,* which broke ground by emphasizing atmosphere over plot coherency (and first cast David Duchovny as a G-man). But *Kolchak* was first to pit modern police, political, and medical bureaucracies against the supernatural. Like *X-Files, Kolchak* was unique in its day. With only three TV networks, all replete with cops and docs, gumshoes and sitcoms, if you wanted a spooky scare it was *Kolchak* or nothing.

To modern viewers, *Kolchak* may compare poorly against *The X-Files*'s slick production values, but *Kolchak* was produced without computer effects and subject to greater network censorship (it's unlikely the quadriplegic in *X-Files*'s "The Walk" could have aired in 1974). While both shows stress creative lighting, set design, and editing, *Kolchak* relies more heavily on these traditional techniques to build its scares.

In "The Sentry," dark lighting and lonely tunnels recall Val Lewton's less-is-more expressionism. And when the lizard monster shatters lights as it approaches Kolchak, it not only makes sense storywise, it also conceals what, even in silhouette, looks like a clumsy rubber suit.

Lacking morph technology, "The Youth Killer" uses cutaways to rapidly age a woman during her calisthenics. Dipping below a railing, she always arises older. (*The X-Files* didn't require morphing in "Dod Kalm" because Mulder and Scully's rapid aging spanned days rather than minutes—so "The Youth Killer's" effects are more ambitious, however cheesy.)

Kolchak is saved from cheesiness by its strongest point, the indomitable and incorrigible character of Carl Kolchak, played by then 52-year-old Darren McGavin. We watch *The X-Files* for its creepy sensibility. We watch *Kolchak* for Kolchak.

Like *The X-Files, Kolchak* reflects its decade. Woodward and Bernstein had lionized journalists in public consciousness (it's questionable if Mulder and Scully could have been heroes when the FBI was personified by G. Gordon Liddy). Yet Kolchak is stubbornly pre-Watergate. He's no journalist; he's a reporter. Lacking Mulder and Scully's advanced education, Kolchak compensates with street smarts. He reflects an era when newspapermen were working class. A Truman liberal with conservative cynicism, stuck in pre-women's lib. Kolchak balks when partnered with the publisher's daughter, is unimpressed with her Columbia School of Journalism degree, and promptly locks her in the trunk of his car to keep her out of his hair. A confirmed bachelor, he recoils from matchmakers. Like Mulder, he has no close ties.

Yet Kolchak is not so much misogynist as wounded misanthrope. His last fiancée was chased away by Big Brother. Aside from the maternal Miss Emily, he trusts no one. He works alone, an outcast challenging the powers that be, sacrificing a normal life for the truth. An iconoclast of Polish extraction, he is purely American.

Rice says *Kolchak*'s theme is the misuse of power. Likewise, *The X-Files.* Carter terms Watergate his most formative childhood event, naming one character Deep Throat. But whereas Mulder and Kolchak both challenge Consensus Reality, Mulder is an insider. Kolchak stands outside, without police backup, gun privileges, or powers of arrest. Armed solely with a wooden stake, his wiles, and the First Amendment.

Kolchak's cynicism bolstered viewer suspension of disbelief. If he bought into UFOs, so could they. Yet his skepticism seemed dubious after twenty monsters. Some contend it doomed *Kolchak* to early cancellation, whereas one vampire pursued episode to episode might have prolonged the show. Although, that *Fugitive* structure didn't extend *Werewolf* beyond one season. (Curiously, Kolchak's vampire and Eric Cord's werewolf nemesis are both named Janos Skorzeny.)

The X-Files borrows both approaches, alternating weekly monsters with a continuing story arc, Scully's skepticism reinforced by a *Twin Peaks* aura of uncertainty. Kolchak's findings were never so inconclusive. He succeeds where Mulder fails. Pity they never met.

But then, Kolchak works alone.

Five Paranoiacs, All in a Row . . .

"I knew the operation was risky, but no one expects to die."

"But you did die."

Frank nodded, sweat glistening on his balding scalp.

Dr. Milo spoke softly. "Go on. We're here to help."

Frank fidgeted noisily in his vinyl chair. "Like I said, I was in cardiac arrest, floating over my body, then down a tunnel of blue light, toward a white light. I met my dead wife there."

"That must have been a great comfort."

"I felt peaceful."

"Good. Remember that peace."

"Even felt bad about being revived." Frank laughed tensely. "Felt bad ever since I got here."

"You mean, since you returned?"

"Yeah."

"Back amongst the living."

Frank nodded.

"Not an uncommon reaction." Dr. Milo glanced among the five somber patients, murky faces under dim fluorescent lights. "Depression is commonplace after the euphoria of an out-of-body experience." He beckoned to an elderly woman. "Tell us about your experience, Marsha."

"I already told everyone."

"I think we have a new member."

A young man, skinny and long-haired, warily raised a hand.

Marsha looked at him. "My experience wasn't so good."

The stark fluorescent tubes underneath the pockmarked ceiling tiles flickered and buzzed. Dr. Milo nodded his encouragement. "Tell us about it, Marsha."

"It seems that's all I do."

"It helps to talk."

Marsha sighed. "Like I said before, I met my dead sister at that white light, but she just waved good-bye. Soon I was beyond the light, surrounded by darkness. I called for help, but there was only . . . I don't know how I knew this, because I couldn't see anything, but I knew I was completely alone. Inside infinite emptiness." She wiped away a tear. "I knew I was in Hell."

"That must have been a terrifying realization." Dr. Milo scribbled into his spiral notebook. "But you returned."

"I thought I was damned for eternity."

"Don't dwell on it. Remember your relief after the crash."

"I don't even remember the crash."

"After the crash. In the hospital."

"It's hard to remember anything. So confusing."

"That's nothing to worry about." Dr. Milo scanned the five sullen patients squeaking against vinyl seats. "Disorientation is also normal following an out-of-body experience." He glanced among his five patients, focused on the newcomer. "Tell us about your experience, Bobby."

"I don't know if this will make any sense."

"Don't worry about making sense. Tell us your story."

"Yesterday, I went out for a walk . . . " He tugged at his faded army jacket, his hollow voice barely audible. "Something weird happened."

"Tell us what happened."

"I felt a sudden blow, saw sparks. Next thing, I'm floating over my body, looking down at some guy searching my pockets! I screamed for help, but nobody heard. I entered the blue tunnel."

Dr. Milo scribbled into his notebook.

"At that white light, I saw my dead mom, looking sad, waving good-bye. I floated through that empty darkness." He looked at Marsha. "Like you said, alone in Hell."

Marsha gripped her handkerchief, her old knuckles bone white underneath the fluorescent lights.

"And then what happened?" asked Dr. Milo.

"The journey ended."

"You left the darkness."

Bobby nodded.

"And now here you are."

Bobby nodded.

"How do you feel about that?"

Bobby shrugged.

"Don't be afraid to talk about it." Dr. Milo perused his five patients. "Out-of-body experiences can be both depressing and disorienting, but you'll find it helps to talk." He looked at Bobby squirming silently against vinyl. "How do you feel about your experience?"

"This is all pretty new."

"Don't use that as an excuse not to contribute. We all talk here. Describe your impression of the afterlife."

Bobby glanced about the office. "Well, this is it."

"How do you mean?"

"I mean *this is it!* I entered Hell, and here I am. *This* is my afterlife."

Scribbling furiously, Dr. Milo scanned all five patients. "Recall what I said about disorientation." He focused on Bobby. "How do you feel right now?"

"Weird."

"Disoriented?"

"Kind of."

"Describe it."

"Like I'm floating, but being pulled back. I hear doctors' voices. I smell medicine."

"That's nothing to worry about. Periodically, subconscious memories from your revival at the hospital will resurface. Not an uncommon phenomenon."

The fluorescent lights flickered into grayness.

Dr. Milo turned to his four patients. "Tell us about your experience, Lisa."

A timid young woman glanced at the other three patients. "I already told everyone here."

Dr. Milo opened a fresh notebook. "Tell it to us again."

The Pragmatic Aesthetics of Low-Budget Horror Cinema

Hollywood money is supposed to result in superior filmmaking, superior to anything independents can afford to produce. This supposition holds true for most film genres. *2001: A Space Odyssey* and *Blade Runner* for science fiction, *Conan the Barbarian* for fantasy, James Bond for thrillers, *Gallipoli* for war films. The slick production values and sheer spectacle in each of these films overwhelm the low-budget indie entries in their respective genres, of which you'll find many forgettable titles at the local video shop. There are exceptions, sci-fi films such as *The Quiet Earth, The Navigator, Mad Max.* But for most film genres, Hollywood studio product represents the best of that genre.

Horror breaks that rule. The bulk of horror's finest films, its most influential, effective, and innovative works, have been low-budget efforts produced by filmmakers who were forced to cut corners. The best of these filmmakers put their technical compromises to artistic effect, their pragmatic choices to aesthetic service.

Night of the Living Dead's (1968) grainy high-contrast black and white images, its harshly reverberant soundtrack, and its rough handheld camera work convey an urgent documentary sensibility, conferring an immediacy to its story and an intimacy with its actors. It's as though we're watching real people in live combat, much as the Vietnam conflict appeared to TV audiences of its day. Yet Romero's choices were dictated by his budget. A meticulously lit color film with slick sound and set design was beyond his purse. Film stock, gore, even the genre itself, were determined by financial considerations. Romero historian Paul R. Gagne writes, "[T]he decision to use black and white was always a budgetary rather than an aesthetic consideration . . . The decision to do a horror film was made purely for commercial reasons . . . Similarly, the decision to take a direct, visceral approach to the gore was purely an attempt to make the film noticeable, to make it the kind of film that kids would tell their friends they *had* to see; it wasn't a political or artistic statement or anything else that critics have read into it."[1]

Yet *Night of the Living Dead* emerged as a horror film classic precisely because many of its pragmatically motivated technical limitations serve aesthetic functions, whether intentional on the part of Romero or being "one of the film's many critical appeals that they stumbled into for simple lack of money."[2] Moreover, *Night of the Living Dead* is but one of the better known examples of the pragmatic aesthetics of the low-budget horror film.

Consider *The Jar* (1984, aka *Carrion*), a surrealistic horror art film about an unassuming young man (Paul, played by Gary Wallace) who chances upon a jar containing a pickled demon-thing. *The Jar* chronicles Paul's progressive mental deterioration as he struggles to understand and overcome the demon's creeping psychic encroachment. Paul is tormented by surreal visions: Blood arises in his bathtub and a boy emerges from the blood; water drips in a grotto; a restaurant wall transmutes into a doorway of glowing pebbles; children ride a merry-go-round; a youth kills a boy in a foggy urban park and escapes with Paul; black-robed monks trudge toward a crucifixion in the desert; during a hairy Vietnam battle, a tuxedoed yuppie sipping wine observes Paul's neighbor landing in a helicopter to rescue him.

Because low-budget filmmakers can easily obtain actors willing to work for no pay or deferred pay (often the same thing), and because unpaid camera crews are often willing to "loan" their equipment into the bargain, securing appropriate *locations* remains one of the low-budget filmmaker's greatest concerns.

Director Bruce Tuscano's outdoor locations are impressive: a Colorado desert; a Vietnam battlefield (albeit a distinctly non-tropical one), an urban park. And as outdoor venues are equally impressive whatever the filmmaker's budget, many low-budget films utilize them (note all the summer camp slasher films). As Roger Corman concurs: "My theory, as I began studying some of my own films that were shot in studios, was that if I continued to shoot primarily in studios, my films would always look cheap. Budgets were so low and the sets we could afford were so small that we'd wind up giving the picture away as a

---

[1] *The Zombies that Ate Pittsburgh: The Films of George A. Romero,* by Paul R. Gagne, Dodd, Mead & Company, New York, 1987, pp. 21, 23.

[2] Ibid. p. 21.

low-budget film from the very first shot. You just knew it was going to be a little picture. If I filmed on natural locations, I wouldn't have such a low budget look."[3]

In *The Jar* Tuscano takes full advantage of outdoor locations when available: He pans across the widely-spaced monks in the desert, then tracks the American platoon's trek along a Vietnam river. He reverts to a tight frame when he must hide his less impressive (or nonexistent) locations in offscreen space.

Aside from the inexpensive majesty of nature, another reason many low-budget filmmakers shoot outdoors is because it's generally easier to obtain permission to film (or avoid getting caught filming) at a public outdoor location than inside a private home, office, or place of business (that you don't own). Easier still when filming at night as there will be fewer cops or pesky passersby. Filming without permits or insurance is termed *guerrilla filmmaking.* An example is *Carnival of Souls* (1962), regarding which Jeff Hillegass writes, "A small crew allowed the filmmakers to sneak in and out of settings in order to grab a few shots, without having to bother to obtain permits and close streets for shooting."[4] *The Jar*'s end credits indicate that Tuscano obtained all necessary permits. Nevertheless, this inexpensive but risky option is why some low-budget films are shot in barren urban areas during early hours, or on remote beaches, or in forests.

Tuscano's *tight framing* merits special attention. *The Jar* begins with an auto accident involving Paul and a strange old man (who resembles *Phantasm*'s Angus Scrimm). Closeups of stationary car lights are all we see of the "accident." Tuscano's frame follows Paul leading the old man into Paul's car, but Tuscano does not show us the accident wreckage, or other cars on the road, or even the road itself. Tightly framed and darkly lit, Paul's car might simply be sitting in Tuscano's driveway as Paul "drives" down the highway, a garden hose showering the windshield to fabricate rain. Later in the film, Paul is "running" in the rain, possibly in the middle of the highway. Surrounded by darkness and a tight frame, he appears to be running in place (as he most probably is), possibly in Tuscano's backyard. Tuscano uses his tight frame pragmatically, to hide artificial locations, yet this artifice (tight framing of incongruous locales) supports *The Jar*'s expressionism.

Aside from tight framing, *The Jar* shows its low-budget seams in other areas. Editing is rough. Paul smiles blissfully, we jump cut to a radically different angle, same scene, and now he's no longer smiling. Other jump cuts leave story elements missing, as though we've skipped over a plot point. Jump cuts are

---

[3] *The Films of Roger Corman: Brilliance on a Budget,* by Ed Naha, Arco Publishing, New York, 1982, p. 16.

[4] *Cinematic Hauntings,* edited by Gary J. and Susan Svehla, Midnight Marquee Press, Baltimore, 1996, p. 23.

underscored by subtle changes in lighting and color hues from shot to shot, within the same scene. It's as if Tuscano used different film stocks within the same scene, or shot on different days and was unable to recreate the previous day's lighting setup.

Seamless editing is expensive. To ensure a final edit without jump cuts, a director will often film several *master shots*[5] from different angles, followed by various medium shots, closeups, and insert shots of that same scene. Low-budget filmmakers may attempt to save on film stock by only shooting the necessary minimum of footage. If they foresee using a closeup in the final edit, they will forego a master shot which might have ensured a smooth transition.

Likewise, while Hollywood directors avoid using different film stocks within the same film (unless there is a specific aesthetic motivation for it, as in *Natural Born Killers*), low-budget filmmakers often have no choice. Film stock is costly, and money can be saved by buying *short ends* and *recans.*[6] Money can also be saved by using film stock donated by studios, manufacturers, labs, cooperatives, and arts councils. Often, a low-budget filmmaker uses whatever he or she gets, making do with film stocks of different ASA from different manufacturers.

Happily, *The Jar*'s unpolished production values aesthetically support the story's surrealism. Paul is battling demonic possession and its concomitant mental breakdown. He laments to Crystal (Karen Sjoberg), his neighbor and nascent girlfriend, that he no longer knows what's real, what's imagined. The deterioration of his subjective reality is effectively conveyed by his (dis)placement in expressionistic locales, and by the jump cuts and changing color hues.

The Jar's soundtrack merits attention: (1) The film seems to have been shot MOS,[7] with the dialogue dubbed in afterwards, and (2) the scenes contain no ambient sound.

Every location, indoors or out, has an ambient sound. Every room "makes" a sound, even when empty and "silent." Professional filmmakers, upon finishing with a location, will record its ambient sound. This way, come time to edit, the

---

[5] A *master shot* is the entire scene filmed in one uninterrupted take, usually framed as a wide shot.

[6] *Short ends* are unexposed leftover film stock that are sold to film dealers (at about 25% of retail value) then resold to filmmakers (at about 50% retail value). *Recans* are film stock that has been opened and loaded into a magazine (the camera's film container) but then recanned, unused. Recans are usually of full or nearly full magazine length, since the roll has not been shot. Short ends are leftover pieces from rolls that have been partially shot, thus short ends occupy less than a full magazine.

[7] MOS means: without synchronized sound. The term is believed to have originated from one of old Hollywood's many German emigre directors who referred to scenes shot "mit out sound." His crews mimicked his accent, but the acronym gained acceptance. *The Film Encyclopedia,* by Ephraim Katz, Crowell, New York, 1979, p. 835.

sound editor will be able to fill in the breaks between the actors' dialogue with the same ambient sound as exists while the actors are speaking their synchronized lines.

MOS filming saves on labor and sound equipment, and is often utilized by Hollywood filmmakers when there is no dialogue in a scene. Not having dialogue to mix, ambient sound can be recorded from any location or gotten from a sound effects library. Only a very low-budget filmmaker shoots scenes containing dialogue MOS, and even then, one can still mix in ambient sound from another source. Yet not only did Tuscano appear to shoot *The Jar* MOS, he also avoided mixing in ambient sound from *any* sources.

Tuscano's unsynchronized sound yields two aesthetic effects: (1) Dialogue is limited. Many of *The Jar*'s scenes only depict Paul and his visions. His screams are easily dubbed. Unsynchronized "voice overs" of his thoughts are used in lieu of monologues; this works, because characters talking to themselves may appear artificial. If necessary, it's best to shoot unsynchronized dialogue via long shots, whence the actors' lips are difficult to discern, or to obscure their mouths if possible. Tuscano sometimes blocks an actor's mouth with another actor's head. (2) The lack of ambient sound imparts a disembodied background silence to *The Jar,* as though we were listening to the actors at high altitude, with our ears congested. And although the dubbing is respectable, it's rough enough so that the unsynchronized voices, conjoined with the disembodied silence, support Paul's slow disassociation from reality. Paul's conversations with Crystal and Jack (his boss) resonate with Pink Floyd's line: "Your lips move but I cannot hear what you're saying." Paul hears what they're saying, but the subtle vocal desynchronization creates an impression that the fabric of his universe is disintegrating. These unsynchronized voices are not noted by Paul, but they lie within the film's subtext, however aesthetically unintentional.

The Jar's lack of ambient sound evokes *Carnival of Souls,* a low-budget film shot largely MOS about a woman whose soul is disconnecting from reality. Although film critic Jeff Hillegass considered lead actress Candace Hilligoss's detached performance appropriate to her role of a lost soul trapped between life and death, he also wrote that, "Much of the audio had to be post-dubbed, which led to unfortunate difficulties in sync which remain in the final film."[8] While I concur with Hillegass's assessment of Hilligoss's performance, I believe the imprecise sound synchronization contributes to the film for the same reason: It reinforces the impression of a soul trapped in an imprecise twilight world, one in which material reality is always on the verge of slipping away. Unfortunately, it is the film's initial scene, wherein Hilligoss is still alive, that is the most poorly synched.

---

[8] *Cinematic Hauntings*, ibid, p. 26.

While *Carnival of Souls* fills its silences with eerie organ music, *The Jar* compensates with discordant sound effects (unearthly breathing, wheezing, and whining), a technique used to greater extent, and greater effect, in David Lynch's *Eraserhead* (1978).

Comparisons to Lynch are apposite. As with *Eraserhead,* Tuscano's images only appear arbitrary. A water motif predominates: Paul running in the rain, taking a shower, blood filling a bathtub, the dripping grotto, the water from the waiter, spilled liquid from the broken jar, even the parched desert. Water often connotes sex, and Paul is conflicted over Crystal, whom he desires but spurns. As with *Eraserhead, The Jar* reveals a fascination with texture. Extreme closeups of Paul's faucet and drain are synched to unearthly reverberations. Extreme closeups transmogrify Jack's cigarette into an orange glow burning in an incongruous black void. For further emphasis, his one act of cigarette-lighting is depicted repeatedly, as is Paul's jar-smashing, thus evoking *Potemkin* (Soviet 1925). Also apposite, because Eisenstein too was a low-budget filmmaker; Soviet montage was developed in response to a shortage of film stock, necessitating creative editing of whatever stock footage was available.[9]

Fewer excuses can be made for Tuscano's occasionally out of focus shots, as when Crystal enters Paul's apartment and the camera tries desperately to bring her into focus. Most likely Tuscano simply couldn't afford a retake. Yet even these blurry images contribute to *The Jar*'s surreal sensibility. Because it is Paul's POV on Crystal that is out of focus, this further suggests his weakening grip on reality.

As with outdoor locations, colored lights are an inexpensive way to enhance an impoverished film. Tuscano makes heavy use of colored lighting, toward two aesthetic effects, both functionally consistent with his story: (1) As in Dario Argento's *Suspiria* (Italian 1976), colored lights suggest the presence of an evil entity. Paul looks in a mirror and sees the old man, lit in blue from a low angle. Then when Jack knocks on Paul's door, a quick flash of blue light from under Jack's chin intimates that Jack is now targeted by the demon; (2) As in Norman J. Warren's *Terror* (British 1978), much of Tuscano's colored lighting is *nondiegetic.*[10] When Paul drives the old man away from the accident, Paul is lit from below in yellow-green, the old man in red-orange. As in *Terror,* nondiegetic colored lights contribute a stylish sheen to this low-budget film's unpolished production values. But more importantly, the colored lights support *The Jar*'s expressionism and Paul's mental deterioration.

---

[9] *A Short History of the Movies,* by Gerald Mast, Bobbs-Merrill Company, Indianapolis, Second Edition 1978, p. 182.

[10] *Nondiegetic* lighting originates from outside the story; most films incorporate nondiegetic sound (as in a musical soundtrack), while comparatively few utilize nondiegetic lighting.

Traditional Hollywood lighting has two aesthetic goals: (1) Lighting should be unobtrusive; it should not draw attention to itself. The emphasis is on story rather than technique, content over form. The theory is that unobtrusive lighting better enables audiences to suspend disbelief and enjoy the story, much as a magic show is more enjoyable if you aren't distracted by the strings.[11] This contrasts with continental European cinema, which has been more experimental, stylish, and self-conscious. Regarding Roger Vadim's *Blood and Roses,* David Hogan writes, "Like many other European directors who have worked in the [horror] genre, Vadim sacrificed logic and narrative at the altar of imagery."[12] (2) Lighting should glamorize star actors (while remaining unobtrusive—audiences should believe the actors are photographed as they appear in real life).

Traditional Hollywood lighting begins with the classic *three-point setup.* A *key light* provides the primary illumination of an actor. A less intense *fill light* shines from some point opposite the key, in order to soften the key's harsh shadows. A *backlight* from behind the actor outlines his body and creates a sense of three-dimensional space. Otherwise, scenes look flat, as in *Blood Feast* (1964, aka *Feast of Flesh*) and *Splatter University* (1984). Flat lighting has long been common to low-budget porno films, so it is unsurprising that *Blood Feast*'s director, Herschell Gordon Lewis, learned his craft on "nudie" flicks.[13]

Three-point lighting is a time-consuming process, made more so because: (1) Each principal actor in a shot must have his or her own key, fill, and backlight, (2) these lights must be reset whenever an actor changes position, and (3) lights other than an actor's "three points" require attention.

Although some of this difficulty can be mitigated by having one light serve several functions in a scene, it requires an experienced (and expensive) crew to quickly set and reset lights between shots. Even so, many Hollywood producers are thrilled to shoot two or three pages of script a day.

Low-budget filmmakers cannot afford to shoot so few pages a day. Ironically, they can even less afford the large and expensive crews required to shoot even those few. Once again, corners must be cut. Regarding lighting setups, Roger Corman was noted for asking his DPs, "How long to get it perfect? How long to get it good? How long to get an image?" Then he would opt for the image.

As did Sam Raimi for *The Evil Dead* (1983). In a scene with a couple on a couch, the harsh shadows on their faces and on the wall behind them indicate a

---

[11] Analogously, traditional Hollywood editing has been referred to as *invisible editing* because its cuts are meant to pass unnoticed by the audience.

[12] *Dark Romance: Sexuality in the Horror Film,* by David J. Hogan, McFarland, Jefferson, NC, 1986 p.155.

[13] *The Amazing Herschell Gordon Lewis and His World of Exploitation Films,* by Daniel Krogh with John McCarty, FantaCo Enterprises, Albany, 1983, pp. 6-11.

lack of fill lights. Although real life has its harsh shadows, such shadows in a film detract our attention from the story. Ideally no item, shadows included, should be filmed unless the filmmaker intends for that item to be onscreen, serving some purpose to the story. In *Evil Dead* these shadows seem sloppy and arbitrary, causing the scene to feel ugly and cheap, like a video shot in some amateur's basement. Raimi correctly surmised that his audience would forgive his unpolished lighting due to *Evil Dead*'s many other merits. The lighting also creates a sense of intimacy with his characters. But such intimacy is easily attained in low-budget films because rough production values evoke a "you are there" documentary/home movie sensibility. Character intimacy aside, *Evil Dead*'s harsh lighting offers little aesthetic benefit to its story, unlike in *Night of the Living Dead,* wherein the contrasty lighting accentuated the story.

Harsh lighting works better in *Children Shouldn't Play with Dead Things* (1972, aka *Revenge of the Living Dead*). Set entirely at night, *Children* opens on an island cemetery, whereon a corpse attacks a caretaker. The scene switches to a small boat arriving from Miami carrying a theatrical troupe and its tyrannical director (Alan Ormsby). Alan (*Children*'s characters share first names with the actors portraying them) disinters a corpse for his play, then has his troupe beseech Satan to raise the dead. Mocking and disbelieving, they expect nothing. But as in many horror films, somebody listens.

Children's budgetary compromises function aesthetically and are complemented by the film's other elements. For instance, the harshly lit contrasts are unsoftened by fill lights. Supporting (rather than mitigating) this is *night-for-night* photography that creates a pitch black canvas to accentuate these contrasts.[14] A single white bulb atop the boat's mast provides the troupe's only oasis against the dark. Lanterns and street lamps pierce the blackness of the cemetery. These stark lights within black night contribute to a spooky otherworldly atmosphere.

Interiors are also harshly lit. When Orville attacks Alan, their stark shadows contrast well against a white wall, underscoring the harsh desperation of Alan's situation. *Evil Dead*'s shadows play against a drab wall, in a murkily dim room. *Children* takes the shadows it cannot afford to soften with fills, then heightens and uses them.

Children Shouldn't Play with Dead Things effectively employs wide-angle lens photography. Wide-angle lenses may be considered the low-budget filmmaker's lens of choice. Compared to telephoto and normal lenses, wide-angle lenses admit more light, thus fewer lights are required to illuminate a set. Wide-angle lenses have greater depth-of-field, so less crew time is spent

[14] *Night-for-night* means filming nighttime scenes at night, as opposed to *day-for-night,* the filming of nighttime scenes under daylight, a technique that cannot capture the true black of night.

measuring and "pulling" focus. Finally, its wide viewing angle is useful for filming within cramped spaces. This may not be an issue for producers who can afford to rent a studio. The camera can always be pulled back from the missing "fourth wall" to view the entire set. But low-budget filmmakers often film in actual apartments or houses, lent by family and friends. They cannot pull back the camera very far without knocking out a real wall.

While *Children*'s wide-angle lens pragmatically captures the proceedings within the confined cabin, it's also put to aesthetic use. Wide-angle lenses magnify images near their surface. After Alan reestablishes his dictatorial authority over his troupe, he adds, "The revolution is dead. Long live the king!" punctuating his remark by thrusting his hand, Nazi-style, toward the lens. Here, the distorted magnification of Alan's hand underscores and adumbrates the perversity and hubris eventuating in his downfall.

Children's producers appear not to have rented a sound stage or, apparently, sound blankets. Thus, interior shots reverberate with that hollow low-budget sound. A lack of master shots yields some rough edits. All this, plus the harsh lighting and amateurish acting, contribute to a sense of intimacy and immediacy that works with the story: We feel we are viewing an actual troupe of low-grade performers preparing for a low-budget play. This rough verisimilitude is then interrupted by some beautifully atmospheric extreme wide-angle/slow-motion photography of arising corpses, reinforced by eerie music and unearthly noises. Besides distracting from the corpses' gruesome but amateurish makeup, this suddenly stylish photography parallels a shift in story, a surreal supernatural event intruding upon crass reality.

Two other examples of aesthetically pragmatic lighting merit attention. Although night-for-night photography typically works better than day-for-night in a horror film (because it better conveys the true black of night), *The Grim Reaper* (Italian 1981, aka *Anthropophagus, The Anthropophagus Beast,* and *Man Eater*) cleverly uses day-for-night photography to simulate lightning: Tisa Farrow (Mia's sister) is chasing Zora Kerova through a forest during a storm. Because Farrow's costume and the trees are nearly white, their images are recorded despite the film stock being underexposed. We see only the bright trees and Farrow, the underexposed surroundings appearing lost in nighttime darkness. But every so often director Aristide Massaccesi (Joe D'Amato on some prints) opens the lens aperture—briefly!—to admit more light. When such instances are synched with thunder on the soundtrack, the impression is of lightning illuminating the landscape. But freeze the frame on your VCR and you'll see the "lightning" is daylight, the entire landscape evenly lit. Compare this to *Suspiria*'s night-for-night lightning when a ballet student escapes through a forest. She and the trees are lit, but the background remains black.

Suspiria's lightning effects are both more realistic and more fantastic than those in *Grim Reaper.* But waiting for real lightning is expensive and the results unpredictable. And simulating lightning at night requires additional crew and equipment. Massaccesi's day-for-night lightning serves well as a thrifty alternative.[15]

Lemora—The Lady Dracula (1973, aka *The Legendary Curse of Lemora* and *Lemora—A Child's Tale of the Supernatural*) apparently intercuts day-for-night with night-for-night photography during Lila Lee's (Cheryl Smith) bus ride through werewolf-infested woods. As with Farrow, Smith is blond and costumed in white, allowing for greater underexposure of film while simultaneously emphasizing Lila's virginal persona. But a more noteworthy instance of low-budget lighting is when the vampire Lemora (Lesley Gilb) addresses Lila in a darkened room. We don't see Lemora, only her burning torch, her voice emanating from darkness. And because there are no lips to synchronize, the scene can be shot MOS, saving on crew and equipment. Even Lesley Gilb need not be present during actual filming. And while Lemora's "voice from the dark" is technologically similar to those "voice overs" that reveal a character's thoughts (a perennial low-budget crutch), its aesthetic application is imaginative and appropriate. What makes it so is its surreal sensibility within the context of a child's bizarre nightmare. Filming this scene MOS not only saved money, it supported *Lemora*'s dramatic premise.[16]

Conversely, a laughably cheesy "voice over" that saves money but contributes little aesthetically is evident in *Return from the Past* (1966, aka *Gallery of Horrors, Dr. Terror's Gallery of Horrors, Alien Massacre, The Blood*

---

[15] Actually, I am assuming Massaccesi achieved this "lightning effect" by opening the lens aperture during filming. It may also have been done in the lab during post-production. However, low-budget filmmakers will appreciate that while post-production work would have allowed for greater certitude and control, opening the lens aperture during filming would have been the cheapest way to simulate such lightning.

[16] Something about *Lemora* invites misinterpretation. The film's been described as "leavened with a fierce anti-Catholicism" (*The Overlook Film Encyclopedia: Horror,* edited by Phil Hardy, Overlook Press, Woodstock, 1995, p. 279). And Barry Kaufman writes "the entire plot of the film reeks of anti-Catholicism" (*Demonique #4,* FantaCo Enterprises, Albany, 1983, p. 3) and recounts Lemora "shedding Lilah of her Catholic inhibitions" (sic; *ibid* p. 4). Yet Lila's guardian is a southern Protestant minister, and Lila specifically refers to herself as a Baptist. Both Hardy and Kaufman state that the Catholic Film Board condemned *Lemora,* but a CFB condemnation does not alter the story, converting Baptist characters into Catholics. Silver and Ursini further obfuscate matters, writing that Lila wishes "to escape the sexual advances of the minister" (*The Vampire Film: From Nosferatu to Bram Stoker's Dracula,* by Alain Silver and James Ursini, Limelight, New York, 1993, p. 194). However, the minister makes no advances. It is Lila who embraces him, while he recoils in guilt and disgust. Silver and Ursini also write that *Lemora* was condemned by the Catholic Legion of Decency, rather than by the Catholic Film Board. On this matter I don't know who is correct; Hardy and Kaufman, or Silver and Ursini.

Drinkers, and *The Blood Suckers*). This horror omnibus includes a story that is largely one strip of stock footage (of a horse-drawn carriage) endlessly repeated while an unseen corpse within the carriage recounts the bulk of the tale. Also consider the stock footage and MOS shots in *Hydra* (1972, aka *Attack of the Swamp Creatures, Blood Waters of Dr. Z,* and *ZaAT*), played over the purple tirade of a mad marine biologist. Nevertheless, while neither film utilizes MOS sequences aesthetically, they both hold certain charms for Z-movie aficionados. Notably, *Return from the Past* features John Carradine and Lon Chaney Jr.

Although a monograph on film aesthetics typically emphasizes technical issues (probably because the technical is what distinguishes cinema from theater), attention should also be paid to acting and writing. In the art of low-budget horror cinema, few excuses can be made for compromising on either.

Skilled actors of every "type" are available, union and non, who are willing to work unpaid for the chance to be seen. Even small towns often have community colleges with theater departments full of trained talent. And if a low-budget filmmaker can't find appropriate talent, he can still *tailor the script* to his cast's abilities. Not every actor can deliver a subtle performance, but most can deliver *something.* Thus, a horror scripter may foresee and allow for characters to be played in a "bad" hammy fashion. Consider the "bad actor" characters in *Children Shouldn't Play with Dead Things,* appropriately portrayed by bad actors. Also consider the hammy delivery of lines in the *Friday the Thirteenth* film series ("You're doomed! Doomed!") and *Intruder* ("I'm just crazy about this store!").

A scripter may even "spoof" the genre, utilizing poor acting as a source of comedy. But a caveat: Bad acting and incompetent moviemaking have limited comedic appeal, otherwise video stores would teem with amateur home videos. Cheapo "spoofs," "sendups," and "takeoffs" of famous films or cultural icons rarely result in a comedy classic such as *This Is Spinal Tap,* but more often in something unwatchable.

Tailoring a script to a limited budget may be a filmmaker's most pragmatic "compromise." A completed film is a work of art, be it good or bad. The elements within that film "work" only to the extent that they contribute toward achieving the film's goals. Those goals are set by the script. The script establishes the themes and ideas to be communicated and the emotions to be conveyed, then it charts the dramatic events through which those themes, ideas, and emotions emerge.

Additionally, and perhaps unfairly, while good writing benefits all films, low-budget films need it more. Shortly after the release of *Twister,* a column in *Daily Variety* mocked the dialogue in many of 1996's summer blockbusters, replete with lines such as "Watch out!" and "Hurry!" and "Look out—run, run!" It's evident from the success of such extravaganzas that a large segment of the audience is satisfied with simple pyrotechnics, the actors existing mainly to provide a vantage point from which to view the destruction caused by twisters, dinosaurs, aliens, lava, rockets, and bombs.[17] This is all well and good for the major studios. But because low-budget producers can at best afford only cheesy stock footage of mass devastation, the quality of dialogue assumes greater importance.

Bad dialogue costs the same as good dialogue. A clever line is no more expensive to type than lame remarks. Much of *Re-Animator*'s (1985) widespread appeal lies in its sharply scripted black humor ("Who's going to believe a talking head? Get a job in the circus!"). Dialogue also enriches a film with its subtext. The dialogue in *Deathdream* (1972, aka *The Night Walk, Dead of Night, The Night Andy Came Home,* and *The Veteran*) functions on two levels: It relates the story of a KIA Vietnam vet returned as a vampire, and it comments on the war. When Andy (Richard Backus) murders his family physician, he punctuates it with, "I died for you, Doc. Why shouldn't you return the favor?" And when the decaying Andy finally surrenders to his grave, his mother rationalizes, "Andy's home. Some boys never come home."

A clever script is a filmmaker's cheapest budgetary compromise because it is no compromise at all. Even as crowds flock to expensive spectaculars, a concurrent boom in low-budget independent fare indicates that audiences still appreciate small films with fresh stories. In pragmatic terms, this means that horror filmmakers should write or buy the highest quality scripts possible, compromising only to the extent of tailoring its elements to the best locations, crew, equipment, and actors they can afford. To the extent the final technical execution supports the dramatic vision, the film works aesthetically.

---

[17] The storyline of almost every Hollywood summer popcorn movie can be summarized as: Beautiful people engage in sex and high-speed chases amidst huge explosions.

The Actor as Horror Villain

A pretty young blond production manager rejects an actor's amorous advances, so she may finish her paperwork. After he departs, the lights go out. Now alone in a darkened theater, she groans, "Bloody actors, all the same. Bloody kids." Dismissing what would be a portent in any slasher film (in this case, *Stage Fright,* aka *Nightmares,* Australian 1983), she merely notes what others have long observed: The acting field attracts a strange crowd of neurotics. And as neurosis is one step short of psychosis, actors make for natural and colorful horror film villains.

Stage Fright was produced at the peak of the 1978-86 slasher cycle, and it follows form. A little girl, Helen, is traumatized upon seeing her mother fornicating with a man. Later, Helen's unsuspecting daddy bids goodbye as Helen and mommy drive off. That night, Helen awakens in the back seat to espy the man fondling mommy's thighs while she's driving. Helen panics and intervenes. Mommy is thrown through the windshield in the resulting accident. When Helen tries to drag mommy back into the car, she inadvertently slits mommy's throat against windshield shards.

Recovering in a hospital, Helen overhears a nurse mention that she killed her mom. Daddy accuses Helen likewise, apparently ignorant or indifferent that his daughter was defending him from cuckoldom. With all that guilt and ingratitude, what's a girl to do?

Helen attacks a hospital employee with a glass shard.

Upon growing up, she pursues a career in acting. Played by Jenny Neumann (*Hell Night*), the adult Helen is cast in a theatrical "comedy about death."

Actors hide in their roles and Helen is always in character. The character she portrays onstage, and the character of normalcy offstage. In her offstage role, Helen evokes Norman Bates. She strives to remain self-possessed but lives on an emotional edge, her composure masking inner turmoil. Like Norman, she fears her sexuality. She tells Terry, a fellow actor, that she's "Never had a boyfriend. Never been allowed." Suppressing her trauma, Helen allows Terry to kiss her. It's not something she allows lightly. So when she catches Terry peck the production manager at lunch, Helen bolts from the cafeteria, distraught. Terry follows her to her apartment, outside of which he hears Helen arguing.

"I trusted him!" Helen screams.

"Then you're a fool!" a deeper voice responds.

When Helen leaves, Terry knocks on the door. If you've seen *Psycho,* you won't be surprised to learn that no one answers.

Helen also dreams. Dreams of death. Which is curious, because a string of murders is plaguing the theater. When Helen relates her nightmares to Terry, he responds, "You're strange." No kidding.

This exchange occurs in a park. The scene's tightly framed shots indicate the filming was done *sans* permit, passersby just beyond frame. Such tight shots enhance our intimacy with *Stage Fright*'s characters, while fostering a claustrophobic atmosphere. Yet despite the aesthetically beneficial result (beneficial because the claustrophobia enhances the horror), the framing was likely pragmatic. The frame widens whenever there is nothing to hide, as when filming the actors performing on stage. The frame tightens again when the director (George) approaches the stage to thunderous applause. That, and the low camera angle framing his head with the ceiling "behind" him, both emphasizes his vanity and effectively hides the empty theater. (Extras cost money.) The shot simultaneously serves the pragmatic need to conceal an empty theater and the aesthetic goal of illustrating George's character.

Another example of *Stage Fright*'s pragmatic aesthetics is how it avoids aiming the camera into a nonexistent audience by instead shooting the play's rising and falling curtain from myriad stylized angles. These camera angles not only hide the empty theater, but they effectively underscore the emotionally erratic life of actors.

Harsh lighting, because it evokes documentaries, creates a concrete immediacy that heightens intimacy with a film's characters. *Stage Fright*'s characters benefit from such harsh lighting, even if only lit that way because the filmmaker had little time for complicated lighting setups. Stock footage of theater crowds pads the film, along with canned crowd murmur. Offhand remarks mixed into the murmuring are not attributable to any specific theatergoer.

Despite (or perhaps because of) low-budget restraints, *Stage Fright* conveys a poetical lyricism. Scenes are quick, often just a line or two, fading in and out in rapid haiku succession. Helen begins a scene by saying to Terry, "I can't love you. Much as I want to, I can't."

"I can love you," he responds.

"You fool. Cathy won't let you." Fade out.

This minimalist approach, fading in and out of brief scenes, was used to great poetic effect in *Stranger Than Paradise* (1984). Jim Jarmusch developed it due to budget constraints, filming *Stranger Than Paradise* piecemeal, as money was raised.

Stage Fright's stereotypical characters drawn from the world of Theater jell well with what remains a traditional slasher film. Their superstitions and neuroses form the subtext for the slasher's psychosis. An actress traumatizes her peers by whistling backstage. After one murder, she is reminded, "You're to blame! You whistled! This production's jinxed!" George is shocked upon seeing an actor in green ("Never wear green!"). When not insulting his actors, he spouts artsy-fartsy gobbledygook. "The meaning of the lines don't matter. It's the juxtaposition and rhythm of the words." A foppish critic (Bennett) delights in writing negative reviews and propositioning both actors and actresses alike.

Stage Fright applies standard slasher film aesthetics to its theatrical milieu. POV shots conceal the killer's identity. Jarring melodramatic music heralds ominous events. Characters turn stupid at the most inopportune times. The drunken Bennett, staggering through the theater's basement just as the killer bursts through a glass door, simply remarks, "Jesus, why'd you do that for? You scared the fucking daylights out of me." But instead of fretting over this unusual entrance, Bennett ignores his own query and adds, "Well don't just stand there. Help me find my lighter."

Whereupon the killer picks up a glass shard . . .

Her identity is obvious, although *Stage Fright* does end on a surprise twist, similar to that in *Intruder* (1989). *Stage Fright* is marred by crass sadism (victims require prolonged and repeated stabbings to die) and gratuitous nudity, but is an overall enjoyable excursion into the world of Theater, delineating all of its backbiting jealousies, backstage gossip, and petty power politics within a slasher film context. Jenny Neumann makes for a plucky Helen.

While *Stage Fright* concerns an actress at the start of her career, *Curtains* (Canadian 1982) regards a fortysomething actress at her peak and imminent decline (Samantha Sherwood, played by Samantha Eggar). *Curtains* also examines two Hollywood customs practiced mostly by men: Riding a superstar wife's coattails to success, and dumping an aging wife. These aren't necessarily identical. The discarded wife is often a quiet helpmate, not a star. But *Curtains* combines the themes, to fine effect.

Samantha Sherwood buys the film rights to *Audra* (a hot play about a psychotic) for director Jonathan Stryker. It remains unclear whether they are (were?) married, but it seems they shared "something." A house in the wintry woods, for instance.

Feigning insanity, Samantha checks into an asylum to better understand her Audra character. Jonathan leaves her there to rot and sets about casting for a new and younger Audra. Six nubile actresses are scheduled for "a weekend audition at his house." An unknown woman (we never see her face) breaks Samantha free of the asylum. Samantha arrives at the house to audition.

Everyone playacts in *Curtains,* on and off stage. Samantha feigns insanity, Jonathan feigns his intent to release her. An actress is "raped" by a burglar, who turns out to be her boyfriend playacting their usual sex game. O'Connor (the comedian in the group) playacts sex games with hand puppets, the dog cajoling a snake to "give head." Like many comedians, she hides her pained neuroses and burning ambition behind jokes. When the ice-skater discovers Jonathan and Samantha arguing, Jonathan claims they were rehearsing an old play. After Jonathan abuses O'Connor during an interview, she accuses him of playing directorial mind games. He smiles, mum. When Brooke becomes hysterical, claiming to have seen a severed head in her toilet, O'Connor accuses her of "putting on a show, acting like Audra."

Curtains is about people so desperate to "make it" in Hollywood that they are always "in character," their personal identities as contrived as the characters they portray, their selves hidden behind curtains of their own making. After Jonathan has Samantha audition in a crone mask, he yanks off the mask, forces Samantha to face a mirror, and states, "This is a mask too."

Curtains examines those willing to do anything to "make it." It's the theme of O'Connor's standup act. "Have you ever wanted something *so bad* you would do anything to get it? Me, I wanted to be an actress. I wanted to be in pictures so bad, I screwed the guy from Fotomat." Hollywood encourages self-deception, and with this attitude the playacting is constant. One is always in character, projecting an image, the Self ever more elusive.

Samantha suffers and sacrifices to maintain her star status, including a sojourn in the asylum. But the stay affects her, the patients both frighten and move her ("So sad. Even when they're laughing they're sad."). She advises O'Connor to forego a career in show business, to "get married and grow old together."

O'Connor suspects Samantha of trying to thin the competition, but more likely Samantha is stating what she might do if she could begin again.

Curtains is an effective slasher film. The wintry location creates a coldly beautiful isolation, reminiscent of *The Shining, Ghost Story,* and *The Brood* (the latter also featuring Eggar). The slasher's crone mask, worn to hide her identity, also augurs these pretty young actresses likely fate, when they too will be discarded. Killings are stylized, shot with lyrical slow-motion. One actress is chased backstage amid mannequins, discovering a dead actress hanging among them (sagacious commentary on Hollywood's meat market?). The subsequent stabbings (off camera) are punctuated by quick jump cuts amid the mannequins. Unlike many slasher films, *Curtains*'s killer is difficult to identify (there's a reason for that).

Curtains also functions as commentary on Samantha Eggar's own career. Named Best Actress at Cannes for her work in *The Collector* (1965), she has gone to slumming in Canadian slasher fare (much to the benefit of the genre). Notably, Eggar's character shares her first name. *Curtains* has other curious "insider" attributes. Actor John Vernon portrays the fictitious Jonathan Stryker, yet *Curtains* is credited to director "Jonathan Stryker." (Actually directed by Richard Ciupka).

Curtains opens with Samantha playacting a scene from *Audra*. She finds closure by performing the scene for real. What has she learned? "That an actress must always be in control," she tells O'Connor. It may be for naught. The final survivor in *Curtains,* the one who has what it takes to "make it" to the end, ends up in an asylum.

Stage Fright depicts acting as a refuge for neurotics, their quirks hidden behind roles onstage or as artistic eccentricities offstage. *Curtains* portrays acting as an outlet for destructive ambitions, a magnet for incomplete people. *Terror* (British 1978) portrays actors as weak victims, easy targets for dark supernatural forces. Hardly a new insight, the theme was used to great effect in *Rosemary's Baby* (1968) wherein an actor sold his wife's womb to Satan for a film role.

Terror comes at the tail end of the *Rosemary's Baby/Exorcist* demonic horror cycle. Its opening scene in seventeenth century England evokes Hammer's supernatural period pieces. As a witch burns at the stake, she implores Satan to curse all members and descendants of the witch hunter's family. Soon resurrected, she strangles the witch hunter and decapitates his wife (Mary Maude, the brown-bloused, sado-fascistic lesbian in *The House that Screamed,* aka *The Boarding School,* Spanish 1969).

We then discover we've been watching a "film within a film" produced by James (John Nolan) and screened at his home in Buttercup Lodge. (The Brits have a habit of naming their houses.) James informs his party guests his film is based on fact. He is the witch hunter's last living direct descendent, his cousin Ann (Carolyn Courage) his only living blood relative.

Talk turns to the supernatural, and to parlor tricks. When Gary pretends to hypnotize Carole, glass shatters throughout the house; the proverbial "opening to the other side." Ann grasps Gary's arm ("She's got a grip like steel!")

demanding that she be hypnotized. To his own amazement, Gary succeeds, unleashing something else in the process. Entranced, Ann attacks James with the sword used in his film, the sword used by the witch three centuries earlier. Subdued and failing to kill James, Ann bolts Buttercup Lodge.

Later that night, *somebody* stabs Carole to death.

Terror plays on the reputation of actors for being flaky, unpredictable, unstable. Ann is an actress, as are her roommates (Viv, Susie), as was Carole. Like *Stage Fright*'s Helen, Ann runs home in a rainstorm, arriving flustered and soaked and not quite remembering what happened. This, on the night of Carole's death. Which is problematic, because Susie notices blood on Ann's hands.

James frets that he knows little about Ann, having only met her last week. Ann never again enters a trance after that night at Buttercup Lodge, yet her roommates worry as others around Ann die violently. An intense introverted brunette, Ann is nice, but quiet. The sort who keeps to herself. As an actress, she shows little ambition, forfeiting auditions so she can concentrate on her day job serving drinks at a strip club ("At least there I don't have to think."). She often broods, a trait she shares with James.

Yet suspicions of Ann are unjustified. Ann is more victim than villain. She frets over her memory loss and suspects the worst. She may have been a conduit for the witch's entry into the present, but Ann isn't possessed. If characters are confused as to Ann's role in the deaths, it's partially because the script is confusing.

If the witch cursed direct descendants, why does she target Ann as well as James? Why kill non-family members before going after Ann and James? Why kill anyone who suspects Ann? Why kill a club patron who offends Ann? Why kill Carole? And if Ann is an instrument of the witch, what of James? James sees a klieg light about to drop in his studio, its ropes loosening as he watches, yet he says nothing, allowing the light to fall on and injure a porn director he wants evicted. Why is the witch helping James manage his studio? An angry glance from either Ann or James can bring death, and neither seems aware of it. If the witch wants to destroy Ann and James, why destroy their enemies?

As best can be determined, Gary unleashed the witch's spirit by hypnotizing Ann (redundant, because Ann was already possessed, as evidenced by her supernaturally strong grip). Afterwards, the witch kills everyone within vicinity of James or Ann. The witch's motive is that she's evil, and dammit, that's what evil spirits do. This simplistic motivation makes her a forerunner to the subsequent decade's slashers, who kill "because he's crazy, and dammit, that's what crazy people do."

Despite some gaping plot holes, *Terror* is stubbornly stylish and enjoyable. Its credits open over eerie music and alternating red, sepia, and aqua-green colors that also suffuse many scenes. Often the lighting makes no dramatic sense, but creates a stylish supernatural atmosphere. James's partner is attacked and captured in a film stock vortex (visually evocative of the unexplained razor wire in *Suspiria,* Italian 1976), then swept through a Rube Goldberg's chain of horror culminating in his decapitation in a freak guillotine accident. Viv spots blood dripping from the ceiling, coming from the room upstairs. Susie goes up to investigate (climbing *two* flights?!) only to discover a can of spilled red paint. A behind-the-scenes look at the making of a porn film is cute and comedic. A Norma Desmond-type who lives in the boarding house with the actresses relates her future projects and current admirers, all illusory. She is both colorful comic relief, and a painful reminder to the young women of their potential future.

For some indiscernible reason, cars are a motif. Susie's car stalls near Buttercup Lodge. She breaks into the house, calls a mechanic, and is frightened by his arrival. A policeman is attacked and killed by his driverless squad car. Ann is safe riding the tube (subway), but once on foot to Buttercup Lodge, she is harassed by gusts. So she breaks into a deserted car on the road. The car levitates, spins, then drops to the ground. Maybe there's a unifying theme to all this. Or maybe it's just that European cars are so lightweight, they make for easy props.

Curtains makes a statement on the acting profession, however unoriginal. *Terror* is more form than substance, stylishly integrating the erratic lives of actors with the chaotic havoc of the supernatural. Its director, Norman J. Warren, also shot *Satan's Slaves* (1976), *Prey* (1977), and the excellent *Inseminoid* (aka *Horror Planet* 1980), the latter a sci-fi slasher film.

But horror's most colorful actor-as-villain is Edward Lionheart (Vincent Price) in *Theater of Blood* (aka *Much Ado About Murder,* British 1972). A hammy Shakespearean actor who botches his suicide attempt after being denied a Critic's Circle award, Lionheart uses his second chance at life to kill his critics by methods drawn from Shakespeare's plays. The deaths are gruesome and inevitable, taking up much screen time. This is why *Theater of Blood,* although arguably a suspense film, may be regarded as horror. Albeit, a horror/black comedy.

Lionheart is the actor as egomaniac, a male Norma Desmond. Opening credits play over old silent film footage of Shakespearean actors. While nothing in *Theater of Blood* indicates that Lionheart ever worked in film (it's stated he never performed anything other than Shakespeare), Lionheart, like Desmond, belongs to an earlier era. Silent cinema and old theatrical productions encouraged melodramatic performances. The rise of the Method in the 1950s popularized a more "natural" acting, often derided by practitioners of "classical theatrical style" as producing actors who dressed dirty and mumbled incoherently. (Marlon Brando and James Dean were accused of such.) Lionheart accuses his critics of denying him the award to give it to a youth "who can barely grunt his way through an incomprehensible performance."

Lionheart's egomania is manifest when he kills one critic by cutting out his heart, thereby altering *The Merchant of Venice.* Lionheart's arch-foe, critic Peregrine Devlin (Ian Hendry) remarks, "Only Lionheart would have the temerity to rewrite Shakespeare." Not having a son to christen Edward Jr., Lionheart names his daughter Edwina (Diana Rigg). That Lionheart wanted a son is implied by Edwina's usual disguise of male clothing and mustache, by her incessant (insecure) desire to please him, and by finally dying happily in his appreciative arms, happy to have served him well.

A darkly comic commentary on the shared egomaniacal roots of artists and political activists is drawn when Lionheart concludes a thunderous oratory to his ragged street devotees, followed by a recording of a speech by Hitler (a former artist) inadvertently played on Lionheart's applause machine.

Theater of Blood depicts an actor's exaggerated view of critics. They can afford expensive homes and lavish offices, exploit young actresses for sex, and expend more effort in writing clever insults than in staying awake to see a complete play. They enjoy hurting actors. Devlin confesses to the detective inspector that when Lionheart broke into the Critic's Circle meeting after losing the Best Actor Award, they had fun at his expense.

Critics are twice criticized for their abuse of power. Once when the detective inspector suggests motives for why someone may want to kill them. And once when Lionheart justifies his murders to Devlin. In both instances, the point is made that a negative review can close a production, ruin reputations, bankrupt people, destroy lives. Few, if any, critics wield such power today (perhaps more so in theater than in film, more so in Britain than in the U.S.). But to insecure actors in an insecure profession, reviews take on exaggerated importance.

If Lionheart is an egomaniac, his critics are worse. They too have egos, but they lack Lionheart's cunning intelligence and perverse imagination. One lecherous old man readily accepts that a young actress (Edwina) is flirting with him. Another is unsuspicious when Lionheart selects him alone to report the exclusive story of Lionheart's comeback. Another sees nothing amiss with a TV crew arriving unannounced at his house, himself the center of attention. Another shrugs off Princess Margaret's hairdresser coming in after-hours, especially for her. Another agrees to help police evict squatters, because the police need someone with an air of authority (something the police lack!). All traps by Lionheart, all successful because these critics' egos block their brains.

The one critic who survives is Devlin, who doesn't trust Edwina's pretty but frightened daughter act. Devlin tells her there is a homing device in the car's glove compartment, but not about the police constable in the trunk. He is also the only critic, of those given time to recant, who refuses to revise his opinion of Lionheart's performances (all others deny their past reviews or readily agree to Lionheart's revisions).

There is a nascent astrology motif. One critic's wife cautions him about his horoscope. Another critic wears a huge gold Scorpio medallion around his neck. Most likely, these references merely reflect the period.

Theater of Blood's gruesome murders are leavened with campy black comedy. Even as Lionheart decapitates one critic, he rolls eyes at Edwina's theatrical handling of medical instruments. A stage father critiquing his daughter's performance in his show. And Lionheart's forcing one effete critic (Robert Morley) to eat his poodles, baked in a pie, is classic horror black comedy.

Theater of Blood is a sumptuous production with lavish sets and costumes. Extreme high and low camera angles heighten the melodrama. The sudden switch from a straight-on to extreme high angle, just as the critics open the drapes to view Lionheart set to jump off the balcony, creates an impression that we are looking down onto a stage with the curtain opening upon a performance. Anthony Greville-Bell's literate script artfully integrates select Shakespearean dialogue into contemporary proceedings that are alternately macabre, comic, or poignant. The music supports the story, shifting from gentle to dramatic as required, without ever overwhelming events onscreen. However melodramatically the music swells, Lionheart matches it. Vincent Price shines.

A year later, tables were turned on Price in *Madhouse* (1972, aka *The Revenge of Doctor Death*). In this film, Price is a has-been horror film star victimized by frustrated writer Peter Cushing. Yet while vengeful writers have their own subgenre, *Theater of Blood*'s enduring fame compared to *Madhouse*'s relative obscurity demonstrates why actors get the glory while writers more often toil in anonymity. Lionheart's extroverted exuberance, shameless scene-stealing, and indestructible ego is a crowd-pleaser, easily steamrollering over the vengeance meted out by cool Cushing's introverted writer. As the tabloids have long known, actors make for colorful villains, which is why they get the cover while writers must settle for a byline.

The Lady Who Ate Dolls

"Bixby's really quite stupid. But he's so pushy. Sticking his face everywhere. Trying to get our boss to notice him. He steals my ideas. He steals a lot of things from me."

"Did you complain to your boss?"

"No. It wouldn't do any good. He hates me."

"But I don't hate you, Arthur. You were right to come to me. I can help you."

"I believe you." Arthur shifted on the low cushion, feeling ridiculous. The table before him was too low, leaving no room for his legs. His balance was off. He struggled to avoid toppling. "At first I wasn't sure about seeing a witch, but now I know I made the right decision."

"It was the right decision. But only because it wasn't your decision." Cheavan lay sprawled on a high couch, gazing down on him. Long blond hair cascading upon her blood-red robe, gold occult pendants hanging from a slender neck and waist. An attractive fortysomething. "Fate brought you here. Destiny. Yours and mine. Do you believe in destiny, Arthur?"

Shrugging, Arthur wiped his trench coat's sleeve against his sweaty forehead. "You're the expert."

Cheavan smiled. "I'm glad you understand that. Not everyone does." Rising, tall and statuesque in her high-heeled pumps, she approached the big dollhouse in the corner of her parlor. "Especially not men."

"Why especially not men?"

"I don't know." Avoiding his gaze, Cheavan fingered some dolls within the dollhouse. "It's just been my experience that men put less faith in destiny."

"What kind of experience do you—?"

"My *professional* experience."

Nodding, Arthur scanned the dozens of dolls populating her parlor: porcelain-faced antique dolls, modern action figures, manufactured talking dolls, handcrafted colonial dolls. "You really like dolls."

"They help me in my work." Cheavan picked up a Ken doll, stroked him with her long fingers, caressed him with her long fingernails. "Obedient little people. Never hurtful. Always supportive. With my dolls, I shall destroy your enemy. Through them, I channel my power."

"So . . . you have a lot of power?"

"More than you can imagine." Tightening her grip on Ken, Cheavan's voice choked. "But it wasn't easy. I devoted years developing it. Decades mastering the occult arts and sciences. So you see, I understand what it must be like for you. It can be very lonely, being so devoted to your work."

Arthur nodded, not knowing how to respond. Behind the heavy scarlet drapes, he knew a violet neon sign glowed into the night: *SORCERESS: Let Me Help You.* Arthur had contemplated that sign in a second-story window of Cheavan's antiquated house every night on his way home from work, for over two years. Tonight it had rained. Storm clouds obscured the moon and stars, and without streetlights in this part of town, the sign provided the sole illumination. Its purple glow shimmered upon wet pavement.

It took two years to muster courage, but tonight he entered her house.

Gently, Cheavan replaced Ken inside the dollhouse. "You don't have many friends, Arthur, do you?"

"Same as everyone else, I guess. Same as you."

"I don't have any friends. None."

Arthur fidgeted. "But you're an extremely attractive woman, Cheavan." Especially for forty-plus.

Cheavan blushed. "Thank you. But I've never felt completely at ease with most people." She strained a smile. "I guess I just haven't had the time to get to know too many of them."

Arthur nodded, avoiding her eyes, glancing about the parlor, at her crystal ball and tarot cards, searching for a less personal topic. "Rain seems to have cleared up."

"It cleared up before you arrived."

"Oh good." Arthur rose from his cramped position, trying to do so nonchalantly. He stumbled over the low table, struggled to stay upright while appearing suave. "I think I better get going. I haven't even had dinner yet."

"Neither have I," said Cheavan, a bit too quickly.

Arthur considered her. She *was* attractive. And probably no more than fifteen, sixteen years older.

Cheavan's smiled wavered. "I don't like eating alone."

Arthur found himself smiling back. "I don't either."

* * *

"Arthur, it was such a good idea of yours to come here." Cheavan drew closer to him in the corner booth. "The food is quite delicious. How do you know so much about restaurants?"

Arthur reddened. "I don't really. I've never been here before. Usually, I just go to a diner."

"I want to know all your favorite spots and secret places. You obviously know the best places to eat. But why didn't you take me to one of your delectable diners?"

Because, Arthur thought, the only reason he favored diners was because diner crowds didn't stare at guys eating alone.

Arthur shrugged. "I just thought you deserved someplace nice."

Cheavan beamed. "Well you chose an excellent place. Thank you again for your fine judgment."

"Arthur made a fine judgment?" A tall man with an easy grin stepped into view.

"Oh, hello Roy," Arthur stammered. "Ah, Cheavan, *this* is Roy Bixby."

Leering, Bixby shook Cheavan's hand. "Hello Cheavan. It *is* a pleasure to meet you." He slapped Arthur's back. "Hey Arthur, where have you been hiding this lady? She's gorgeous. Mind if I join you for a minute?"

Bixby slid into the booth beside Cheavan. She pulled back, but was confined by the booth. Bixby pressed closer to her than necessary. The sorceress scowled.

"I'm with a client," said Bixby, "but he went to the washroom, so I have time to spare. So Arthur, looks as if you're doing all right. You found a replacement quick enough."

Arthur missed Cheavan's questioning glance.

"But, love 'em and leave 'em," said Bixby. "That's the way of the world, am I right? *Hey there!* Not too friendly!" He grinned at Cheavan. "I already have a lady. Right, Arthur?"

Cheavan smiled graciously. "Just some hairs on your lapel."

Bixby winked at Arthur. "Hey, this one really does know how to pamper her man. Better take care of her, Arthur, or someone will take care of her for you."

Neither man saw the sorceress wrap the hairs into a napkin, then slide the napkin into a small drawstring pouch.

"Ah, there's my client," said Bixby. "I've got to get back. It's a work night and all. I don't suppose you'd know anything about work, Arthur?" Bixby leered at Cheavan. "But, I don't suppose I can blame ol' Art, just for tonight. Bye, Cheavan." He punctuated his farewell with a quick squeeze of her thigh, then returned to his client.

"Lord, I hate the man," Arthur stammered. "I can't think of anything he hasn't tried to steal from me."

"Don't worry, darling," Cheavan assured him. "He could never steal me. I'm on your side."

"It's bad enough seeing him at the office every day, without seeing him after work as well."

"I'm glad he came here. He saved us much time and effort."

"What do you mean?"

"Never mind the details, darling. Just know that it wasn't a coincidence, your enemy coming here tonight. He came because *we* came. *Our* destiny, united, was strong enough to ensnare his destiny, and pull him in here. Into my web, spun for your benefit. His presence proves what I said earlier about our fate. I know the signs."

Contemplating his water glass, Arthur shrugged. "You're the expert."

"I'm *so* glad you understand. *So* glad you agree."

* * *

They parted after dinner. Cheavan ambled home, down lonely rain-drenched streets. Most stores closed by now. Time seemed to have forgotten this part of town, where storefronts remained unchanged after twenty, thirty years. A comforting thought, but deceptive. The stores were aging beneath their sun-bleached signs, just as surely as she was.

Cheavan halted before a bridal shop, saw a mannequin wearing a traditional white wedding gown. Cheavan positioned her body to superimpose her reflection over the mannequin. She smiled at the doll and felt happy for it.

A twenty-four hour grocery stood at the corner of the next block. Its pale light the only sign of life on the dark street. Cheavan was in no hurry to return home.

Inside the grocery, an old woman wearing thick yellowed eyeglasses sat behind the counter, near an antique cash register. A minister preached from a cracked AM radio. Engrossed in last week's tabloid, the old woman ignored Cheavan.

The store's only other occupant was a fat ugly cat.

The cat snarled at Cheavan.

"Shut up!" the storekeeper snapped. "You had your dinner."

Arching its back, the cat hissed.

Cheavan strolled the aisles, browsing sparse shelves. She found nothing of interest. A black rotary phone sat on a dusty wooden table at the back of the store. The aged storekeeper up front either lacked the money to relocate the jack, or the need. But neither would Cheavan's machine record any messages tonight. That gloomy prospect stirred Cheavan to buy something, anything, for herself. She dare not return to her empty house empty-handed.

Cheavan laid her items on the counter. Setting aside her tabloid, the storekeeper totaled the items on the vintage cash register. Cheavan gazed out the window into the black night, seemingly lost in thought.

The old woman punched an extra item.

"Eleven eighty-seven."

Startled, Cheavan quickly smiled. "Wait a minute. That can't be right."

"Eleven eighty-seven."

"No, look. A box of tea. Milk. Oh, let me see the receipt."

The storekeeper was hastily stuffing the items into a bag. "No receipt. Don't make receipt paper for registers this old."

"Wait!" Cheavan grabbed the bag, tore it, spilling items across the counter. "Look. A box of tea, a carton of . . . Why there's not even seven dollars worth of groceries here!"

"If you don't want it, get out!" the woman yelled.

Cheavan stared at the storekeeper, puzzled anyone would want to cheat her. Difficult to understand, yet she should stop being so naïve. Her soft voice was without anger. "You tried to cheat me."

"Get out of my store!"

"But you don't understand. That's not right."

"Oh shut up!"

The cat snarled from a corner.

"You too!"

Cheavan seized the woman's hair, *slamming* her head onto the counter. "I SAID THAT'S NOT RIGHT!"

Again and again, the sorceress slam-banged the grizzled gray head against the counter, jackhammering the old woman's face upon the hard linoleum surface. UP DOWN SMASH! UP DOWN SMASH! A red puddle blossomed. Shattered eyeglass shards adorned and embedded the old woman's face, contributing to the crimson pool fed by her crushed nose.

Absorbed in head-banging frenzy, Cheavan never noticed the blood spattering her face, even as she yanked and pulled the old woman across the counter, the eldster flailing and screaming and gurgling blood, but no match for a woman thirty years younger. Cheavan dragged the eldster up, over, across the countertop . . .

The woman crashed to the floor and lay still at Cheavan's feet.

Cheavan saw clumps of gray hair with red roots entangling her fingers. Smiling, she removed a handcrafted doll from her leather pouch, began wrapping the hairs around the doll in an intricate web pattern.

Cheavan did not see the storekeeper's eyes squint open.

Eyeglasses broken, blinking blood and seeing a pink blur, then recognizing familiar shapes, the old woman began dragging her battered body, as quietly as possible, toward the phone at the back of the store.

Engrossed in her Craft, diligently wrapping the old woman's hairs about the doll, Cheavan gleefully anticipated her ownership of the storekeeper. The elaborate pattern of crisscrossing gray strands must be set just so. It was this fastidious attention to detail that separated amateurs from true practitioners of The Craft.

Glancing up, Cheavan saw the storekeeper's progress down the aisle, renewed rage exploded within the sorceress, she chased the limping eldster, pounced against her frail body with full force, *slamming* the old woman against shelves, Cheavan falling upon her, cans of produce tumbling around them, Cheavan grabbed a can, *smashing* it against the woman's skull, blood spraying Cheavan's hands and face—*how dare the old hag attempt to escape her punishment!*—Cheavan repeated wild hammer blows until the old woman's struggle subsided.

Confident the old woman would finally sit still, Cheavan sat on the floor, cross-legged, gripped her blood-stained doll, resumed weaving hair, in and around, over and under. Tie a knot here. Twist and pull. Cheavan stuck out her tongue, performing her task with childish glee.

Twenty minutes passed. Cheavan never noticed. The task was nearly done. Her doll, her property, to do with as she pleased.

The storekeeper could barely crawl but crawl she did, dizzy and dazed, made slow and painful progress toward the phone, knew the general direction, beyond that she just had to hope, heard a minister in the background, Jesus loved her, her gnarled old hand reached a leg of the dusty table, groped and found the telephone cord, pulled and the phone *crashed* to the ground.

Cheavan jumped to her feet, bolted toward the woman, kicked the receiver from her arthritic hand with a force that sent it shattering into a dozen pieces against the wall.

"LEAVE IT YOU BITCH!" screamed Cheavan.

Assuming fetal position, the old woman cowered at the feet of the enraged sorceress, whimpering.

Cheavan glared at her rag doll, savage eyes flaring hate, cold eyes pitiless and beyond appeal.

The old woman's whimpering subsided until it could be heard no more, at least not by normal-sized people.

Cheavan cast her gentle eyes away from the doll, gazed down at the old woman, now all of six inches tall.

Cheavan set her foot gently atop the old woman, positioning her gold pump just so, shifted her weight . . . *CRUNCH!*

The sorceress removed her foot from the red mess, saw movement, set the tip of her high heel over a skull the size of a walnut, stepped down, heard and felt the walnut *crack!*

Cheavan scraped the sole and heel of her gold pump against the edge of a shelf.

A cat meowed.

Cheavan crouched, calling softly, "Here little kitty."

The fat ugly cat attacked the fresh red meat with voracious hunger.

"Just a little trouble I stamped out for you," purred the sorceress, petting the cat.

* * *

"You had three calls this morning. Frank wants to know when the chart will be ready. He's been waiting since Thursday. You promised you'd get it to him two days ago."

Arthur nodded, slouched behind his desk, shifting uncomfortably in an ill-fitting suit.

Lindsay flipped a page in her message pad. "George is still waiting for the Miami Market Analysis."

Arthur nodded again. He shared the office with Bixby, which was decorated with Bixby's corporate awards and trophies. And he shared Lindsay, their secretary, who occupied the anteroom.

Lindsay flipped a page. "And Lyona still isn't pleased with your San Diego survey. She wanted to see you first thing this morning. She can't understand why you're late again."

Groaning, Arthur glanced at his clock radio. 10:16 a.m.

Lindsay began leaving, then spun around on her heel, twirling her tawny hair through the air. "Oh! Roy told me he saw you at Chez Antoine's last night. He said you were with a girl. Did you have fun?"

"It was all right."

"Good." Lindsay turned to leave.

"Oh . . . Lindsay."

"Yes, Arthur?"

"We're just friends."

"Oh. Well, I hope things work out for you eventually."

"I think they will. She's going to help me."

Lindsay scowled, then brightened. "Good. I want you to be happy." She returned to her anteroom.

Arthur watched the door long after Lindsay left.

* * *

Cheavan entered her kitchen at about the same time. It was as dark and cluttered as the rest of her house. Window shrouded behind plants and curtains. Jars containing potions and herbs strewn across the counter.

Cheavan set down her Ken doll and unfolded the napkin from Chez Antoine's. She removed Bixby's hairs, began her elaborate craftwork on Ken. This morning's webbing would be quicker than last night's. Cheavan planned a different fate for the man who troubled Arthur so. The hair pattern binding Ken's naked torso would be simpler. Same basic outline, but less intricate crossovers.

Not that Cheavan was sloppy. On the contrary, it was precisely because she took so much pride in her Craft that she refused to repeat old patterns. She was an artist. Each new subjugation was an opportunity for experimentation. She had never practiced this morning's magickal mastery before. Already envisioning his bondage to her will, her fingers trembled. Her ice-blue witch's eyes gazed with girlish glee at Ken. Her long tongue licked her moist lips at the thought of delicious pleasures to come.

Sorcery was poetry.

* * *

"Well, I'm off to another presentation." Bixby exited his office shortly before eleven. His stride conveyed energy and confidence. His slate gray power suit fit like skin. He kissed Lindsay on the cheek. "Wish me luck."

"Luck. Not that you need it."

"Can't hurt. Market's getting tight. Stiff competition."

"You'll pull through. It's poor Arthur I'm worried about."

"Hey, I thought you were my lady."

Lindsay pecked Bixby's cheek. "You know I am. It's just that, I feel sorry for Arthur."

"You're too sweet for your own good. But, I guess that's what I love about you."

Back in her kitchen darkness, Cheavan ran her tongue across Ken's naked waist, licking his loins, pressing her tongue between his little legs, pushing her long tongue against his tiny groin, swallowing his legs, moving her moist lips over his hard plastic body, caressing him with her teeth.

Lindsay and Bixby were kissing, embracing, tonguing, wanting to do more, resisting temptation—they were in an office! Neither had trouble curbing their desires until just a moment ago. Very strange. Bixby buried his face in Lindsay's hair and inhaled her scent. Their breathing and passion intensified, even as they fought to restrain themselves.

Arthur sat numb behind his desk, clenching a pencil, glaring at the anteroom door. He heard their moaning, items being shoved aside on Lindsay's desk, her suppressed shouts, someone kicking her desk. Arthur pressed his thumb against his pencil, rubbed its spine . . .

The phone rang!

Arthur jumped, snapping the pencil in two, dropped its pieces, grabbed the receiver. "Hello!" he bellowed, then meekly, "No George, the market analysis is not quite ready . . . I know it's been a while . . . "

The moaning and groaning from the anteroom intensified.

In her kitchen, Cheavan sucked Ken into her wide mouth, head first, twirling him upon and massaging him with her tongue. When she extracted him, slowly, her saliva glistened like sweat on his naked body. She clenched him in her hands, swallowed hard, smacking her lips in anticipation, eyeing him hungrily.

Lindsay and Bixby forced themselves apart, their lust now manageable if not absent. They gazed at one another, uncomprehending. Bixby zipped his pants and departed wordlessly. Lindsay stared dumbstruck after him.

No longer on the phone, Arthur sat motionless, ears perked. He heard Bixby leave. Arthur picked up his phone. "Lindsay? Can you come in here for a second?"

Lindsay entered a minute later.

"Sit down."

Lindsay sat down.

"So . . . I need . . . " Arthur snatched the broken pencil. "Can you please sharpen this for me?"

Lindsay took the pencil, slid it into the electric sharpener on Arthur's desk.

Arthur watched it sharpen, wondering what to say next.

* * *

Out in the hall, Bixby pressed aboard an elevator carrying an early lunchtime crowd. A tight squeeze, just enough room for all. An express elevator. No further stops until the lobby.

Back in the kitchen, Cheavan clenched her molars over Ken's arm, not tearing, just grinding, gyrating his arm slowly between her teeth. She growled lustily.

Inside the elevator, an obese woman bumped into Bixby's arm.

Bixby winced.

"Oh, I'm sorry," the obese woman apologized, then saw his wrist. "Oh, that's a lovely watch! I was thinking of buying one just like that for my nephew. May I see it?"

Smiling, Bixby extended his hand.

The woman took his wrist. "Just lovely." She turned to her friend. "Look at this."

Cheavan ripped the doll's arm from its socket.

As the woman pulled Bixby's arm over to her friend, his arm fell from its socket.

Bixby stared at his arm, at the woman holding his arm, shock overpowering pain, until the blood cascading from his torn socket hit home. Bixby screamed.

The woman stared at Bixby's arm, hanging limply in her hand. She whimpered, dropped it, then joined his screaming.

Other passengers were already screaming, shoving against each other and away from Bixby, even as Bixby's blood splashed and drenched them all.

Cheavan inserted the doll deep into her wet mouth, squishing him this way and that, crushing him under her molars, biting him with her incisors, gnawing, grinding, chewing.

Bixby crumpled to the floor, shaking like an epileptic fish out of water, flopping under passengers' legs. Passengers pounded vainly on the elevator doors. People pressed buttons at random. Someone pressed the alarm. No use. This express elevator would stop for no one until ground floor.

Bixby's suit shred and tore away from his body, giant teeth marks sank into his flesh, red gashes opened along his chest and stomach.

Cheavan pulled Ken from her mouth until only his soft plastic head remained hidden past her moist lips. She ran her tongue around his head a few times, then slid Ken deeper into her mouth, slowly lowering her molars, squishing his head out of shape, moaning in ecstasy as his head collapsed under her teeth.

Bixby gripped his head as it collapsed, screaming insanely as his skull cracked and splintered and fell into his brain, screamed as brain matter poured through his broken skull, first forming pustules beneath his scalp, then exploding gray brain pus. His hands were shaking, his body quaking, trembling from neurological trauma. Yet still, Bixby held his head, even as brain matter poured past his fingers.

The obese woman swooned, faint, nauseated. Her corpulence struck the wall with a thud, and she disgorged torrents of half-digested donuts and coffee, vomiting upon Bixby's exploding head and oozing brain pus. As if to cork the woman, Bixby's eyeball popped from his head into her mouth.

Cheavan slid Ken from her moist mouth, saliva glistening along his wet nakedness. She carried him to her blender.

In the lobby, a crowd awaited the elevator. A building engineer had arrived in response to the alarm. The elevator's descent appeared normal. The engineer expected a false alarm.

Cheavan dropped Ken into the blender.

The elevator reached the lobby. People shifted toward its doors. The engineer made a slight effort to hold everyone back until he could confirm all was well.

Cheavan pressed a button. The blender came to life.

The elevator doors opened.

A torrent of blood and organs splashed from the elevator and into the waiting crowd, followed by a panic-stricken mob rushing from the elevator, colliding into the crowd, spreading pandemonium throughout the lobby. Drenched in Bixby's blood, the exiting passengers resembled airline disaster victims.

An arm shot from the elevator, landing in a woman's purse. The woman gaped, then screamed when she realized the severed arm was bobbing about her purse with a life of its own, chunks of it slicing off and flung about the lobby.

Bixby's crushed head bounced from the elevator like a punctured basketball, rolling willy-nilly across the lobby, bits of it chipping off and zig-zagging along their own courses.

A blood-red whirlpool swirled inside the elevator. Bixby's bone fragments and organ chunks twirling and twisting within its crimson vortex.

* * *

That evening, Cheavan sat watching from her parlor window, her anxious face lit by the violet glow of her neon sign. Outside, the street was dark and empty. She only dared smile when she espied Arthur running toward her house, his unbuttoned trench coat flapping in the wind.

"Cheavan, it was horrible!" Arthur cried upon entering her parlor, sweating profusely, eyes red and glistening.

"My poor darling, you look dreadful." Cheavan led him to a low cushion, seating him as though directing a child. He was too numb to resist. Cheavan sat on the couch before him, folding her arms across her lap, gazing lovingly down on him.

Arthur held his head in trembling hands. "Flesh flying out the window. Blood splashing against walls. Torn apart piece by piece."

Cheavan clapped her hands. "Oh Arthur! How wonderfully you describe it! I wish I had been there to see Bixby."

"I'm not talking about Bixby! I'm talking about Lindsay!"

"Lindsay? Arthur, who's Lindsay?"

"Lindsay was our secretary. Mine and Bixby's."

Cheavan grew concerned. "But how is Bixby?"

"He was torn apart too."

She brightened. "Well then, there's no problem!"

"Why did you kill her? I didn't ask you to harm Lindsay."

"Oh darling, it's perfectly simple. Some of the hairs on Bixby's jacket must have been Lindsay's. So now Bixby's dead and so is his little tramp."

"And I'm responsible!" Arthur covered his face. "Oh God, I don't want to live!"

"Arthur, you mustn't say that! You had no way of knowing who Bixby was fucking." Cheavan shrugged. "And if he was porking Lindsay, well then so what? Lindsay was tied to your enemy's destiny. *Our* destiny delivered her to us."

"But I loved Lindsay. I wanted to marry her."

Cheavan's smile froze. Her eyes widened. Her mouth slackened. Her faint voice barely audible over the buzzing neon sign. "But Arthur. What about us?"

Arthur did not hear her.

She reached a trembling hand across the low table separating them. "Arthur darling?"

Arthur brushed aside her hand without thought.

"BASTARD!" She leapt to her feet, flinging the table across the room, scattering tarot cards, shattering a crystal ball. She grabbed Arthur's head, yanked him up, burying her long fingers in his hair. "I love you! Doesn't that mean anything to you?"

Too late, Arthur noticed her.

Clenching his hair, Cheavan pulled him low, glaring down on him as if he were a slug. "How can you do this to me? How can you betray me after all I've done for you? You *saw* what I did!"

Arthur had seen. And felt Lindsay's blood splatter him as he tried to help. And heard her screams up until her misshapen tawny head disintegrated in a final, merciful death . . .

Legs quivering, Arthur stammered, "Cheavan, please let me go."

"How dare you take my love and throw it back in my face?"

"I like you, Cheavan. I really do. Let's be best friends."

"I never wanted to be your *best friend!*"

Arthur clasped his hands, begging. "Please don't hurt me."

"You men are all alike. Full of betrayal and ingratitude."

"I'm very grateful—"

"LIAR!" Yanking her hands away, Cheavan turned her back to him, arms folded. She was trembling. So was he. An uncomfortable silence ensued.

Arthur crept toward the door, trying desperately not to make noise. The floorboards creaked with every step.

Cheavan seemed not to notice. From behind, she seemed to be praying. Or crying. Arthur couldn't know for sure. He reached the door, tried to open it without a sound. *CREAK!*

Cheavan did not turn around, said with more pain than anger, "Don't go."

Arthur left the parlor, closing the door behind him.

Cheavan heard his footsteps recede down the hall, down the stairs. She opened her hands, saw his hair.

She reached for a rag doll.

At the bottom of the stairs, Arthur glanced back nervously. She wasn't following. He felt safer.

Cheavan chose a simple pattern to entwine the doll, crude but strong. Anger and hurt made her impatient. And with him so near, no elaborate knots were required to subjugate him. He was comfortably within her range of control. A few twirls to own his flesh, secure his soul, bind his destiny . . .

Arthur opened the front door, exiting into the cool dark night. Free at last. He shut the door behind him.

She was finished. She wrapped her fingers around the doll, kneading it in anticipation.

Arthur hurried toward the front gate, grabbed his stomach . . . some sort of pain . . .

Seating the rag doll on the floor, Cheavan encircled a long finger around the doll's belly, *yanking violently!*

Arthur was at the front gate when a force gripped his belly, yanking him backward. He screamed upon realizing he'd failed to escape, felt cold terror as the invisible force dragged him back toward the house. He tried to grab something, but only scraped his hands against the concrete path. The force hammered Arthur against the front door until it had smashed a hole, pulling and dragging Arthur through the hole, cutting and bruising him upon splinters . . .

Cheavan squeezed the tiny doll, gazing hungrily at it. She struggled not to chew or devour it in one bite.

Downstairs, Arthur lay immobilized on the floor, felt giant fingers restraining him. He turned blue, breathing difficult.

Cheavan rubbed a thumbnail over the doll, pressing its soft cloth. She heard a shriek from downstairs. She dug her nails into the doll, began tearing it open.

Arthur's clothes were shredding, tearing away from his body. Wounds opened along his torso. His eyes bulged as he remembered the giant teeth marks on Lindsay's torso . . .

Cheavan held the doll's arms against its sides, dug her long fingernails into its body, opening tears along its belly.

His arms pinned against him, Arthur watched new wounds open along his body.

Cheavan slid a gold pump off her foot, lay the doll flat on the floor, set the shoe's high heel on the doll's belly. "That should keep you in your place."

Arthur was still pinned to the floor when Cheavan descended the stairs. She approached him, gazed down on him, stated icily, "You can't go. You still owe me."

Arthur whimpered.

Cheavan knelt beside him, touched his wounds.

Arthur was begging, then screaming as the sorceress slid her fingers into a gash, digging ever deeper past his rib cage, until her entire hand was inside Arthur's body, followed by her other hand. With both hands inside him, she rummaged for his organs, smiled coldly at his red-and-blue screaming face. Blood flowed from his torso, across her wrists, onto the parquet floor.

"You can't go like this," Cheavan gently laughed. "You're hurt." She pulled tendons from his body. "Look at this! You're coming apart at the seams."

Arthur screamed and cried. "*Please* don't kill me!"

"Arthur darling, I would never hurt you. You belong to me."

* * *

Cheavan stood by the window, smiling at a new day. Outside, the sun was shining. It lent a warm glow to her face. Not that she ever planned to go outside. Ever. She was content where she was. She had everything she would ever need.

"You disappointed me, Arthur. But I understand. You were confused about our destiny. I guess I should just stop expecting men to get it right away." Cheavan released the scarlet drapery, sinking the room back into comfortable darkness. She approached her dollhouse, crouched before it. "I forgive you," she smiled. "We certainly understand each other now."

Cheavan peered into the dollhouse.

Arthur lay tied with string to a toy bed, his tiny arms and legs securely bound to its plastic bedposts. Covered with dried blood. He forced his eyes open, saw the giant sorceress peering in on him.

"And Arthur," she trilled. "We are going to be together for a very long time. Isn't that wonderful, Arthur?"

Something was wrong. He did not answer her.

Frowning, Cheavan reached into the dollhouse, pinched him with her long fingernails.

Arthur emitted a mouselike squeal.

"I asked you a question, Arthur! Isn't it wonderful?" She heard a faint reply, pinched him again. "I can't hear you." She placed her giant fingernails between his legs, and each time she repeated her question, she pinched. "Isn't it wonderful? Isn't it? Isn't it . . . ?"

About the Author

Thomas M. Sipos was born in Queens, NY, to Hungarian refugees from Communism. He attended Catholic schools, and graduated NYU's film school. His childhood visits to family in Communist Transylvania served to inspire his horror/black comedy novel, *Vampire Nation,* a Prometheus Award nominee.

Sipos's fiction has appeared in *Wicked Mystic, 100 Wicked Little Witch Stories*, and *Horrors! 365 Scary Stories*; his nonfiction in *The Journal of Horror Cinema, Tangent, Horror, Midnight Marquee, Horrorfind.com Green-Tentacles.com, Liberty, Filmfax*, and *Sci-Fi Universe.* Some of it reprinted in this volume.

Sipos belongs to the Horror Writers Association, the Science Fiction & Fantasy Writers of America, the National Writers Union, the Libertarian Futurist Society, and the Academy of Science Fiction, Fantasy & Horror Films. He lives in Los Angeles, where his sitcom and horror scripts (including *Halloween Candy*) have won awards.

Lightning Source UK Ltd.
Milton Keynes UK
UKOW02n1330271014

240695UK00006BA/48/P

9 780759 637481